W9-DAS-802

Date: 5/11/16

GRA 741.5 GIJ V.2
Van Lente, Fred,
G.I. Joe. Threat matrix /

THREAT MATRIX

**PALM BEACH COUNTY
LIBRARY SYSTEM**
3650 Summit Boulevard
West Palm Beach, FL 33406-4198

Special thanks to Hasbro's Ed Lane, Joe Furfaro, Heather Hopkins, and Michael Kelly for their invaluable assistance.

ISBN: 978-1-61377-866-1

17 16 15 14   1 2 3 4

Ted Adams, CEO & Publisher
Greg Goldstein, President & COO
Robbie Robbins, EVP/Sr. Graphic Artist
Chris Ryall, Chief Creative Officer/Editor-in-Chief
Matthew Ruzicka, CPA, Chief Financial Officer
Alan Payne, VP of Sales
Dirk Wood, VP of Marketing
Lorelei Bunjes, VP of Digital Services
Jeff Webber, VP of Digital Publishing & Business Development

Facebook: facebook.com/idwpublishing
Twitter: @idwpublishing
YouTube: youtube.com/idwpublishing
Instagram: instagram.com/idwpublishing
deviantART: idwpublishing.deviantart.com
Pinterest: pinterest.com/idwpublishing/idw-staff-faves

www.IDWPUBLISHING.com
IDW founded by Ted Adams, Alex Garner, Kris Oprisko, and Robbie Robbins

G.I. JOE, VOLUME 2: THREAT MATRIX. FEBRUARY 2014. FIRST PRINTING. HASBRO and its logo, G.I. JOE, and all related characters are trademarks of Hasbro and are used with permission. © 2014 Hasbro. All Rights Reserved. IDW Publishing, a division of Idea and Design Works, LLC. Editorial offices: 5080 Santa Fe St., San Diego, CA 92109. The IDW logo is registered in the U.S. Patent and Trademark Office. Any similarities to persons living or dead are purely coincidental. With the exception of artwork used for review purposes, none of the contents of this publication may be reprinted without the permission of Idea and Design Works, LLC. Printed in Korea. IDW Publishing does not read or accept unsolicited submissions of ideas, stories, or artwork.

Originally published as G.I. JOE VOLUME 3 issues #6–11.

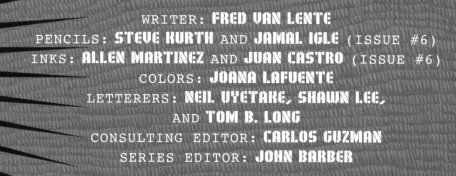

WRITER: **FRED VAN LENTE**
PENCILS: **STEVE KURTH** AND **JAMAL IGLE** (ISSUE #6)
INKS: **ALLEN MARTINEZ** AND **JUAN CASTRO** (ISSUE #6)
COLORS: **JOANA LAFUENTE**
LETTERERS: **NEIL UYETAKE, SHAWN LEE,**
AND **TOM B. LONG**
CONSULTING EDITOR: **CARLOS GUZMAN**
SERIES EDITOR: **JOHN BARBER**

COLLECTION COVER ARTIST: **JAMAL IGLE**
COLLECTION COVER COLORIST: **ROMULO FAJARDO, JR.**
COLLECTION EDITORS: **JUSTIN EISINGER** AND **ALONZO SIMON**
COLLECTION DESIGNER: **CHRIS MOWRY**

CHAPTER ONE

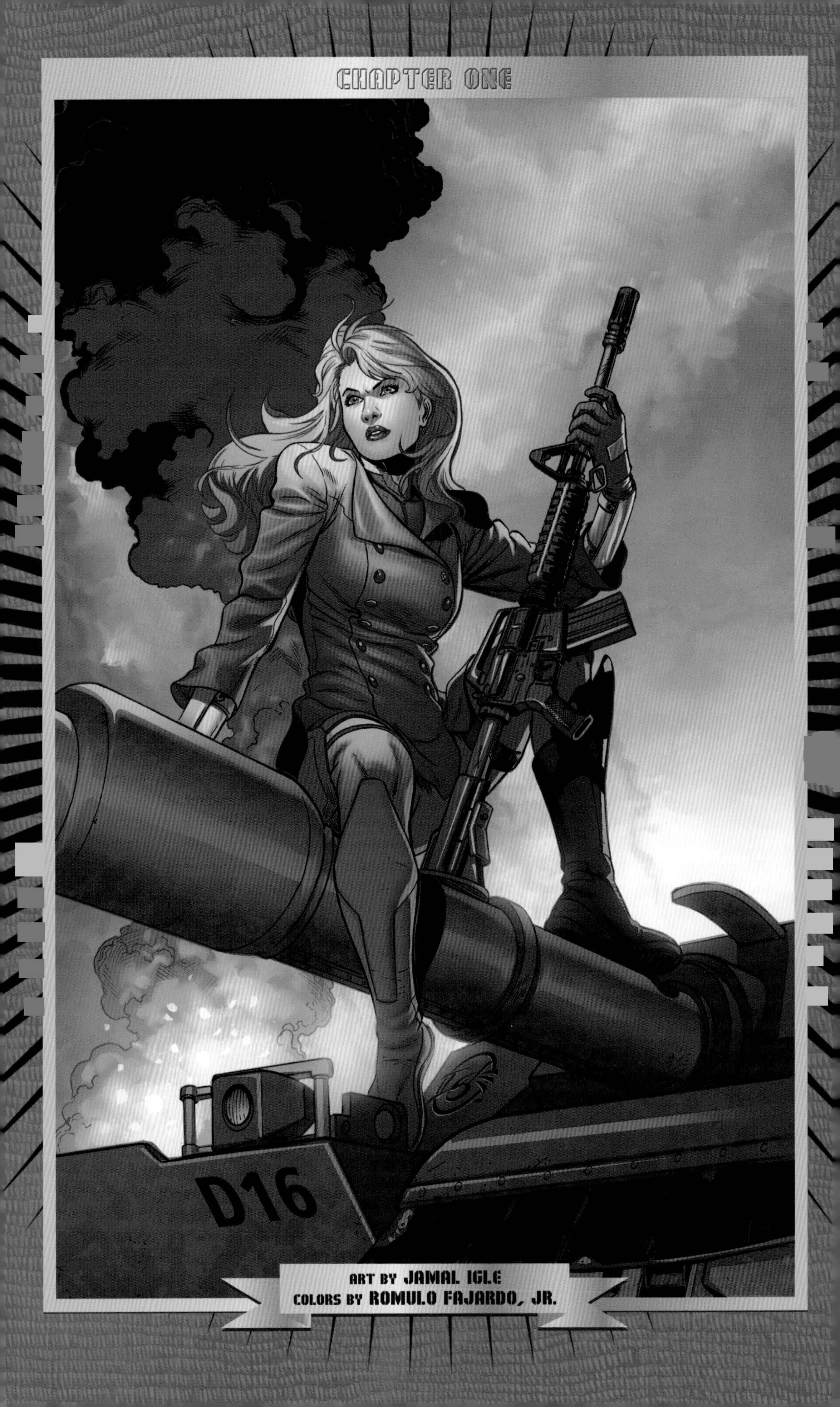

D16

ART BY JAMAL IGLE
COLORS BY ROMULO FAJARDO, JR.

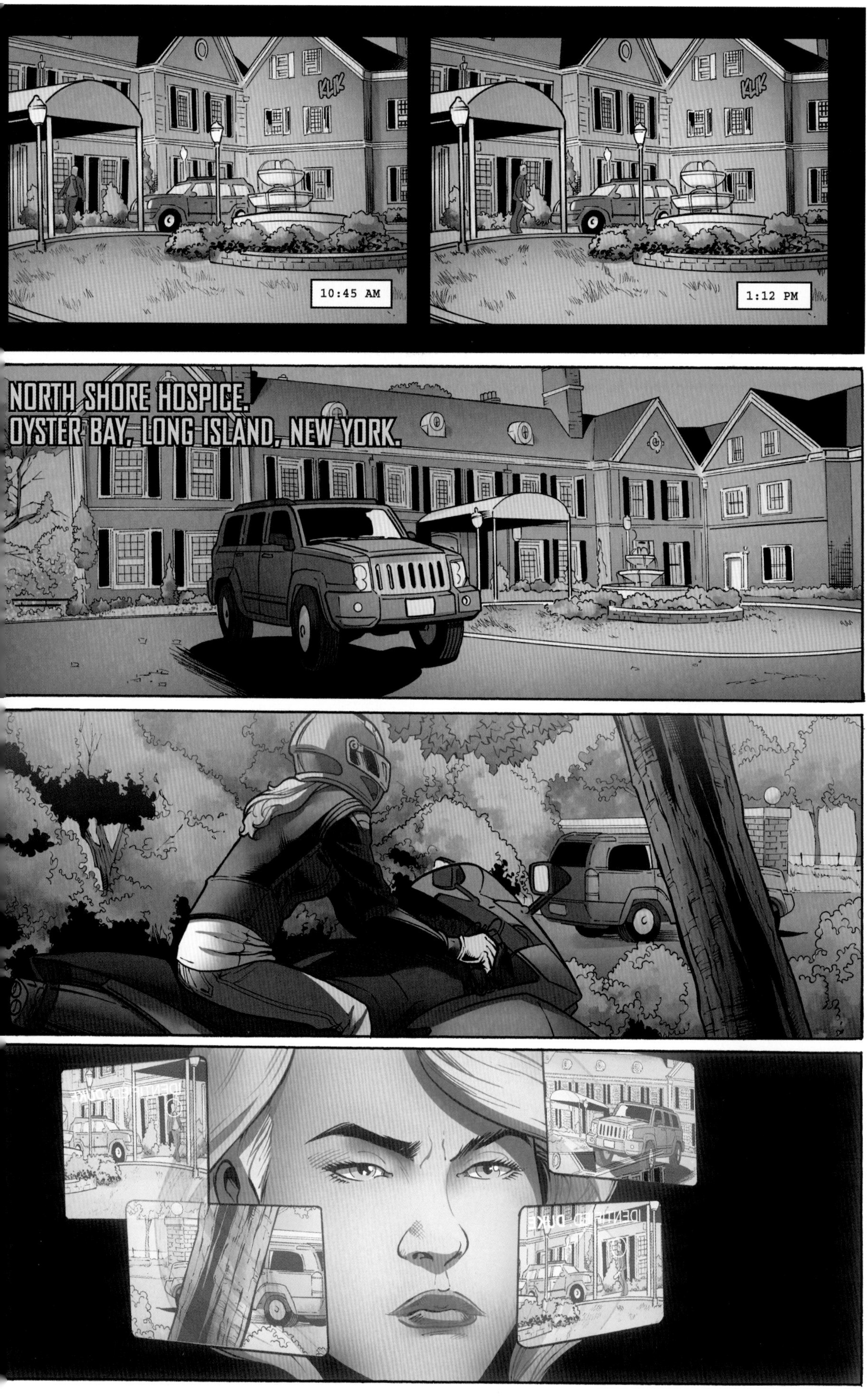
KLIK
10:45 AM
KLIK
1:12 PM
NORTH SHORE HOSPICE.
OYSTER BAY, LONG ISLAND, NEW YORK.

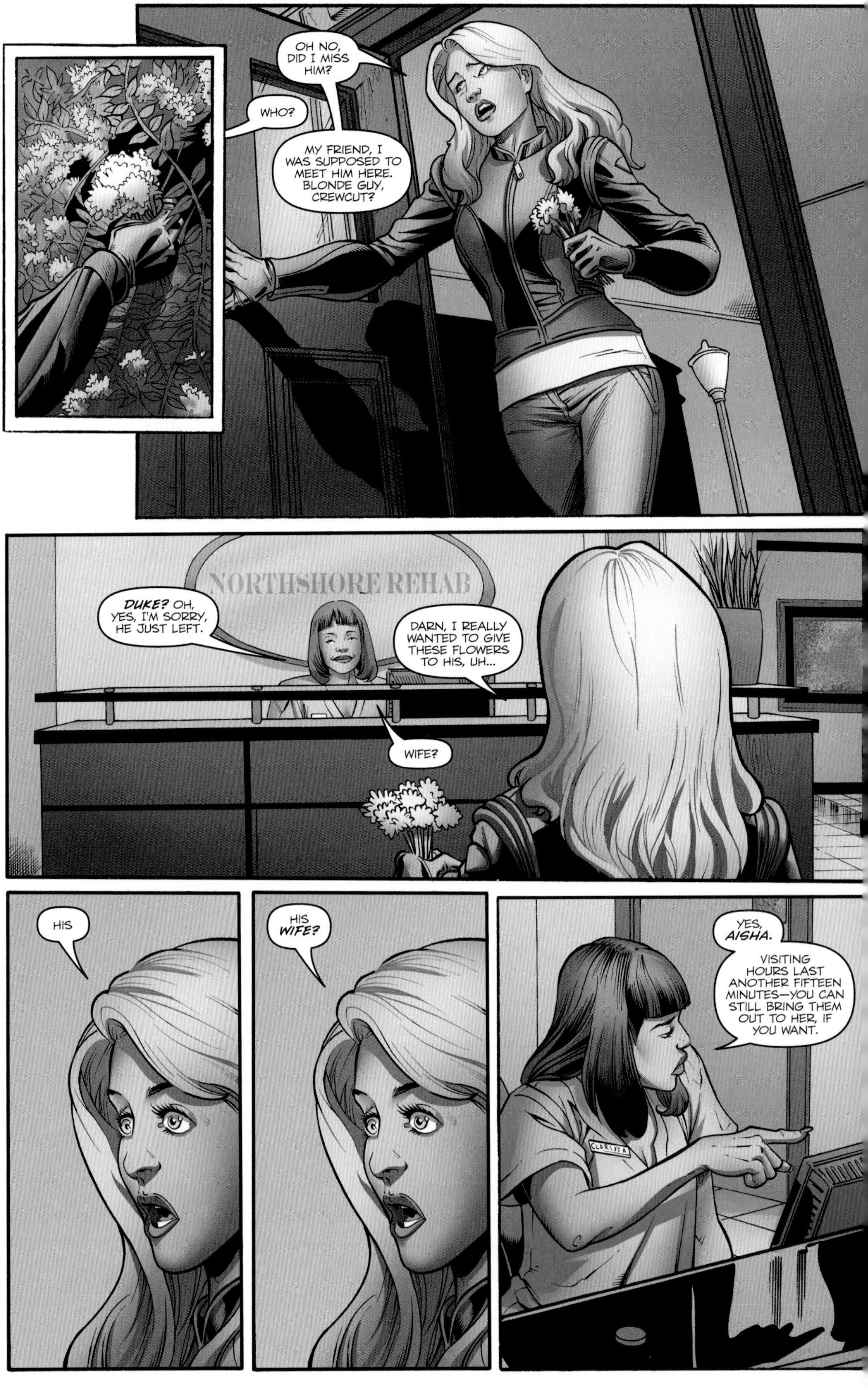
OH NO, DID I MISS HIM?
WHO?
MY FRIEND, I WAS SUPPOSED TO MEET HIM HERE. BLONDE GUY, CREWCUT?
NORTHSHORE REHAB
DUKE? OH, YES, I'M SORRY, HE JUST LEFT.
DARN, I REALLY WANTED TO GIVE THESE FLOWERS TO HIS, UH...
WIFE?
HIS
HIS WIFE?
YES, AISHA.
VISITING HOURS LAST ANOTHER FIFTEEN MINUTES—YOU CAN STILL BRING THEM OUT TO HER, IF YOU WANT.
CLARISSA

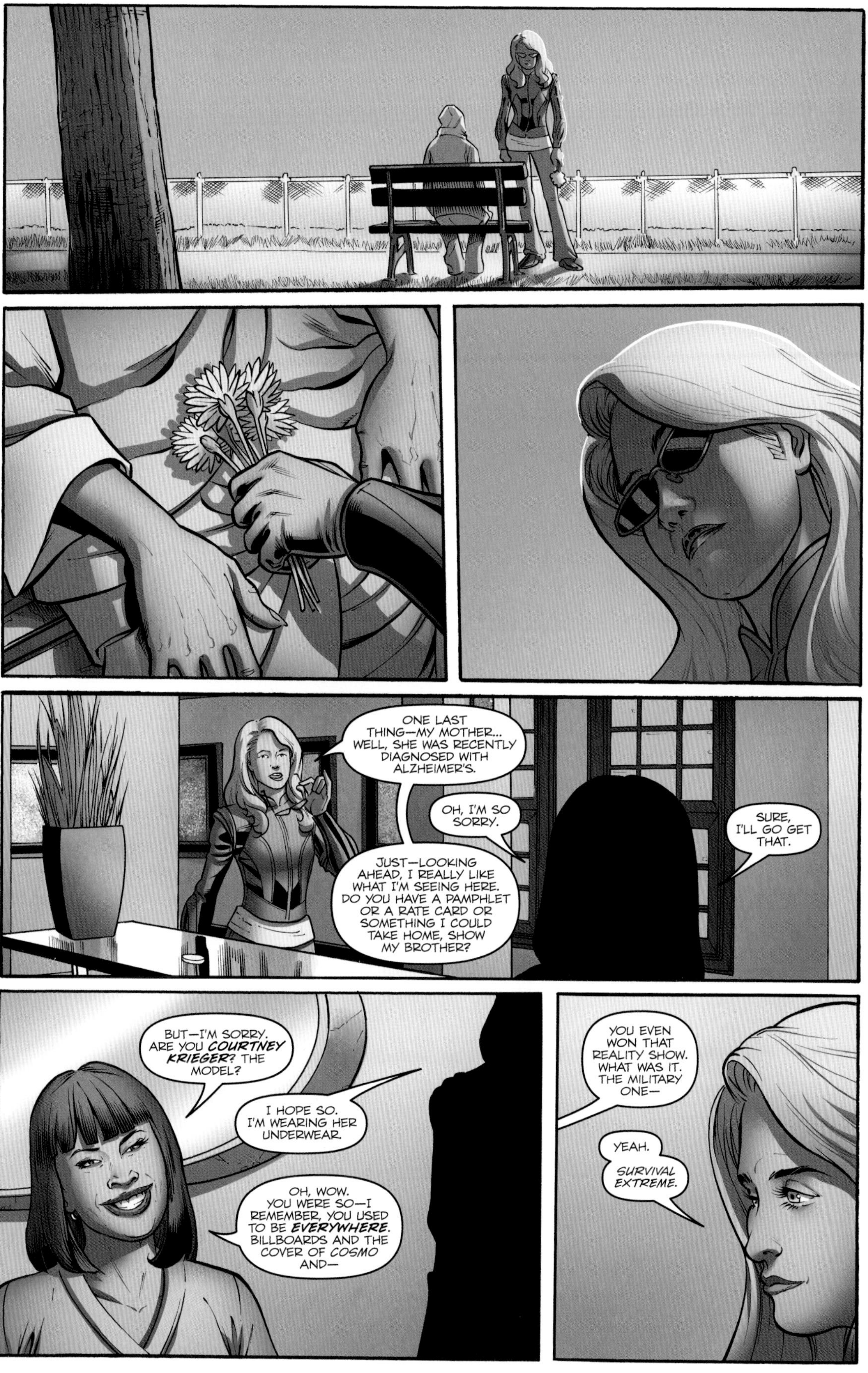
ONE LAST THING—MY MOTHER... WELL, SHE WAS RECENTLY DIAGNOSED WITH ALZHEIMER'S.
OH, I'M SO SORRY.
JUST—LOOKING AHEAD, I REALLY LIKE WHAT I'M SEEING HERE. DO YOU HAVE A PAMPHLET OR A RATE CARD OR SOMETHING I COULD TAKE HOME, SHOW MY BROTHER?
SURE, I'LL GO GET THAT.
BUT—I'M SORRY. ARE YOU COURTNEY KRIEGER? THE MODEL?
I HOPE SO. I'M WEARING HER UNDERWEAR.
OH, WOW. YOU WERE SO—I REMEMBER, YOU USED TO BE EVERYWHERE. BILLBOARDS AND THE COVER OF COSMO AND—
YOU EVEN WON THAT REALITY SHOW. WHAT WAS IT. THE MILITARY ONE—
YEAH. SURVIVAL EXTREME.

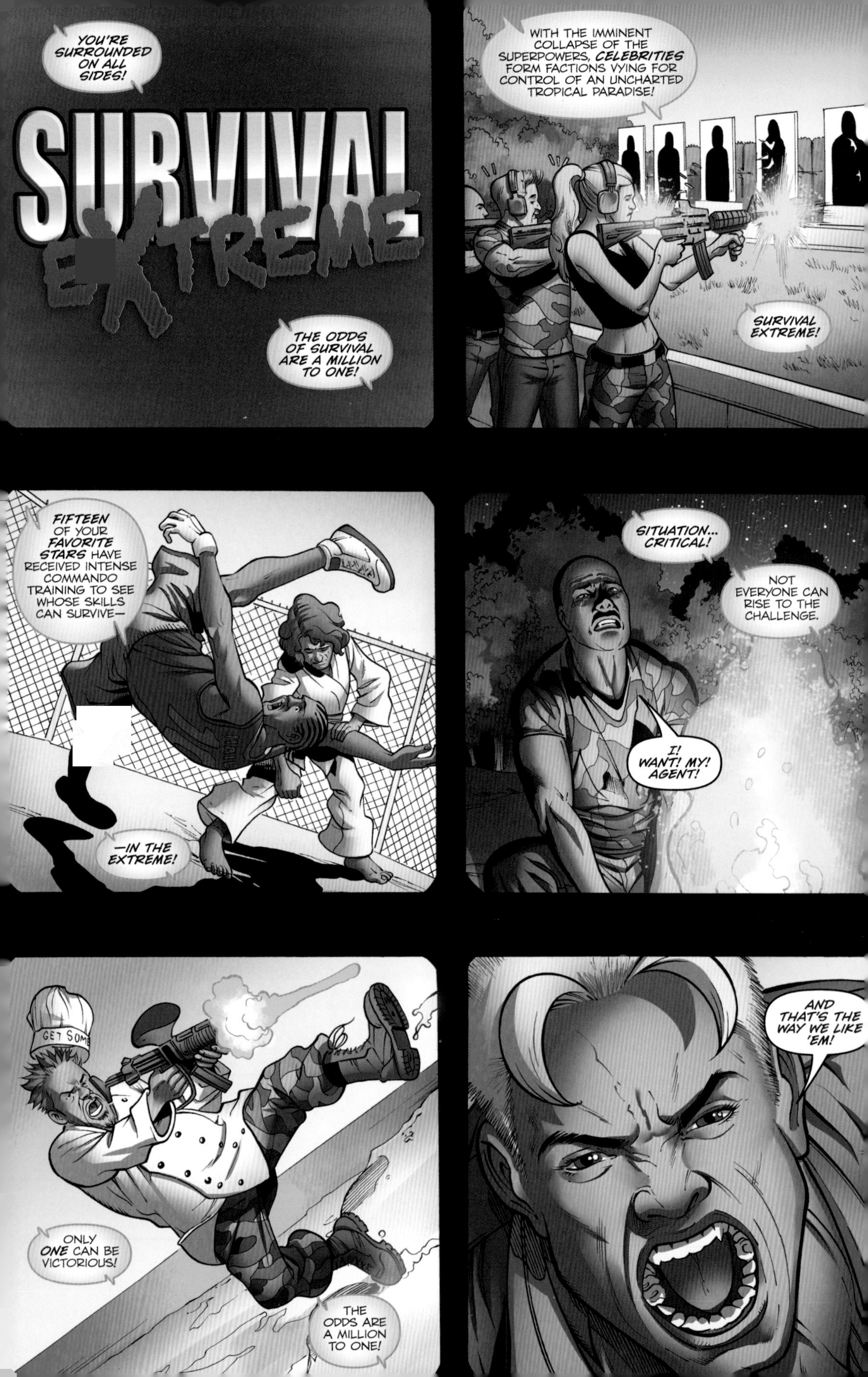

YOU'RE SURROUNDED ON ALL SIDES!
SURVIVAL
EXTREME
THE ODDS OF SURVIVAL ARE A MILLION TO ONE!
WITH THE IMMINENT COLLAPSE OF THE SUPERPOWERS, CELEBRITIES FORM FACTIONS VYING FOR CONTROL OF AN UNCHARTED TROPICAL PARADISE!
SURVIVAL EXTREME!
FIFTEEN OF YOUR FAVORITE STARS HAVE RECEIVED INTENSE COMMANDO TRAINING TO SEE WHOSE SKILLS CAN SURVIVE—
—IN THE EXTREME!
SITUATION... CRITICAL!
NOT EVERYONE CAN RISE TO THE CHALLENGE.
I! WANT! MY! AGENT!
GET SOME
ONLY ONE CAN BE VICTORIOUS!
THE ODDS ARE A MILLION TO ONE!
AND THAT'S THE WAY WE LIKE 'EM!

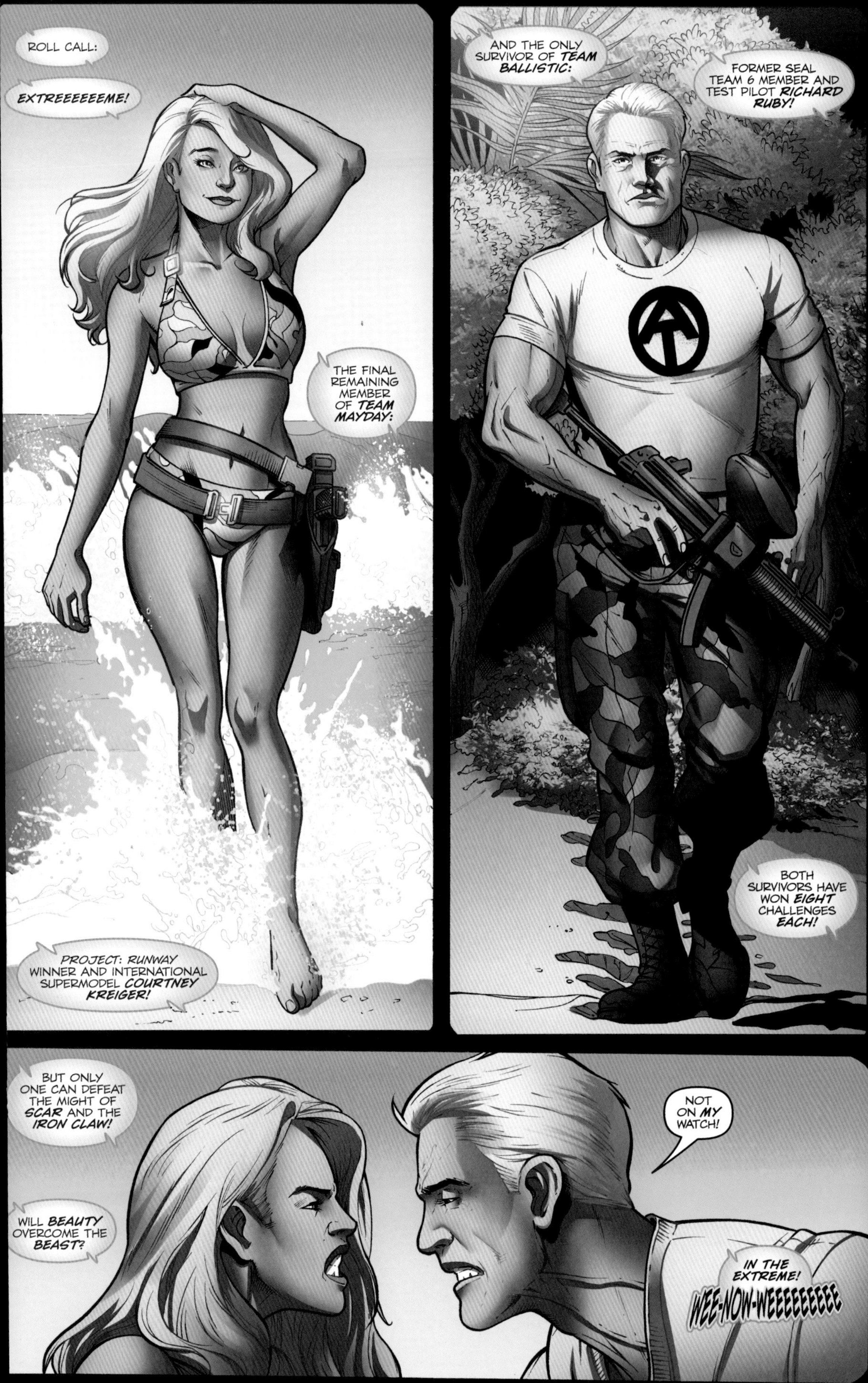
ROLL CALL:
EXTREEEEEEEME!
THE FINAL REMAINING MEMBER OF TEAM MAYDAY:
PROJECT: RUNWAY WINNER AND INTERNATIONAL SUPERMODEL COURTNEY KREIGER!
AND THE ONLY SURVIVOR OF TEAM BALLISTIC:
FORMER SEAL TEAM 6 MEMBER AND TEST PILOT RICHARD RUBY!
BOTH SURVIVORS HAVE WON EIGHT CHALLENGES EACH!
BUT ONLY ONE CAN DEFEAT THE MIGHT OF SCAR AND THE IRON CLAW!
WILL BEAUTY OVERCOME THE BEAST?
NOT ON MY WATCH!
IN THE EXTREME!
WEE-NOW-WEEEEEEEEE

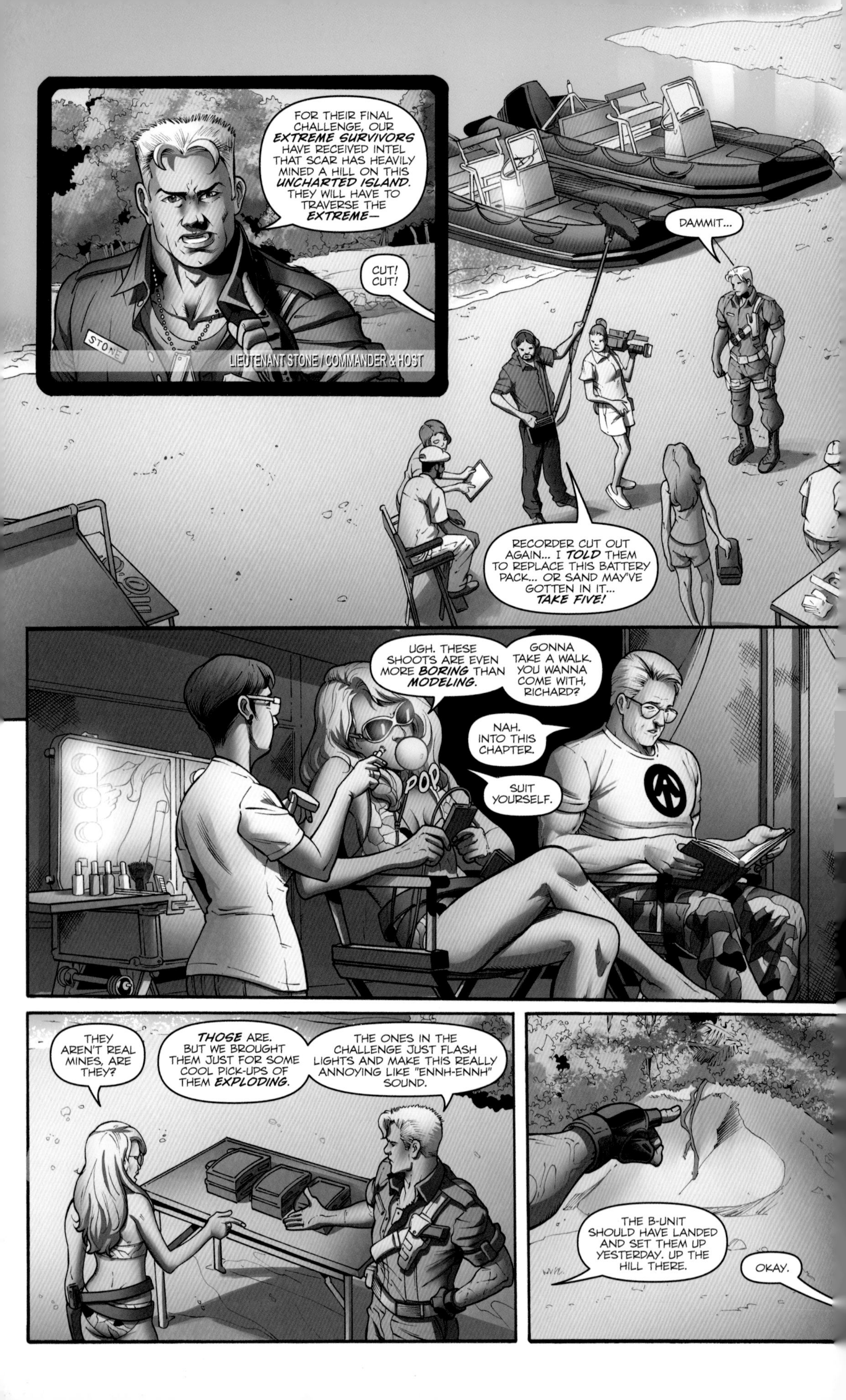

FOR THEIR FINAL CHALLENGE, OUR EXTREME SURVIVORS HAVE RECEIVED INTEL THAT SCAR HAS HEAVILY MINED A HILL ON THIS UNCHARTED ISLAND. THEY WILL HAVE TO TRAVERSE THE EXTREME—
STONE
LIEUTENANT STONE / COMMANDER & HOST
CUT! CUT!
DAMMIT...
RECORDER CUT OUT AGAIN... I TOLD THEM TO REPLACE THIS BATTERY PACK... OR SAND MAY'VE GOTTEN IN IT... TAKE FIVE!
UGH. THESE SHOOTS ARE EVEN MORE BORING THAN MODELING.
GONNA TAKE A WALK. YOU WANNA COME WITH, RICHARD?
NAH. INTO THIS CHAPTER.
SUIT YOURSELF.
POP
THEY AREN'T REAL MINES, ARE THEY?
THOSE ARE. BUT WE BROUGHT THEM JUST FOR SOME COOL PICK-UPS OF THEM EXPLODING.
THE ONES IN THE CHALLENGE JUST FLASH LIGHTS AND MAKE THIS REALLY ANNOYING LIKE "ENNH-ENNH" SOUND.
THE B-UNIT SHOULD HAVE LANDED AND SET THEM UP YESTERDAY. UP THE HILL THERE.
OKAY.

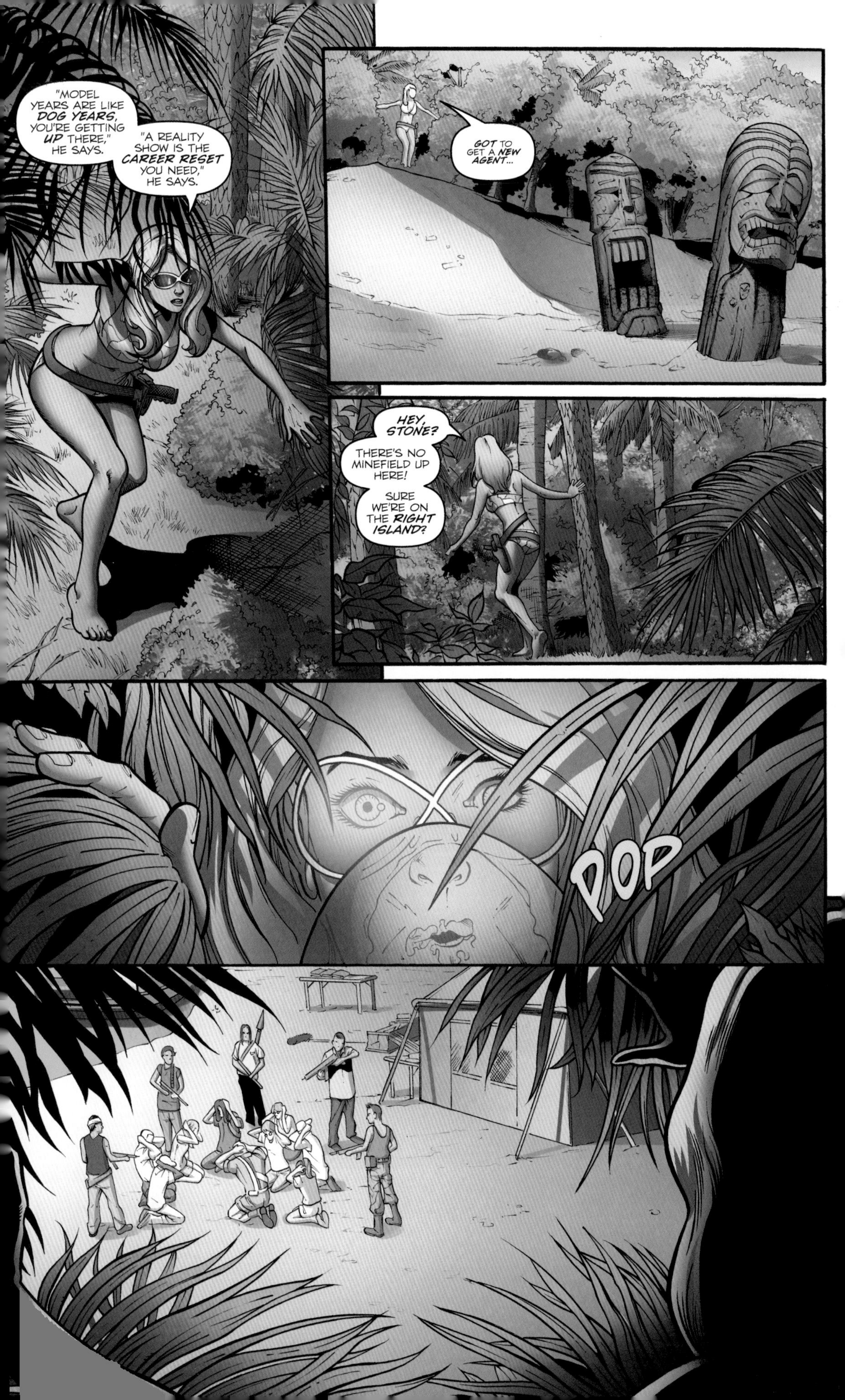

"MODEL YEARS ARE LIKE DOG YEARS, YOU'RE GETTING UP THERE," HE SAYS.
"A REALITY SHOW IS THE CAREER RESET YOU NEED," HE SAYS.
GOT TO GET A NEW AGENT...
HEY, STONE?
THERE'S NO MINEFIELD UP HERE!
SURE WE'RE ON THE RIGHT ISLAND?
POP

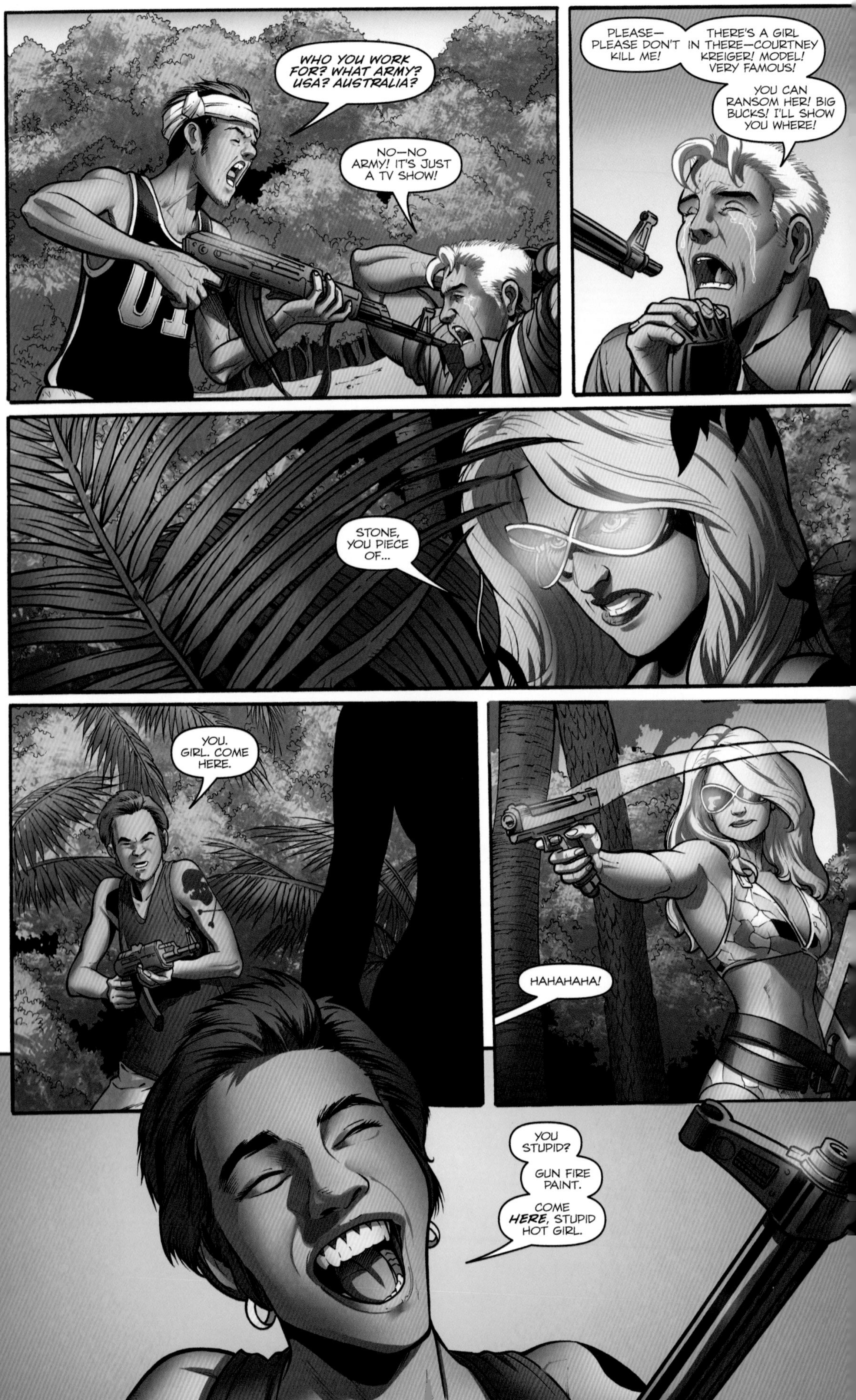
WHO YOU WORK FOR? WHAT ARMY? USA? AUSTRALIA?
NO—NO ARMY! IT'S JUST A TV SHOW!
PLEASE— PLEASE DON'T KILL ME!
THERE'S A GIRL IN THERE—COURTNEY KREIGER! MODEL! VERY FAMOUS!
YOU CAN RANSOM HER! BIG BUCKS! I'LL SHOW YOU WHERE!
STONE, YOU PIECE OF...
YOU. GIRL. COME HERE.
HAHAHAHA!
YOU STUPID?
GUN FIRE PAINT.
COME *HERE*, STUPID HOT GIRL.

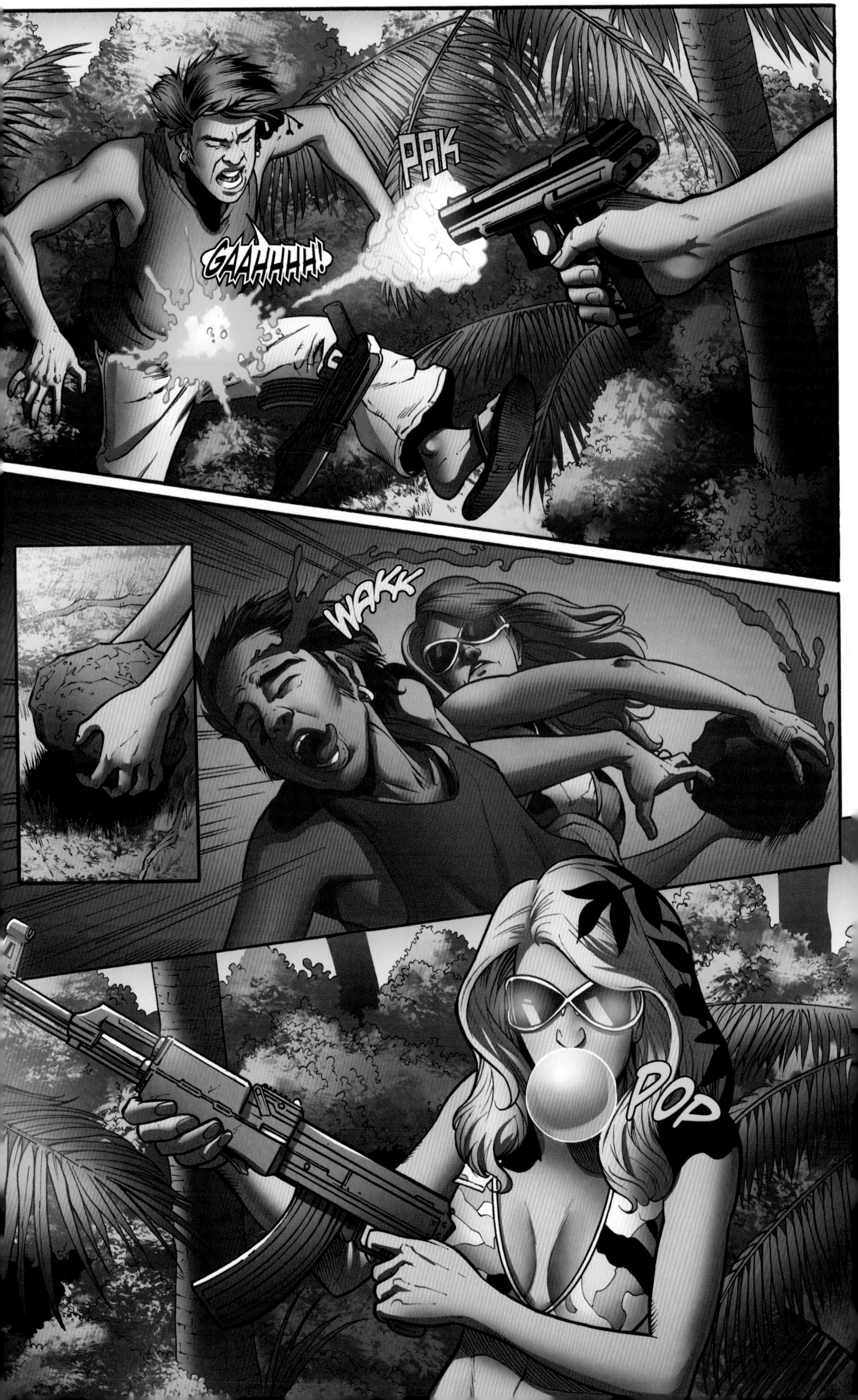
PAK
GAAHHHH!
WAKK
POP

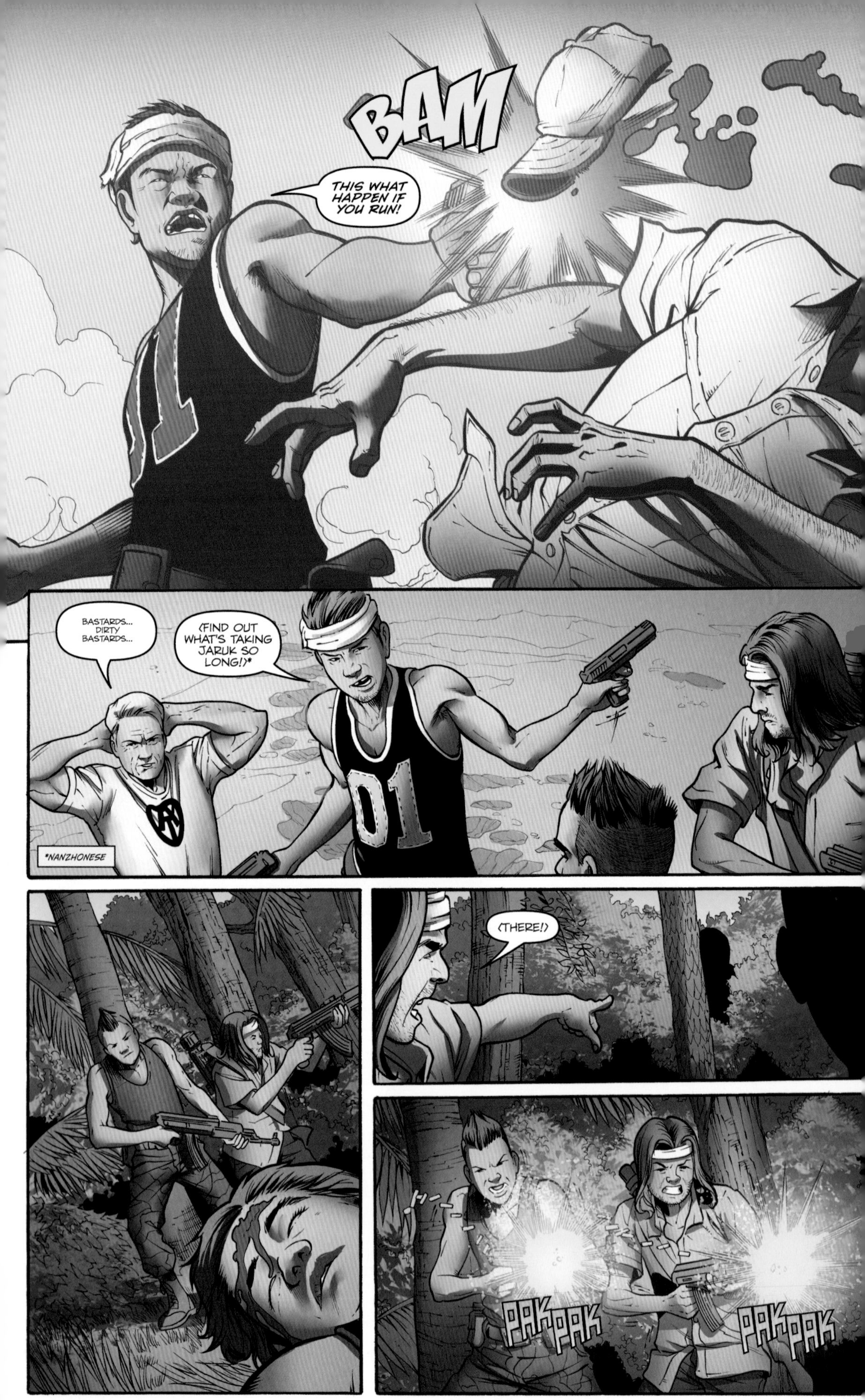
BAM
THIS WHAT HAPPEN IF YOU RUN!
BASTARDS... DIRTY BASTARDS...
(FIND OUT WHAT'S TAKING JARUK SO LONG!)*
*NANZHONESE
(THERE!)
PAKPAK
PAKPAK

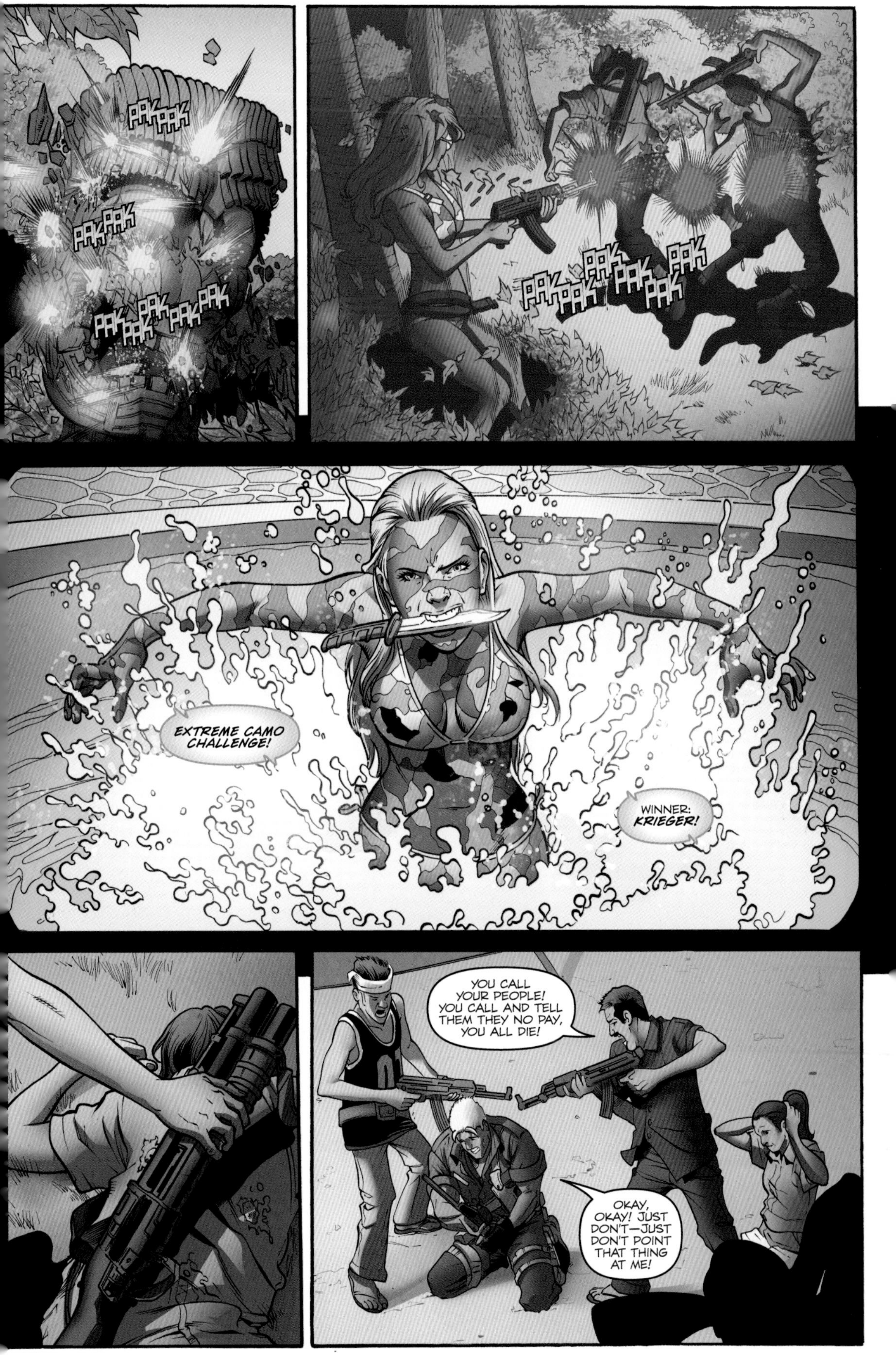
PAK PAK
PAK PAK
PAK PAK PAK PAK PAK
PAK PAK PAK PAK PAK PAK
EXTREME CAMO CHALLENGE!
WINNER: KRIEGER!
YOU CALL YOUR PEOPLE! YOU CALL AND TELL THEM THEY NO PAY, YOU ALL DIE!
OKAY, OKAY! JUST DON'T—JUST DON'T POINT THAT THING AT ME!

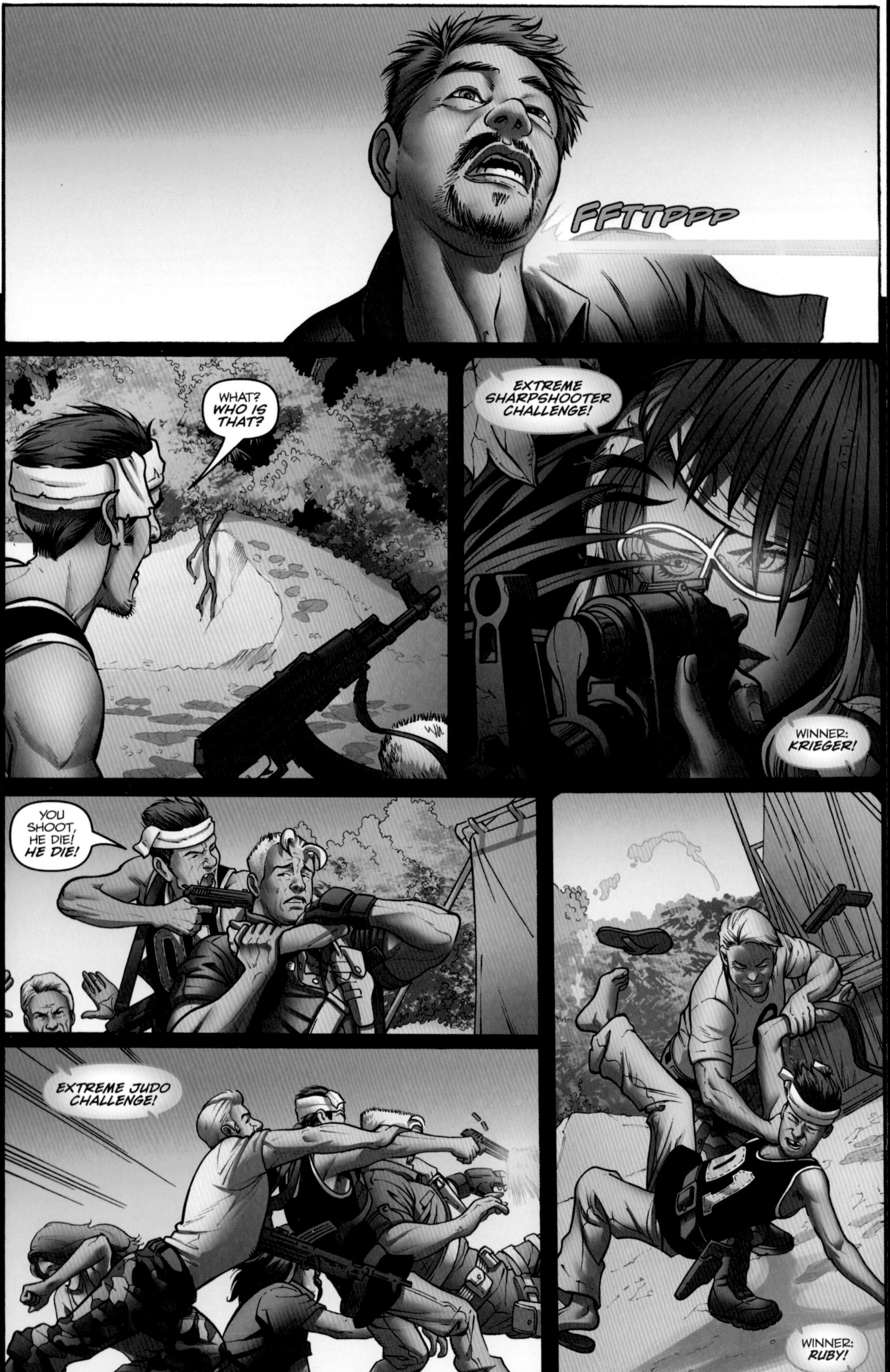
FFTTPPP
WHAT? WHO IS THAT?
EXTREME SHARPSHOOTER CHALLENGE!
WINNER: KRIEGER!
YOU SHOOT, HE DIE! HE DIE!
EXTREME JUDO CHALLENGE!
WINNER: RUBY!

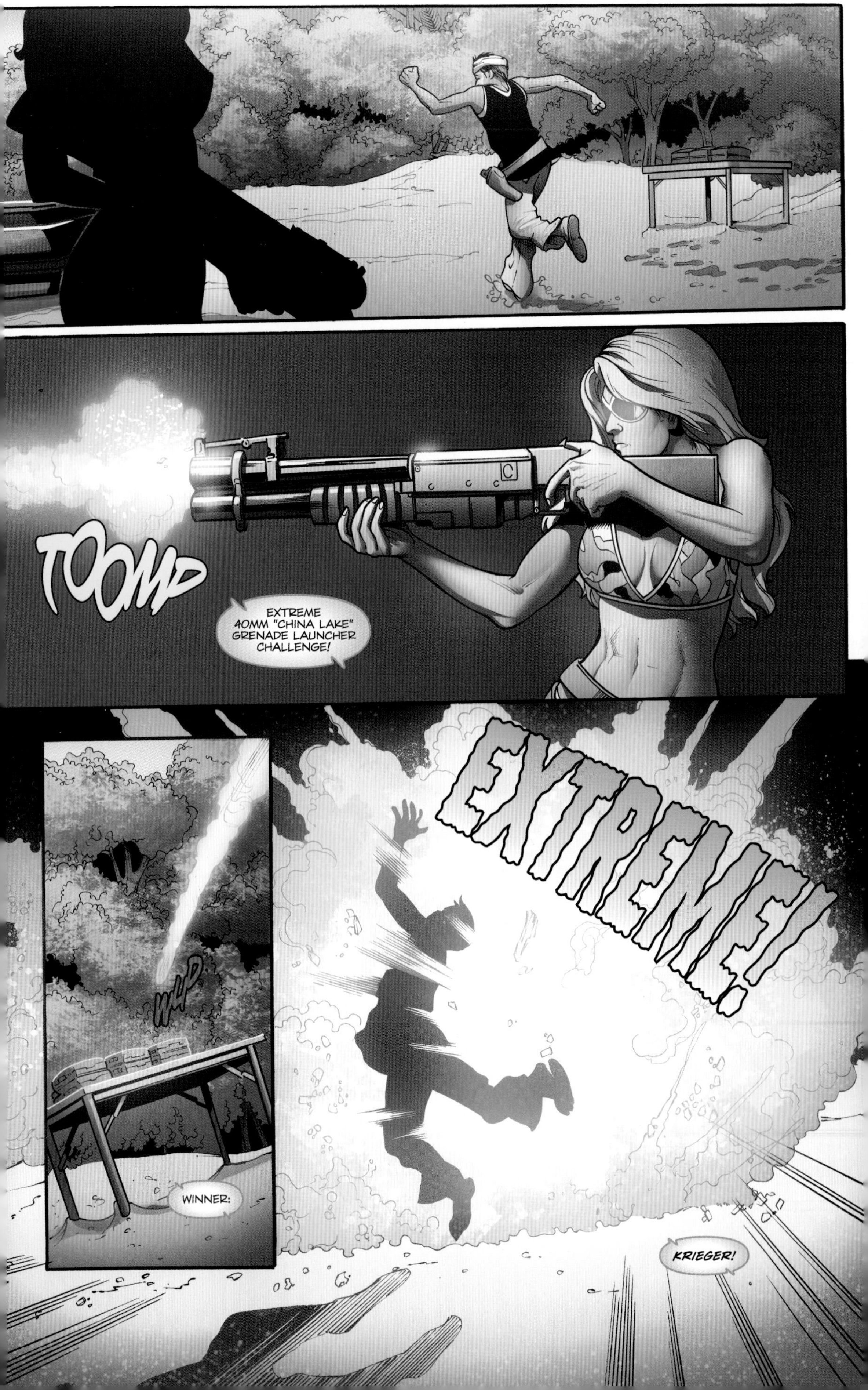
TOOMP
EXTREME 40MM "CHINA LAKE" GRENADE LAUNCHER CHALLENGE!
WHIP
WINNER:
EXTREME!!
KRIEGER!

PIRATES.

FROM *NANZHOU*, FROM THE SOUND OF THEIR LANGUAGE. NOT TOO FAR FROM HERE.

GUESS WE LANDED ON THEIR BASE BY ACCIDENT.

COURTNEY...

WHAT'S THAT, STONE? I HEAR A HIGH-PITCHED, WHINING SOUND.

NOT UNLIKE *AIR* ESCAPING FROM A *BALLOON*.

THAT WAS... IMPRESSIVE.

WHAT, JUST BECAUSE I PAID ATTENTION WHEN THEY PUT US THROUGH FAUX-BASIC TRAINING?

THAT WAS ABOVE AND BEYOND. YOU'RE A NATURAL.

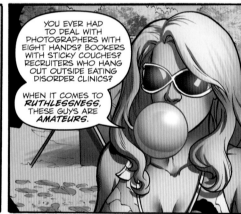

YOU EVER HAD TO DEAL WITH PHOTOGRAPHERS WITH EIGHT HANDS? BOOKERS WITH STICKY COUCHES? RECRUITERS WHO HANG OUT OUTSIDE EATING DISORDER CLINICS?

WHEN IT COMES TO *RUTHLESSNESS*, THESE GUYS ARE *AMATEURS*.

IF YOU EVER WANT TO CHANGE CAREERS, I KNOW A GUY TO TALK TO.

THESE DAYS HE GOES BY "HAWK."

YEAH? WHAT KINDA CAREER ARE YOU REFERRING TO? I NEVER CAUGHT WHAT YOU WERE FAMOUS *FOR*, RICHARD.

OH.

OH, WOW.

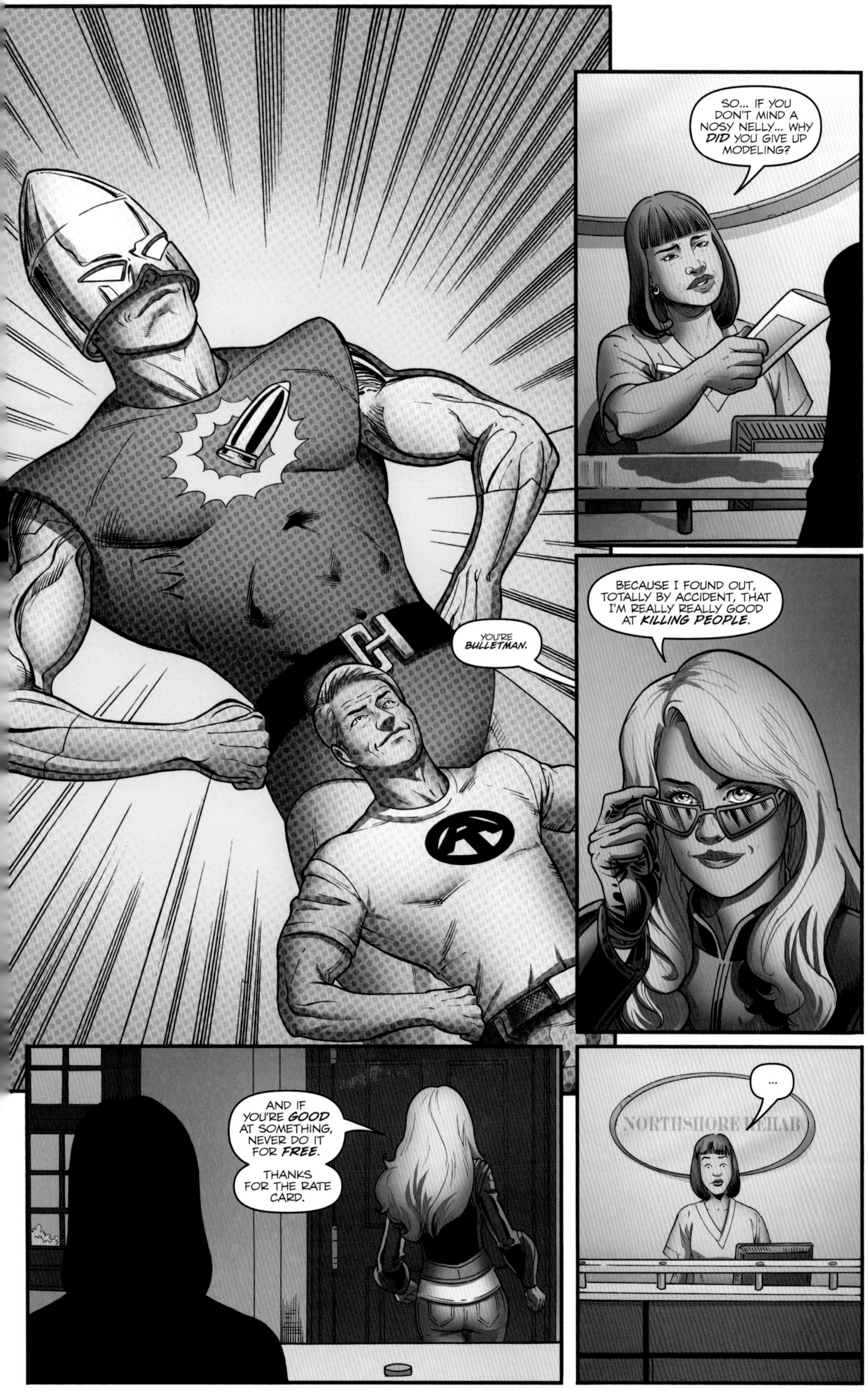
YOU'RE BULLETMAN.
SO... IF YOU DON'T MIND A NOSY NELLY... WHY DID YOU GIVE UP MODELING?
BECAUSE I FOUND OUT, TOTALLY BY ACCIDENT, THAT I'M REALLY REALLY GOOD AT KILLING PEOPLE.
AND IF YOU'RE GOOD AT SOMETHING, NEVER DO IT FOR FREE.
THANKS FOR THE RATE CARD.
...
NORTHSHORE REHAB

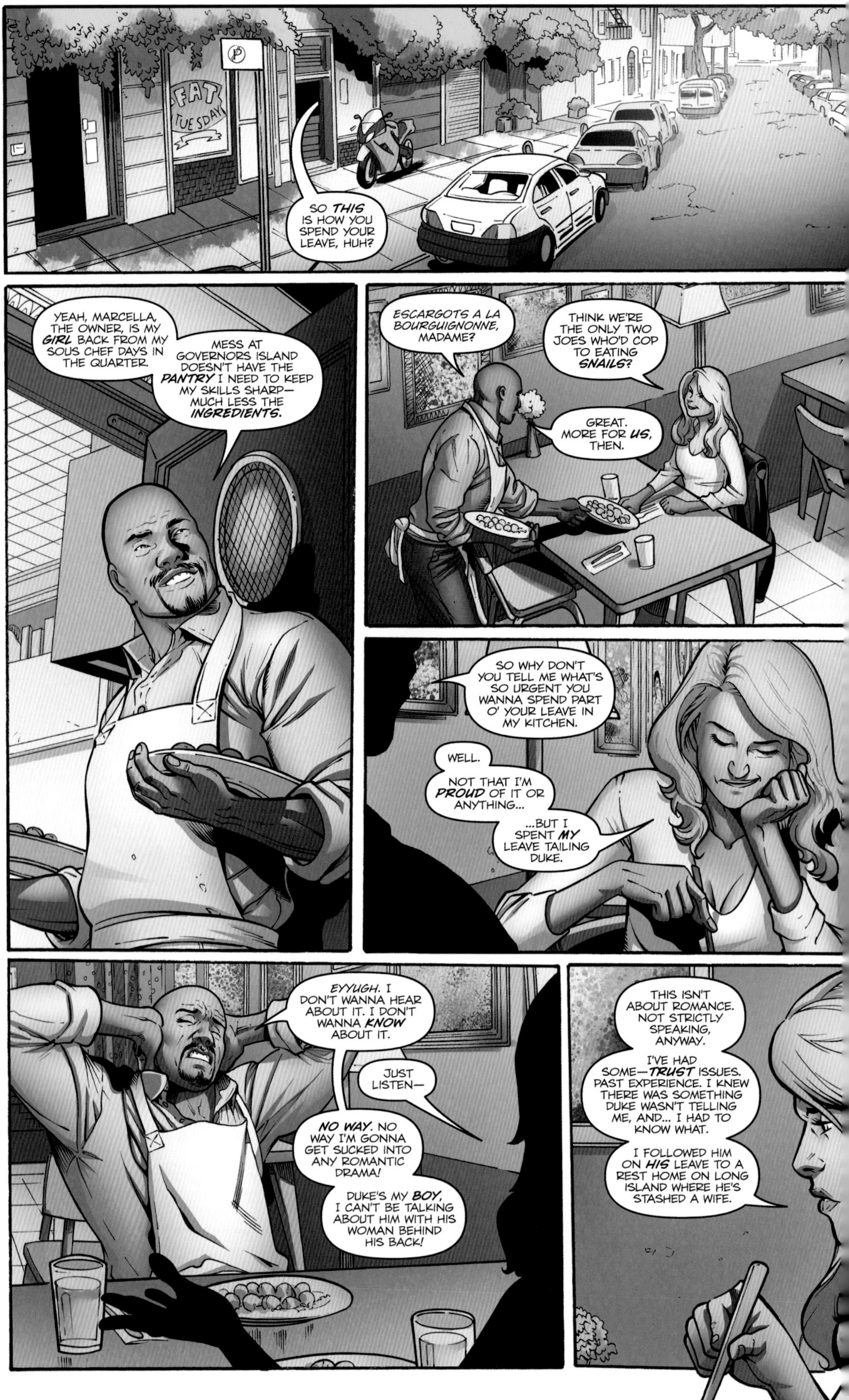
FAT TUESDAY
SO THIS IS HOW YOU SPEND YOUR LEAVE, HUH?
YEAH, MARCELLA, THE OWNER, IS MY GIRL BACK FROM MY SOUS CHEF DAYS IN THE QUARTER.
MESS AT GOVERNORS ISLAND DOESN'T HAVE THE PANTRY I NEED TO KEEP MY SKILLS SHARP— MUCH LESS THE INGREDIENTS.
ESCARGOTS A LA BOURGUIGNONNE, MADAME?
THINK WE'RE THE ONLY TWO JOES WHO'D COP TO EATING SNAILS?
GREAT. MORE FOR US, THEN.
SO WHY DON'T YOU TELL ME WHAT'S SO URGENT YOU WANNA SPEND PART O' YOUR LEAVE IN MY KITCHEN.
WELL.
NOT THAT I'M PROUD OF IT OR ANYTHING...
...BUT I SPENT MY LEAVE TAILING DUKE.
EYYUGH. I DON'T WANNA HEAR ABOUT IT. I DON'T WANNA KNOW ABOUT IT.
JUST LISTEN—
NO WAY. NO WAY I'M GONNA GET SUCKED INTO ANY ROMANTIC DRAMA!
DUKE'S MY BOY, I CAN'T BE TALKING ABOUT HIM WITH HIS WOMAN BEHIND HIS BACK!
THIS ISN'T ABOUT ROMANCE. NOT STRICTLY SPEAKING, ANYWAY.
I'VE HAD SOME—TRUST ISSUES. PAST EXPERIENCE. I KNEW THERE WAS SOMETHING DUKE WASN'T TELLING ME, AND... I HAD TO KNOW WHAT.
I FOLLOWED HIM ON HIS LEAVE TO A REST HOME ON LONG ISLAND WHERE HE'S STASHED A WIFE.

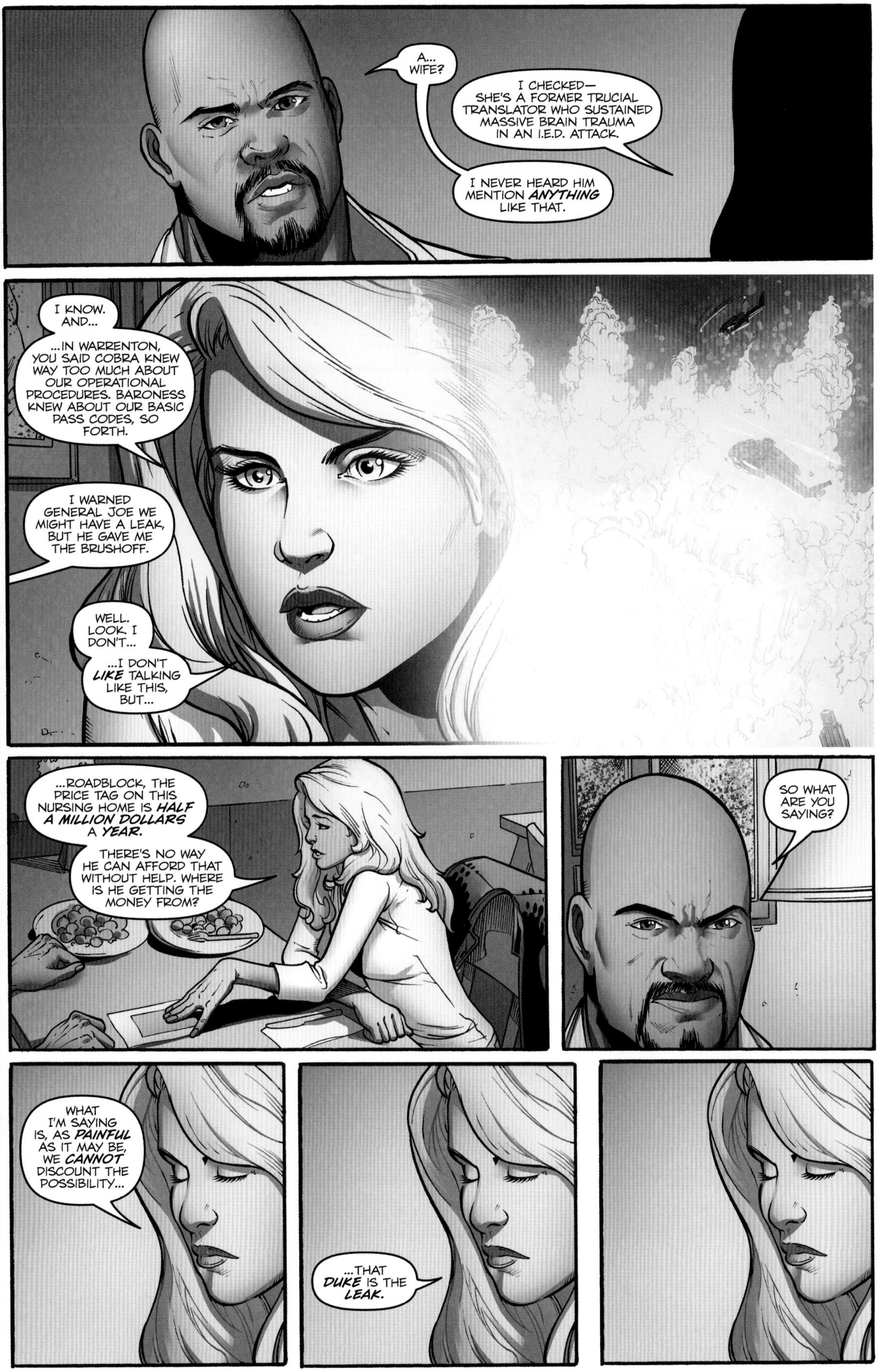
A... WIFE?
I CHECKED— SHE'S A FORMER TRUCIAL TRANSLATOR WHO SUSTAINED MASSIVE BRAIN TRAUMA IN AN I.E.D. ATTACK.
I NEVER HEARD HIM MENTION ANYTHING LIKE THAT.
I KNOW. AND...
...IN WARRENTON, YOU SAID COBRA KNEW WAY TOO MUCH ABOUT OUR OPERATIONAL PROCEDURES. BARONESS KNEW ABOUT OUR BASIC PASS CODES, SO FORTH.
I WARNED GENERAL JOE WE MIGHT HAVE A LEAK, BUT HE GAVE ME THE BRUSHOFF.
WELL. LOOK. I DON'T...
...I DON'T LIKE TALKING LIKE THIS, BUT...
...ROADBLOCK, THE PRICE TAG ON THIS NURSING HOME IS HALF A MILLION DOLLARS A YEAR.
THERE'S NO WAY HE CAN AFFORD THAT WITHOUT HELP. WHERE IS HE GETTING THE MONEY FROM?
SO WHAT ARE YOU SAYING?
WHAT I'M SAYING IS, AS PAINFUL AS IT MAY BE, WE CANNOT DISCOUNT THE POSSIBILITY...
...THAT DUKE IS THE LEAK.

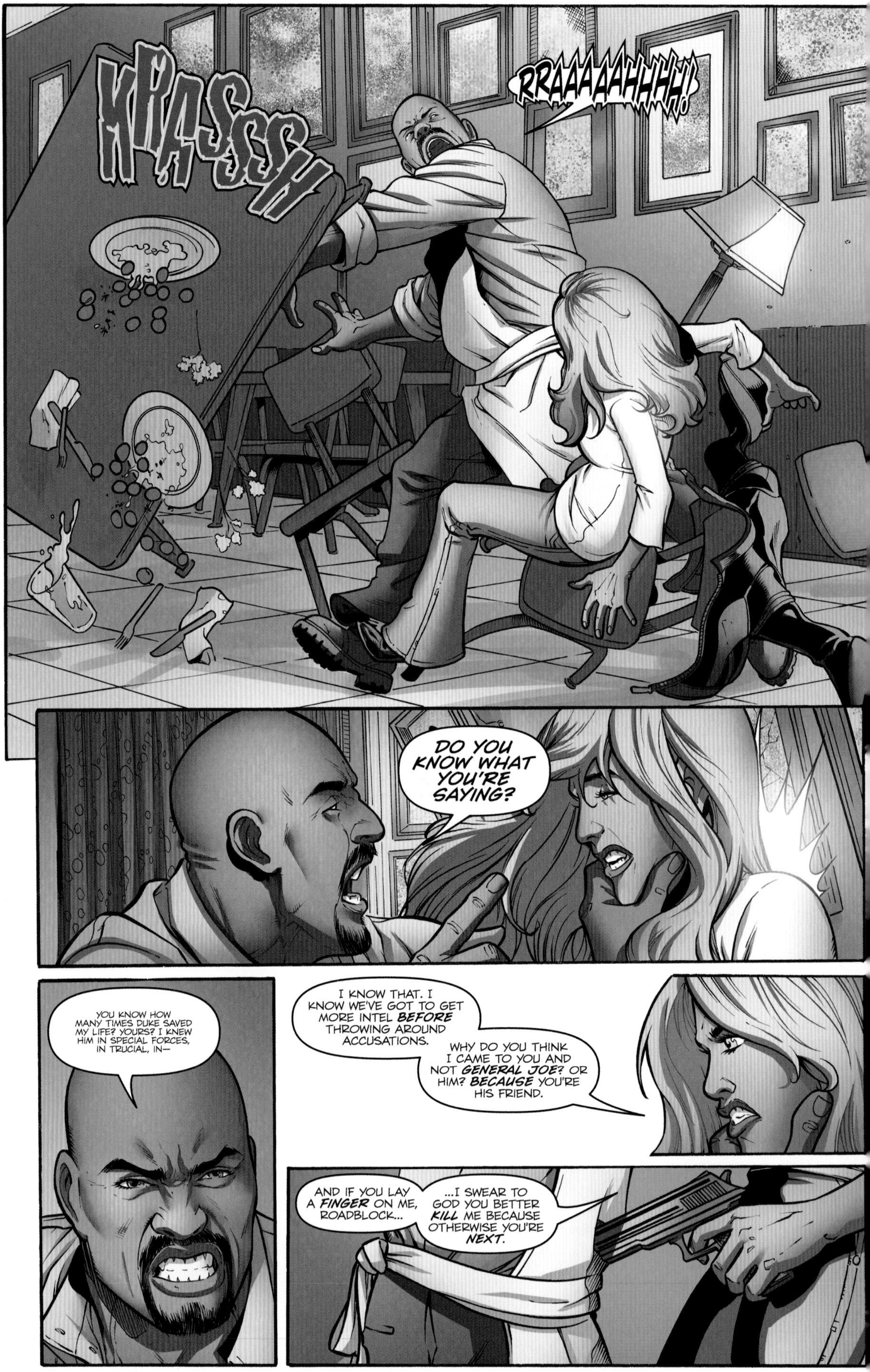
KRASSSH
RRAAAAAHHHH!
DO YOU KNOW WHAT YOU'RE SAYING?
YOU KNOW HOW MANY TIMES DUKE SAVED MY LIFE? YOURS? I KNEW HIM IN SPECIAL FORCES, IN TRUCIAL, IN—
I KNOW THAT. I KNOW WE'VE GOT TO GET MORE INTEL BEFORE THROWING AROUND ACCUSATIONS.
WHY DO YOU THINK I CAME TO YOU AND NOT GENERAL JOE? OR HIM? BECAUSE YOU'RE HIS FRIEND.
AND IF YOU LAY A FINGER ON ME, ROADBLOCK...
...I SWEAR TO GOD YOU BETTER KILL ME BECAUSE OTHERWISE YOU'RE NEXT.

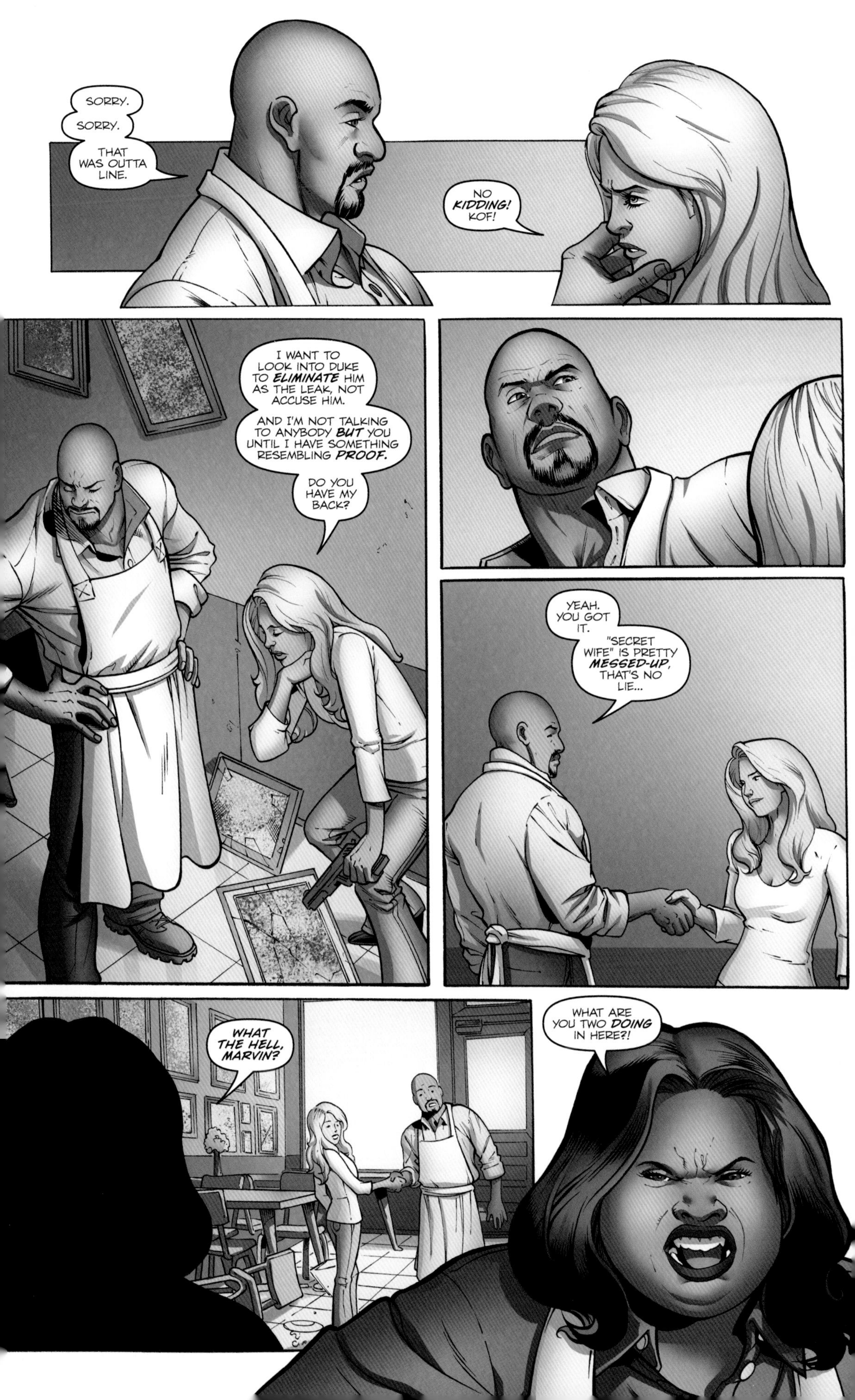
SORRY.
SORRY.
THAT WAS OUTTA LINE.
NO KIDDING! KOF!
I WANT TO LOOK INTO DUKE TO ELIMINATE HIM AS THE LEAK, NOT ACCUSE HIM.
AND I'M NOT TALKING TO ANYBODY BUT YOU UNTIL I HAVE SOMETHING RESEMBLING PROOF.
DO YOU HAVE MY BACK?
YEAH. YOU GOT IT.
"SECRET WIFE" IS PRETTY MESSED-UP, THAT'S NO LIE...
WHAT THE HELL, MARVIN?
WHAT ARE YOU TWO DOING IN HERE?!

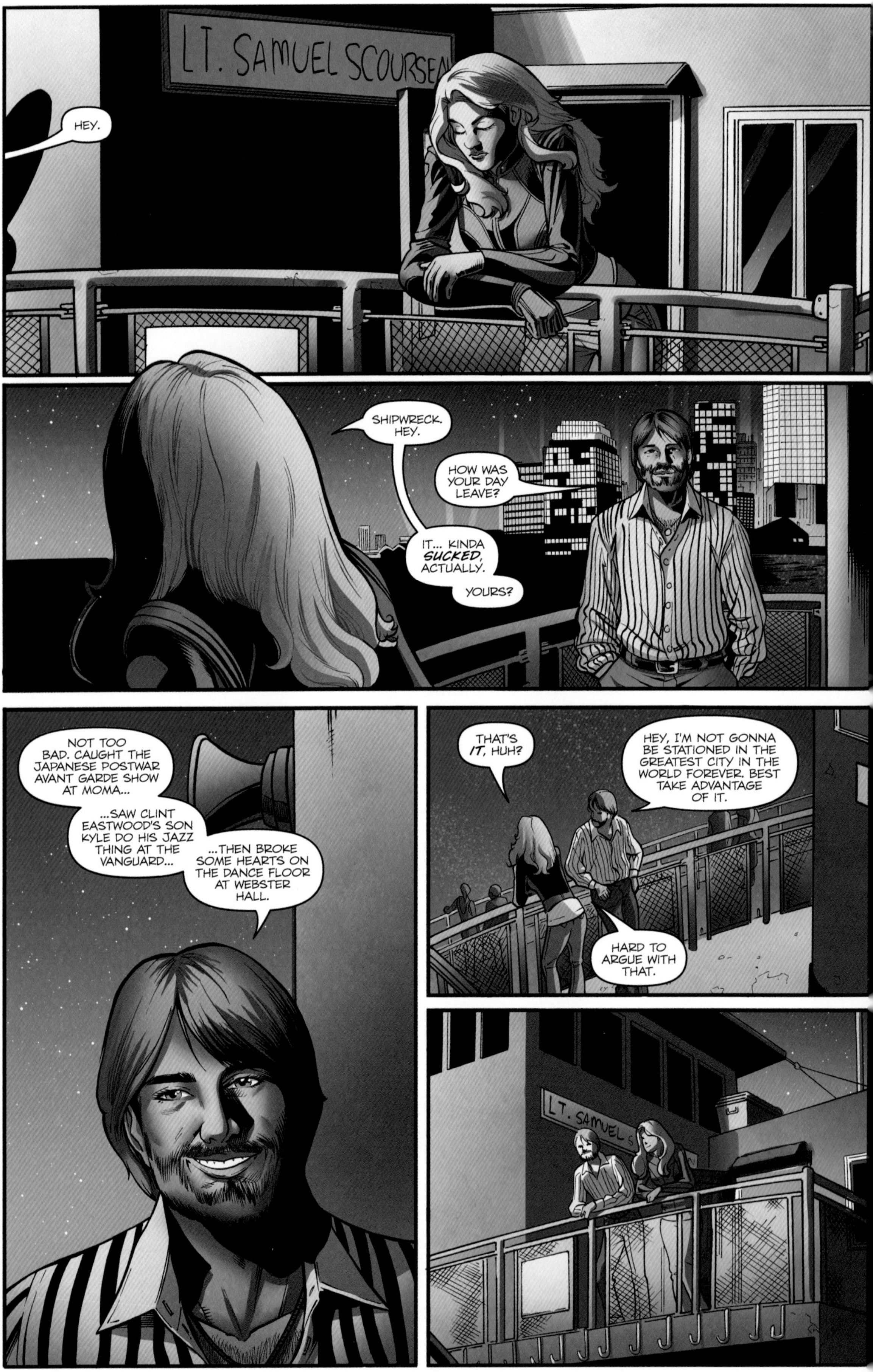

LT. SAMUEL SCOURSEA
HEY.
SHIPWRECK. HEY.
HOW WAS YOUR DAY LEAVE?
IT... KINDA *SUCKED*, ACTUALLY.
YOURS?
NOT TOO BAD. CAUGHT THE JAPANESE POSTWAR AVANT GARDE SHOW AT MOMA...
...SAW CLINT EASTWOOD'S SON KYLE DO HIS JAZZ THING AT THE VANGUARD...
...THEN BROKE SOME HEARTS ON THE DANCE FLOOR AT WEBSTER HALL.
THAT'S *IT*, HUH?
HEY, I'M NOT GONNA BE STATIONED IN THE GREATEST CITY IN THE WORLD FOREVER. BEST TAKE ADVANTAGE OF IT.
HARD TO ARGUE WITH THAT.
LT. SAMUEL S

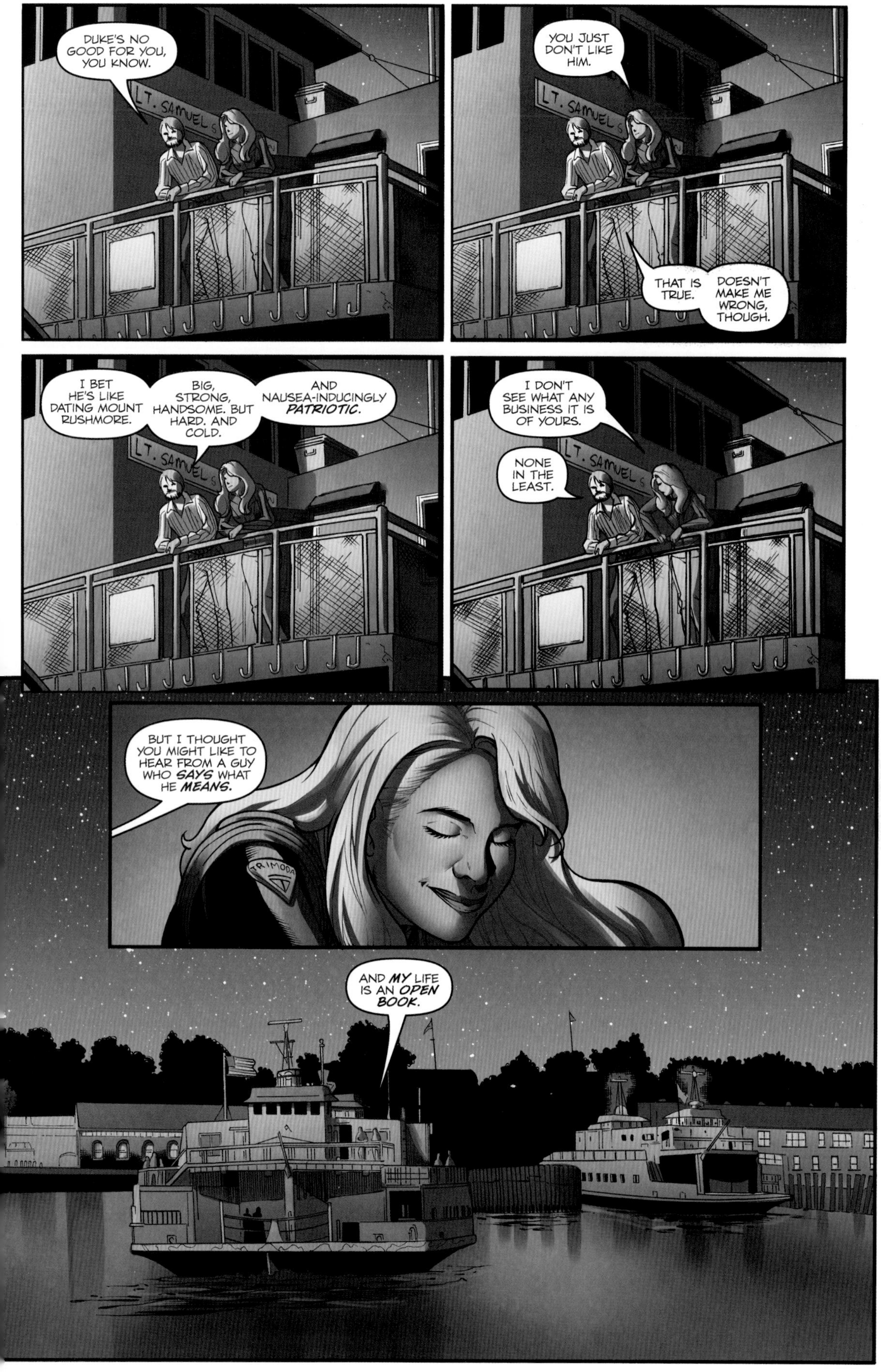

DUKE'S NO GOOD FOR YOU, YOU KNOW.
LT. SAMUEL
YOU JUST DON'T LIKE HIM.
THAT IS TRUE.
DOESN'T MAKE ME WRONG, THOUGH.
I BET HE'S LIKE DATING MOUNT RUSHMORE.
BIG, STRONG, HANDSOME. BUT HARD. AND COLD.
AND NAUSEA-INDUCINGLY *PATRIOTIC*.
I DON'T SEE WHAT ANY BUSINESS IT IS OF YOURS.
NONE IN THE LEAST.
BUT I THOUGHT YOU MIGHT LIKE TO HEAR FROM A GUY WHO *SAYS* WHAT HE *MEANS*.
AND *MY* LIFE IS AN *OPEN BOOK*.

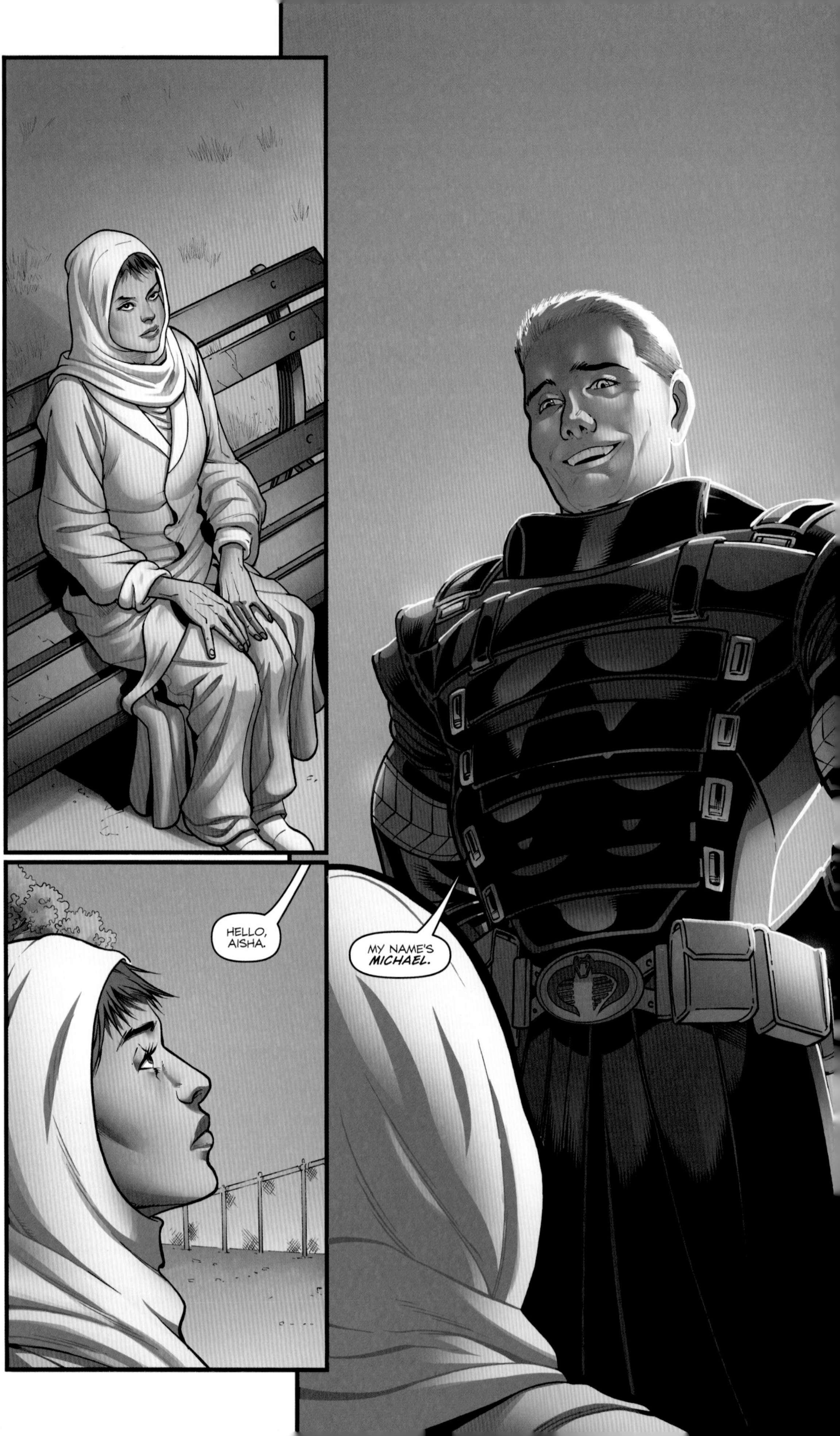
HELLO, AISHA.
MY NAME'S *MICHAEL.*

CHAPTER TWO

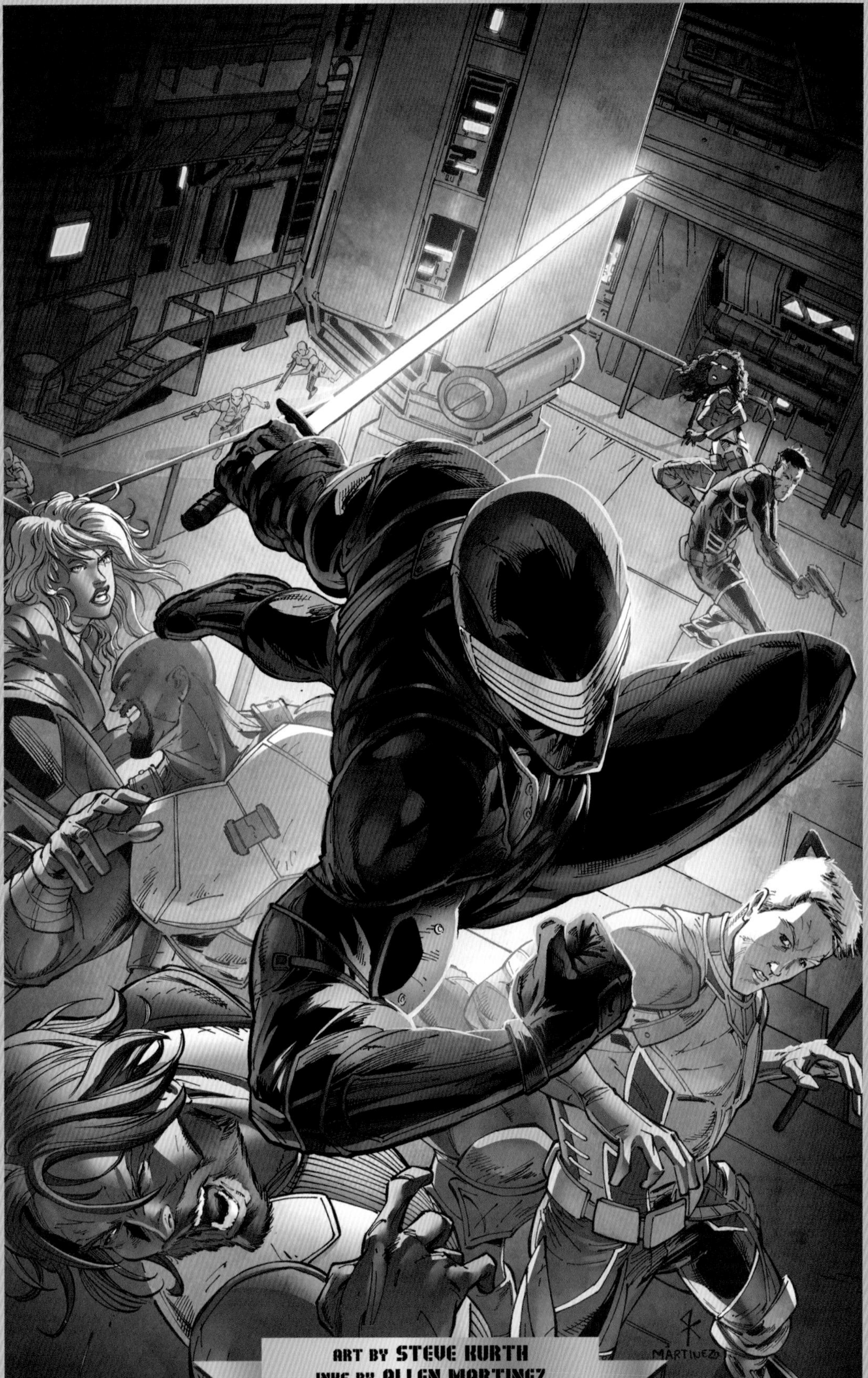

ART BY **STEVE KURTH**
INKS BY **ALLEN MARTINEZ**
COLORS BY **JOANA LAFUENTE**

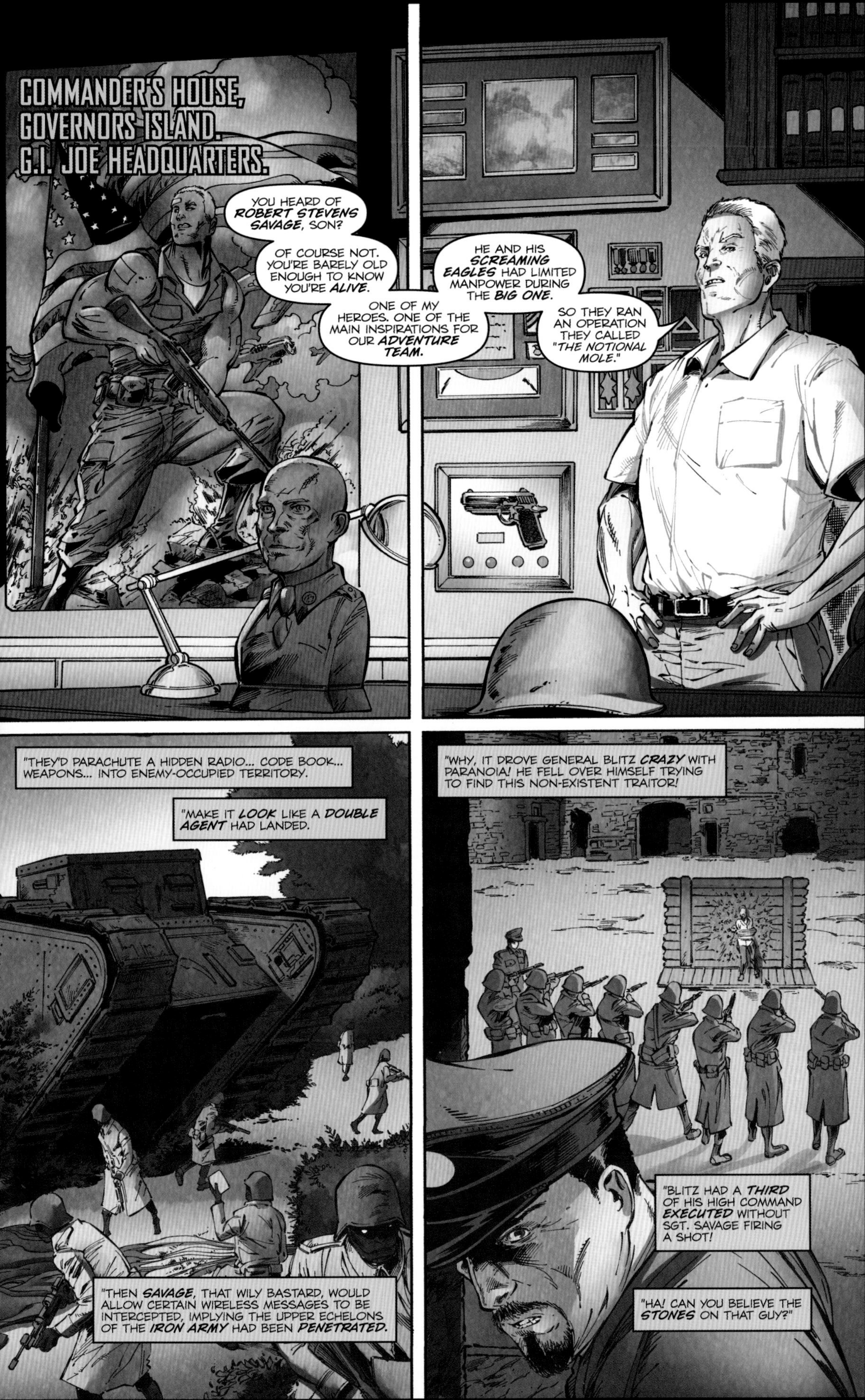
COMMANDER'S HOUSE, GOVERNORS ISLAND. G.I. JOE HEADQUARTERS.
YOU HEARD OF ROBERT STEVENS SAVAGE, SON?
OF COURSE NOT. YOU'RE BARELY OLD ENOUGH TO KNOW YOU'RE ALIVE.
ONE OF MY HEROES. ONE OF THE MAIN INSPIRATIONS FOR OUR ADVENTURE TEAM.
HE AND HIS SCREAMING EAGLES HAD LIMITED MANPOWER DURING THE BIG ONE.
SO THEY RAN AN OPERATION THEY CALLED "THE NOTIONAL MOLE."
"THEY'D PARACHUTE A HIDDEN RADIO... CODE BOOK... WEAPONS... INTO ENEMY-OCCUPIED TERRITORY.
"MAKE IT LOOK LIKE A DOUBLE AGENT HAD LANDED.
"THEN SAVAGE, THAT WILY BASTARD, WOULD ALLOW CERTAIN WIRELESS MESSAGES TO BE INTERCEPTED, IMPLYING THE UPPER ECHELONS OF THE IRON ARMY HAD BEEN PENETRATED.
"WHY, IT DROVE GENERAL BLITZ CRAZY WITH PARANOIA! HE FELL OVER HIMSELF TRYING TO FIND THIS NON-EXISTENT TRAITOR!
"BLITZ HAD A THIRD OF HIS HIGH COMMAND EXECUTED WITHOUT SGT. SAVAGE FIRING A SHOT!
"HA! CAN YOU BELIEVE THE STONES ON THAT GUY?"

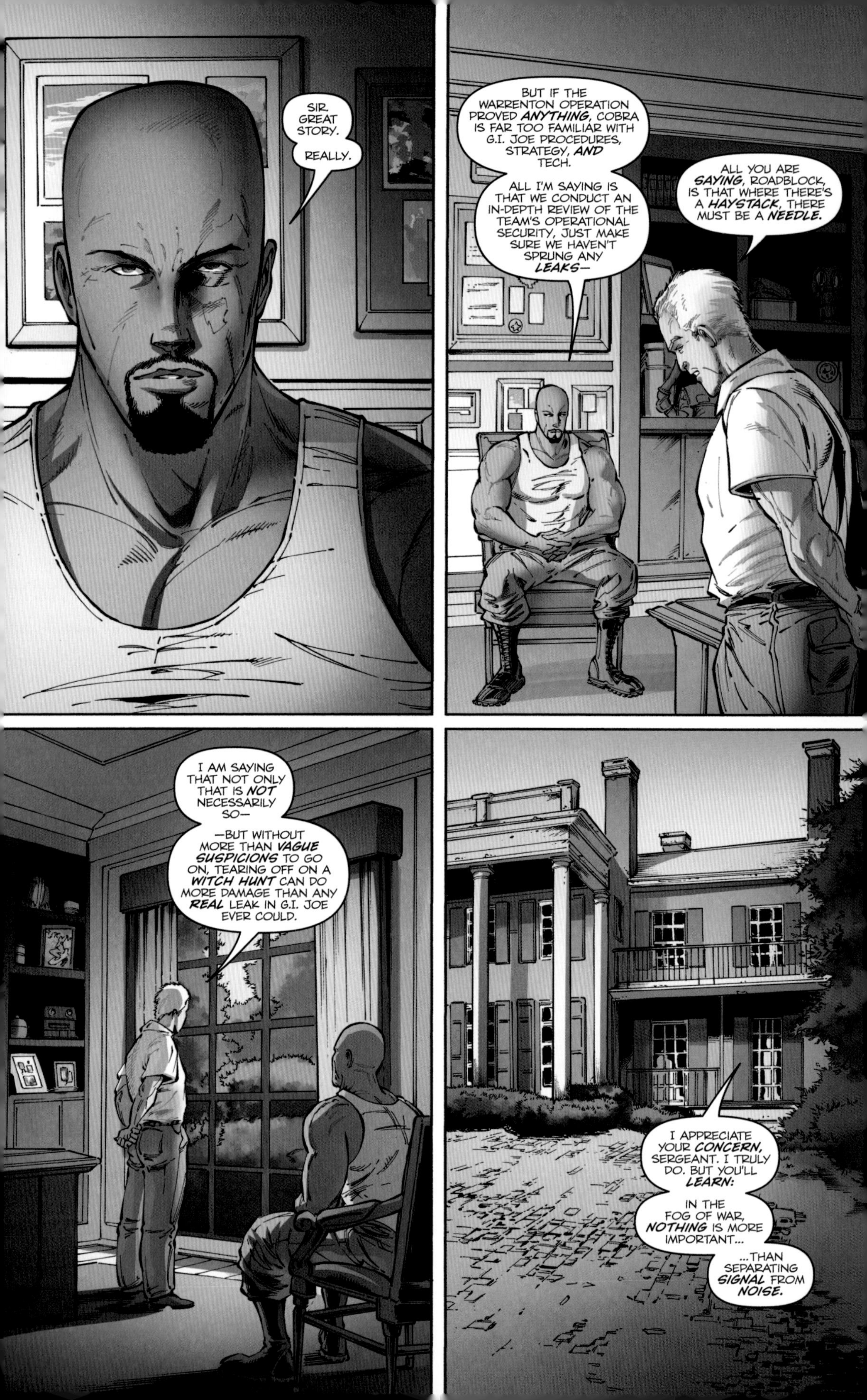
SIR. GREAT STORY.
REALLY.
BUT IF THE WARRENTON OPERATION PROVED ANYTHING, COBRA IS FAR TOO FAMILIAR WITH G.I. JOE PROCEDURES, STRATEGY, AND TECH.
ALL I'M SAYING IS THAT WE CONDUCT AN IN-DEPTH REVIEW OF THE TEAM'S OPERATIONAL SECURITY, JUST MAKE SURE WE HAVEN'T SPRUNG ANY LEAKS—
ALL YOU ARE SAYING, ROADBLOCK, IS THAT WHERE THERE'S A HAYSTACK, THERE MUST BE A NEEDLE.
I AM SAYING THAT NOT ONLY THAT IS NOT NECESSARILY SO—
—BUT WITHOUT MORE THAN VAGUE SUSPICIONS TO GO ON, TEARING OFF ON A WITCH HUNT CAN DO MORE DAMAGE THAN ANY REAL LEAK IN G.I. JOE EVER COULD.
I APPRECIATE YOUR CONCERN, SERGEANT. I TRULY DO. BUT YOU'LL LEARN:
IN THE FOG OF WAR, NOTHING IS MORE IMPORTANT...
...THAN SEPARATING SIGNAL FROM NOISE.

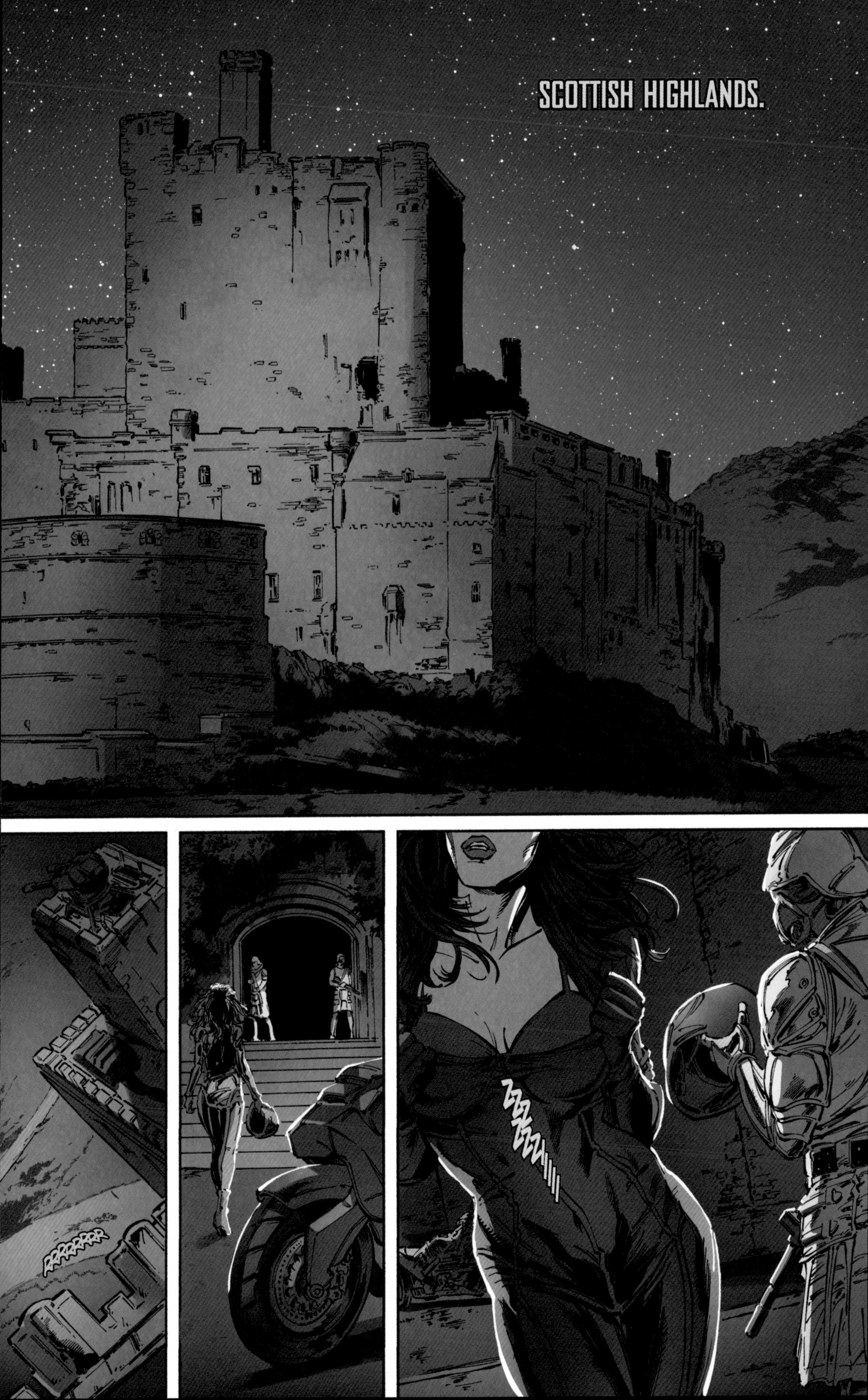
SCOTTISH HIGHLANDS.
RRRRRRRR
ZZZZZ

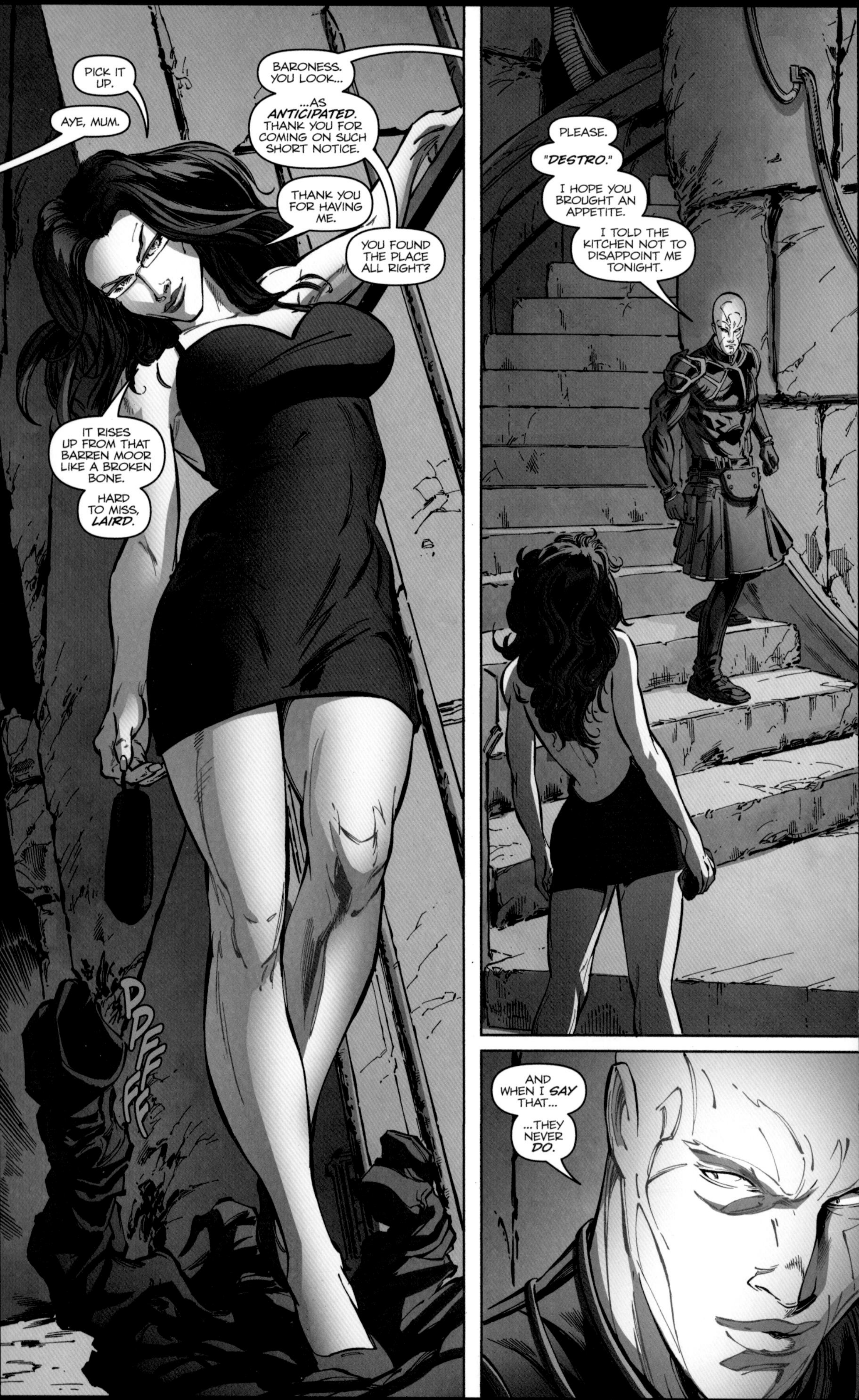
PICK IT UP.
AYE, MUM.
BARONESS. YOU LOOK...
...AS *ANTICIPATED.* THANK YOU FOR COMING ON SUCH SHORT NOTICE.
THANK YOU FOR HAVING ME.
YOU FOUND THE PLACE ALL RIGHT?
IT RISES UP FROM THAT BARREN MOOR LIKE A BROKEN BONE.
HARD TO MISS, *LAIRD*.
PDFFFF
PLEASE.
"*DESTRO.*"
I HOPE YOU BROUGHT AN APPETITE.
I TOLD THE KITCHEN NOT TO DISAPPOINT ME TONIGHT.
AND WHEN I *SAY* THAT...
...THEY NEVER *DO*.

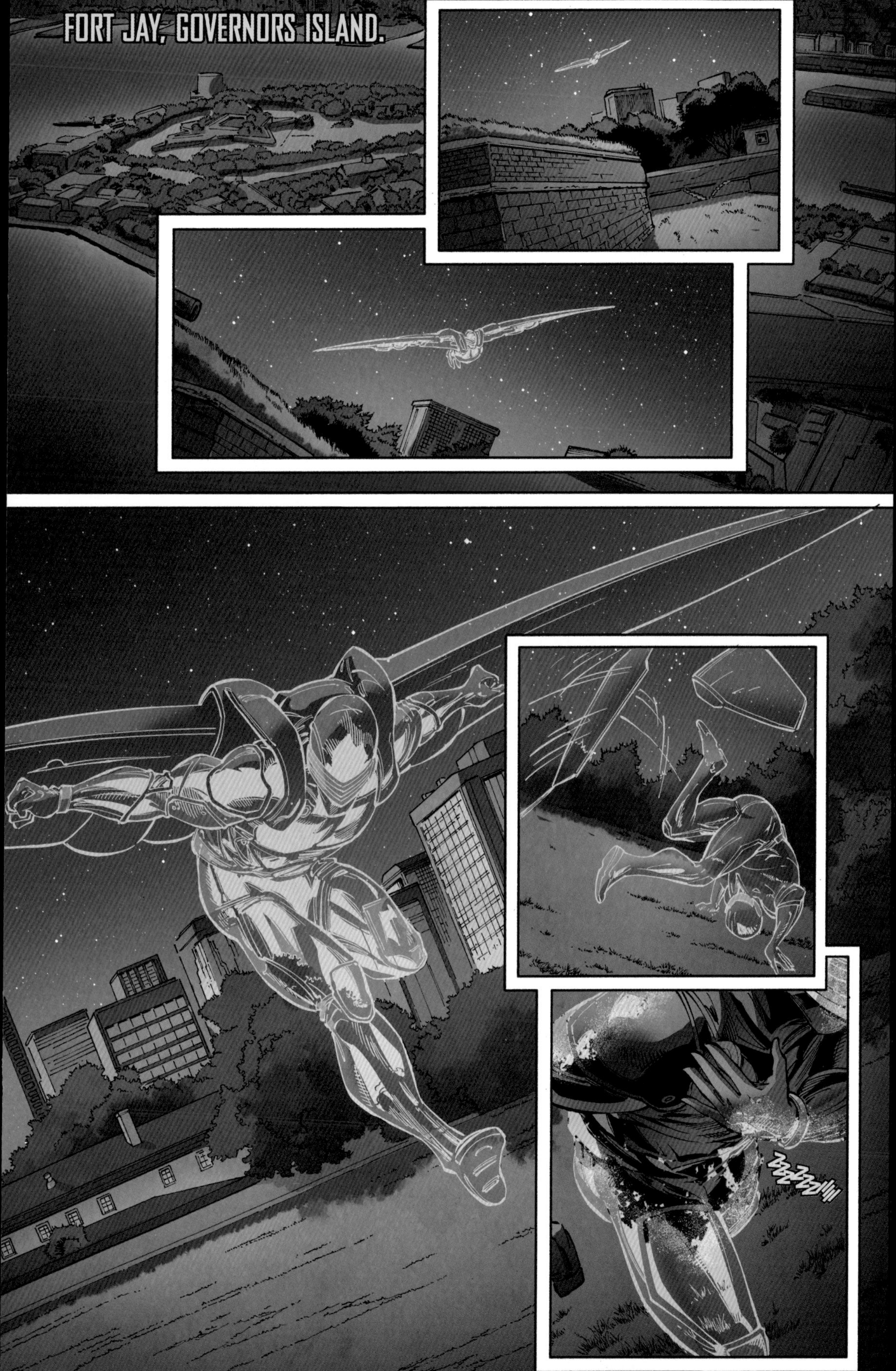
FORT JAY, GOVERNORS ISLAND.
ZZZZZZZ

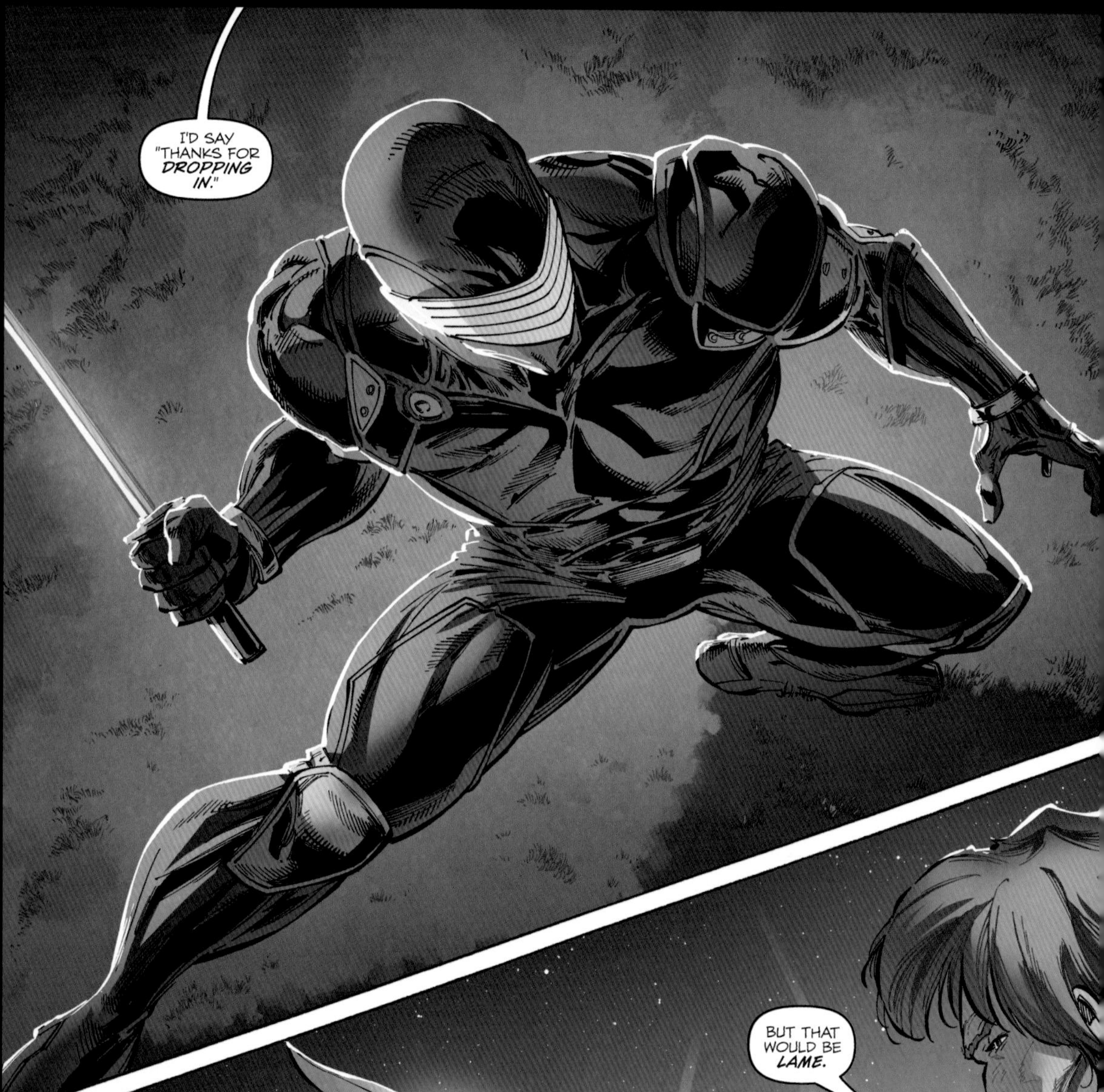
I'D SAY "THANKS FOR DROPPING IN."

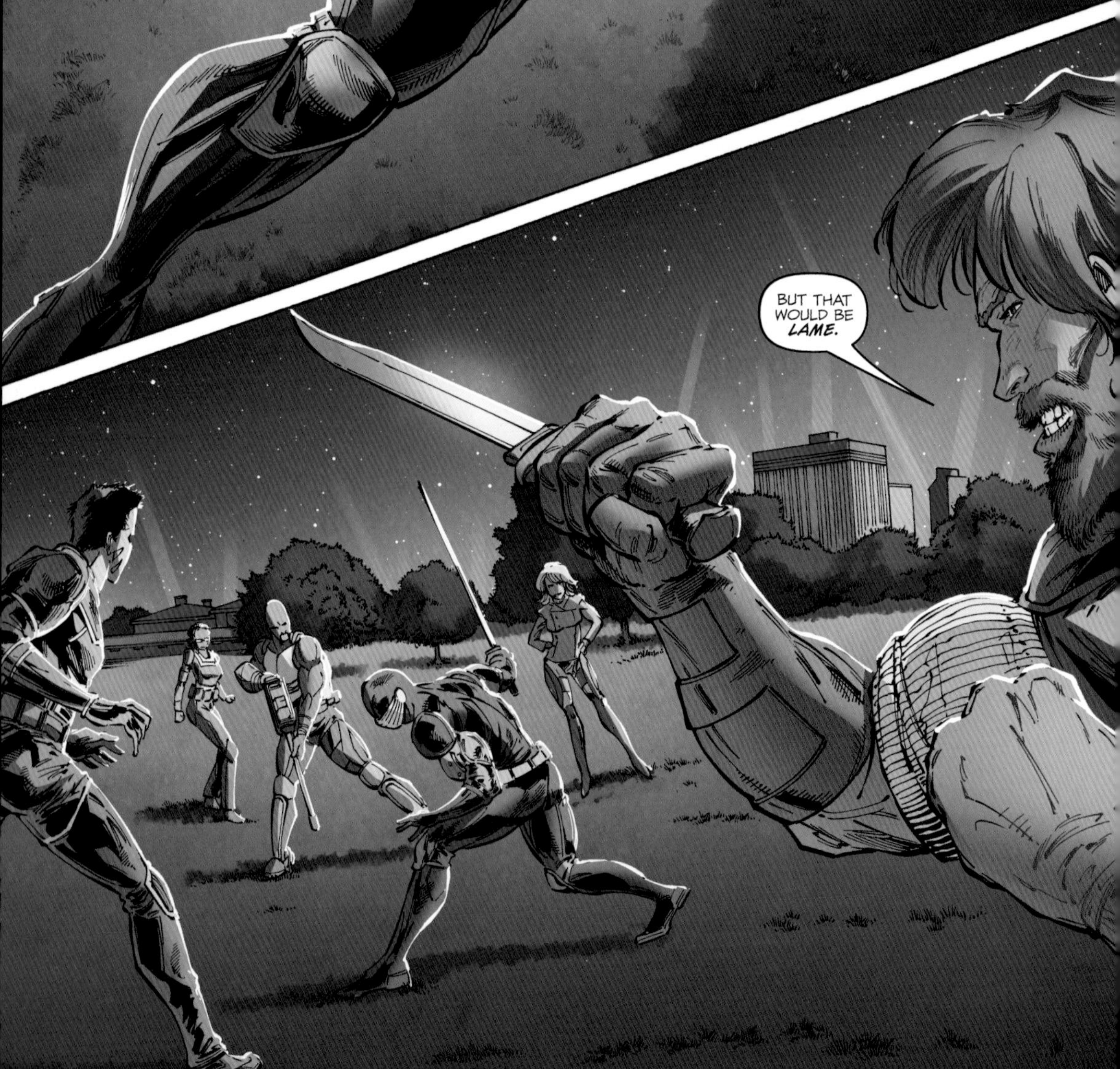
BUT THAT WOULD BE LAME.

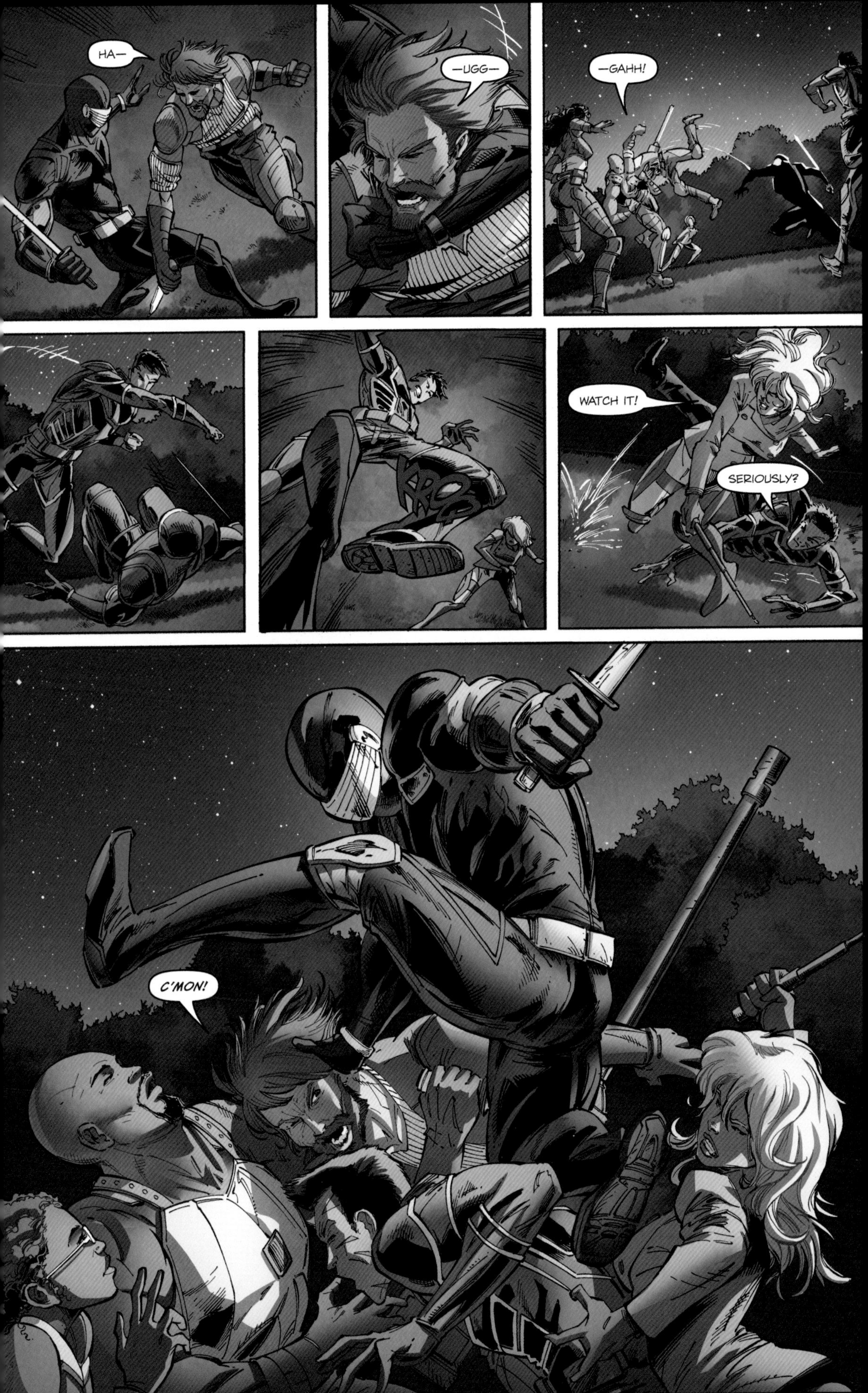
HA—
—UGG—
—GAHH!
WATCH IT!
SERIOUSLY?
C'MON!

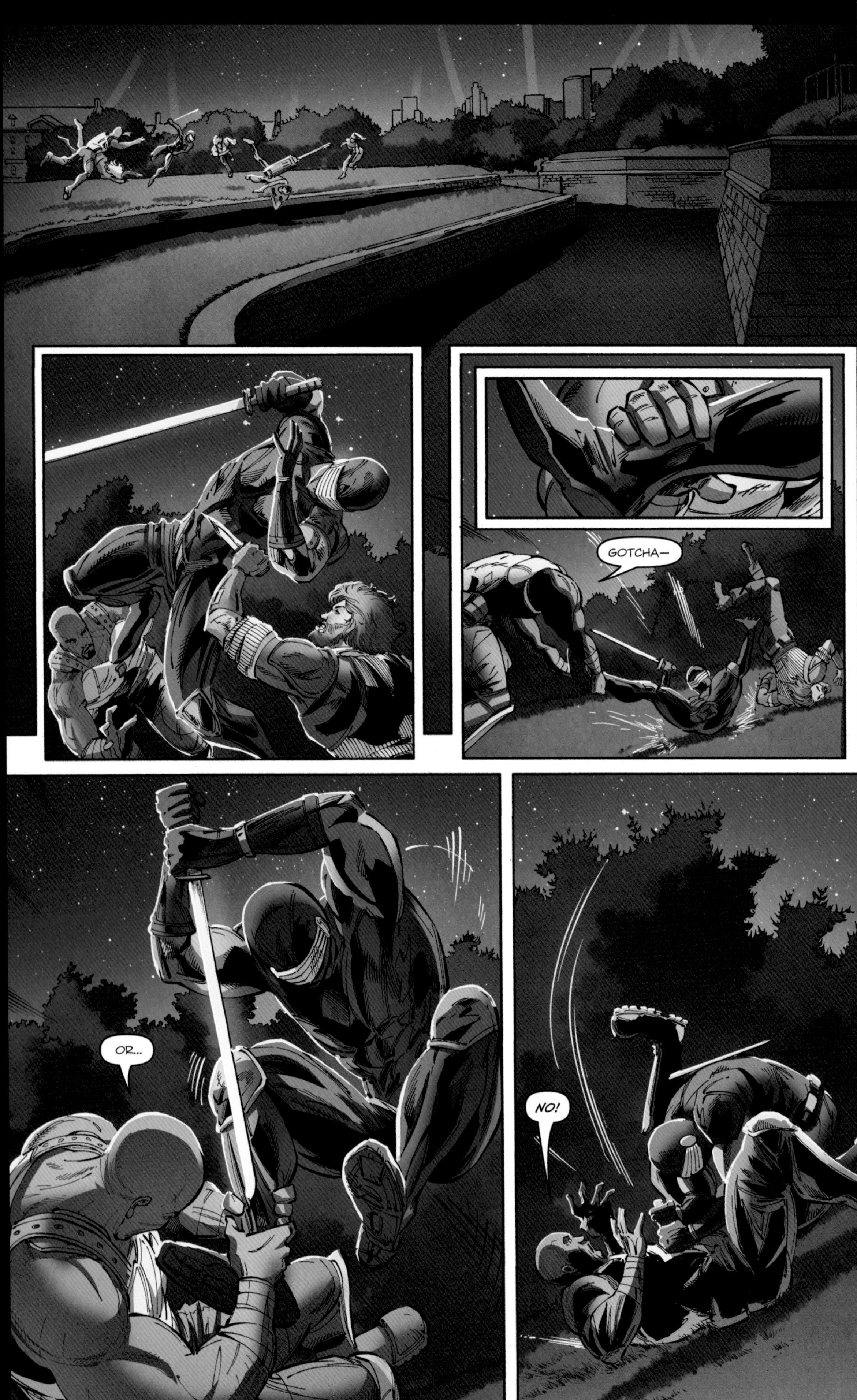
GOTCHA–
OR...
NO!

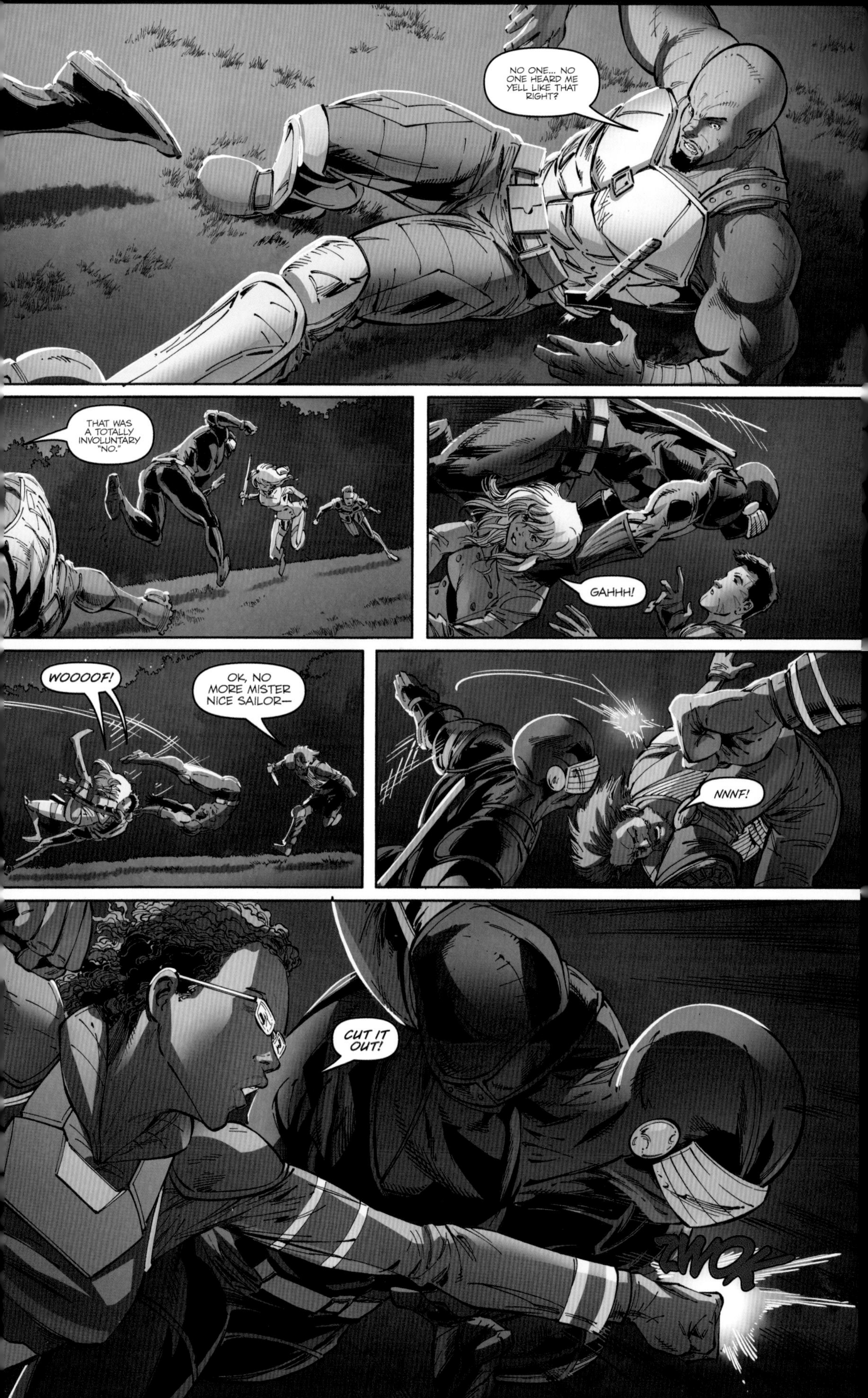
NO ONE... NO ONE HEARD ME YELL LIKE THAT RIGHT?
THAT WAS A TOTALLY INVOLUNTARY "NO."
GAHHH!
WOOOOF!
OK, NO MORE MISTER NICE SAILOR—
NNNF!
CUT IT OUT!
ZWOK

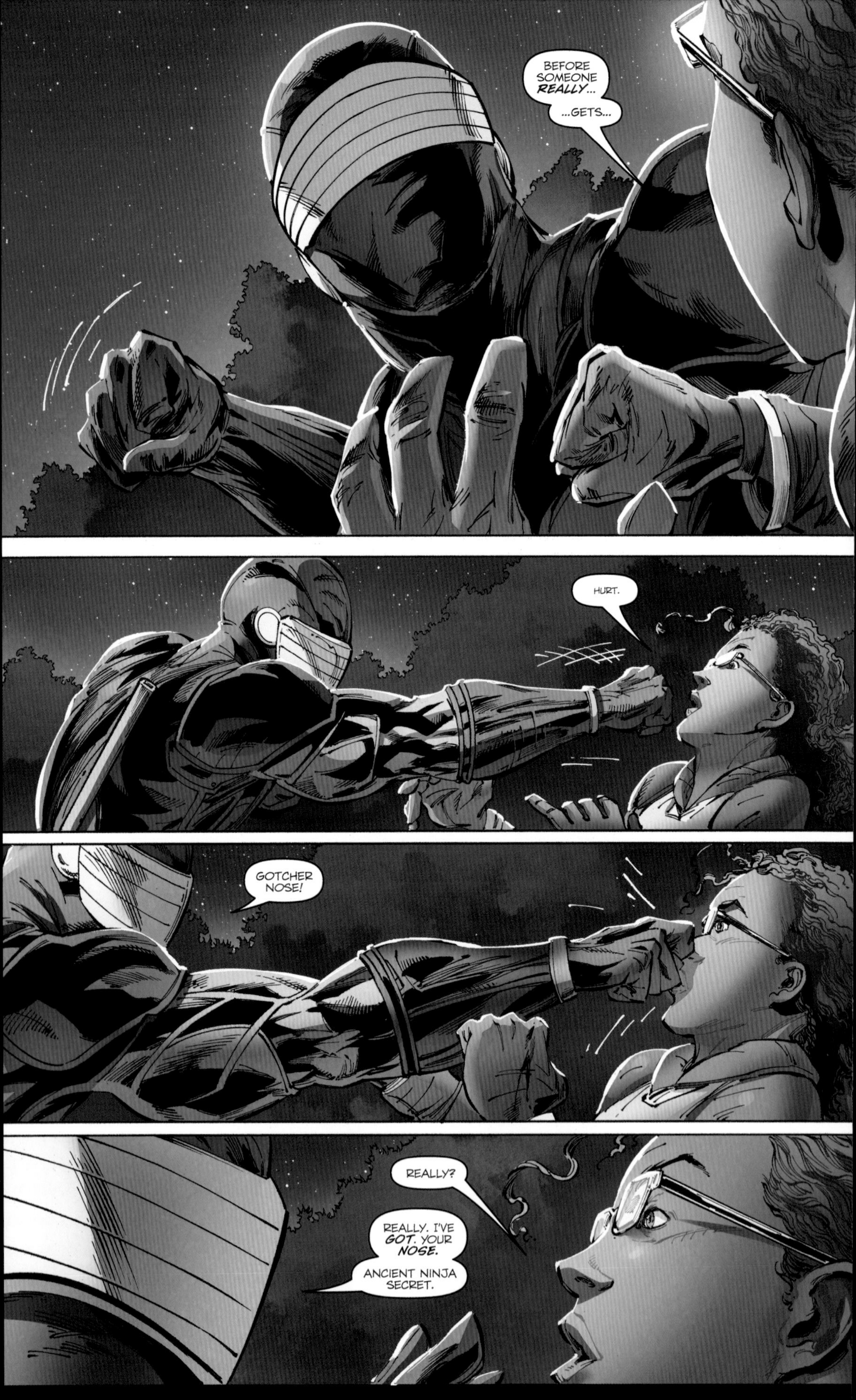
BEFORE SOMEONE REALLY...
...GETS...
HURT.
GOTCHER NOSE!
REALLY?
REALLY. I'VE GOT. YOUR NOSE.
ANCIENT NINJA SECRET.

ALL RIGHT, THAT'S ENOUGH, QUICK KICK...

...OR SHOULD I SAY *"FAKE EYES"*?

CAN I JUST POINT OUT THAT YOU USING "LADIES" IN THAT WAY IS OFFENSIVE TO US *ACTUAL* LADIES?

POINT OF THIS EXERCISE WAS TO TEST OUR *AIR COMMANDO* GLIDER WITH *QUANTUM STEALTH* TECHNOLOGY.

NOT FOR YOU LADIES TO GET INTO A *SLAP FIGHT.*

NO.

LOOKS LIKE THE IMPACT OF LANDING SCRAMBLED THE PIXELS IN THE LIGHT-BENDING FABRIC, DUKE.

SEND IT BACK TO Q-BRANCH FOR AN OVERHAUL! HA!

EVEN THE *REAL* SNAKE EYES—GOD REST 'IM—WOULD'VE BEEN A SITTING DUCK.

WONDERFUL.

HEY! *DUKE!* YOU'RE GONNA WANNA SEE THIS!

WE GOT KIND OF A— *THING.*

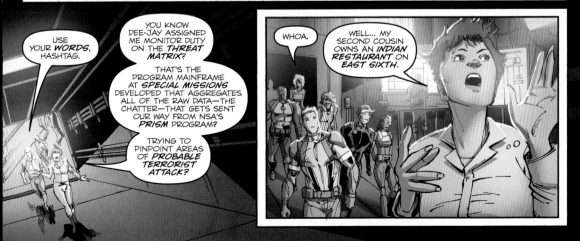

USE YOUR *WORDS,* HASHTAG.

YOU KNOW DEE-JAY ASSIGNED ME MONITOR DUTY ON THE *THREAT MATRIX?*

THAT'S THE PROGRAM MAINFRAME AT *SPECIAL MISSIONS* DEVELOPED THAT AGGREGATES ALL OF THE RAW DATA—THE CHATTER—THAT GETS SENT OUR WAY FROM NSA'S *PRISM* PROGRAM?

TRYING TO PINPOINT AREAS OF *PROBABLE TERRORIST ATTACK?*

WHOA.

WELL... MY SECOND COUSIN OWNS AN *INDIAN RESTAURANT* ON *EAST SIXTH.*

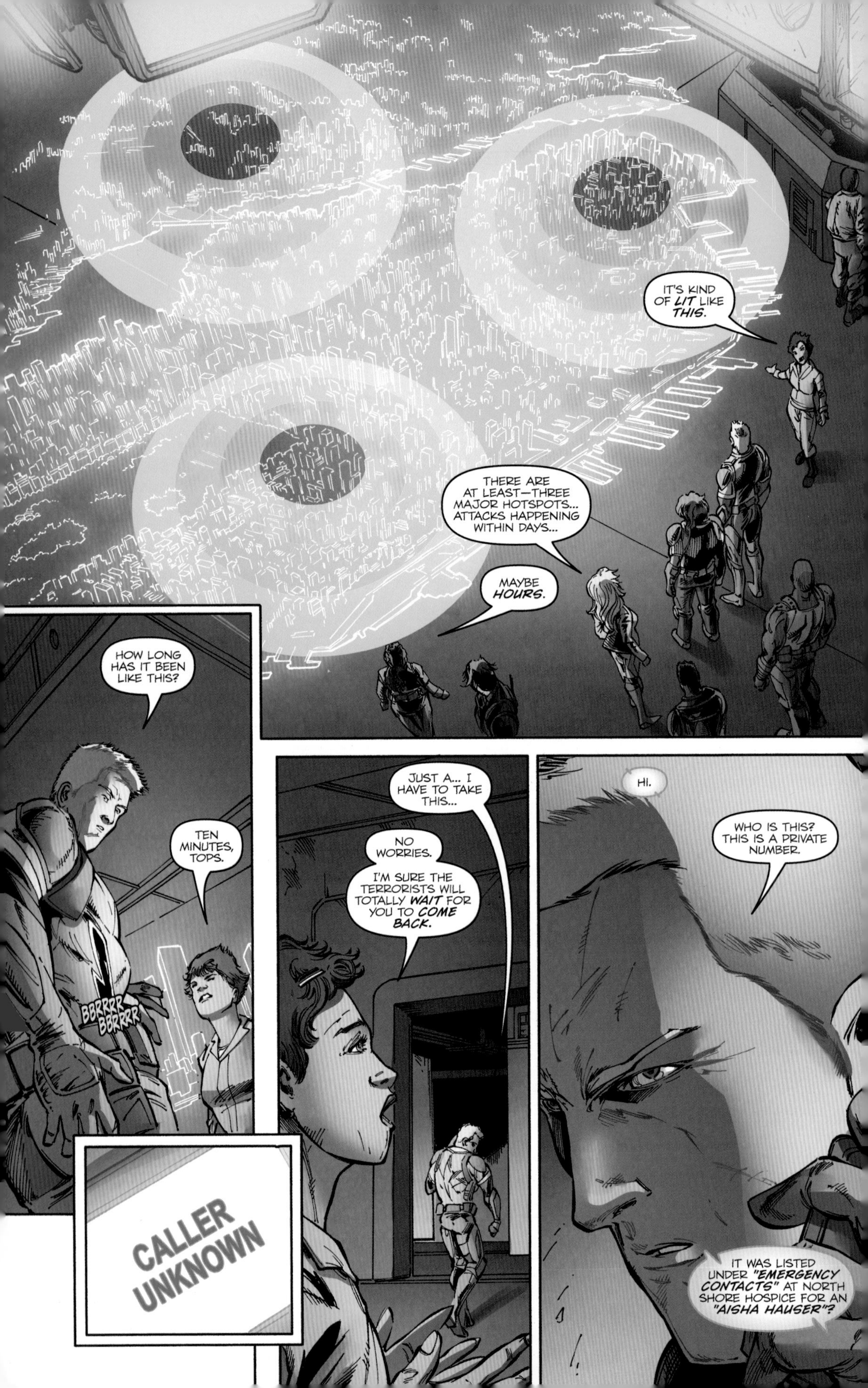

IT'S KIND OF *LIT* LIKE *THIS*.
THERE ARE AT LEAST—THREE MAJOR HOTSPOTS... ATTACKS HAPPENING WITHIN DAYS...
MAYBE *HOURS*.
HOW LONG HAS IT BEEN LIKE THIS?
TEN MINUTES, TOPS.
BBRRRR BBRRRR
CALLER UNKNOWN
JUST A... I HAVE TO TAKE THIS...
NO WORRIES.
I'M SURE THE TERRORISTS WILL TOTALLY *WAIT* FOR YOU TO *COME BACK*.
HI.
WHO IS THIS? THIS IS A PRIVATE NUMBER.
IT WAS LISTED UNDER *"EMERGENCY CONTACTS"* AT NORTH SHORE HOSPICE FOR AN *"AISHA HAUSER"*?

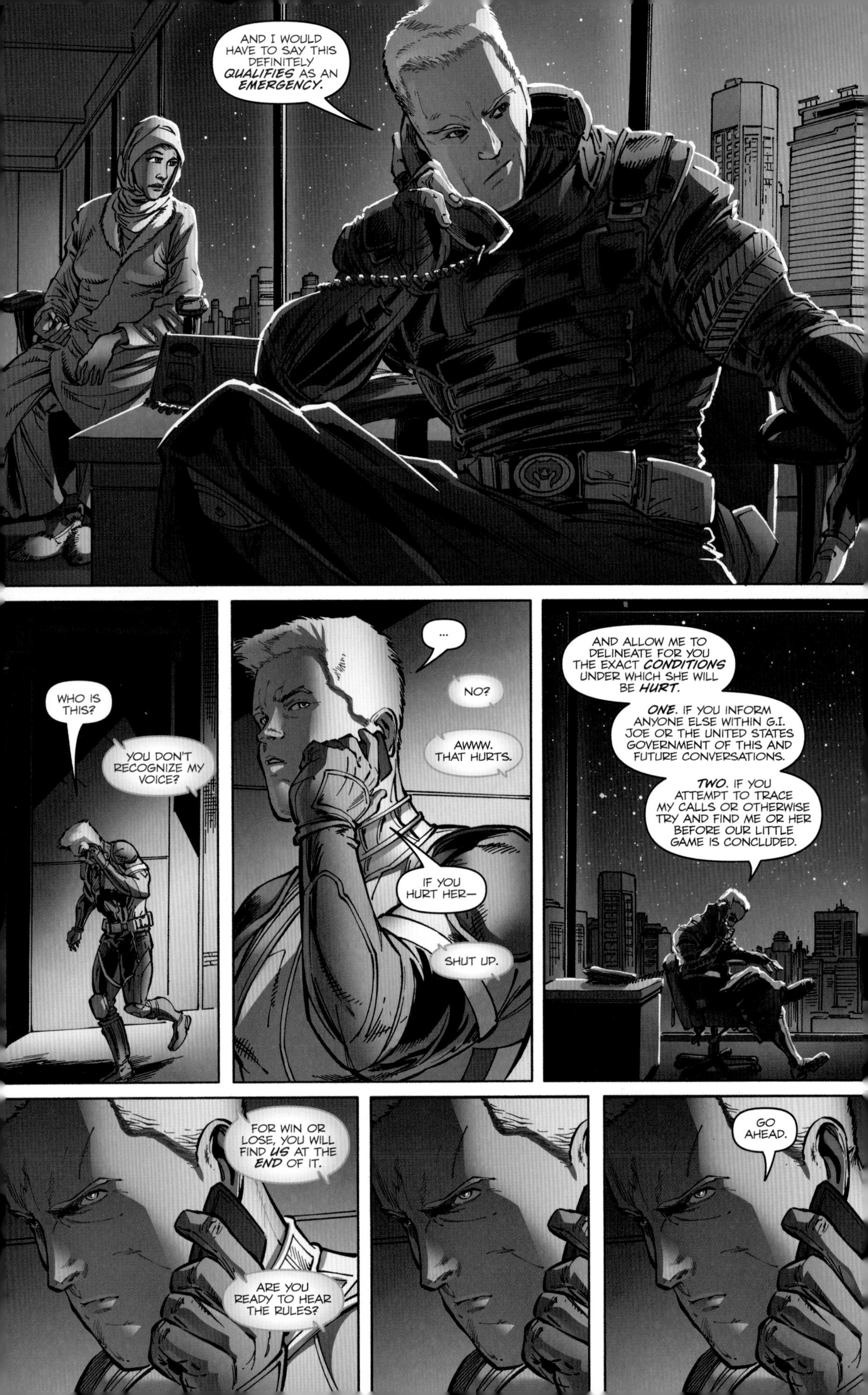
AND I WOULD HAVE TO SAY THIS DEFINITELY QUALIFIES AS AN EMERGENCY.
WHO IS THIS?
YOU DON'T RECOGNIZE MY VOICE?
...
NO?
AWWW. THAT HURTS.
IF YOU HURT HER—
SHUT UP.
AND ALLOW ME TO DELINEATE FOR YOU THE EXACT CONDITIONS UNDER WHICH SHE WILL BE HURT.
ONE. IF YOU INFORM ANYONE ELSE WITHIN G.I. JOE OR THE UNITED STATES GOVERNMENT OF THIS AND FUTURE CONVERSATIONS.
TWO. IF YOU ATTEMPT TO TRACE MY CALLS OR OTHERWISE TRY AND FIND ME OR HER BEFORE OUR LITTLE GAME IS CONCLUDED.
FOR WIN OR LOSE, YOU WILL FIND US AT THE END OF IT.
ARE YOU READY TO HEAR THE RULES?
GO AHEAD.

AS I'M SURE YOU'VE ALREADY NOTICED, I'VE FLOODED YOUR *THREAT MATRIX* WITH CHATTER ABOUT POTENTIAL TERRORIST ATTACKS IN THE NEW YORK CITY AREA TAKING PLACE WITHIN THE NEXT TWENTY-FOUR HOURS.

ONLY *ONE* OF THESE ATTACKS IS *SERIOUS.*

I AM *NOT* GOING TO TELL YOU WHICH ONE.

IN FACT, THE MERE FACT I HAVE TOLD YOU ONE OF THESE ATTACKS *IS* SERIOUS IS BETTER INTEL THAN MOST ANALYSTS GET IN A SINGLE DAY.

DADDY, LOOK.

NEEDLESS TO SAY, IT IS THE *GENUINE* ONE THAT WILL LEAD YOU TO *HER.*

DADDY, YOU'RE *NOT* LOOKING!

MOMMY HELPED ME—

INSIDE VOICE.

MOMMY HELPED ME SPELL *YEESHA.*

THAT'S GREAT, BABY. BUT DADDY'S ON THE PHONE RIGHT NOW.

HELLO? YOU STILL THERE?

RIGHT NOW I'M TEXTING YOU PROOF YOU SHOULD TAKE ME SERIOUSLY.

MOMMY!

IF YOU'RE NOT GOING TO TELL ME WHO YOU ARE...

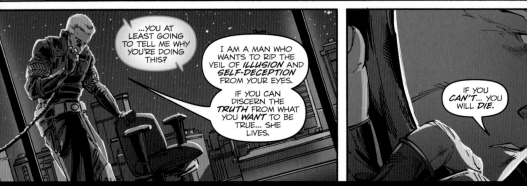

...YOU AT LEAST GOING TO TELL ME WHY YOU'RE DOING THIS?

I AM A MAN WHO WANTS TO RIP THE VEIL OF *ILLUSION* AND *SELF-DECEPTION* FROM YOUR EYES.

IF YOU CAN DISCERN THE *TRUTH* FROM WHAT YOU *WANT* TO BE TRUE... SHE LIVES.

IF YOU *CAN'T*... YOU WILL *DIE.*

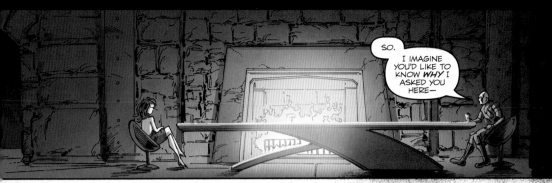

SO.

I IMAGINE YOU'D LIKE TO KNOW *WHY* I ASKED YOU HERE—

BEFORE YOU BEGIN, DESTRO.

I JUST WANT TO MAKE ONE THING CLEAR:

THE COMMANDER ASKED ME TO TAKE A BRIEF LEAVE OF ABSENCE AFTER THE WARRENTON OPERATION. HE SAID HE DID NOT WANT TO KNOW WHERE I WAS GOING.

BUT THE FACT I DID NOT TELL HIM I WAS COMING *HERE* DOES NOT MEAN I BELIEVE IN HIM ANY *LESS* OR *DOUBT* COBRA'S MISSION—

I WOULD NEVER INSULT YOU BY ASKING YOU TO BE DISLOYAL, LASS.

COBRA IS THE SINGLE LARGEST CUSTOMER FOR MY COMPANY'S MUNITIONS.

IT IS IN M.A.R.S.' BEST INTEREST TO SEE THE COMMANDER SUCCEED.

WHICH IS WHY I FIND RECENT DECISIONS OF HIS... DISTURBING.

SUCH AS?

DO YOU KNOW WHO THIS MAN IS?

MICHAEL MONK. *"THE MAD MONK."*

HE IS WHO THE COMMANDER CHOSE OVER ME TO HEAD THE MANHATTAN STATION.

INDEED. AND MONK WAS RECRUITED BY THIS MAN: DR. LESTER HORVATH.

AS WERE MOST OF COBRA'S EARLY RECRUITS.

INDEED. THEN YOU'VE HEARD OF HIS *"LOME TEST"*?

SCORED ON A ONE THROUGH EIGHT, THE TEST MEASURES AN INDIVIDUAL'S ABILITY TO IMAGINE AN ALTERNATIVE WORLDVIEW AND THE ABILITY TO SHAPE THAT REALITY.

A THREE IS PUT INTO COMMAND OF OTHER TWOS, A FIVE OVER FOURS, AND SO ON.

TO REVERSE THE NUMBERS—TO TRY AND MAKE A BUNCH OF SIXES FOLLOW A FIVE, FOR EXAMPLE—WOULD RESULT IN A TOTAL BREAKDOWN OF ORGANIZATIONAL DISCIPLINE AND ORDER.

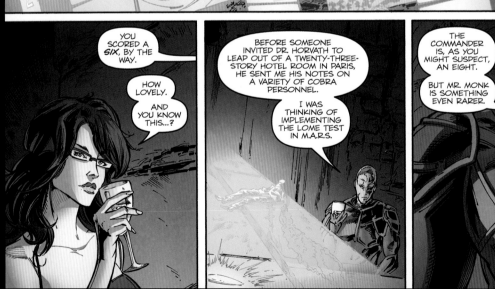

YOU SCORED A *SIX*, BY THE WAY.

HOW LOVELY.

AND YOU KNOW THIS...?

BEFORE SOMEONE INVITED DR. HORVATH TO LEAP OUT OF A TWENTY-THREE-STORY HOTEL ROOM IN PARIS, HE SENT ME HIS NOTES ON A VARIETY OF COBRA PERSONNEL.

I WAS THINKING OF IMPLEMENTING THE LOME TEST IN M.A.R.S.

THE COMMANDER IS, AS YOU MIGHT SUSPECT, AN EIGHT.

BUT MR. MONK IS SOMETHING EVEN RARER.

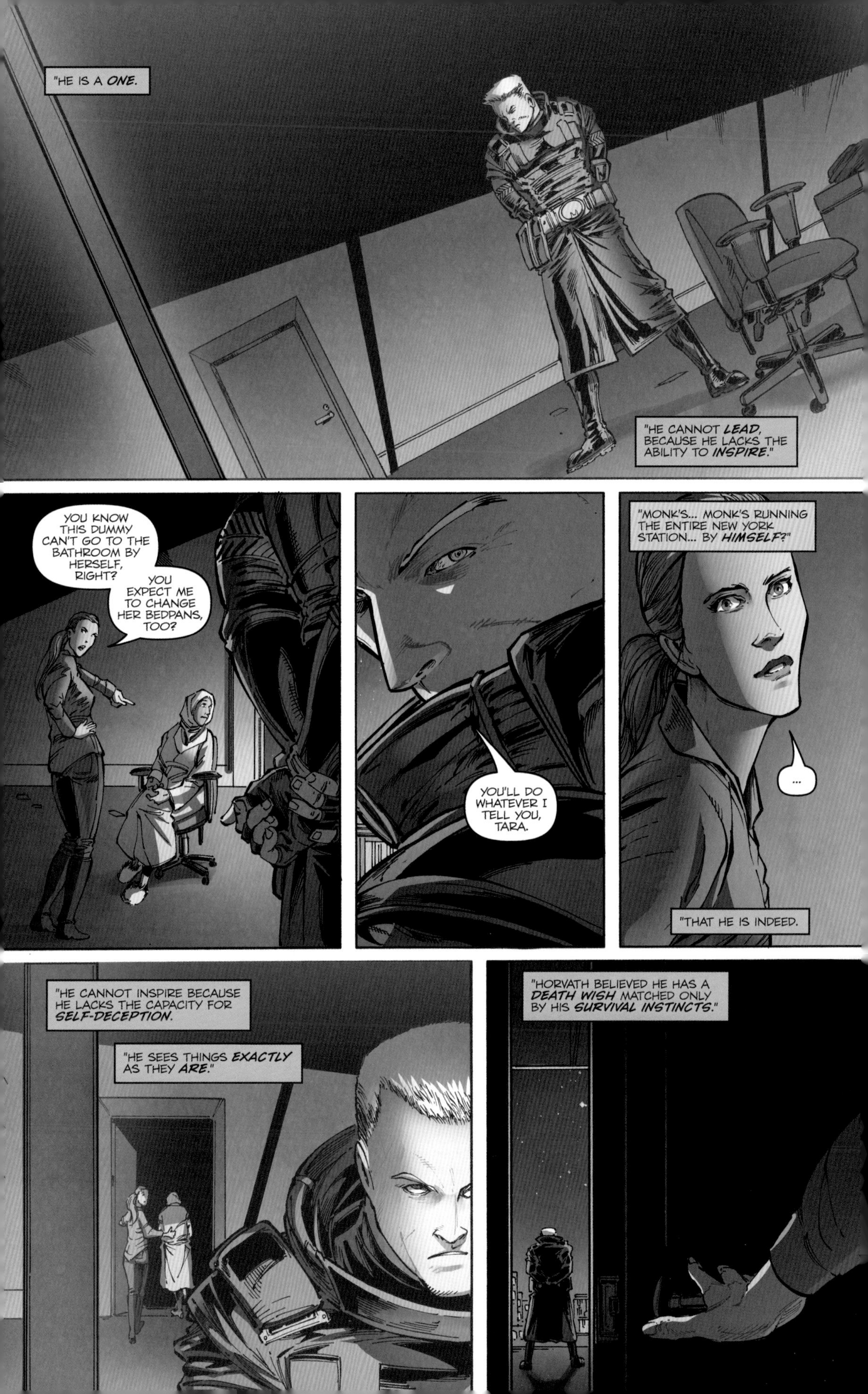
"HE IS A ONE.
"HE CANNOT LEAD, BECAUSE HE LACKS THE ABILITY TO INSPIRE."
YOU KNOW THIS DUMMY CAN'T GO TO THE BATHROOM BY HERSELF, RIGHT?
YOU EXPECT ME TO CHANGE HER BEDPANS, TOO?
YOU'LL DO WHATEVER I TELL YOU, TARA.
"MONK'S... MONK'S RUNNING THE ENTIRE NEW YORK STATION... BY HIMSELF?"
...
"THAT HE IS INDEED.
"HE CANNOT INSPIRE BECAUSE HE LACKS THE CAPACITY FOR SELF-DECEPTION.
"HE SEES THINGS EXACTLY AS THEY ARE."
"HORVATH BELIEVED HE HAS A DEATH WISH MATCHED ONLY BY HIS SURVIVAL INSTINCTS."

WHY LARID DESTRO... ...IT ALMOST SOUNDS LIKE YOU'RE *AFRAID* OF THIS MAN.

THE DESTRO CLAN PERFECTED THE PROCESS OF MAKING STEEL *CENTURIES* BEFORE THE REST OF EUROPE, RIGHT HERE, IN THESE PEAT BOGS FROM WHICH MY CASTLE RISES.

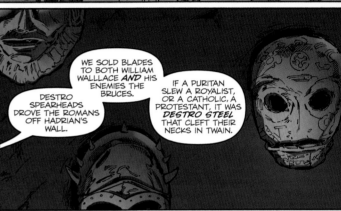

DESTRO SPEARHEADS DROVE THE ROMANS OFF HADRIAN'S WALL.

WE SOLD BLADES TO BOTH WILLIAM WALLLACE *AND* HIS ENEMIES THE BRUCES.

IF A PURITAN SLEW A ROYALIST, OR A CATHOLIC, A PROTESTANT, IT WAS *DESTRO STEEL* THAT CLEFT THEIR NECKS IN TWAIN.

OUR CLAN HAS BEEN FORGED TO FEAR *DISHONOR* OVER *DEATH.*

BUT I TELL YOU THIS *"MAD MONK"* IS *BOTH.*

IN ORDER FOR ME TO SELL *WEAPONS* I NEED A *WORLD* TO SELL THEM *TO.*

IF THE COMMANDER PLACES HIS FAITH IN MEN LIKE MONK, IT IS NOT JUST *COBRA* THAT WILL BE DESTROYED.

CAN I COUNT ON YOU TO HELP ME *SHAKE* THAT FAITH?

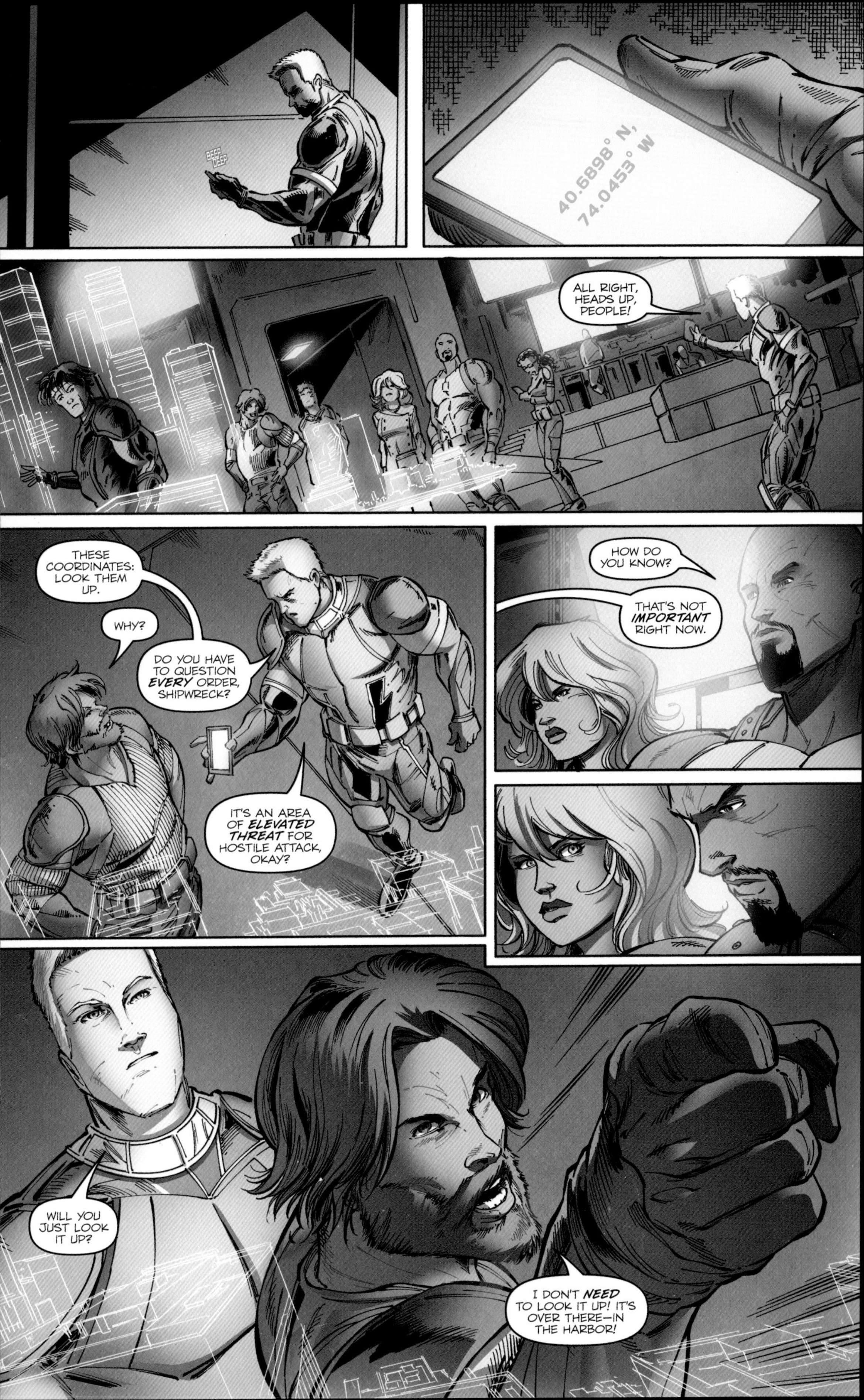
BEEP BEEP
40.6898° N,
74.0453° W
ALL RIGHT, HEADS UP, PEOPLE!
THESE COORDINATES: LOOK THEM UP.
WHY?
DO YOU HAVE TO QUESTION EVERY ORDER, SHIPWRECK?
IT'S AN AREA OF ELEVATED THREAT FOR HOSTILE ATTACK, OKAY?
HOW DO YOU KNOW?
THAT'S NOT IMPORTANT RIGHT NOW.
WILL YOU JUST LOOK IT UP?
I DON'T NEED TO LOOK IT UP! IT'S OVER THERE—IN THE HARBOR!

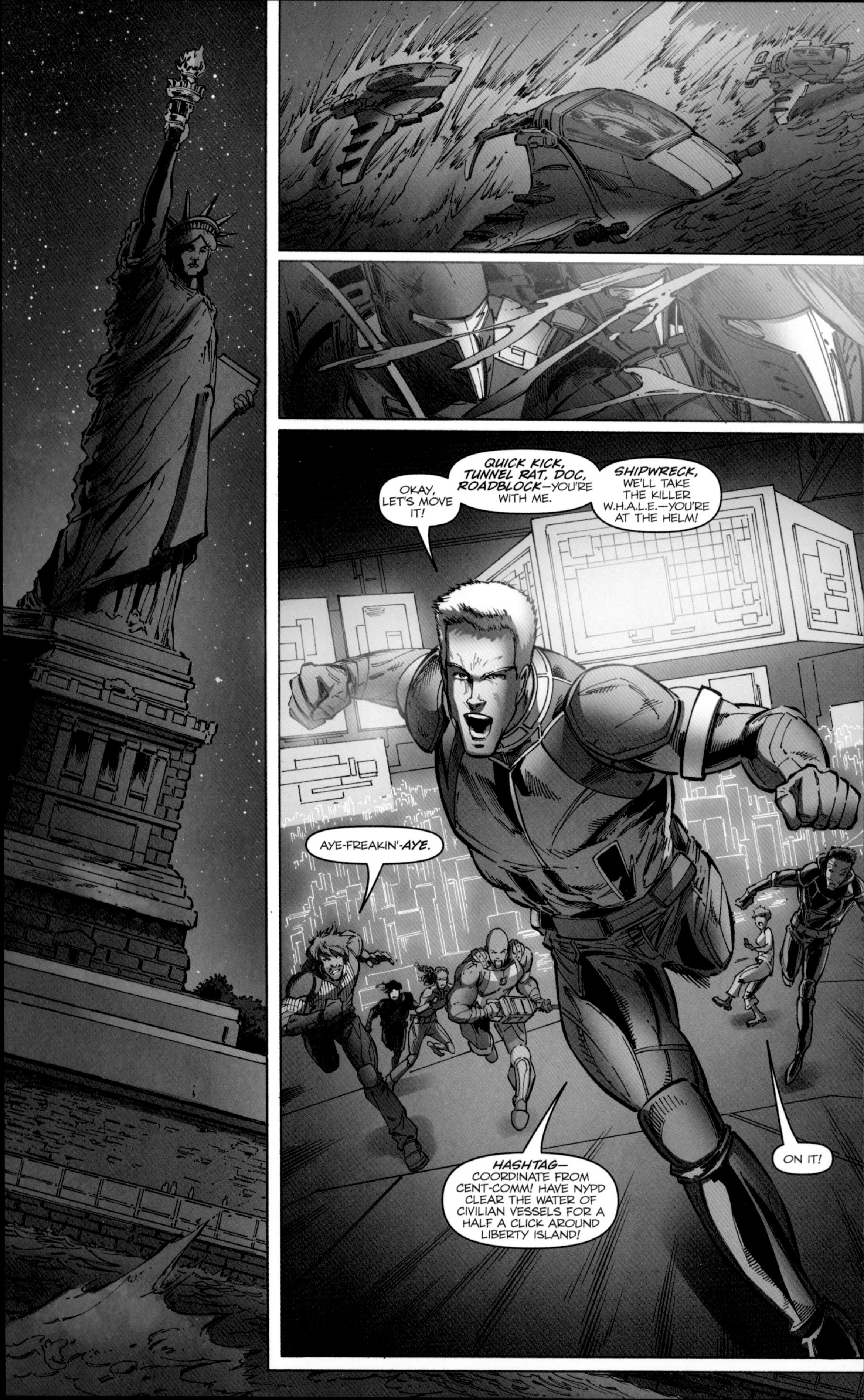
OKAY, LET'S MOVE IT!
QUICK KICK, TUNNEL RAT, DOC, ROADBLOCK—YOU'RE WITH ME.
SHIPWRECK, WE'LL TAKE THE KILLER W.H.A.L.E.—YOU'RE AT THE HELM!
AYE-FREAKIN'-AYE.
HASHTAG—COORDINATE FROM CENT-COMM! HAVE NYPD CLEAR THE WATER OF CIVILIAN VESSELS FOR A HALF A CLICK AROUND LIBERTY ISLAND!
ON IT!

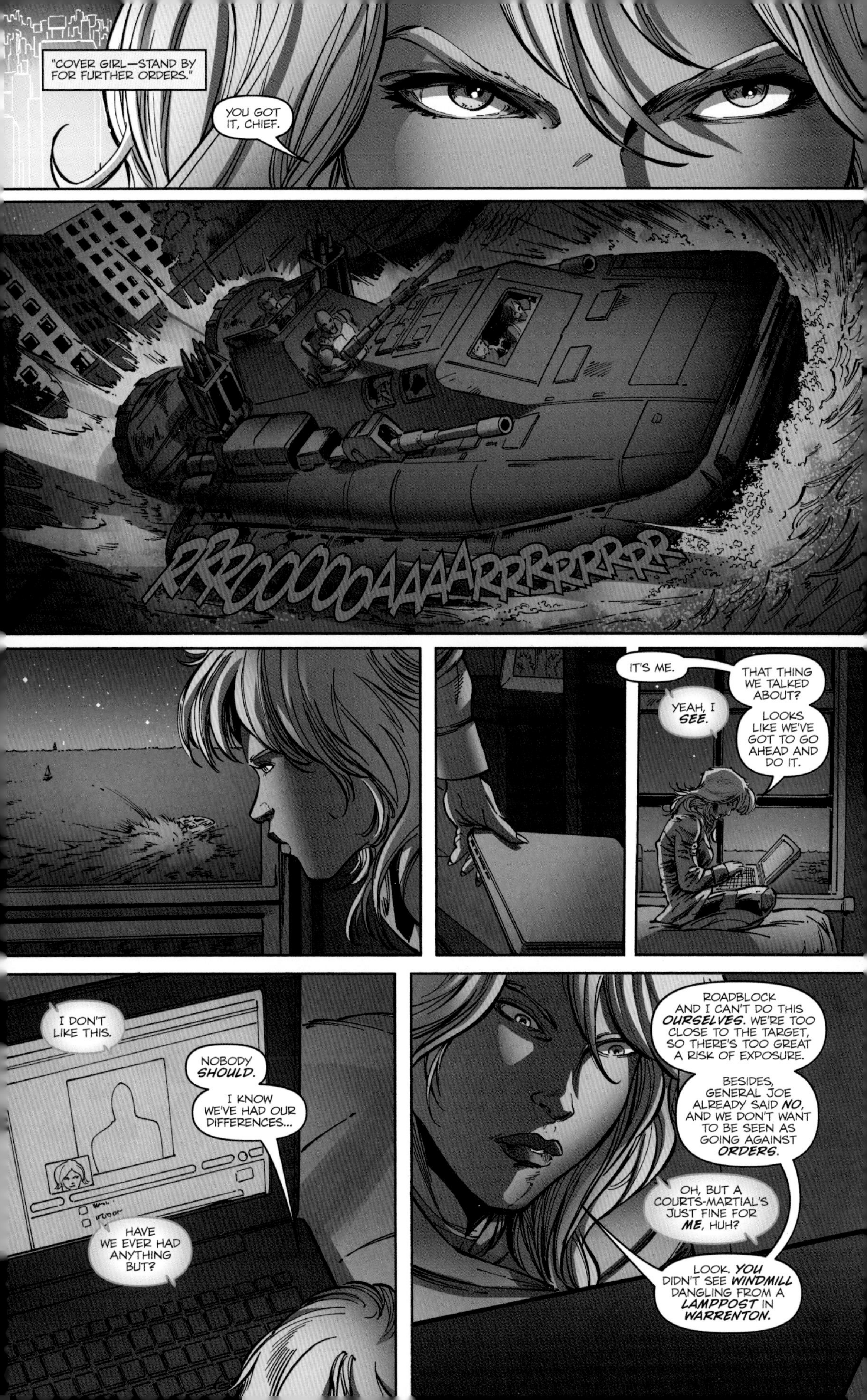
"COVER GIRL—STAND BY FOR FURTHER ORDERS."
YOU GOT IT, CHIEF.
RRROOOOOOAAAARRRRRRR
IT'S ME.
THAT THING WE TALKED ABOUT?
YEAH, I SEE.
LOOKS LIKE WE'VE GOT TO GO AHEAD AND DO IT.
I DON'T LIKE THIS.
NOBODY SHOULD.
I KNOW WE'VE HAD OUR DIFFERENCES...
HAVE WE EVER HAD ANYTHING BUT?
ROADBLOCK AND I CAN'T DO THIS OURSELVES. WE'RE TOO CLOSE TO THE TARGET, SO THERE'S TOO GREAT A RISK OF EXPOSURE.
BESIDES, GENERAL JOE ALREADY SAID NO, AND WE DON'T WANT TO BE SEEN AS GOING AGAINST ORDERS.
OH, BUT A COURTS-MARTIAL'S JUST FINE FOR ME, HUH?
LOOK. YOU DIDN'T SEE WINDMILL DANGLING FROM A LAMPPOST IN WARRENTON.

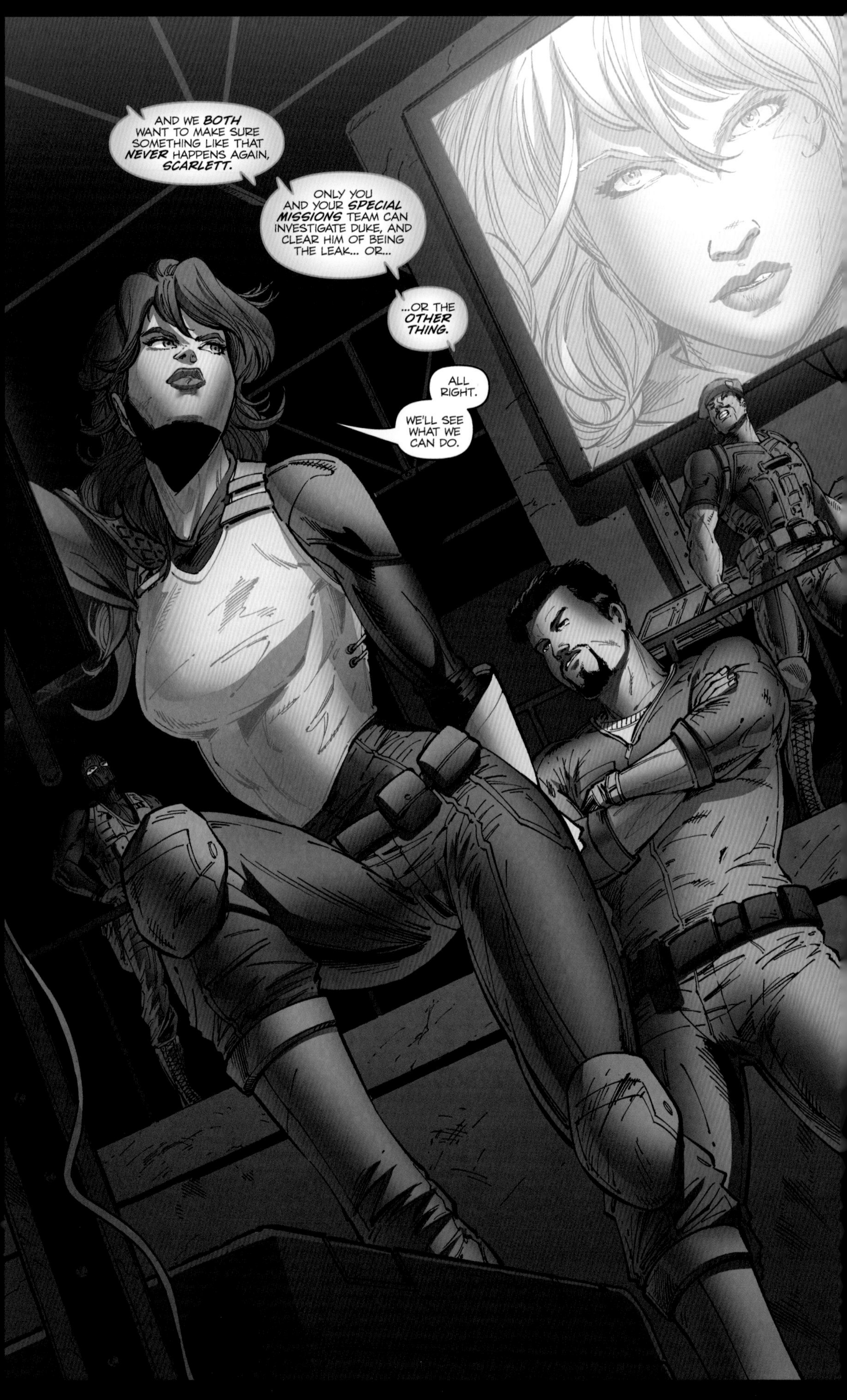
AND WE BOTH WANT TO MAKE SURE SOMETHING LIKE THAT NEVER HAPPENS AGAIN, SCARLETT.
ONLY YOU AND YOUR SPECIAL MISSIONS TEAM CAN INVESTIGATE DUKE, AND CLEAR HIM OF BEING THE LEAK... OR...
...OR THE OTHER THING.
ALL RIGHT.
WE'LL SEE WHAT WE CAN DO.

CHAPTER THREE

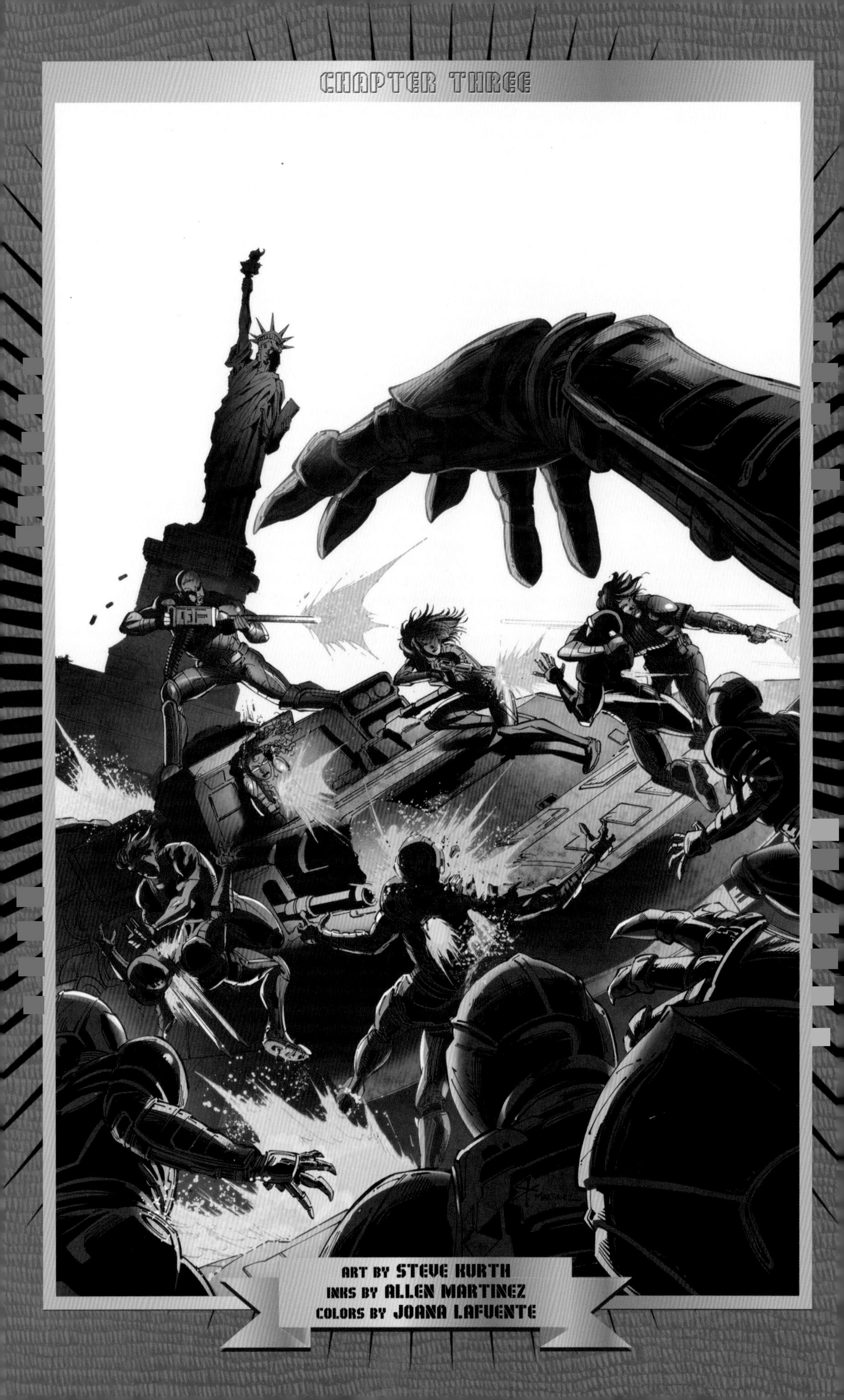

ART BY STEVE KURTH
INKS BY ALLEN MARTINEZ
COLORS BY JOANA LAFUENTE

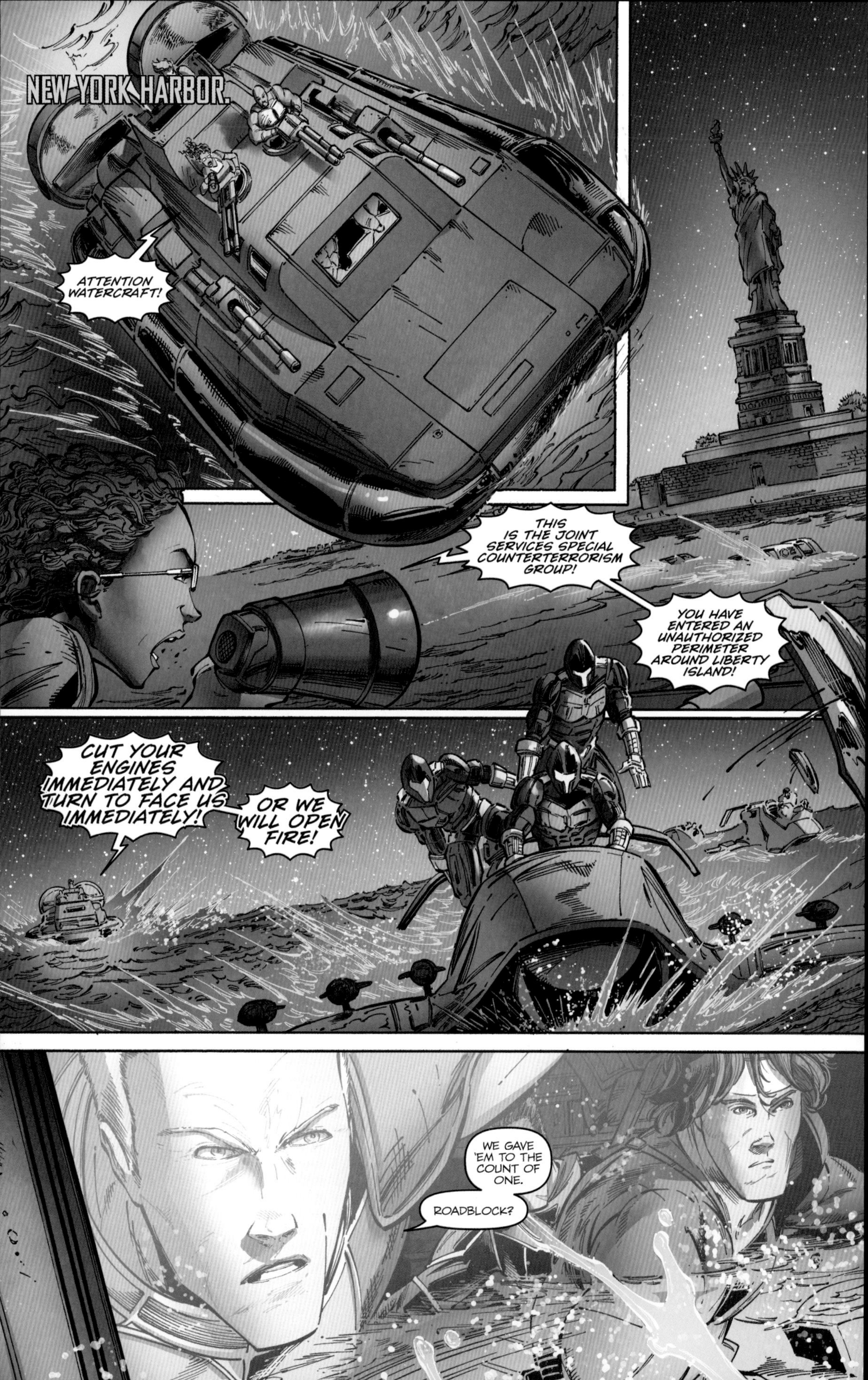
NEW YORK HARBOR.
ATTENTION WATERCRAFT!
THIS IS THE JOINT SERVICES SPECIAL COUNTERTERRORISM GROUP!
YOU HAVE ENTERED AN UNAUTHORIZED PERIMETER AROUND LIBERTY ISLAND!
CUT YOUR ENGINES IMMEDIATELY AND TURN TO FACE US IMMEDIATELY!
OR WE WILL OPEN FIRE!
WE GAVE 'EM TO THE COUNT OF ONE.
ROADBLOCK?

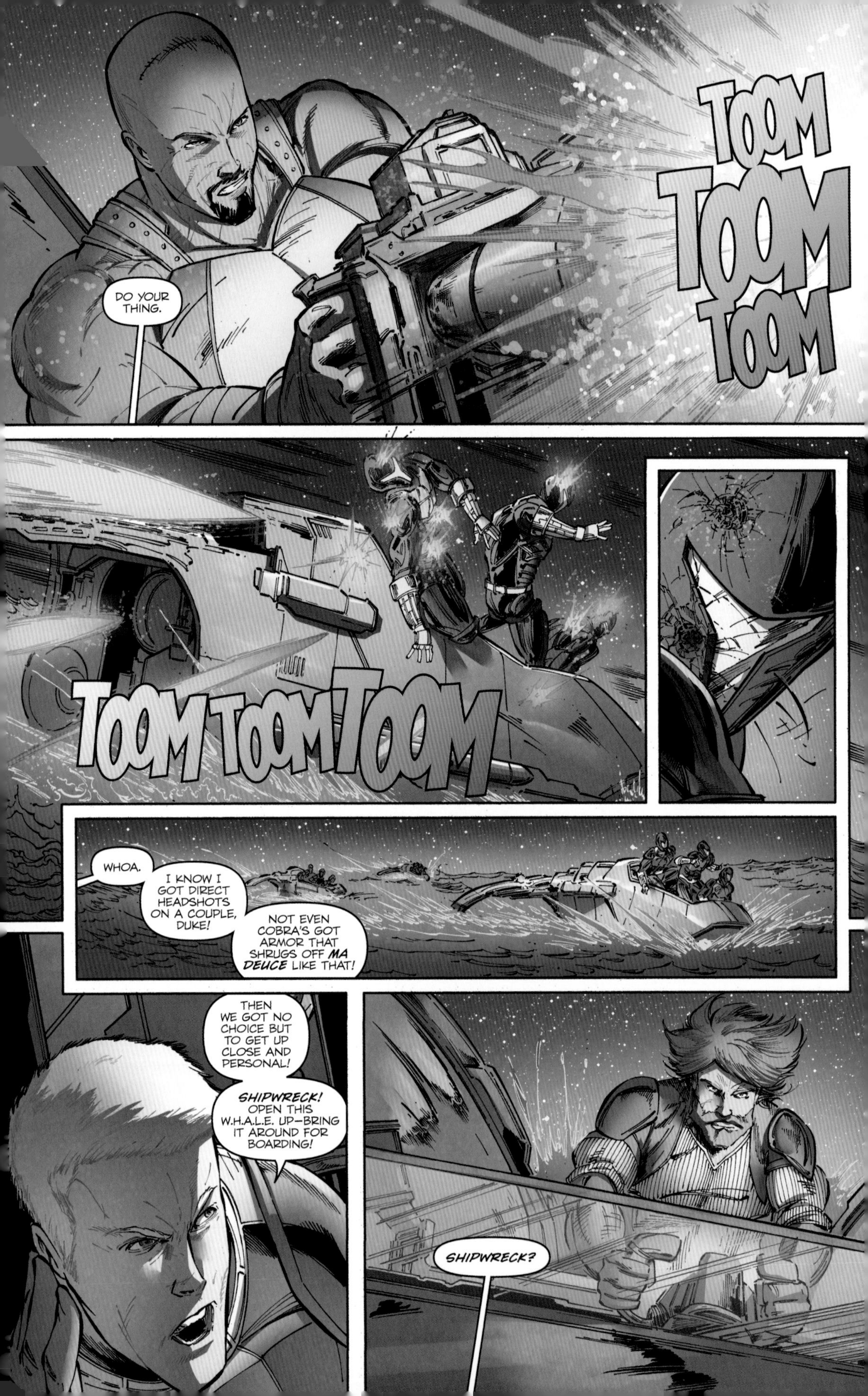
DO YOUR THING.
TOOM TOOM TOOM
TOOM TOOM TOOM
WHOA.
I KNOW I GOT DIRECT HEADSHOTS ON A COUPLE, DUKE!
NOT EVEN COBRA'S GOT ARMOR THAT SHRUGS OFF MA DEUCE LIKE THAT!
THEN WE GOT NO CHOICE BUT TO GET UP CLOSE AND PERSONAL!
SHIPWRECK! OPEN THIS W.H.A.L.E. UP–BRING IT AROUND FOR BOARDING!
SHIPWRECK?

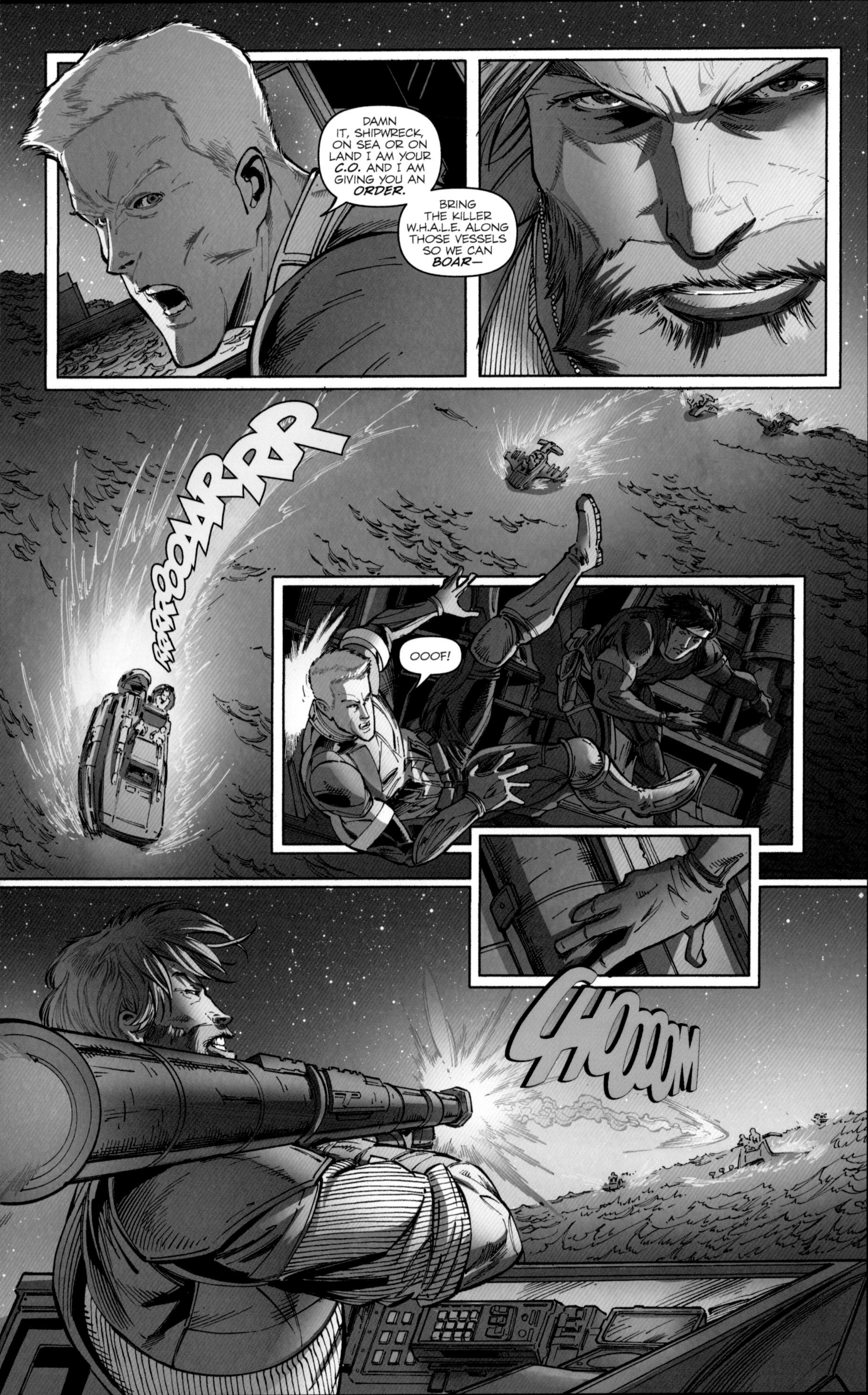
DAMN IT, SHIPWRECK, ON SEA OR ON LAND I AM YOUR *C.O.* AND I AM GIVING YOU AN *ORDER*.
BRING THE KILLER W.H.A.L.E. ALONG THOSE VESSELS SO WE CAN *BOAR—*
BOOARRR
OOOF!
CHOOOM

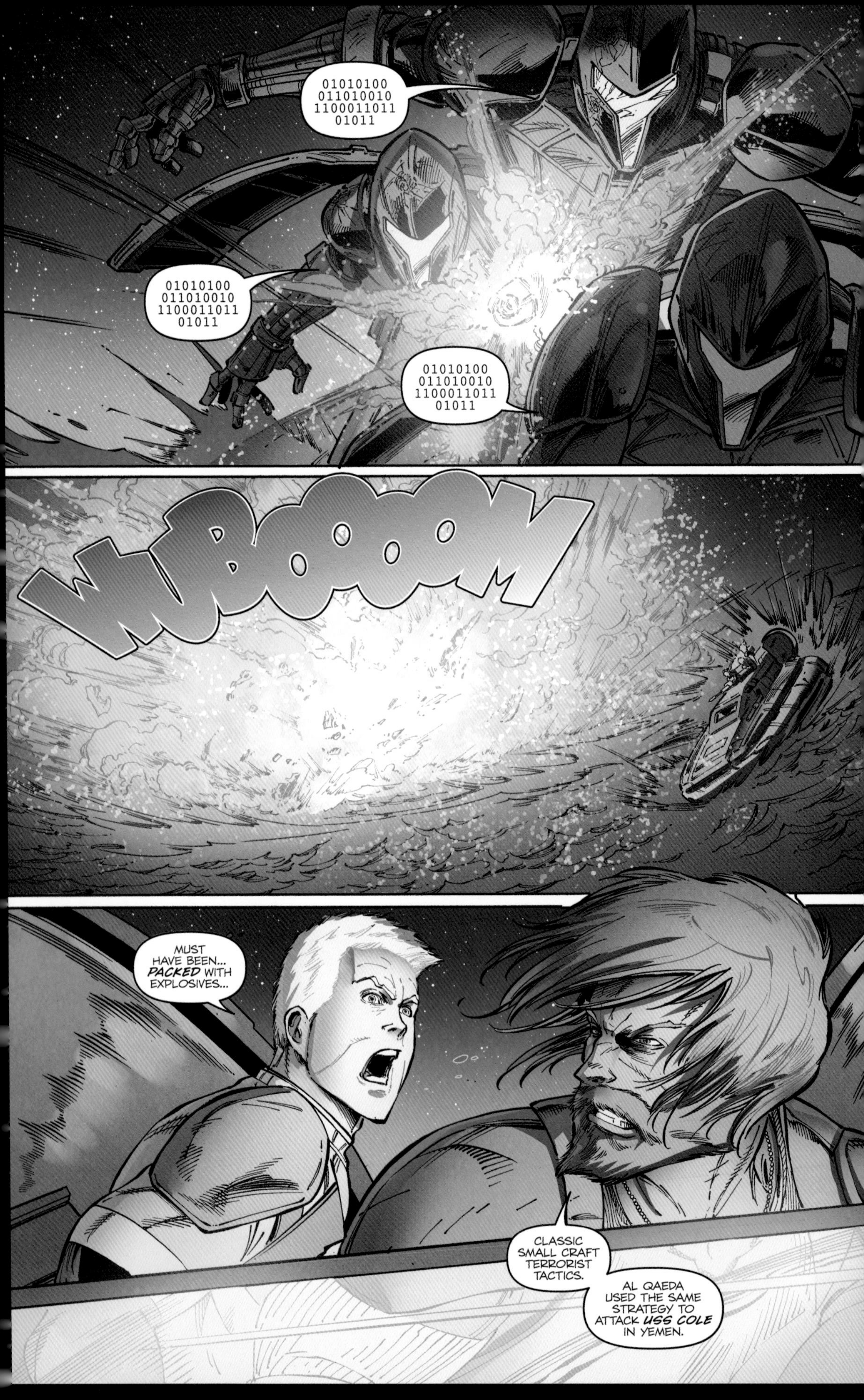
01010100 011010010 1100011011 01011
01010100 011010010 1100011011 01011
01010100 011010010 1100011011 01011
WUBOOOM
MUST HAVE BEEN... PACKED WITH EXPLOSIVES...
CLASSIC SMALL CRAFT TERRORIST TACTICS.
AL QAEDA USED THE SAME STRATEGY TO ATTACK USS COLE IN YEMEN.

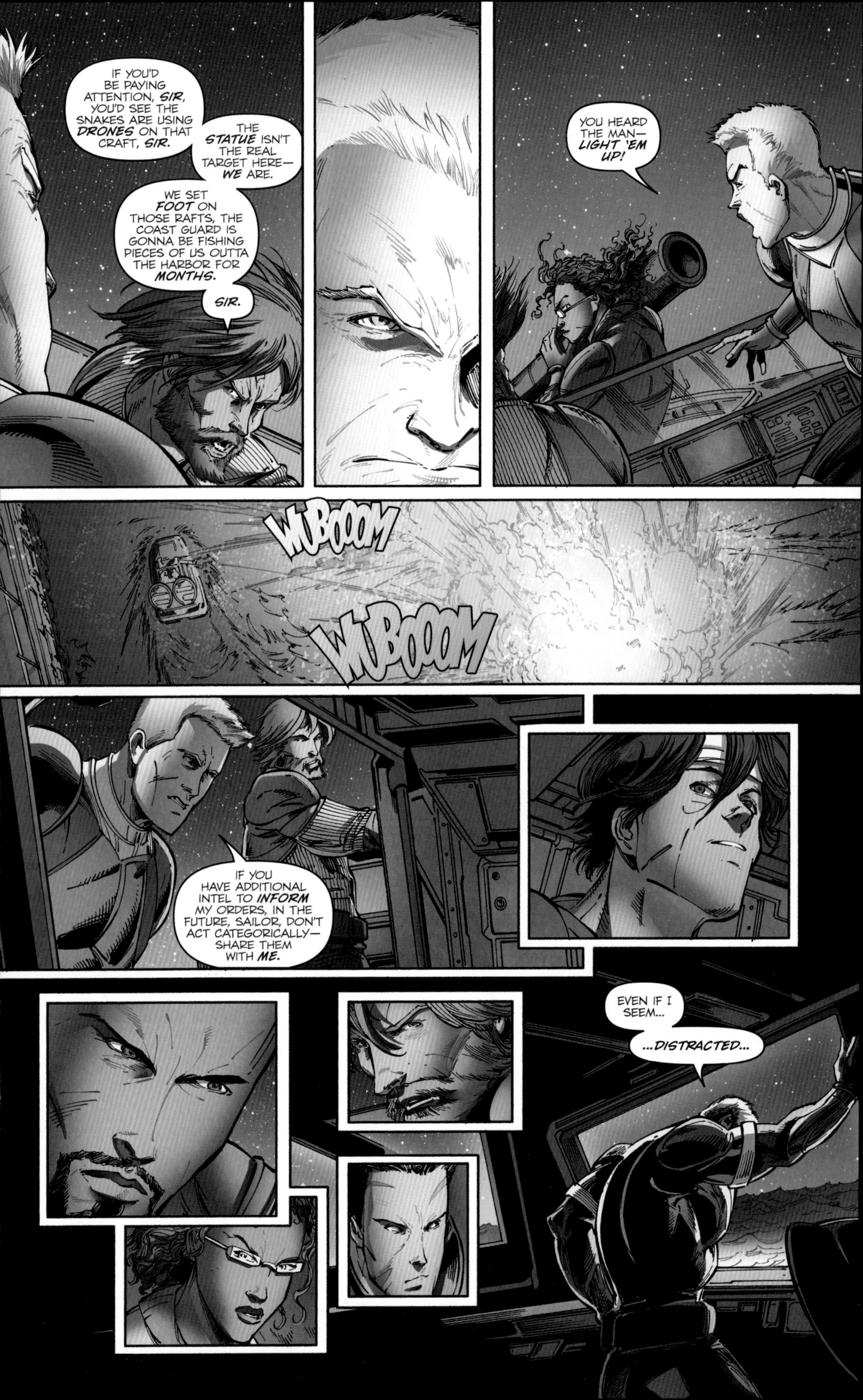
IF YOU'D BE PAYING ATTENTION, SIR, YOU'D SEE THE SNAKES ARE USING DRONES ON THAT CRAFT, SIR.
THE STATUE ISN'T THE REAL TARGET HERE— WE ARE.
WE SET FOOT ON THOSE RAFTS, THE COAST GUARD IS GONNA BE FISHING PIECES OF US OUTTA THE HARBOR FOR MONTHS.
SIR.
YOU HEARD THE MAN— LIGHT 'EM UP!
WHBOOOM
WHBOOOM
IF YOU HAVE ADDITIONAL INTEL TO INFORM MY ORDERS, IN THE FUTURE, SAILOR, DON'T ACT CATEGORICALLY— SHARE THEM WITH ME.
EVEN IF I SEEM...
...DISTRACTED...

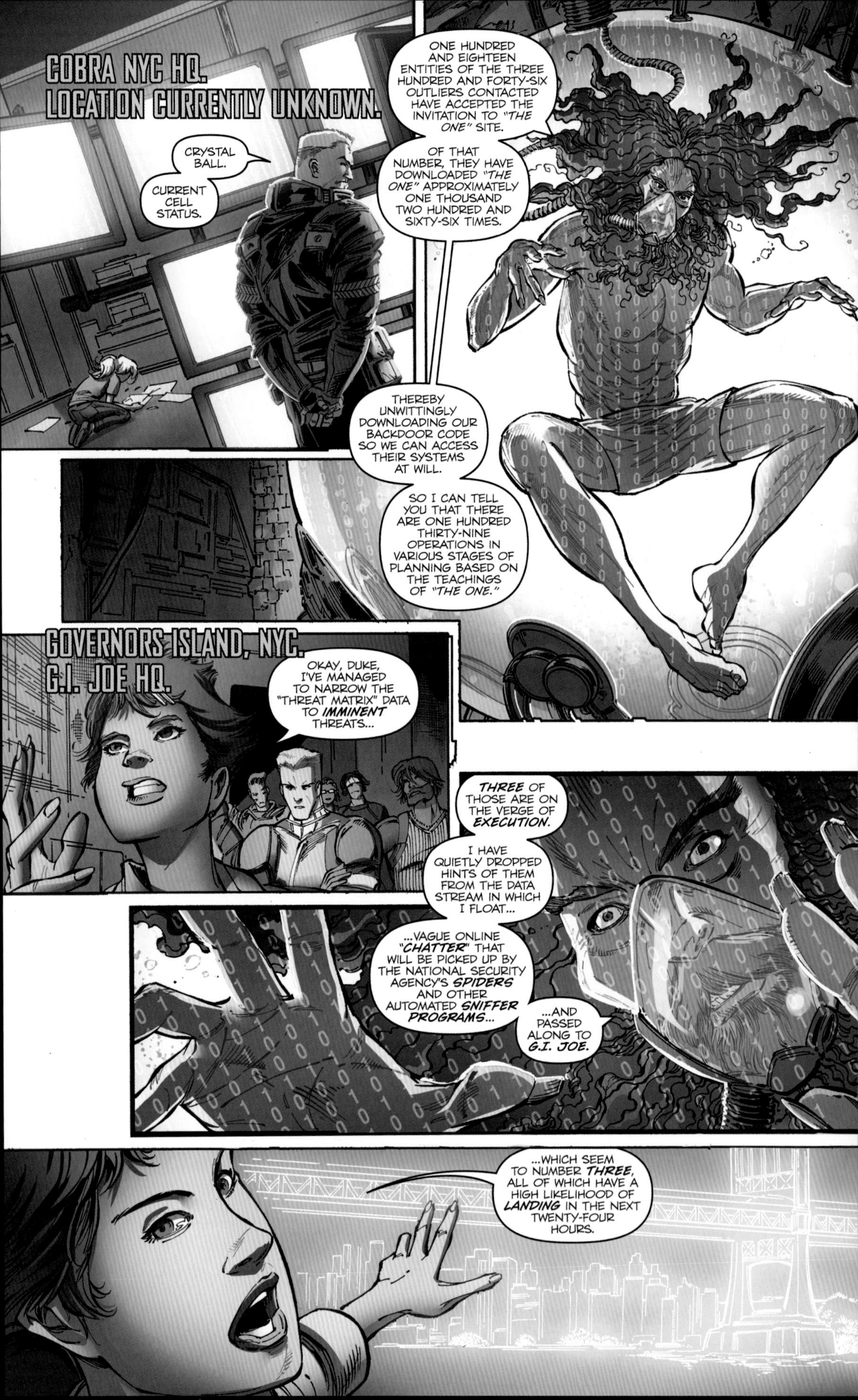
COBRA NYC HQ. LOCATION CURRENTLY UNKNOWN.
CRYSTAL BALL.
CURRENT CELL STATUS.
ONE HUNDRED AND EIGHTEEN ENTITIES OF THE THREE HUNDRED AND FORTY-SIX OUTLIERS CONTACTED HAVE ACCEPTED THE INVITATION TO "THE ONE" SITE.
OF THAT NUMBER, THEY HAVE DOWNLOADED "THE ONE" APPROXIMATELY ONE THOUSAND TWO HUNDRED AND SIXTY-SIX TIMES.
THEREBY UNWITTINGLY DOWNLOADING OUR BACKDOOR CODE SO WE CAN ACCESS THEIR SYSTEMS AT WILL.
SO I CAN TELL YOU THAT THERE ARE ONE HUNDRED THIRTY-NINE OPERATIONS IN VARIOUS STAGES OF PLANNING BASED ON THE TEACHINGS OF "THE ONE."
GOVERNORS ISLAND, NYC. G.I. JOE HQ.
OKAY, DUKE, I'VE MANAGED TO NARROW THE "THREAT MATRIX" DATA TO IMMINENT THREATS...
THREE OF THOSE ARE ON THE VERGE OF EXECUTION.
I HAVE QUIETLY DROPPED HINTS OF THEM FROM THE DATA STREAM IN WHICH I FLOAT...
...VAGUE ONLINE "CHATTER" THAT WILL BE PICKED UP BY THE NATIONAL SECURITY AGENCY'S SPIDERS AND OTHER AUTOMATED SNIFFER PROGRAMS...
...AND PASSED ALONG TO G.I. JOE.
...WHICH SEEM TO NUMBER THREE, ALL OF WHICH HAVE A HIGH LIKELIHOOD OF LANDING IN THE NEXT TWENTY-FOUR HOURS.

"THE SOURCE OF MOST OF THE METH IN EASTERN PENNSYLVANIA, *THE HEATHENS* MOTORCYCLE GANG, IS PLANNING A MAJOR ARMS DEAL ON RANDALL'S ISLAND TONIGHT.

"IN PREP FOR A MUCH LARGER, AND MUCH *NASTIER* PLAN.

"A MILITANT REFUGEE GROUP CLAIMING TO REPRESENT THE SURVIVORS OF THE *NANZHAO* NUCLEAR STRIKE ARE BRAGGING THEY'VE ASSEMBLED A *DIRTY BOMB* IN *FLUSHING.*

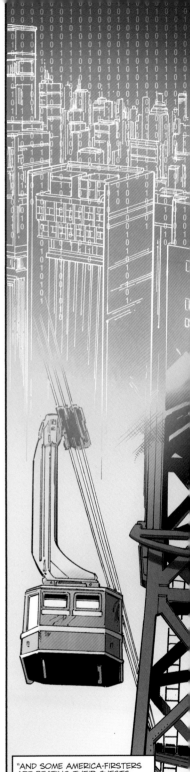

"AND SOME AMERICA-FIRSTERS ARE BEATING THEIR CHESTS ABOUT SOME KIND OF CHEMICAL OR BIOLOGICAL ATTACK ON THE ROOSEVELT ISLAND *TRAMWAY.*

"THE ISLAND IS A POPULAR RESIDENCE FOR *UNITED NATIONS DIPLOMATS,* THAT'S WHY THE RED, WHITE, AND *BROWNSHIRTS* CHOSE IT AS A TARGET..."

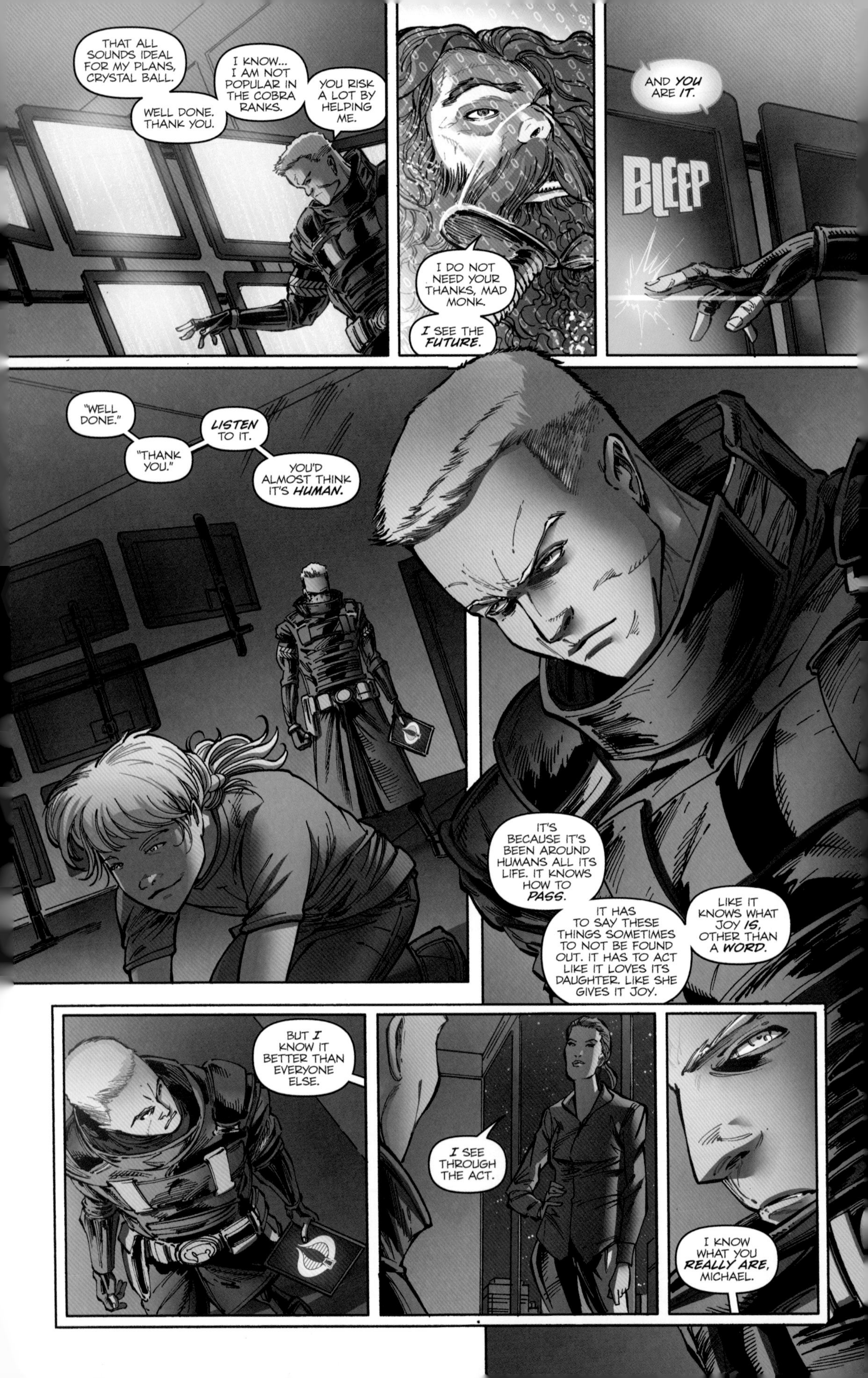
THAT ALL SOUNDS IDEAL FOR MY PLANS, CRYSTAL BALL.
WELL DONE. THANK YOU.
I KNOW... I AM NOT POPULAR IN THE COBRA RANKS.
YOU RISK A LOT BY HELPING ME.
I DO NOT NEED YOUR THANKS, MAD MONK.
I SEE THE FUTURE.
AND YOU ARE IT.
BLEEP
"WELL DONE."
"THANK YOU."
LISTEN TO IT.
YOU'D ALMOST THINK IT'S HUMAN.
IT'S BECAUSE IT'S BEEN AROUND HUMANS ALL ITS LIFE. IT KNOWS HOW TO PASS.
IT HAS TO SAY THESE THINGS SOMETIMES TO NOT BE FOUND OUT. IT HAS TO ACT LIKE IT LOVES ITS DAUGHTER. LIKE SHE GIVES IT JOY.
LIKE IT KNOWS WHAT JOY IS, OTHER THAN A WORD.
BUT I KNOW IT BETTER THAN EVERYONE ELSE.
I SEE THROUGH THE ACT.
I KNOW WHAT YOU REALLY ARE, MICHAEL.

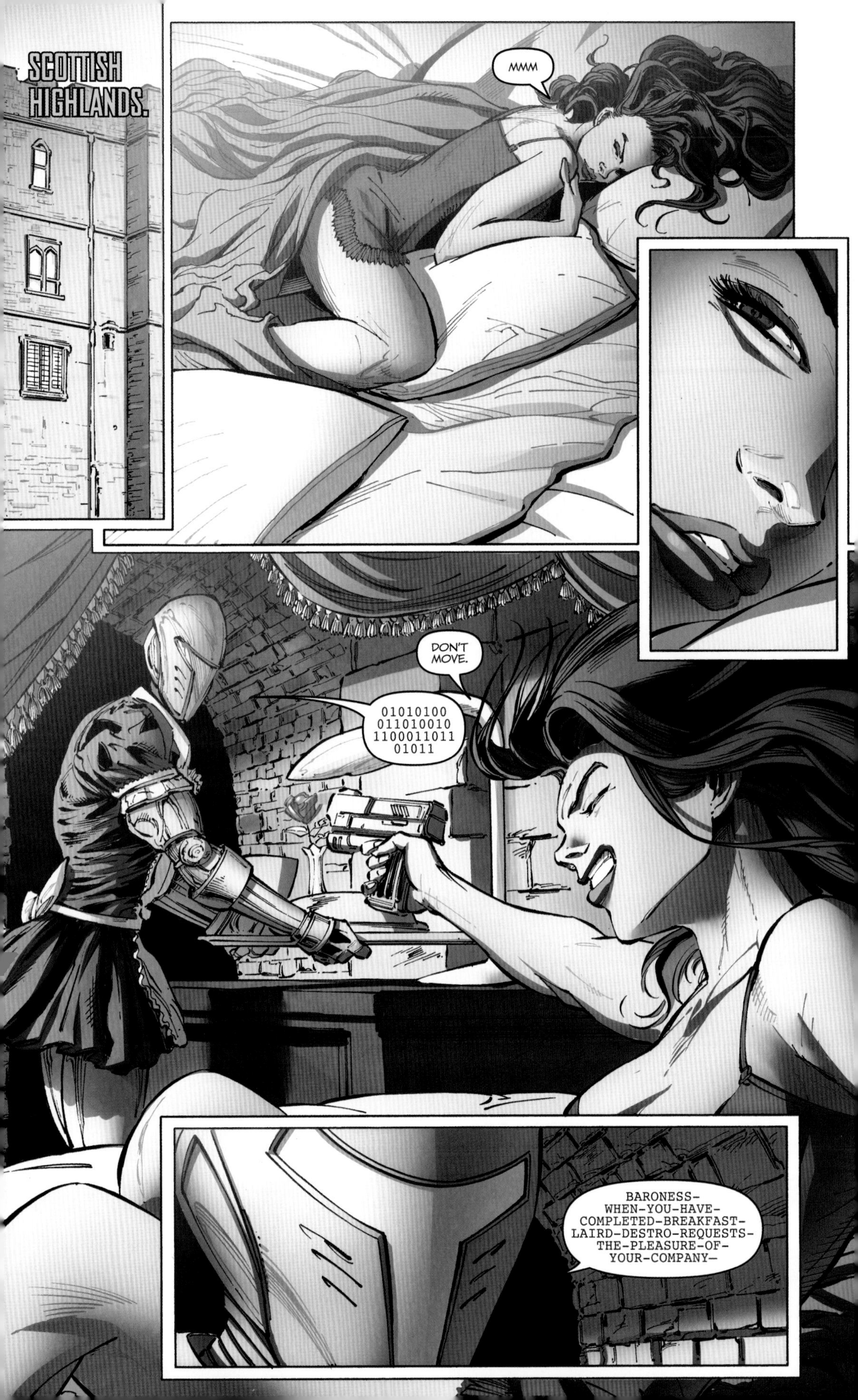
SCOTTISH HIGHLANDS.
MMM
DON'T MOVE.
01010100 011010010 1100011011 01011
BARONESS-
WHEN-YOU-HAVE-
COMPLETED-BREAKFAST-
LAIRD-DESTRO-REQUESTS-
THE-PLEASURE-OF-
YOUR-COMPANY-

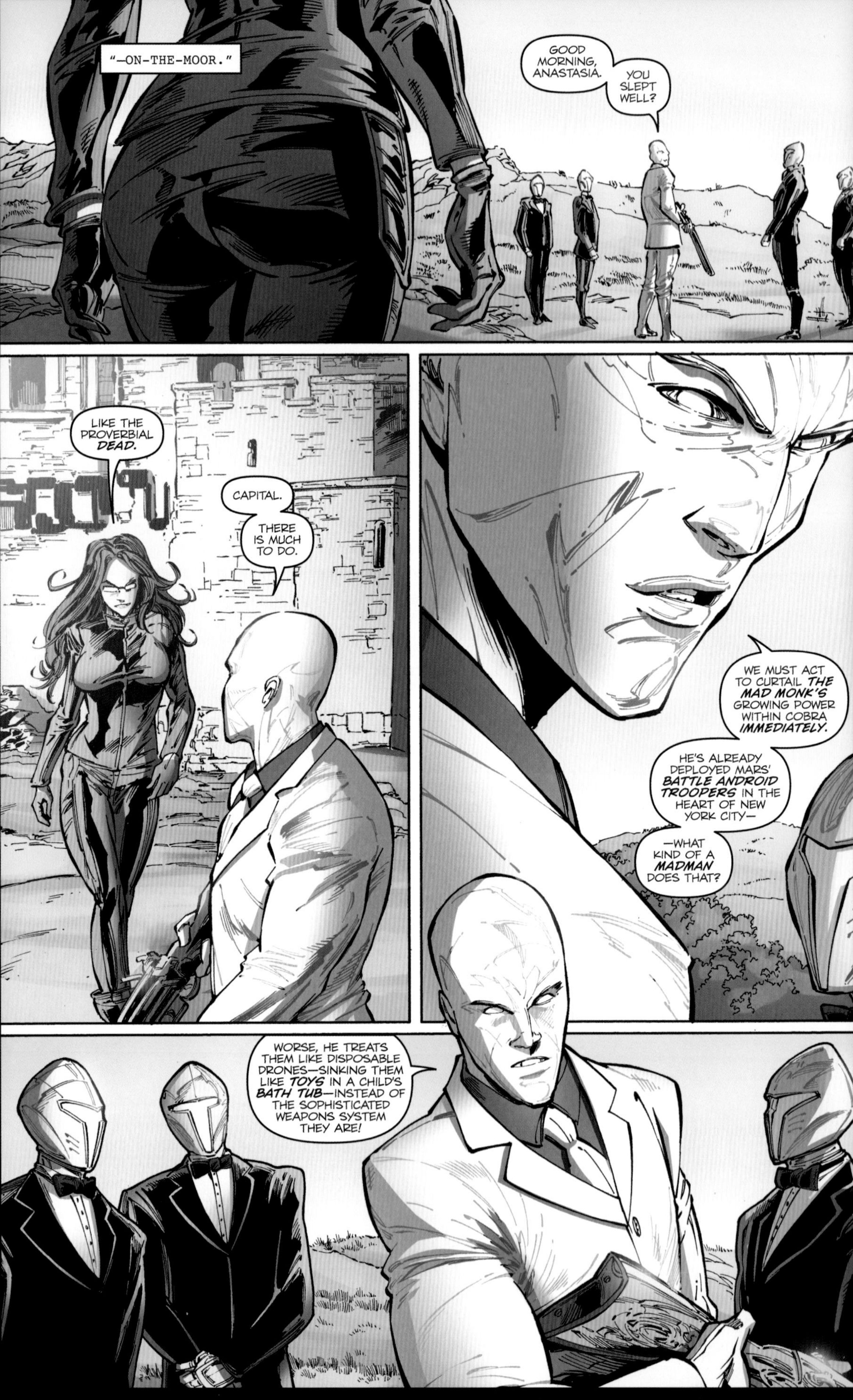
"—ON-THE-MOOR."
GOOD MORNING, ANASTASIA.
YOU SLEPT WELL?
LIKE THE PROVERBIAL DEAD.
CAPITAL.
THERE IS MUCH TO DO.
WE MUST ACT TO CURTAIL THE MAD MONK'S GROWING POWER WITHIN COBRA IMMEDIATELY.
HE'S ALREADY DEPLOYED MARS' BATTLE ANDROID TROOPERS IN THE HEART OF NEW YORK CITY—
—WHAT KIND OF A MADMAN DOES THAT?
WORSE, HE TREATS THEM LIKE DISPOSABLE DRONES—SINKING THEM LIKE TOYS IN A CHILD'S BATH TUB—INSTEAD OF THE SOPHISTICATED WEAPONS SYSTEM THEY ARE!

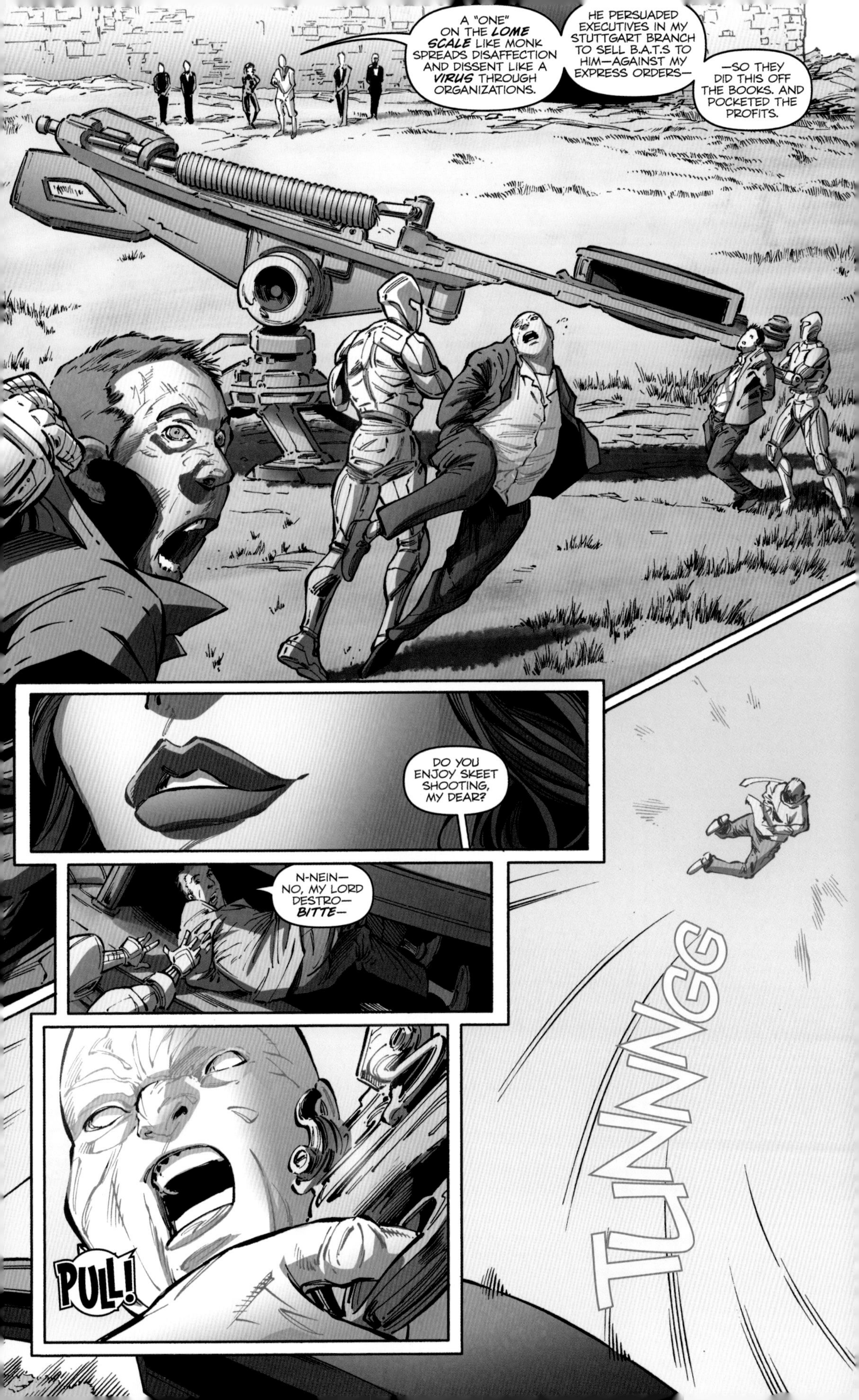
A "ONE" ON THE LOME SCALE LIKE MONK SPREADS DISAFFECTION AND DISSENT LIKE A VIRUS THROUGH ORGANIZATIONS.
HE PERSUADED EXECUTIVES IN MY STUTTGART BRANCH TO SELL B.A.T.S TO HIM—AGAINST MY EXPRESS ORDERS—
—SO THEY DID THIS OFF THE BOOKS. AND POCKETED THE PROFITS.
DO YOU ENJOY SKEET SHOOTING, MY DEAR?
N-NEIN— NO, MY LORD DESTRO— BITTE—
PULL!
TUNNGG

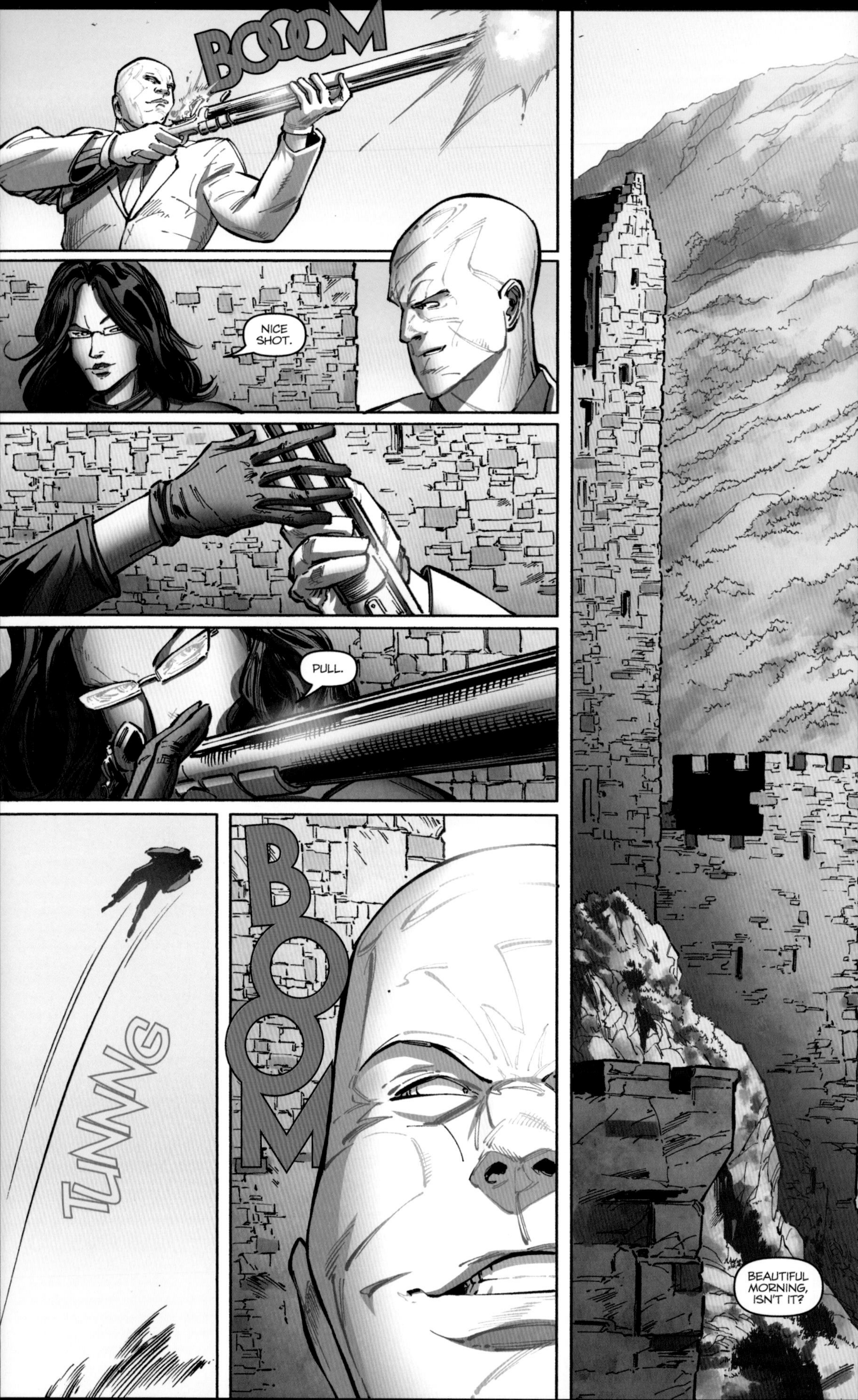
BOOOM
NICE SHOT.
PULL.
TUNNNG
BOOOM
BEAUTIFUL MORNING, ISN'T IT?

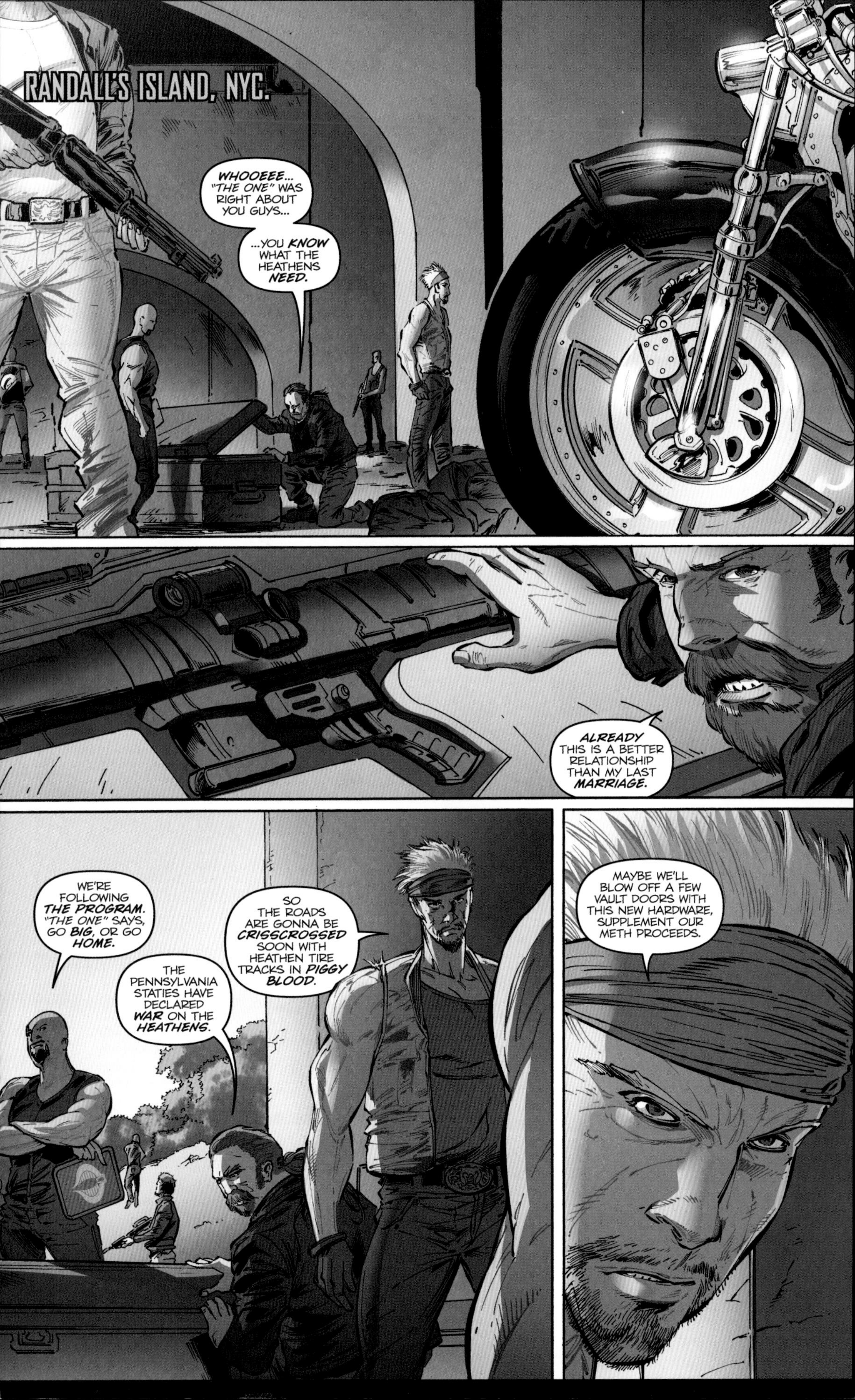
RANDALL'S ISLAND, NYC.
WHOOEEE... "THE ONE" WAS RIGHT ABOUT YOU GUYS...
...YOU KNOW WHAT THE HEATHENS NEED.
ALREADY THIS IS A BETTER RELATIONSHIP THAN MY LAST MARRIAGE.
WE'RE FOLLOWING THE PROGRAM. "THE ONE" SAYS, GO BIG, OR GO HOME.
THE PENNSYLVANIA STATIES HAVE DECLARED WAR ON THE HEATHENS.
SO THE ROADS ARE GONNA BE CRISSCROSSED SOON WITH HEATHEN TIRE TRACKS IN PIGGY BLOOD.
MAYBE WE'LL BLOW OFF A FEW VAULT DOORS WITH THIS NEW HARDWARE, SUPPLEMENT OUR METH PROCEEDS.

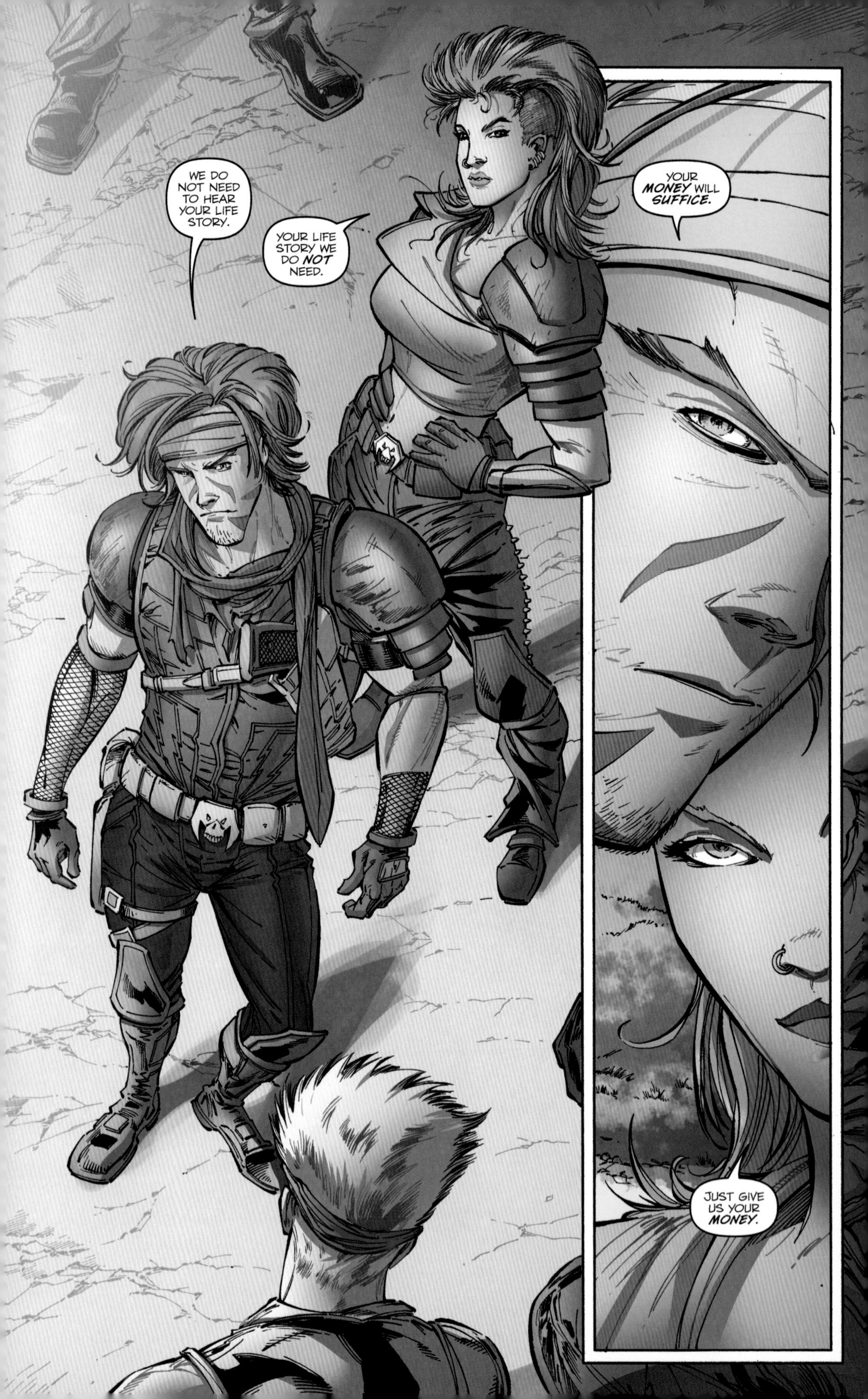
WE DO NOT NEED TO HEAR YOUR LIFE STORY.
YOUR LIFE STORY WE DO NOT NEED.
YOUR MONEY WILL SUFFICE.
JUST GIVE US YOUR MONEY.

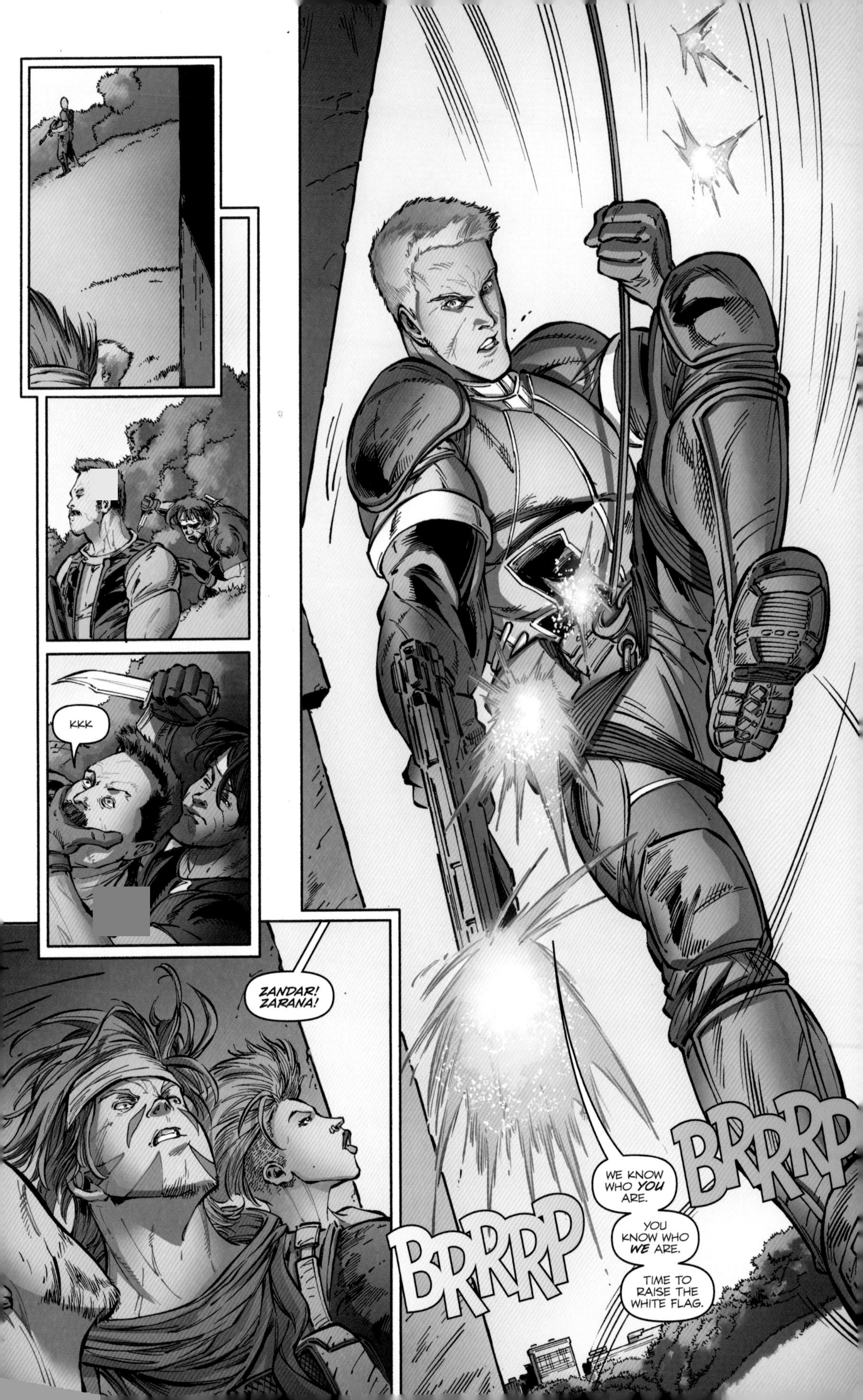
KKK
ZANDAR! ZARANA!
BRRRP
WE KNOW WHO YOU ARE.
YOU KNOW WHO WE ARE.
TIME TO RAISE THE WHITE FLAG.
BRRRP

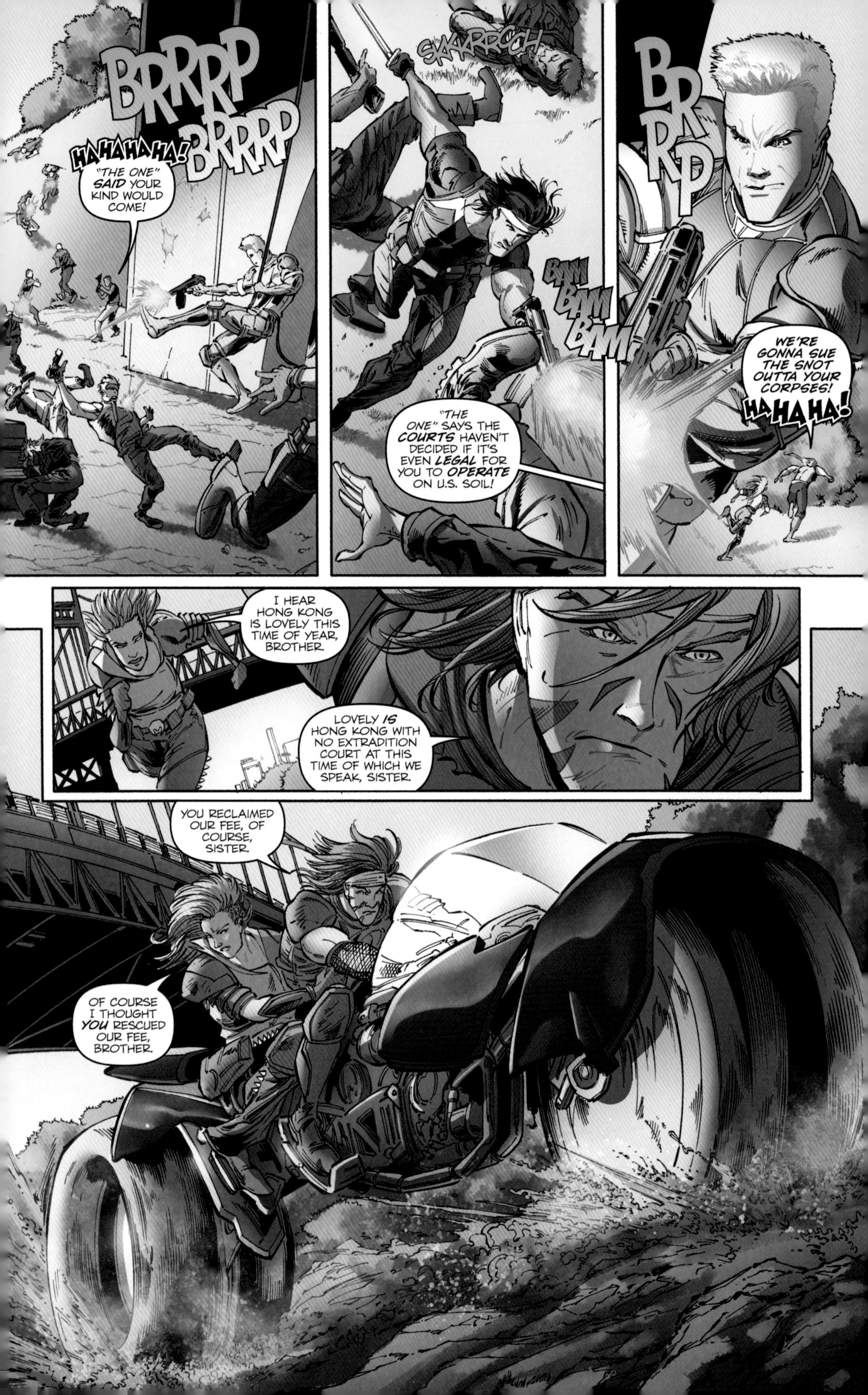
BRRRP BRRRP
HAHAHAHA!
"THE ONE" SAID YOUR KIND WOULD COME!
SKAARRCH
BAM BAM BAM
"THE ONE" SAYS THE COURTS HAVEN'T DECIDED IF IT'S EVEN LEGAL FOR YOU TO OPERATE ON U.S. SOIL!
BRRP
WE'RE GONNA SUE THE SNOT OUTTA YOUR CORPSES!
HAHAHA!
I HEAR HONG KONG IS LOVELY THIS TIME OF YEAR, BROTHER.
LOVELY IS HONG KONG WITH NO EXTRADITION COURT AT THIS TIME OF WHICH WE SPEAK, SISTER.
YOU RECLAIMED OUR FEE, OF COURSE, SISTER.
OF COURSE I THOUGHT YOU RESCUED OUR FEE, BROTHER.

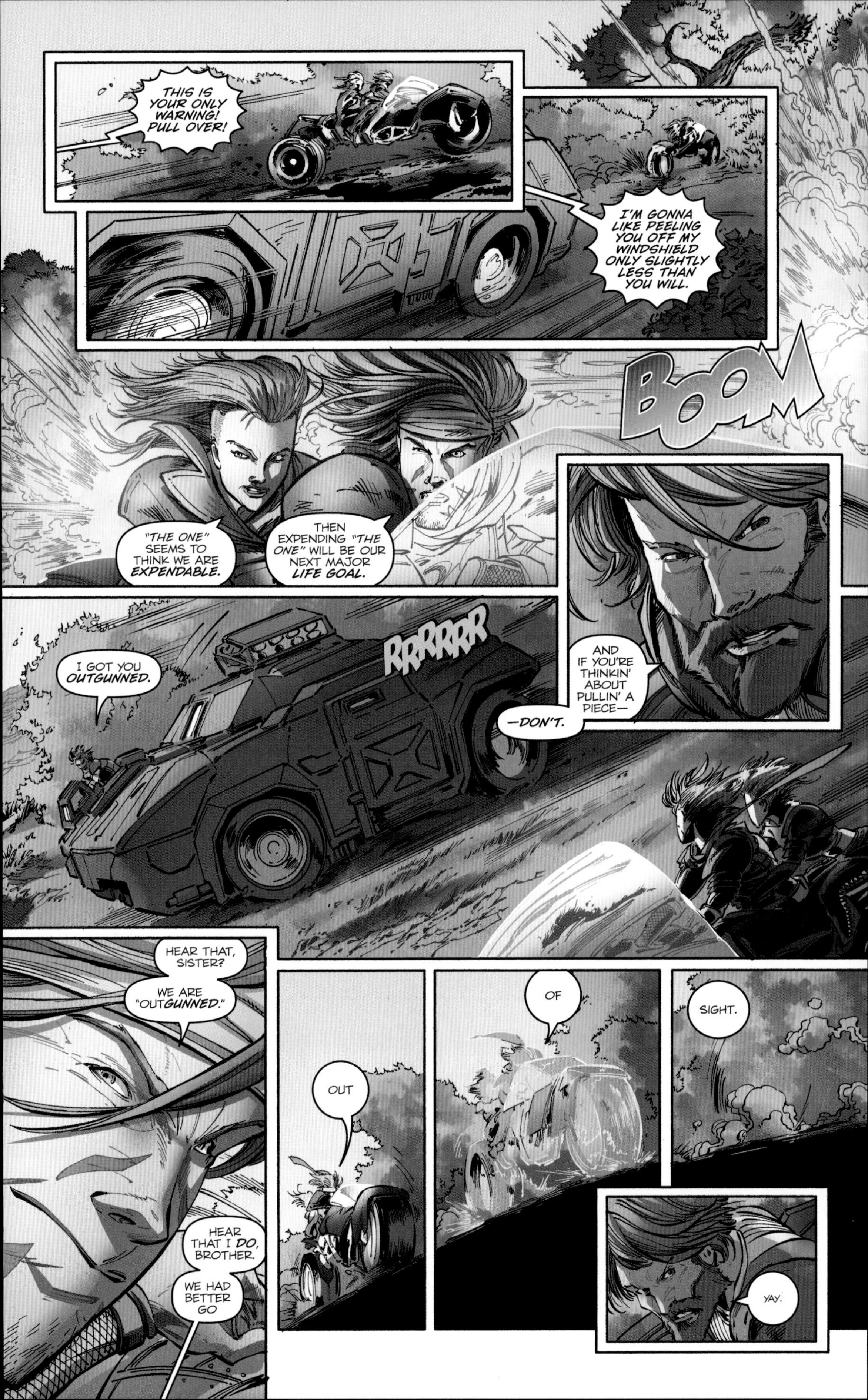

THIS IS YOUR ONLY WARNING! PULL OVER!
I'M GONNA LIKE PEELING YOU OFF MY WINDSHIELD ONLY SLIGHTLY LESS THAN YOU WILL.
BOOM
"THE ONE" SEEMS TO THINK WE ARE EXPENDABLE.
THEN EXPENDING "THE ONE" WILL BE OUR NEXT MAJOR LIFE GOAL.
RRRRRR
I GOT YOU OUTGUNNED.
AND IF YOU'RE THINKIN' ABOUT PULLIN' A PIECE—
—DON'T.
HEAR THAT, SISTER?
WE ARE "OUTGUNNED."
HEAR THAT I DO, BROTHER.
WE HAD BETTER GO
OUT
OF
SIGHT.
YAY.

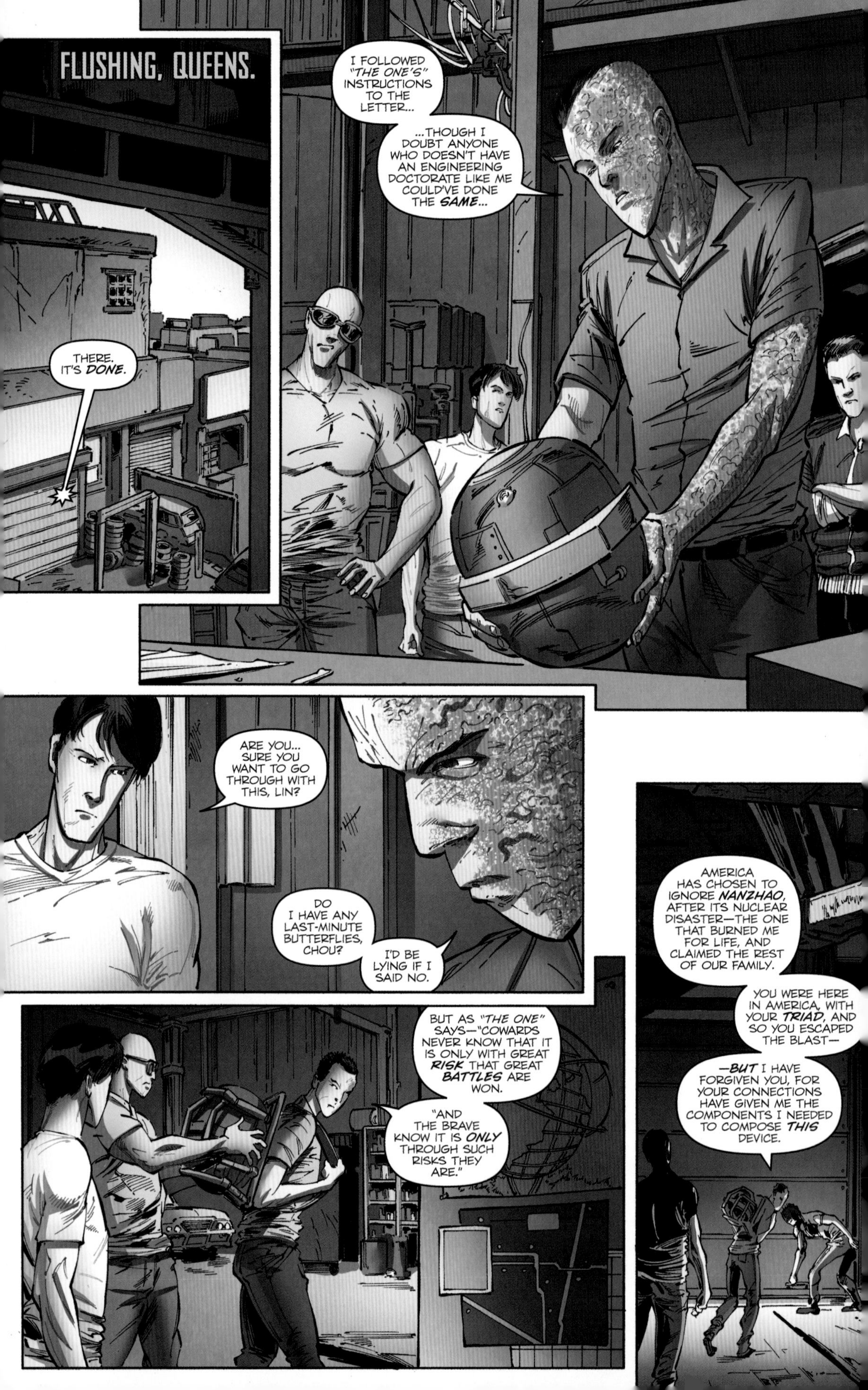
FLUSHING, QUEENS.
THERE. IT'S DONE.
I FOLLOWED "THE ONE'S" INSTRUCTIONS TO THE LETTER...
...THOUGH I DOUBT ANYONE WHO DOESN'T HAVE AN ENGINEERING DOCTORATE LIKE ME COULD'VE DONE THE SAME...
ARE YOU... SURE YOU WANT TO GO THROUGH WITH THIS, LIN?
DO I HAVE ANY LAST-MINUTE BUTTERFLIES, CHOU?
I'D BE LYING IF I SAID NO.
BUT AS "THE ONE" SAYS—"COWARDS NEVER KNOW THAT IT IS ONLY WITH GREAT RISK THAT GREAT BATTLES ARE WON.
"AND THE BRAVE KNOW IT IS ONLY THROUGH SUCH RISKS THEY ARE."
AMERICA HAS CHOSEN TO IGNORE NANZHAO, AFTER ITS NUCLEAR DISASTER—THE ONE THAT BURNED ME FOR LIFE, AND CLAIMED THE REST OF OUR FAMILY.
YOU WERE HERE IN AMERICA, WITH YOUR TRIAD, AND SO YOU ESCAPED THE BLAST—
—BUT I HAVE FORGIVEN YOU, FOR YOUR CONNECTIONS HAVE GIVEN ME THE COMPONENTS I NEEDED TO COMPOSE THIS DEVICE.

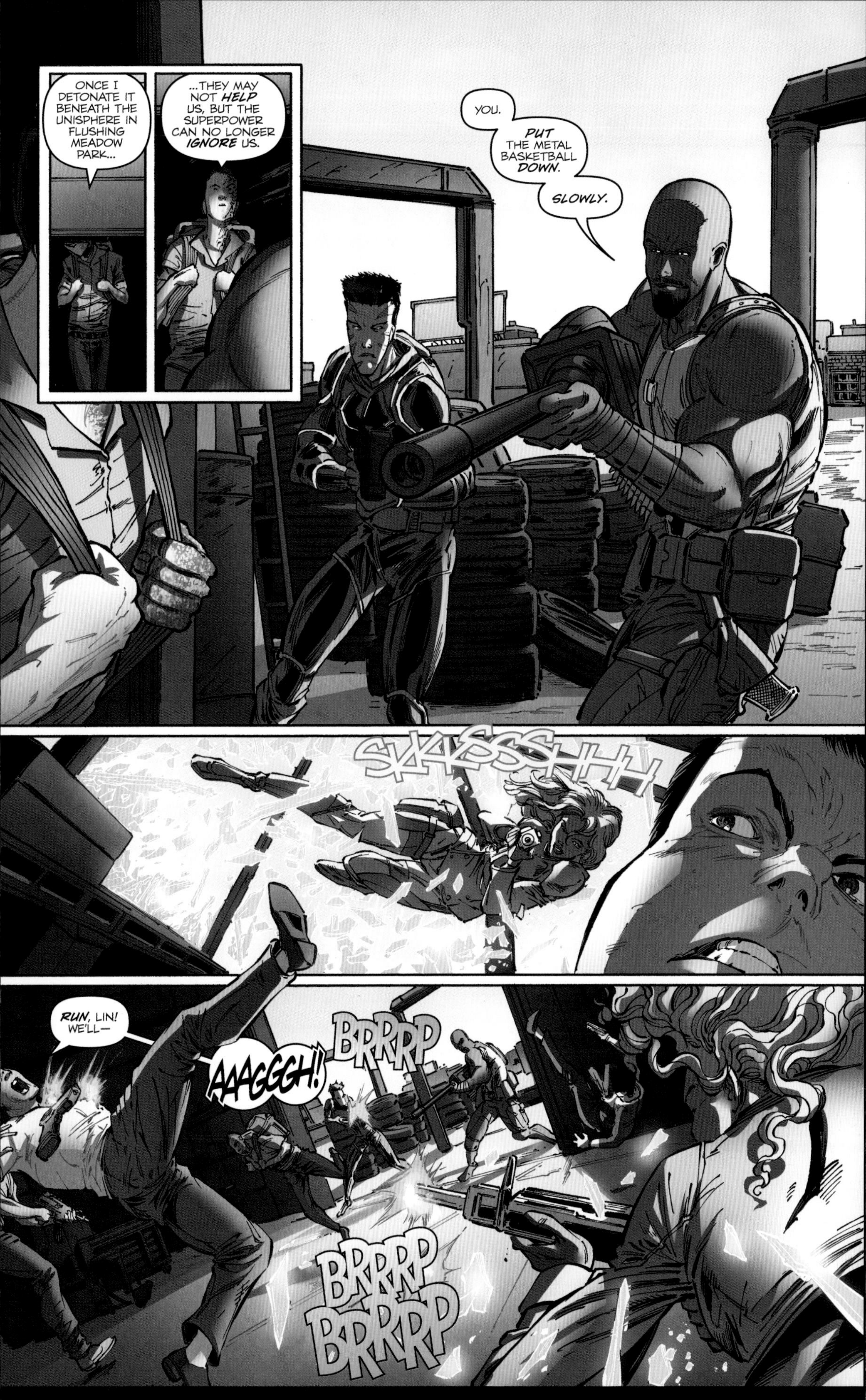

ONCE I DETONATE IT BENEATH THE UNISPHERE IN FLUSHING MEADOW PARK...
...THEY MAY NOT HELP US, BUT THE SUPERPOWER CAN NO LONGER IGNORE US.
YOU.
PUT THE METAL BASKETBALL DOWN.
SLOWLY.
SKASSSHHH
RUN, LIN! WE'LL—
AAAGGGH!
BRRRP
BRRRP
BRRRP

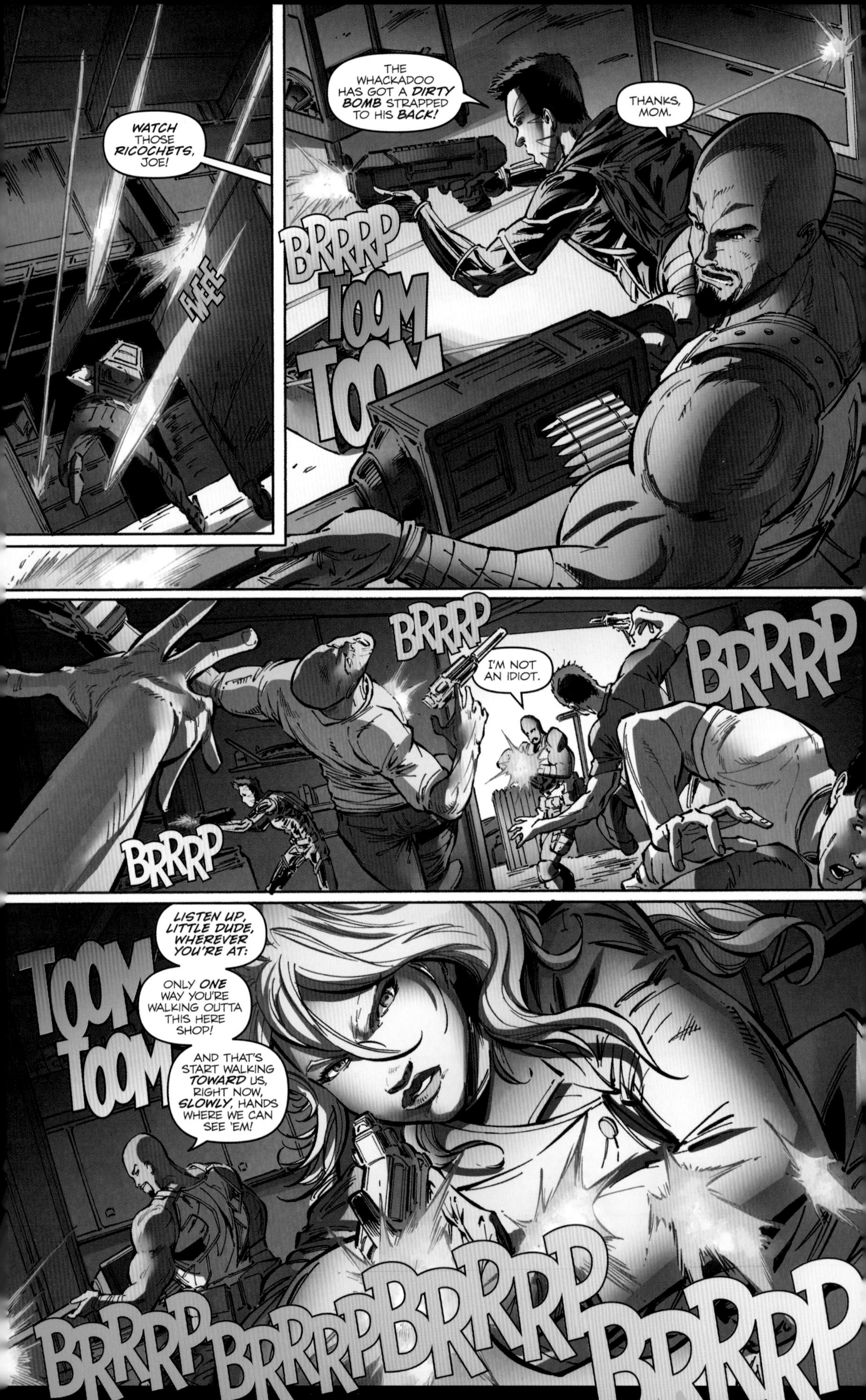
WATCH THOSE RICOCHETS, JOE!
FWEEE
THE WHACKADOO HAS GOT A DIRTY BOMB STRAPPED TO HIS BACK!
THANKS, MOM.
BRRRP
TOOM
TOOM
BRRRP
I'M NOT AN IDIOT.
BRRRP
BRRRP
LISTEN UP, LITTLE DUDE, WHEREVER YOU'RE AT:
ONLY ONE WAY YOU'RE WALKING OUTTA THIS HERE SHOP!
AND THAT'S START WALKING TOWARD US, RIGHT NOW, SLOWLY, HANDS WHERE WE CAN SEE 'EM!
TOOM
TOOM
BRRRP
BRRRRP
BRRRP
BRRRP

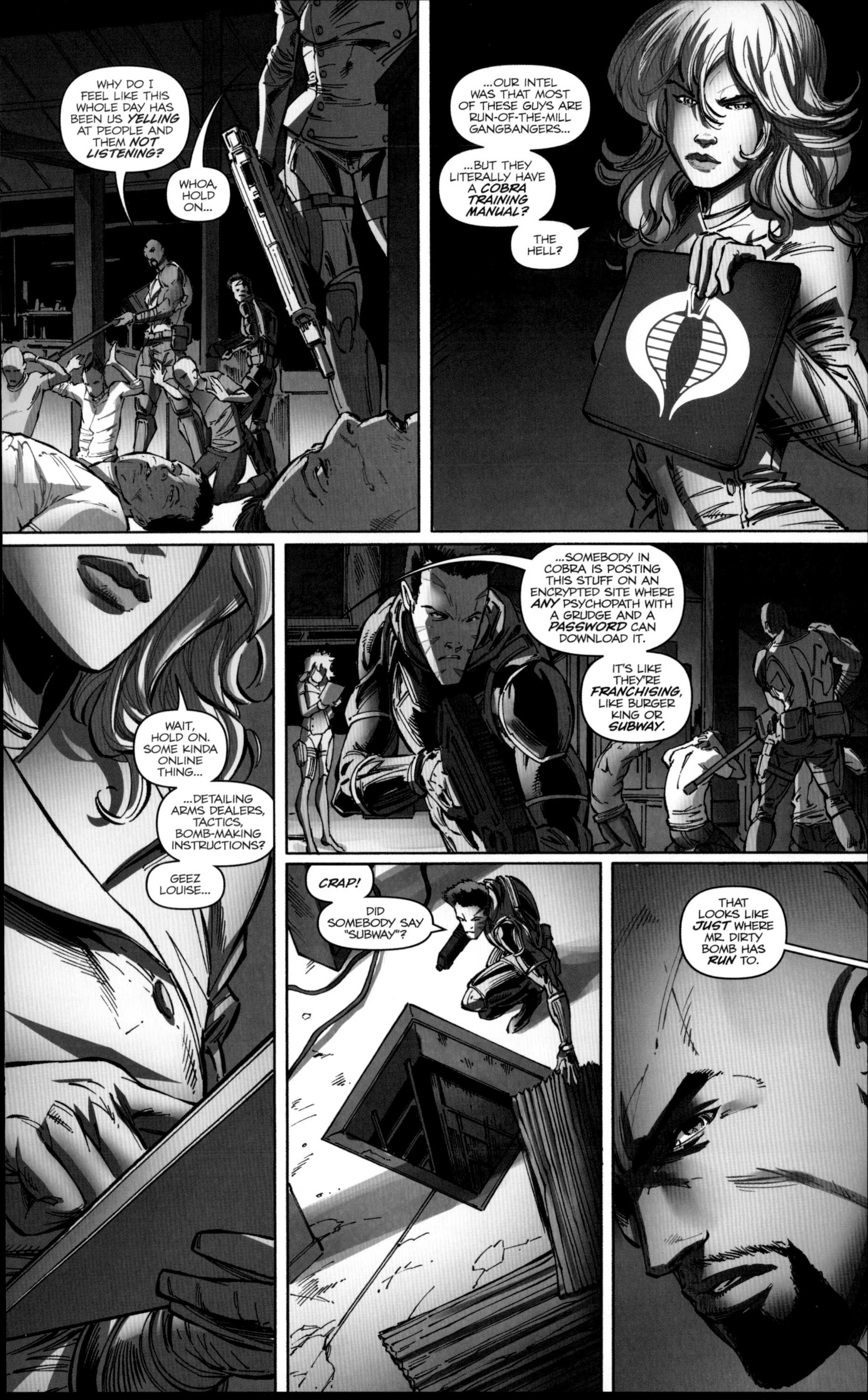

WHY DO I FEEL LIKE THIS WHOLE DAY HAS BEEN US YELLING AT PEOPLE AND THEM NOT LISTENING?
WHOA, HOLD ON...
...OUR INTEL WAS THAT MOST OF THESE GUYS ARE RUN-OF-THE-MILL GANGBANGERS...
...BUT THEY LITERALLY HAVE A COBRA TRAINING MANUAL?
THE HELL?
WAIT, HOLD ON. SOME KINDA ONLINE THING...
...DETAILING ARMS DEALERS, TACTICS, BOMB-MAKING INSTRUCTIONS?
GEEZ LOUISE...
...SOMEBODY IN COBRA IS POSTING THIS STUFF ON AN ENCRYPTED SITE WHERE ANY PSYCHOPATH WITH A GRUDGE AND A PASSWORD CAN DOWNLOAD IT.
IT'S LIKE THEY'RE FRANCHISING, LIKE BURGER KING OR SUBWAY.
CRAP!
DID SOMEBODY SAY "SUBWAY"?
THAT LOOKS LIKE JUST WHERE MR. DIRTY BOMB HAS RUN TO.

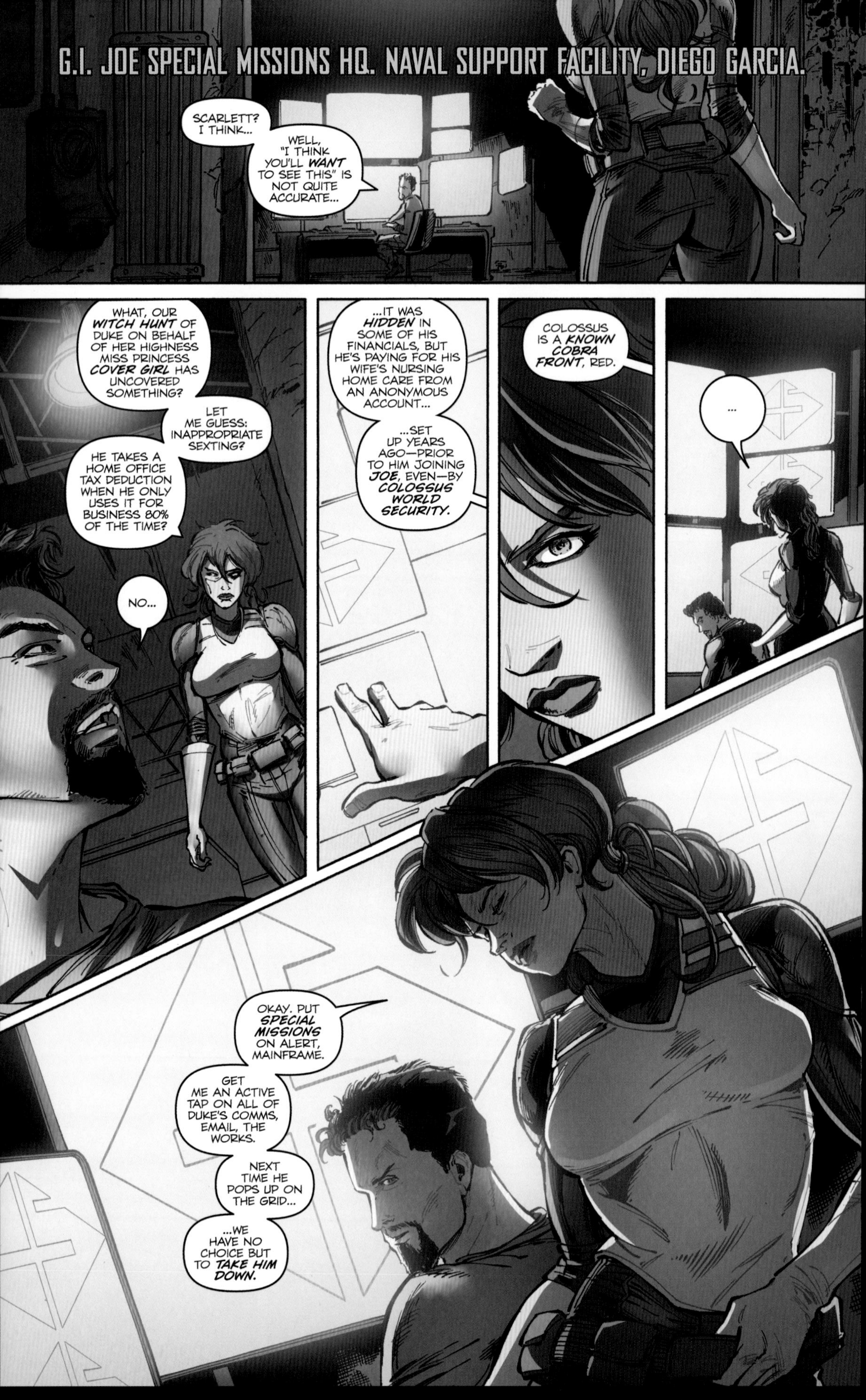
G.I. JOE SPECIAL MISSIONS HQ. NAVAL SUPPORT FACILITY, DIEGO GARCIA.
SCARLETT? I THINK...
WELL, "I THINK YOU'LL WANT TO SEE THIS" IS NOT QUITE ACCURATE...
WHAT, OUR WITCH HUNT OF DUKE ON BEHALF OF HER HIGHNESS MISS PRINCESS COVER GIRL HAS UNCOVERED SOMETHING?
LET ME GUESS: INAPPROPRIATE SEXTING?
HE TAKES A HOME OFFICE TAX DEDUCTION WHEN HE ONLY USES IT FOR BUSINESS 80% OF THE TIME?
NO...
...IT WAS HIDDEN IN SOME OF HIS FINANCIALS, BUT HE'S PAYING FOR HIS WIFE'S NURSING HOME CARE FROM AN ANONYMOUS ACCOUNT...
...SET UP YEARS AGO—PRIOR TO HIM JOINING JOE, EVEN—BY COLOSSUS WORLD SECURITY.
COLOSSUS IS A KNOWN COBRA FRONT, RED.
...
OKAY. PUT SPECIAL MISSIONS ON ALERT, MAINFRAME.
GET ME AN ACTIVE TAP ON ALL OF DUKE'S COMMS, EMAIL, THE WORKS.
NEXT TIME HE POPS UP ON THE GRID...
...WE HAVE NO CHOICE BUT TO TAKE HIM DOWN.

CHAPTER FOUR

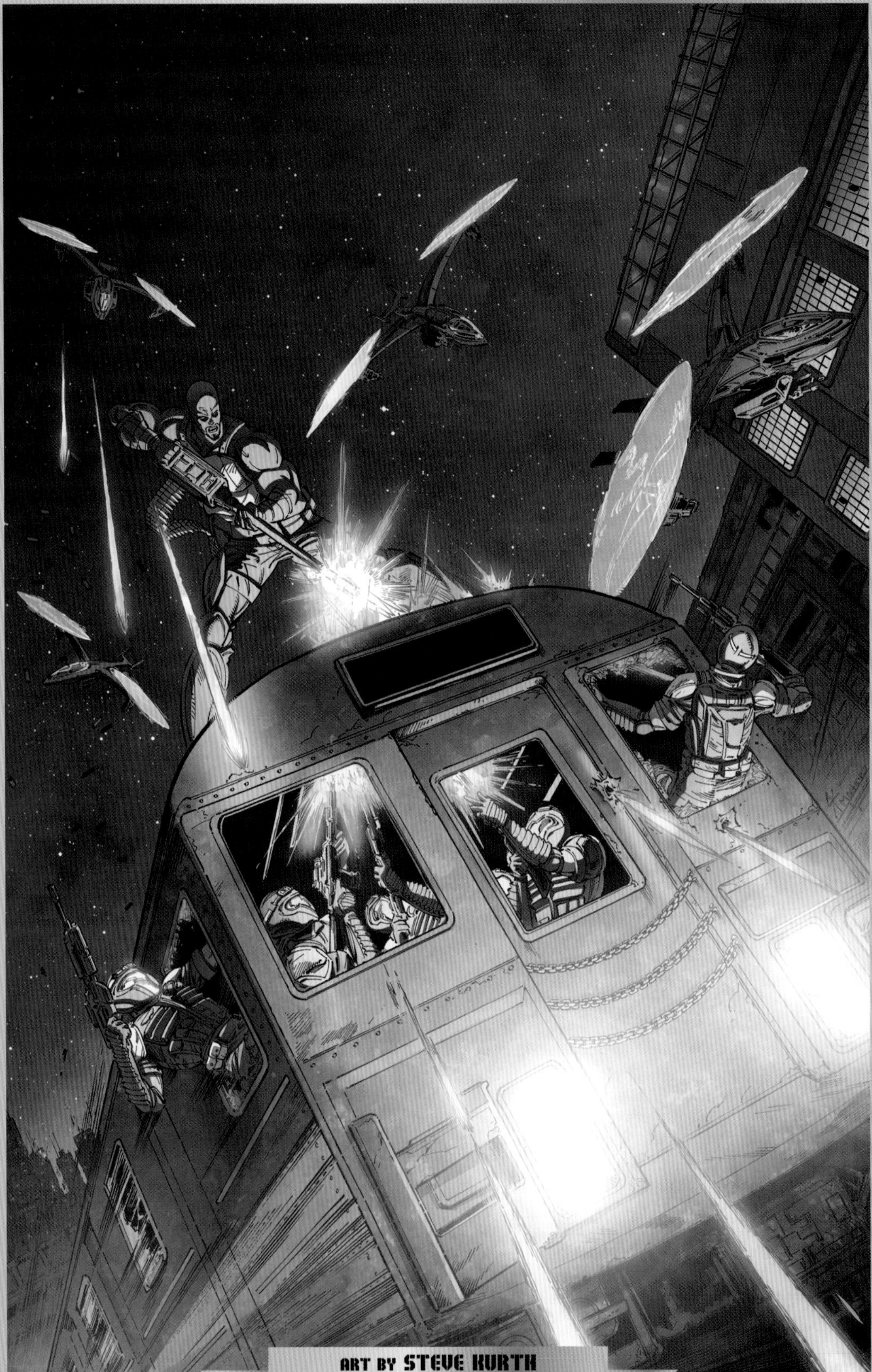

ART BY STEVE KURTH
INKS BY ALLEN MARTINEZ
COLORS BY JOANA LAFUENTE

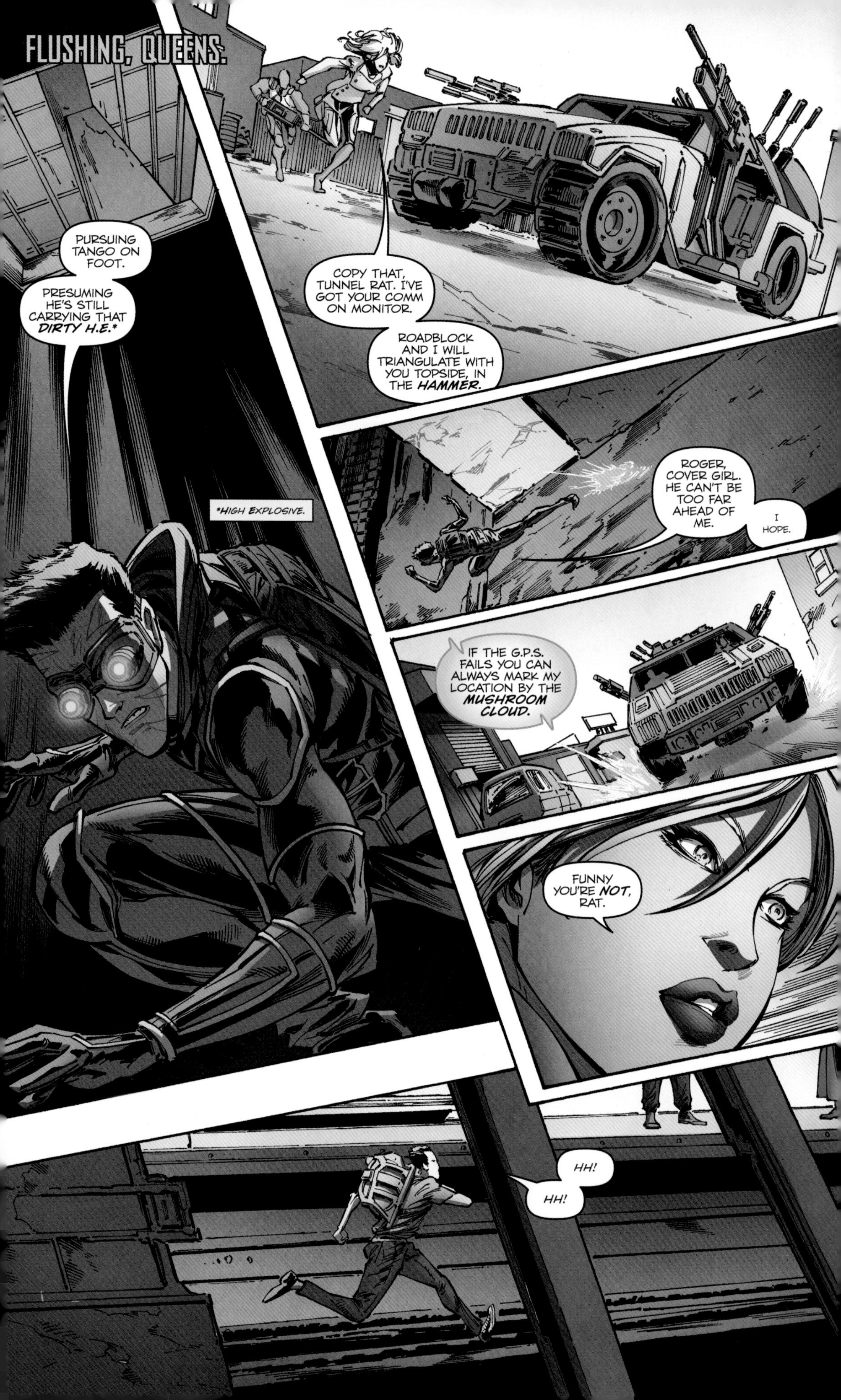
FLUSHING, QUEENS.
PURSUING TANGO ON FOOT.
PRESUMING HE'S STILL CARRYING THAT DIRTY H.E.*
COPY THAT, TUNNEL RAT. I'VE GOT YOUR COMM ON MONITOR.
ROADBLOCK AND I WILL TRIANGULATE WITH YOU TOPSIDE, IN THE HAMMER.
*HIGH EXPLOSIVE.
ROGER, COVER GIRL. HE CAN'T BE TOO FAR AHEAD OF ME.
I HOPE.
IF THE G.P.S. FAILS YOU CAN ALWAYS MARK MY LOCATION BY THE MUSHROOM CLOUD.
FUNNY YOU'RE NOT, RAT.
HH!
HH!

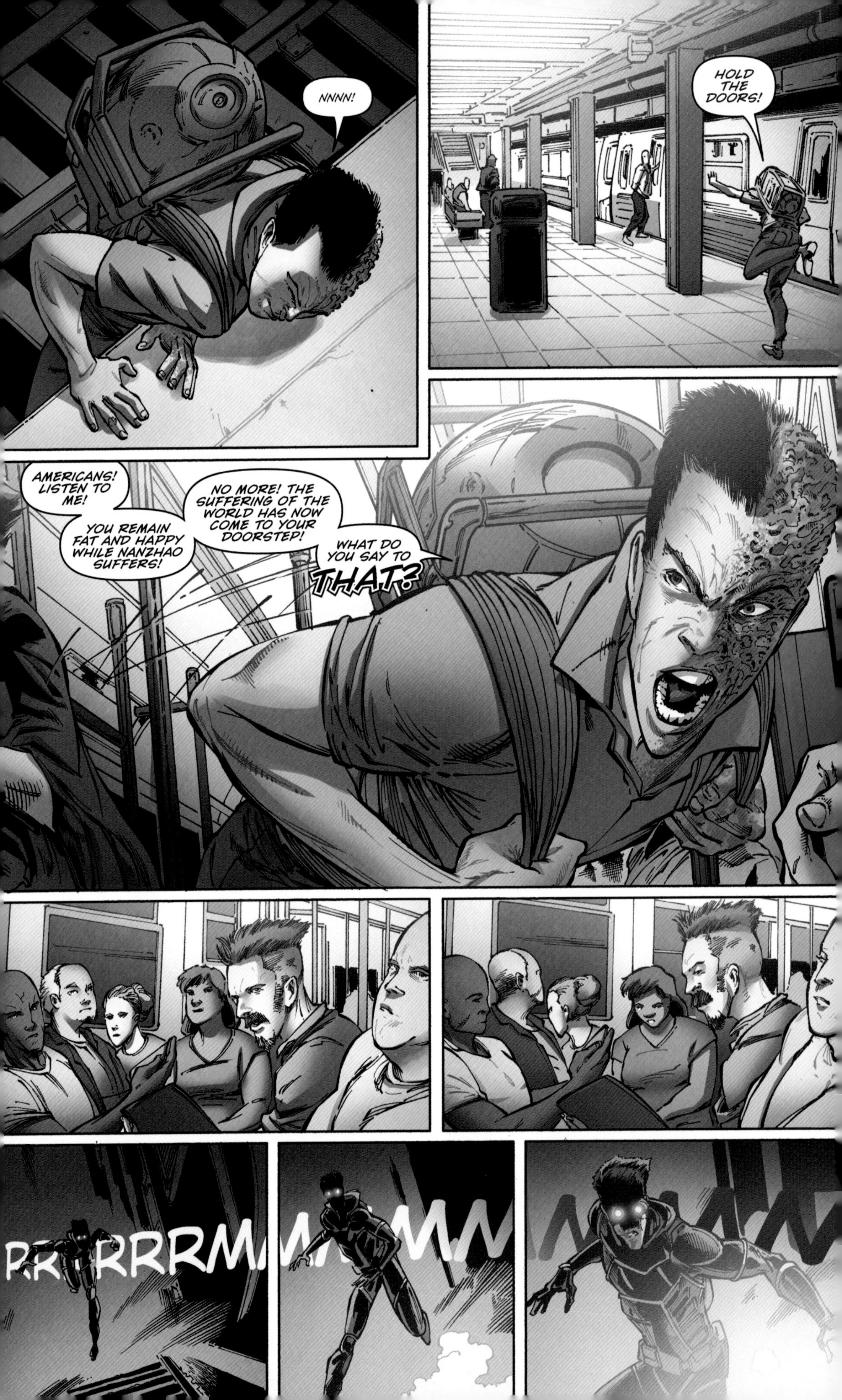
NNNN!
HOLD THE DOORS!
AMERICANS! LISTEN TO ME!
YOU REMAIN FAT AND HAPPY WHILE NANZHAO SUFFERS!
NO MORE! THE SUFFERING OF THE WORLD HAS NOW COME TO YOUR DOORSTEP!
WHAT DO YOU SAY TO THAT?
RRRRRRMMMMMMMMMMMMM

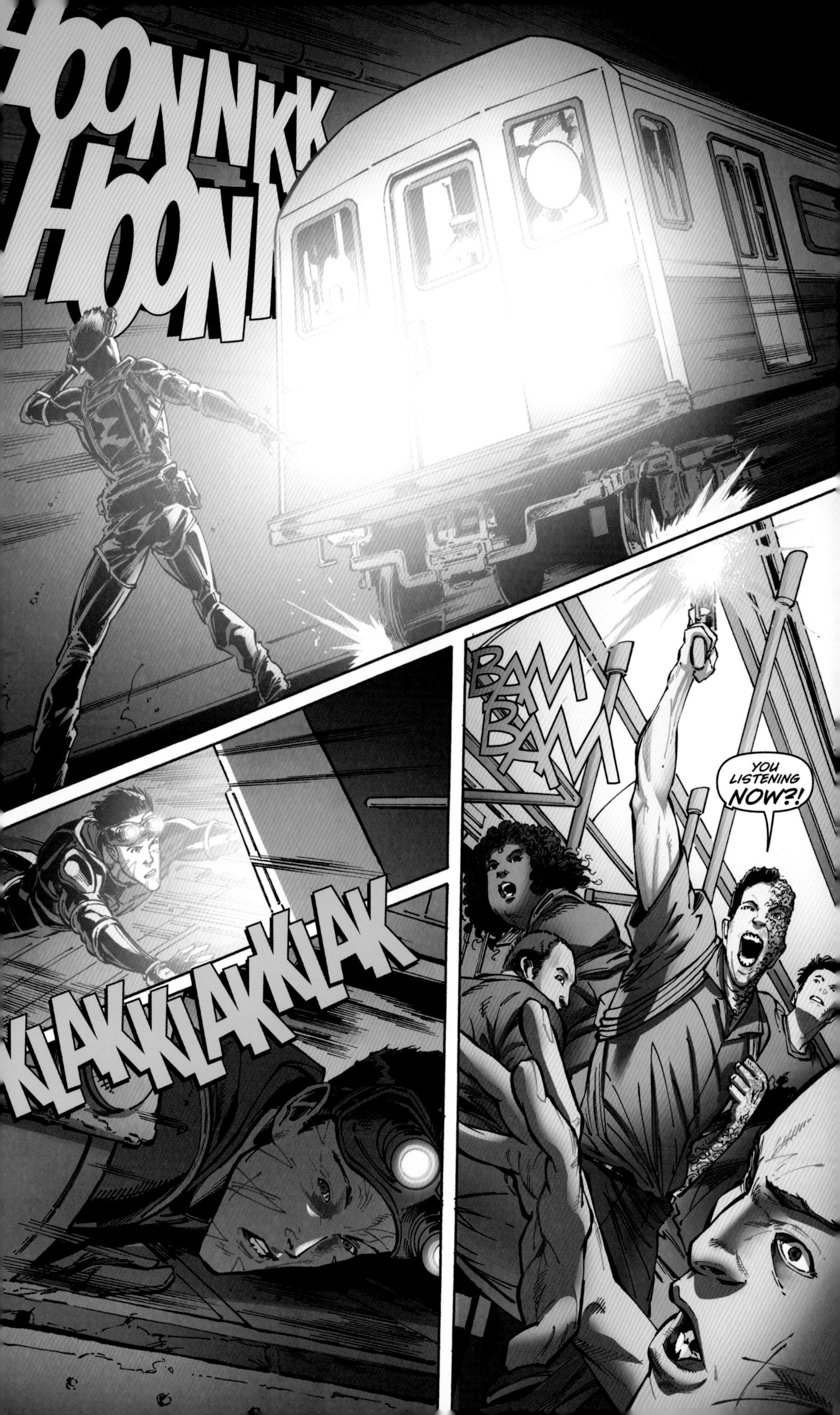
HOONNKK
HOONN
KLAKKLAKKLAKKLAK
BAM
BAM
YOU LISTENING NOW?!

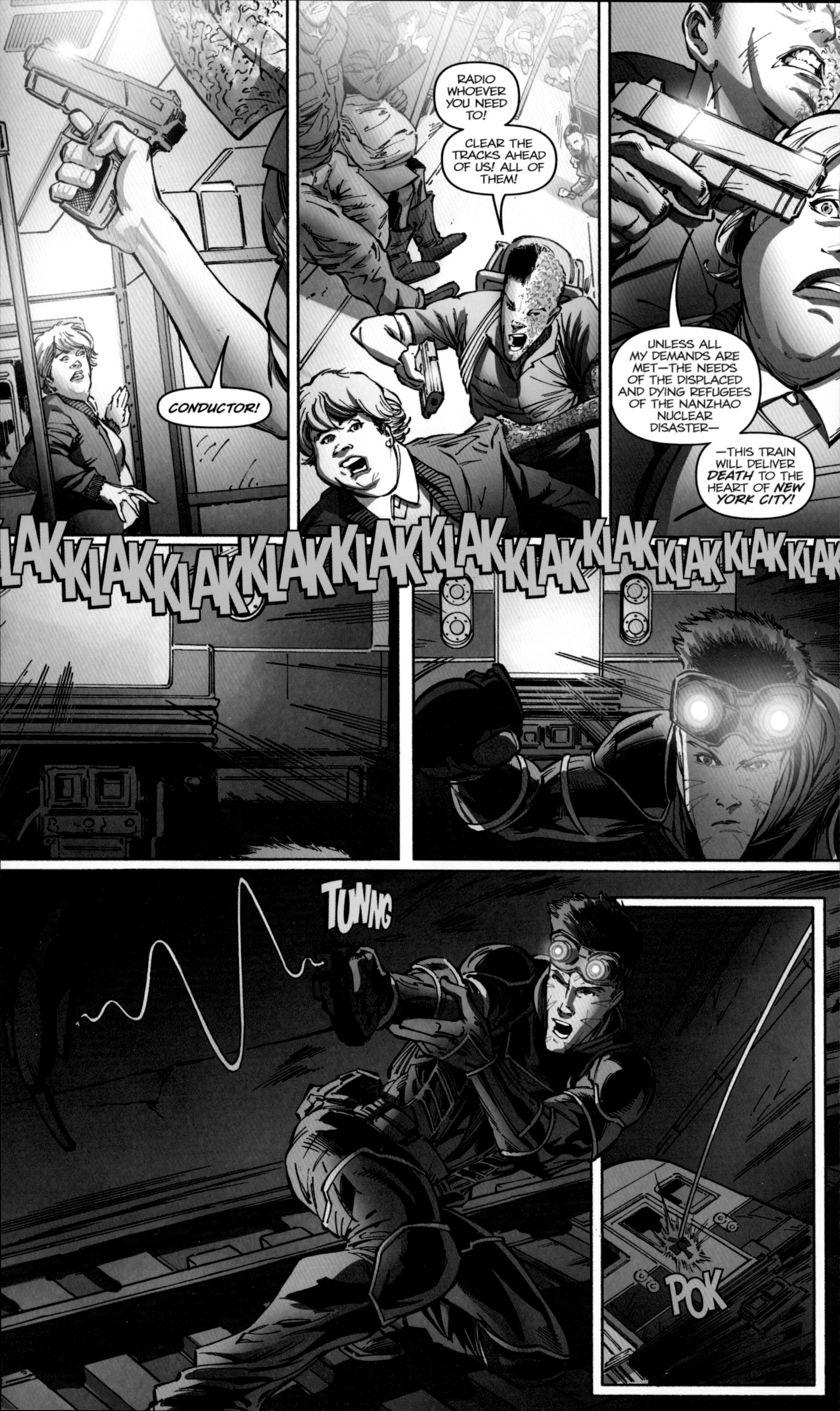
CONDUCTOR!
RADIO WHOEVER YOU NEED TO!
CLEAR THE TRACKS AHEAD OF US! ALL OF THEM!
UNLESS ALL MY DEMANDS ARE MET—THE NEEDS OF THE DISPLACED AND DYING REFUGEES OF THE NANZHAO NUCLEAR DISASTER—
—THIS TRAIN WILL DELIVER DEATH TO THE HEART OF NEW YORK CITY!
KLAK KLAK KLAK KLAK KLAK KLAK KLAK KLAK KLAK KLAK KLAK KLAK
TUNNG
POK

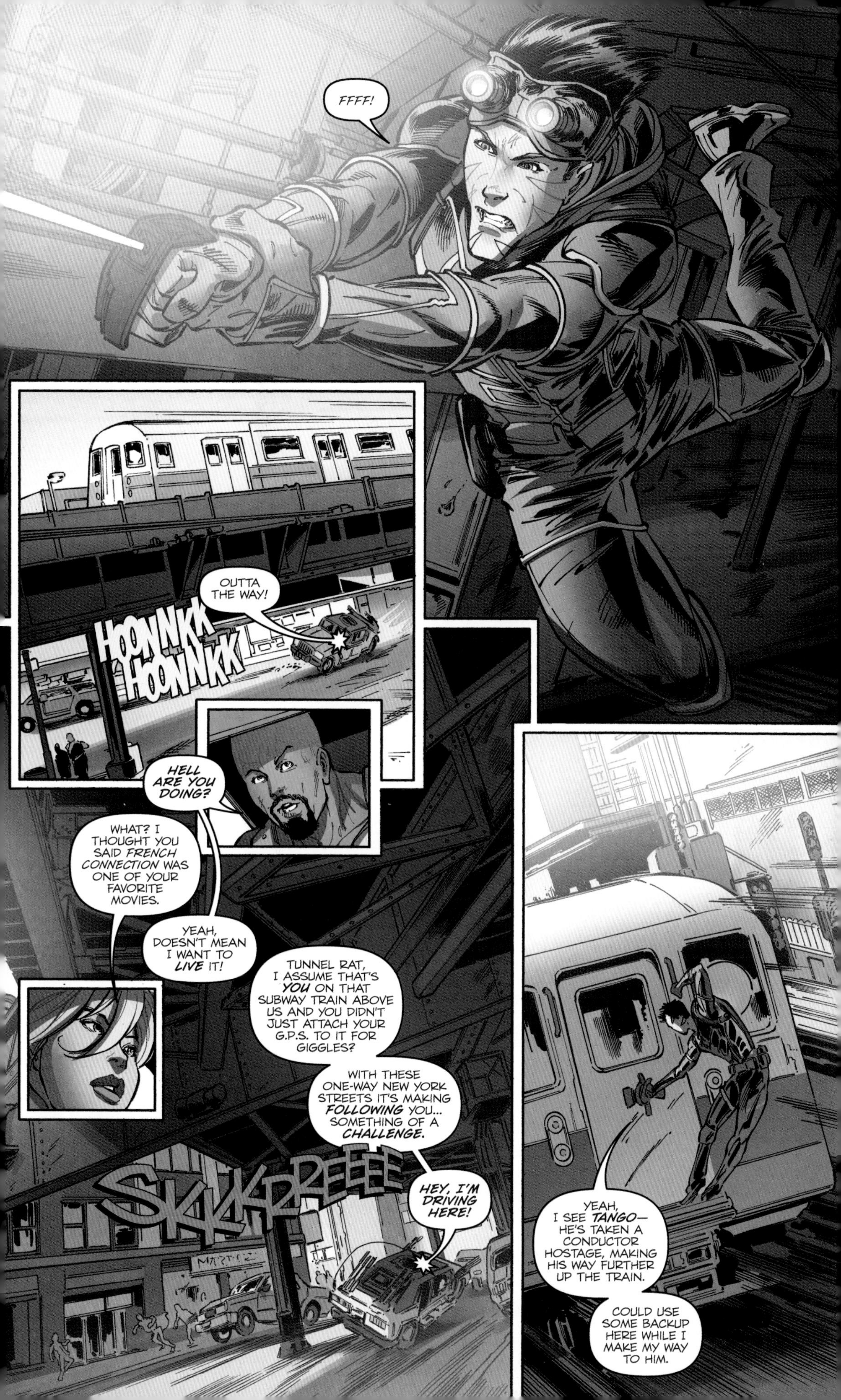

FFFF!
OUTTA THE WAY!
HOONNKK HOONNKK
HELL ARE YOU DOING?
WHAT? I THOUGHT YOU SAID FRENCH CONNECTION WAS ONE OF YOUR FAVORITE MOVIES.
YEAH, DOESN'T MEAN I WANT TO LIVE IT!
TUNNEL RAT, I ASSUME THAT'S YOU ON THAT SUBWAY TRAIN ABOVE US AND YOU DIDN'T JUST ATTACH YOUR G.P.S. TO IT FOR GIGGLES?
WITH THESE ONE-WAY NEW YORK STREETS IT'S MAKING FOLLOWING YOU... SOMETHING OF A CHALLENGE.
SKKKREEEE
HEY, I'M DRIVING HERE!
YEAH, I SEE TANGO— HE'S TAKEN A CONDUCTOR HOSTAGE, MAKING HIS WAY FURTHER UP THE TRAIN.
COULD USE SOME BACKUP HERE WHILE I MAKE MY WAY TO HIM.

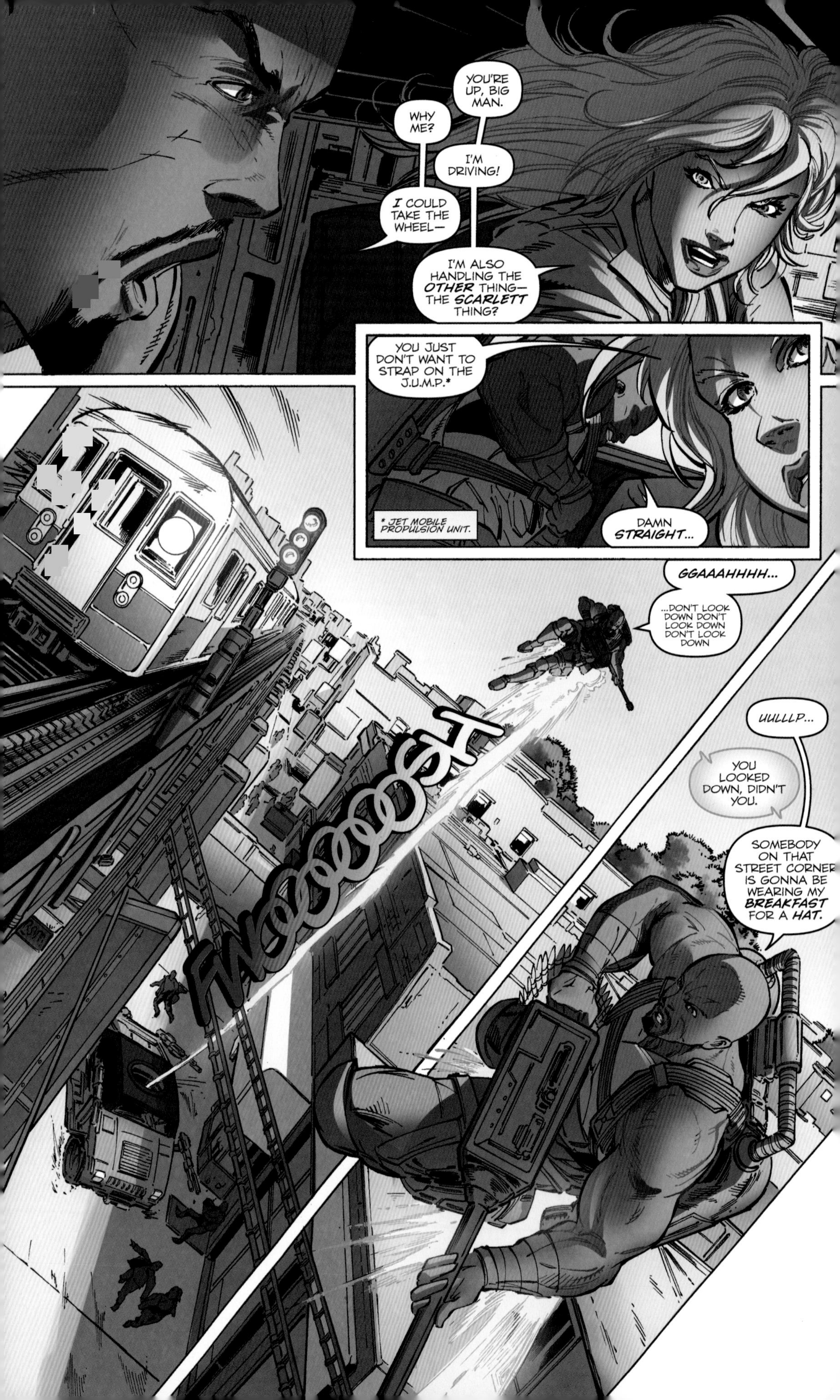

YOU'RE UP, BIG MAN.
WHY ME?
I'M DRIVING!
I COULD TAKE THE WHEEL—
I'M ALSO HANDLING THE OTHER THING—THE SCARLETT THING?
YOU JUST DON'T WANT TO STRAP ON THE J.U.M.P.*
* JET MOBILE PROPULSION UNIT.
DAMN STRAIGHT...
GGAAAHHHH...
...DON'T LOOK DOWN DON'T LOOK DOWN DON'T LOOK DOWN
FWOOOOOOSH
UULLLP...
YOU LOOKED DOWN, DIDN'T YOU.
SOMEBODY ON THAT STREET CORNER IS GONNA BE WEARING MY BREAKFAST FOR A HAT.

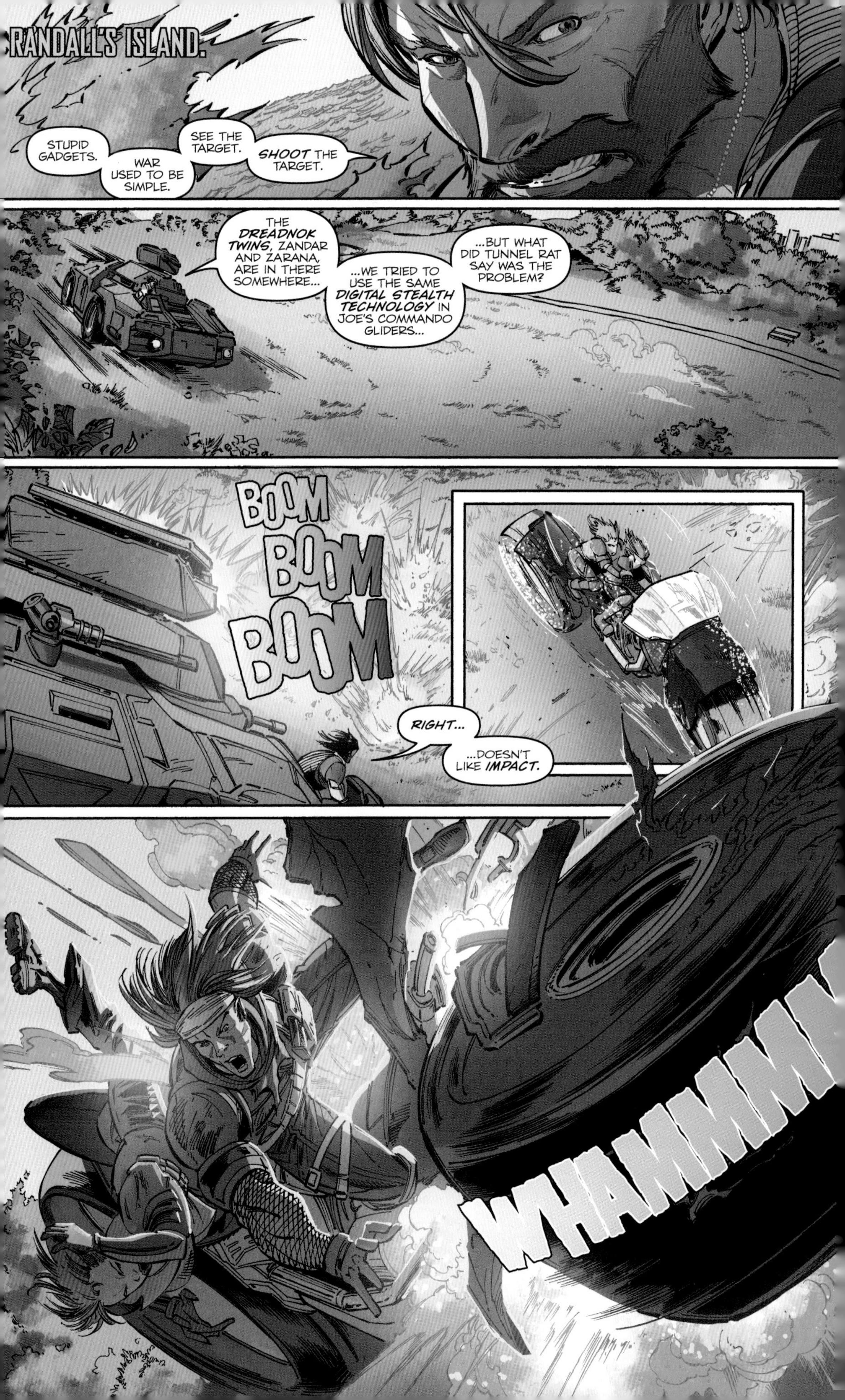
RANDALL'S ISLAND.
STUPID GADGETS.
WAR USED TO BE SIMPLE.
SEE THE TARGET.
SHOOT THE TARGET.
THE DREADNOK TWINS, ZANDAR AND ZARANA, ARE IN THERE SOMEWHERE...
...WE TRIED TO USE THE SAME DIGITAL STEALTH TECHNOLOGY IN JOE'S COMMANDO GLIDERS...
...BUT WHAT DID TUNNEL RAT SAY WAS THE PROBLEM?
BOOM BOOM BOOM
RIGHT...
...DOESN'T LIKE IMPACT.
WHAMMMM

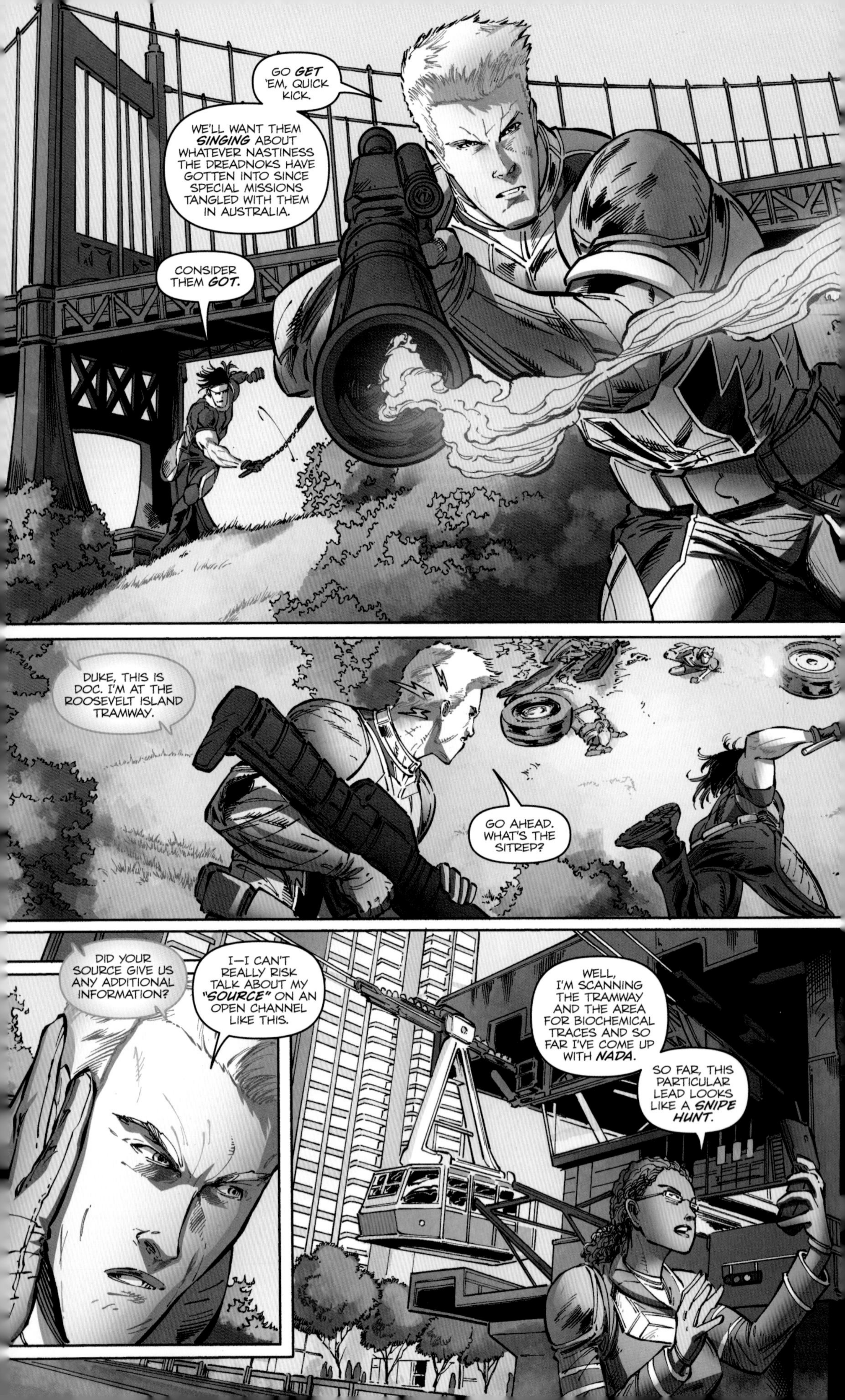
GO GET 'EM, QUICK KICK.
WE'LL WANT THEM SINGING ABOUT WHATEVER NASTINESS THE DREADNOKS HAVE GOTTEN INTO SINCE SPECIAL MISSIONS TANGLED WITH THEM IN AUSTRALIA.
CONSIDER THEM GOT.
DUKE, THIS IS DOC. I'M AT THE ROOSEVELT ISLAND TRAMWAY.
GO AHEAD. WHAT'S THE SITREP?
DID YOUR SOURCE GIVE US ANY ADDITIONAL INFORMATION?
I—I CAN'T REALLY RISK TALK ABOUT MY "SOURCE" ON AN OPEN CHANNEL LIKE THIS.
WELL, I'M SCANNING THE TRAMWAY AND THE AREA FOR BIOCHEMICAL TRACES AND SO FAR I'VE COME UP WITH NADA.
SO FAR, THIS PARTICULAR LEAD LOOKS LIKE A SNIPE HUNT.

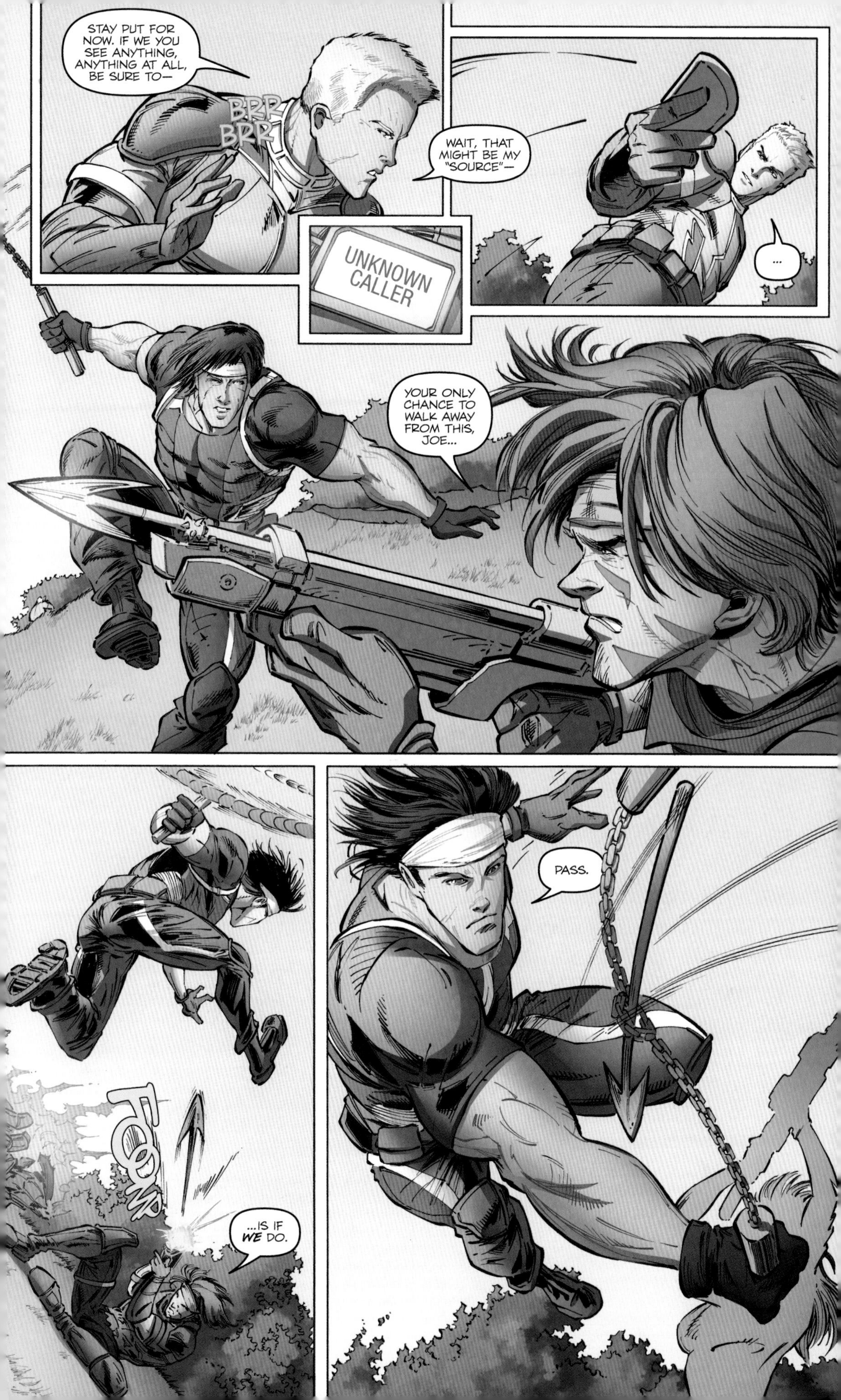
STAY PUT FOR NOW. IF WE YOU SEE ANYTHING, ANYTHING AT ALL, BE SURE TO—
BRR BRR
WAIT, THAT MIGHT BE MY "SOURCE"—
UNKNOWN CALLER
...
YOUR ONLY CHANCE TO WALK AWAY FROM THIS, JOE...
...IS IF WE DO.
FOOMP
PASS.

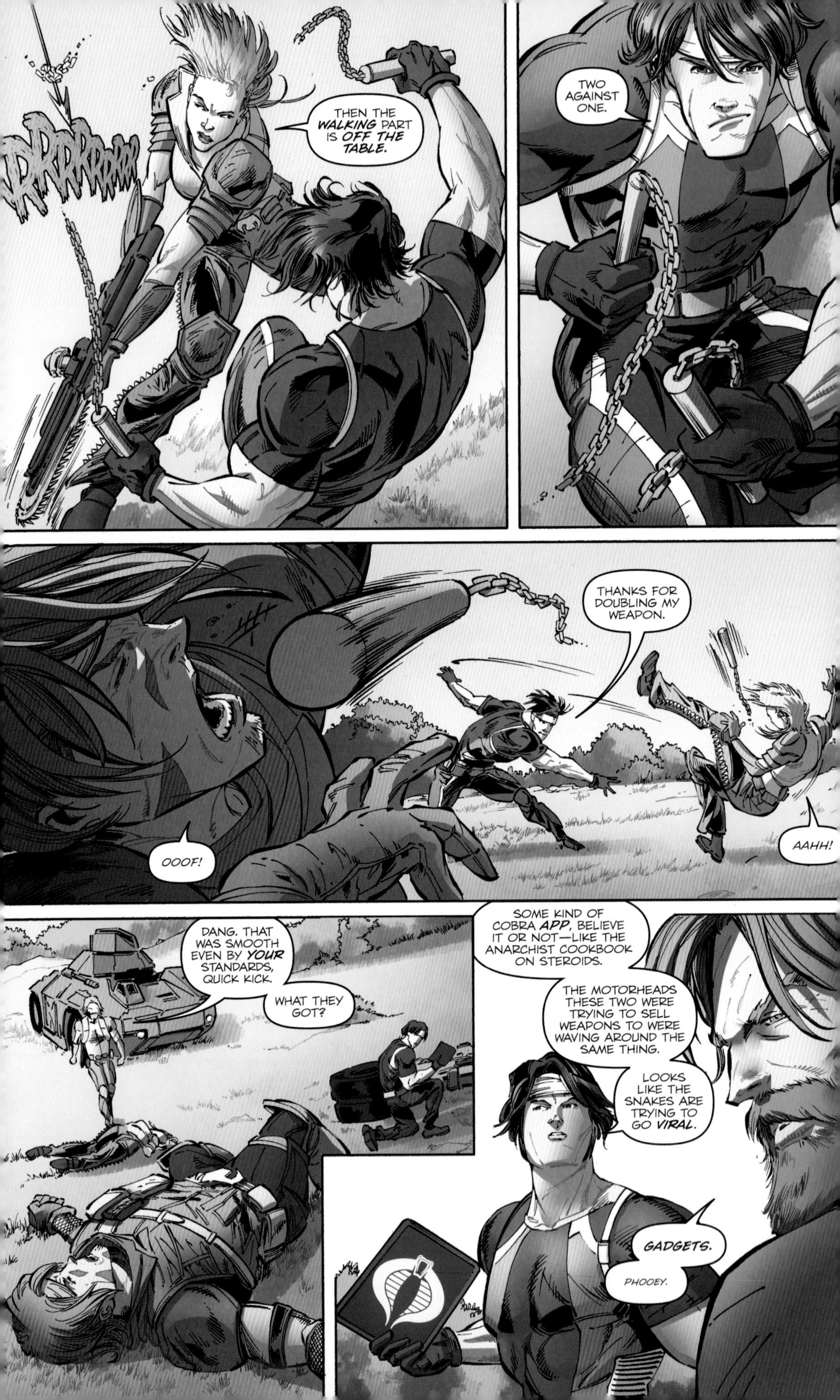

DRRRRRRRR
THEN THE WALKING PART IS OFF THE TABLE.
TWO AGAINST ONE.
THANKS FOR DOUBLING MY WEAPON.
OOOF!
AAHH!
DANG. THAT WAS SMOOTH EVEN BY YOUR STANDARDS, QUICK KICK.
WHAT THEY GOT?
SOME KIND OF COBRA APP, BELIEVE IT OR NOT—LIKE THE ANARCHIST COOKBOOK ON STEROIDS.
THE MOTORHEADS THESE TWO WERE TRYING TO SELL WEAPONS TO WERE WAVING AROUND THE SAME THING.
LOOKS LIKE THE SNAKES ARE TRYING TO GO VIRAL.
GADGETS.
PHOOEY.

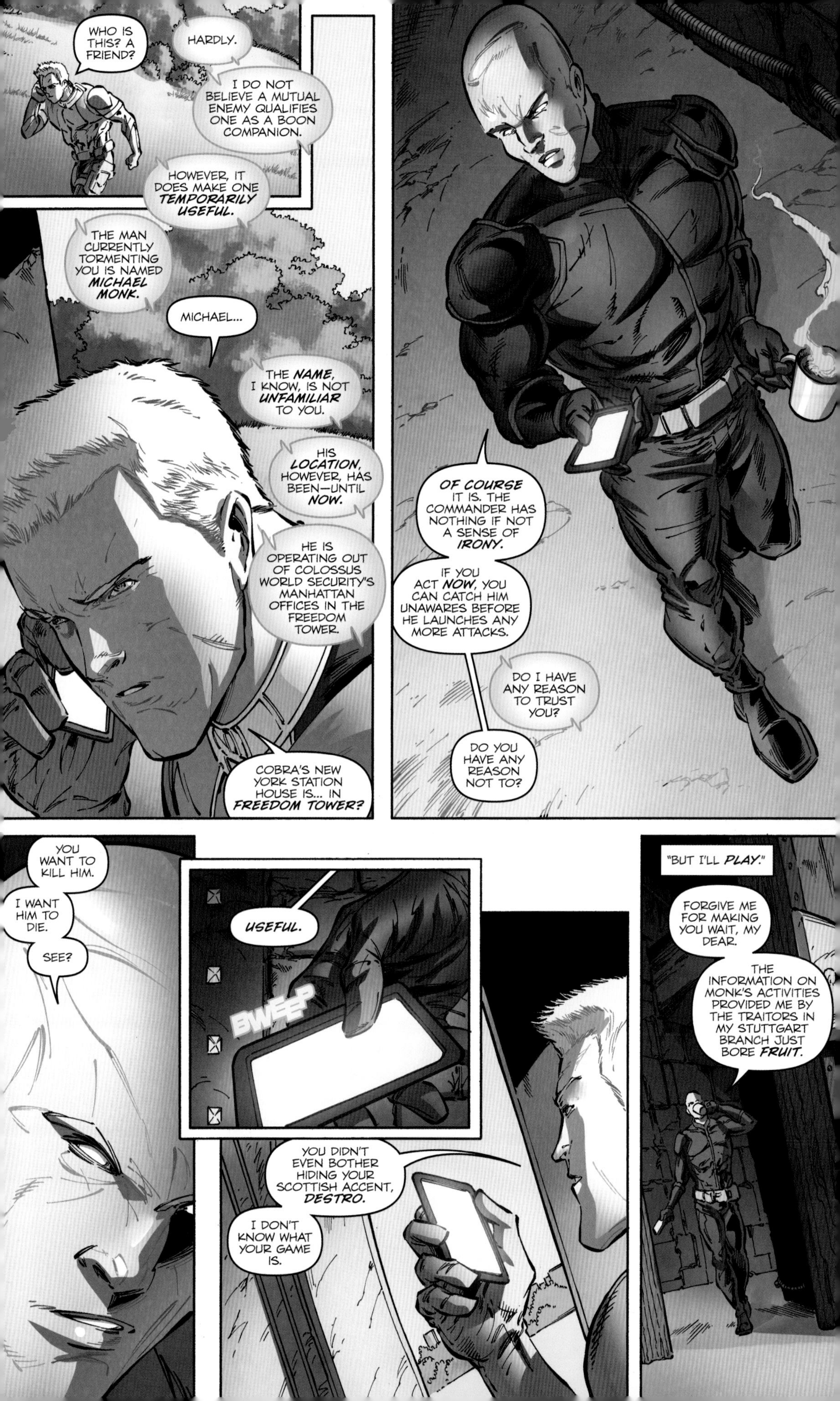
WHO IS THIS? A FRIEND?
HARDLY.
I DO NOT BELIEVE A MUTUAL ENEMY QUALIFIES ONE AS A BOON COMPANION.
HOWEVER, IT DOES MAKE ONE TEMPORARILY USEFUL.
THE MAN CURRENTLY TORMENTING YOU IS NAMED MICHAEL MONK.
MICHAEL...
THE NAME, I KNOW, IS NOT UNFAMILIAR TO YOU.
HIS LOCATION, HOWEVER, HAS BEEN—UNTIL NOW.
HE IS OPERATING OUT OF COLOSSUS WORLD SECURITY'S MANHATTAN OFFICES IN THE FREEDOM TOWER.
COBRA'S NEW YORK STATION HOUSE IS... IN FREEDOM TOWER?
OF COURSE IT IS. THE COMMANDER HAS NOTHING IF NOT A SENSE OF IRONY.
IF YOU ACT NOW, YOU CAN CATCH HIM UNAWARES BEFORE HE LAUNCHES ANY MORE ATTACKS.
DO I HAVE ANY REASON TO TRUST YOU?
DO YOU HAVE ANY REASON NOT TO?
YOU WANT TO KILL HIM.
I WANT HIM TO DIE.
SEE?
USEFUL.
BWEEP
YOU DIDN'T EVEN BOTHER HIDING YOUR SCOTTISH ACCENT, DESTRO.
I DON'T KNOW WHAT YOUR GAME IS.
"BUT I'LL PLAY."
FORGIVE ME FOR MAKING YOU WAIT, MY DEAR.
THE INFORMATION ON MONK'S ACTIVITIES PROVIDED ME BY THE TRAITORS IN MY STUTTGART BRANCH JUST BORE FRUIT.

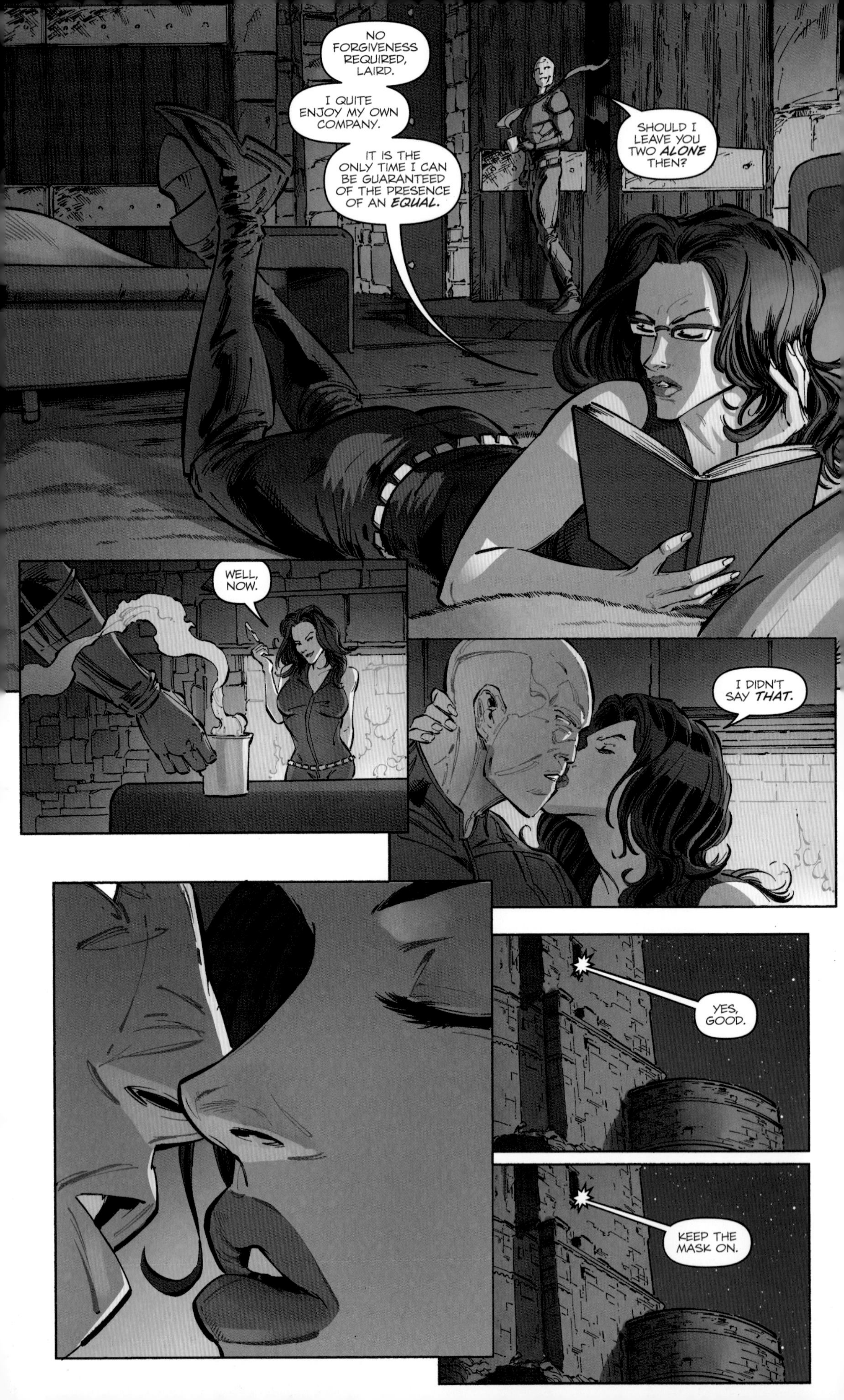
NO FORGIVENESS REQUIRED, LAIRD.
I QUITE ENJOY MY OWN COMPANY.
IT IS THE ONLY TIME I CAN BE GUARANTEED OF THE PRESENCE OF AN *EQUAL.*
SHOULD I LEAVE YOU TWO *ALONE* THEN?
WELL, NOW.
I DIDN'T SAY *THAT.*
YES, GOOD.
KEEP THE MASK ON.

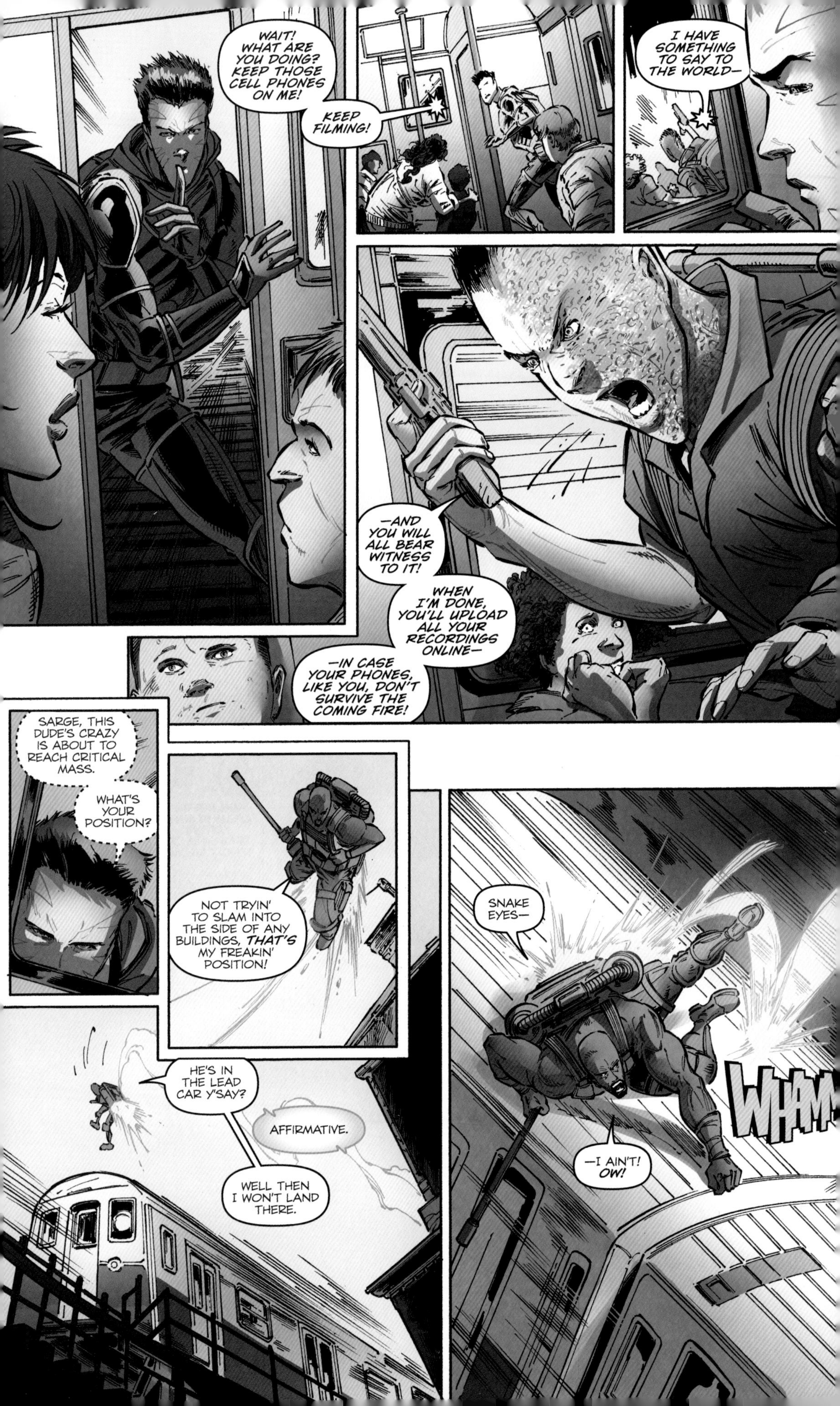
WAIT! WHAT ARE YOU DOING? KEEP THOSE CELL PHONES ON ME!
KEEP FILMING!
I HAVE SOMETHING TO SAY TO THE WORLD—
—AND YOU WILL ALL BEAR WITNESS TO IT!
WHEN I'M DONE, YOU'LL UPLOAD ALL YOUR RECORDINGS ONLINE—
—IN CASE YOUR PHONES, LIKE YOU, DON'T SURVIVE THE COMING FIRE!
SARGE, THIS DUDE'S CRAZY IS ABOUT TO REACH CRITICAL MASS.
WHAT'S YOUR POSITION?
NOT TRYIN' TO SLAM INTO THE SIDE OF ANY BUILDINGS, THAT'S MY FREAKIN' POSITION!
HE'S IN THE LEAD CAR Y'SAY?
AFFIRMATIVE.
WELL THEN I WON'T LAND THERE.
SNAKE EYES—
—I AIN'T! OW!
WHAM

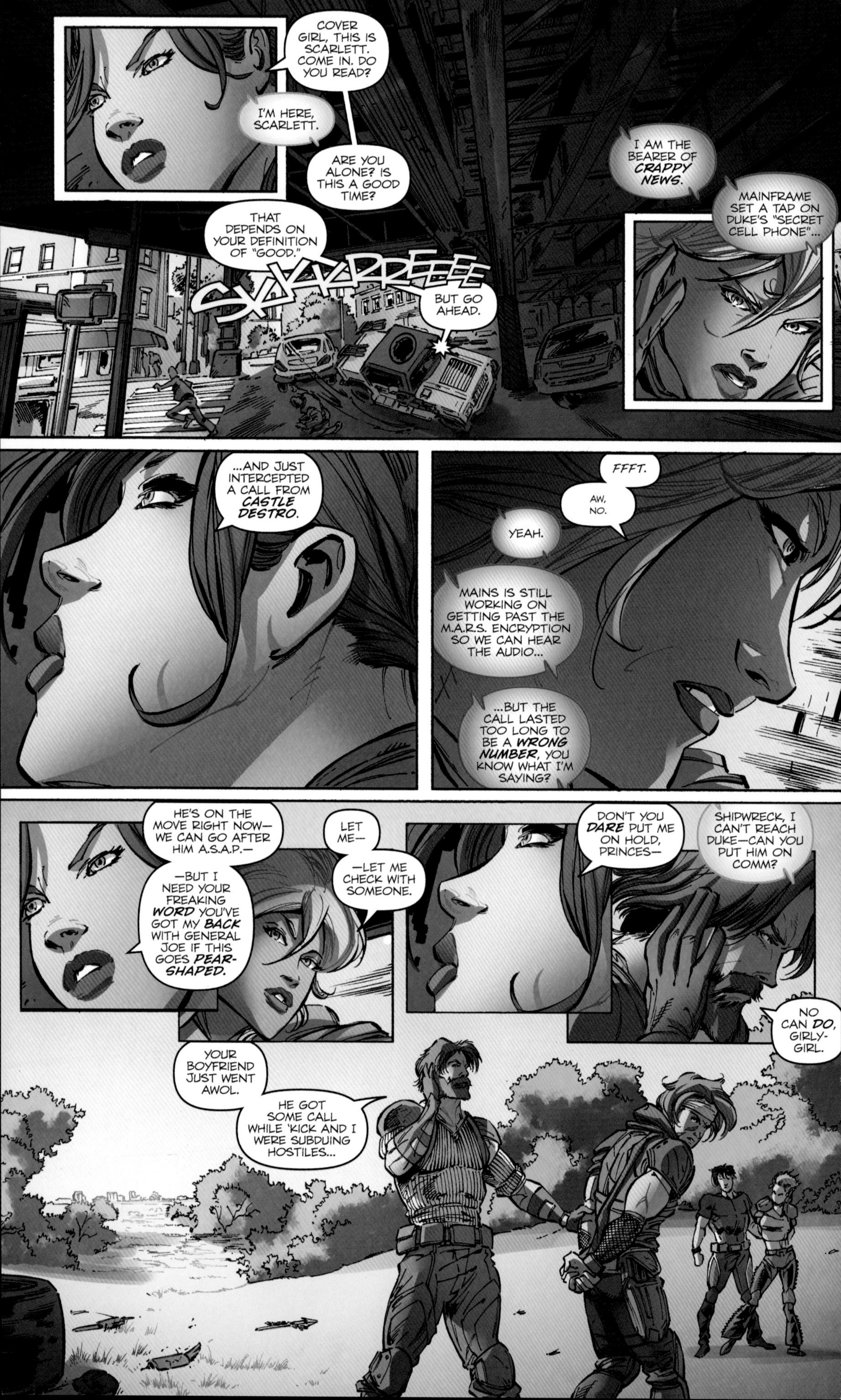
COVER GIRL, THIS IS SCARLETT. COME IN. DO YOU READ?
I'M HERE, SCARLETT.
ARE YOU ALONE? IS THIS A GOOD TIME?
THAT DEPENDS ON YOUR DEFINITION OF "GOOD."
SKKKRREEEE
BUT GO AHEAD.
I AM THE BEARER OF CRAPPY NEWS.
MAINFRAME SET A TAP ON DUKE'S "SECRET CELL PHONE"...
...AND JUST INTERCEPTED A CALL FROM CASTLE DESTRO.
FFFT.
AW, NO.
YEAH.
MAINS IS STILL WORKING ON GETTING PAST THE M.A.R.S. ENCRYPTION SO WE CAN HEAR THE AUDIO...
...BUT THE CALL LASTED TOO LONG TO BE A WRONG NUMBER, YOU KNOW WHAT I'M SAYING?
HE'S ON THE MOVE RIGHT NOW— WE CAN GO AFTER HIM A.S.A.P.—
—BUT I NEED YOUR FREAKING WORD YOU'VE GOT MY BACK WITH GENERAL JOE IF THIS GOES PEAR-SHAPED.
LET ME—
—LET ME CHECK WITH SOMEONE.
DON'T YOU DARE PUT ME ON HOLD, PRINCES—
SHIPWRECK, I CAN'T REACH DUKE—CAN YOU PUT HIM ON COMM?
NO CAN DO, GIRLY-GIRL.
YOUR BOYFRIEND JUST WENT AWOL.
HE GOT SOME CALL WHILE 'KICK AND I WERE SUBDUING HOSTILES...

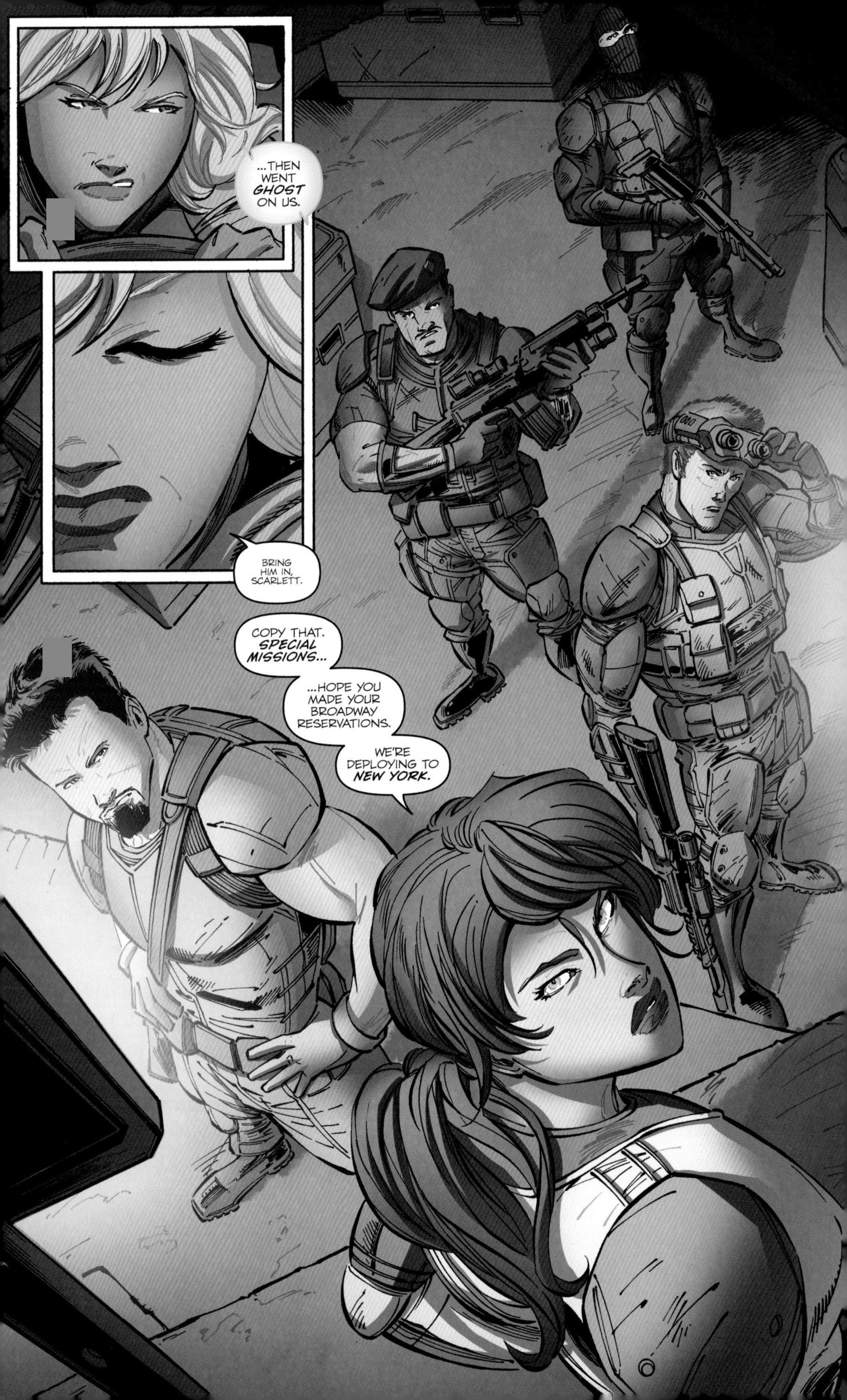
...THEN WENT GHOST ON US.
BRING HIM IN, SCARLETT.
COPY THAT. SPECIAL MISSIONS...
...HOPE YOU MADE YOUR BROADWAY RESERVATIONS.
WE'RE DEPLOYING TO NEW YORK.

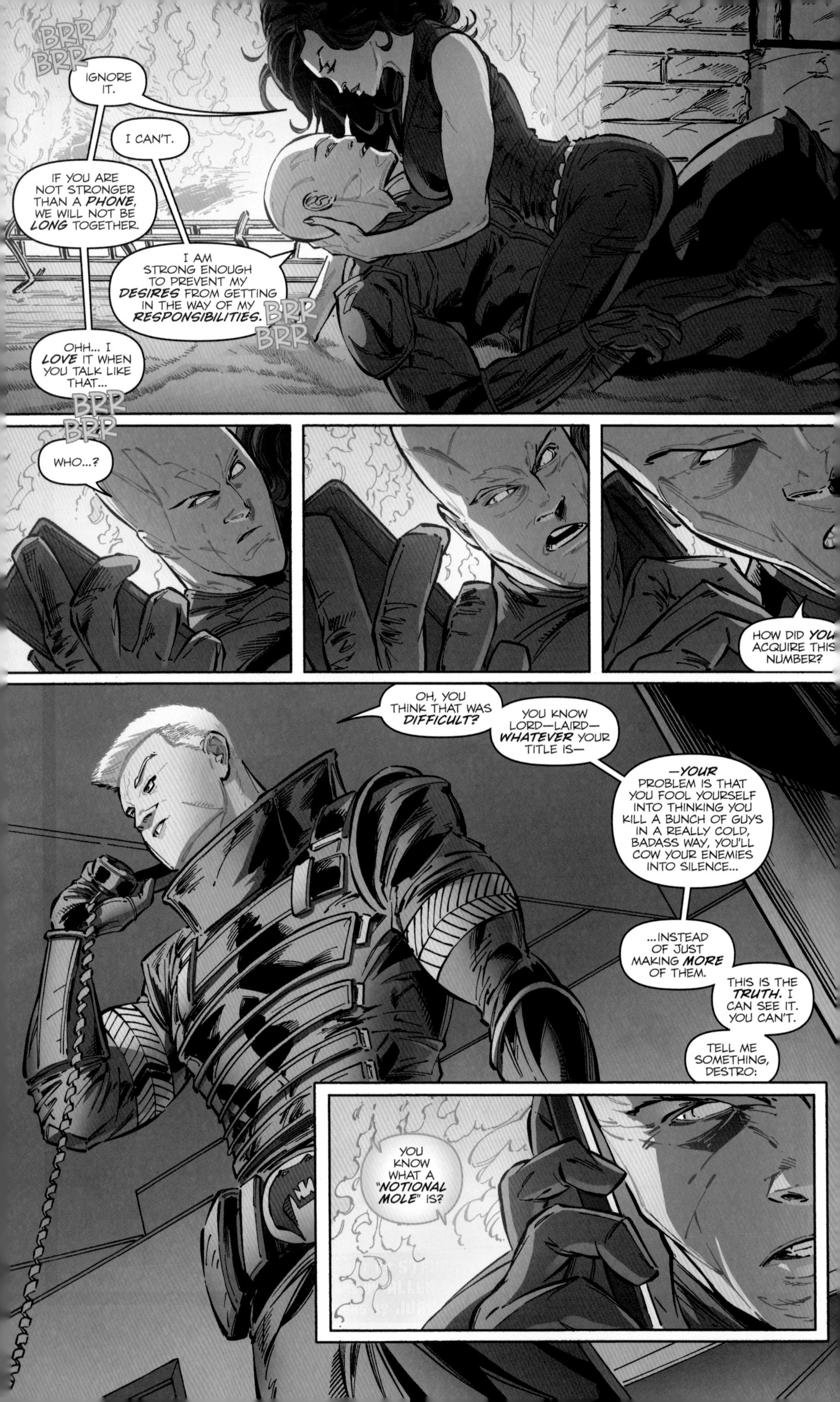
BRR BRR
IGNORE IT.
I CAN'T.
IF YOU ARE NOT STRONGER THAN A PHONE, WE WILL NOT BE LONG TOGETHER.
I AM STRONG ENOUGH TO PREVENT MY DESIRES FROM GETTING IN THE WAY OF MY RESPONSIBILITIES.
BRR BRR
OHH... I LOVE IT WHEN YOU TALK LIKE THAT...
BRR BRR
WHO...?
HOW DID YOU ACQUIRE THIS NUMBER?
OH, YOU THINK THAT WAS DIFFICULT?
YOU KNOW LORD—LAIRD—WHATEVER YOUR TITLE IS—
—YOUR PROBLEM IS THAT YOU FOOL YOURSELF INTO THINKING YOU KILL A BUNCH OF GUYS IN A REALLY COLD, BADASS WAY, YOU'LL COW YOUR ENEMIES INTO SILENCE...
...INSTEAD OF JUST MAKING MORE OF THEM.
THIS IS THE TRUTH. I CAN SEE IT. YOU CAN'T.
TELL ME SOMETHING, DESTRO:
YOU KNOW WHAT A "NOTIONAL MOLE" IS?

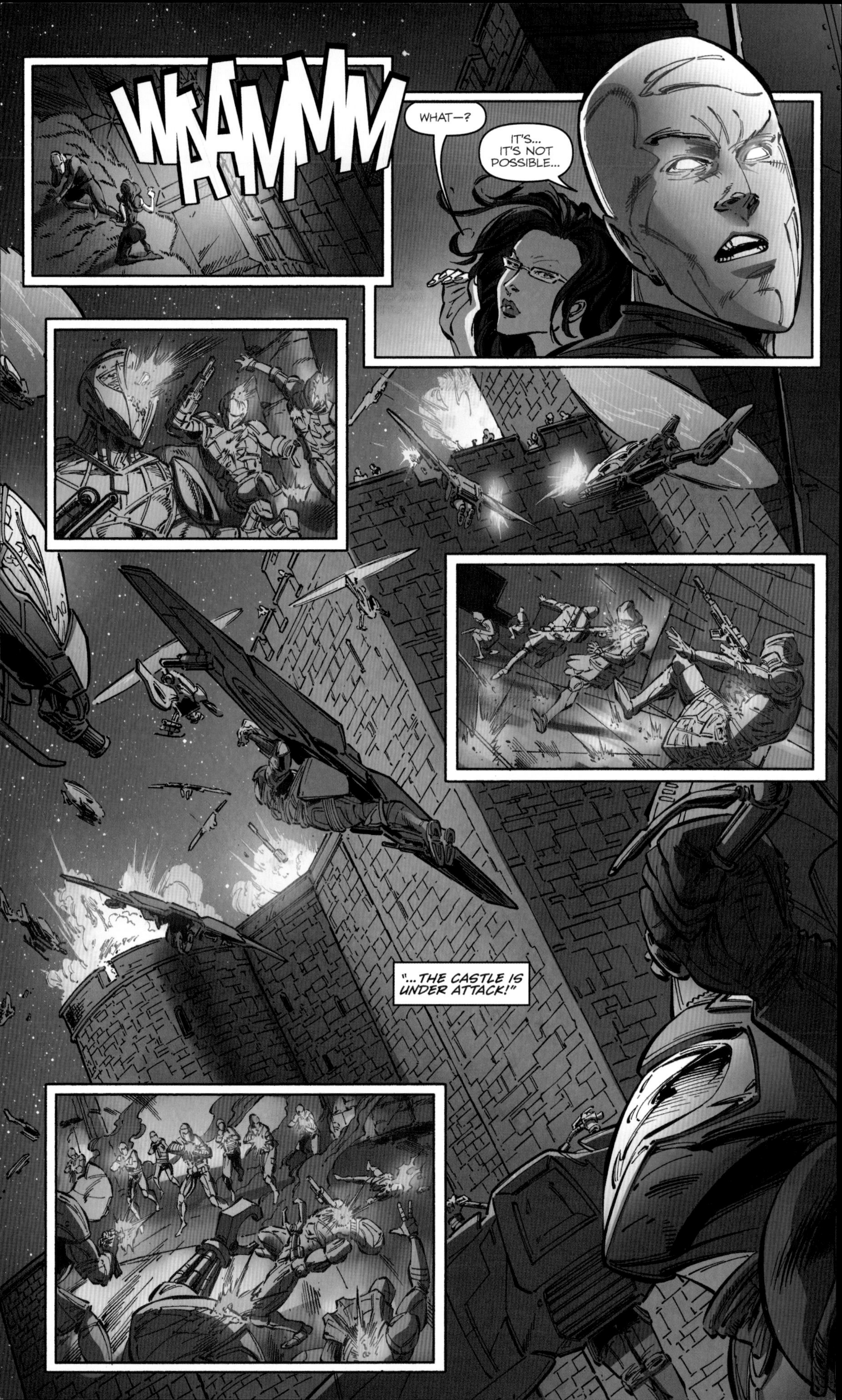

WAAMMM
WHAT—?
IT'S... IT'S NOT POSSIBLE...
"...THE CASTLE IS UNDER ATTACK!"

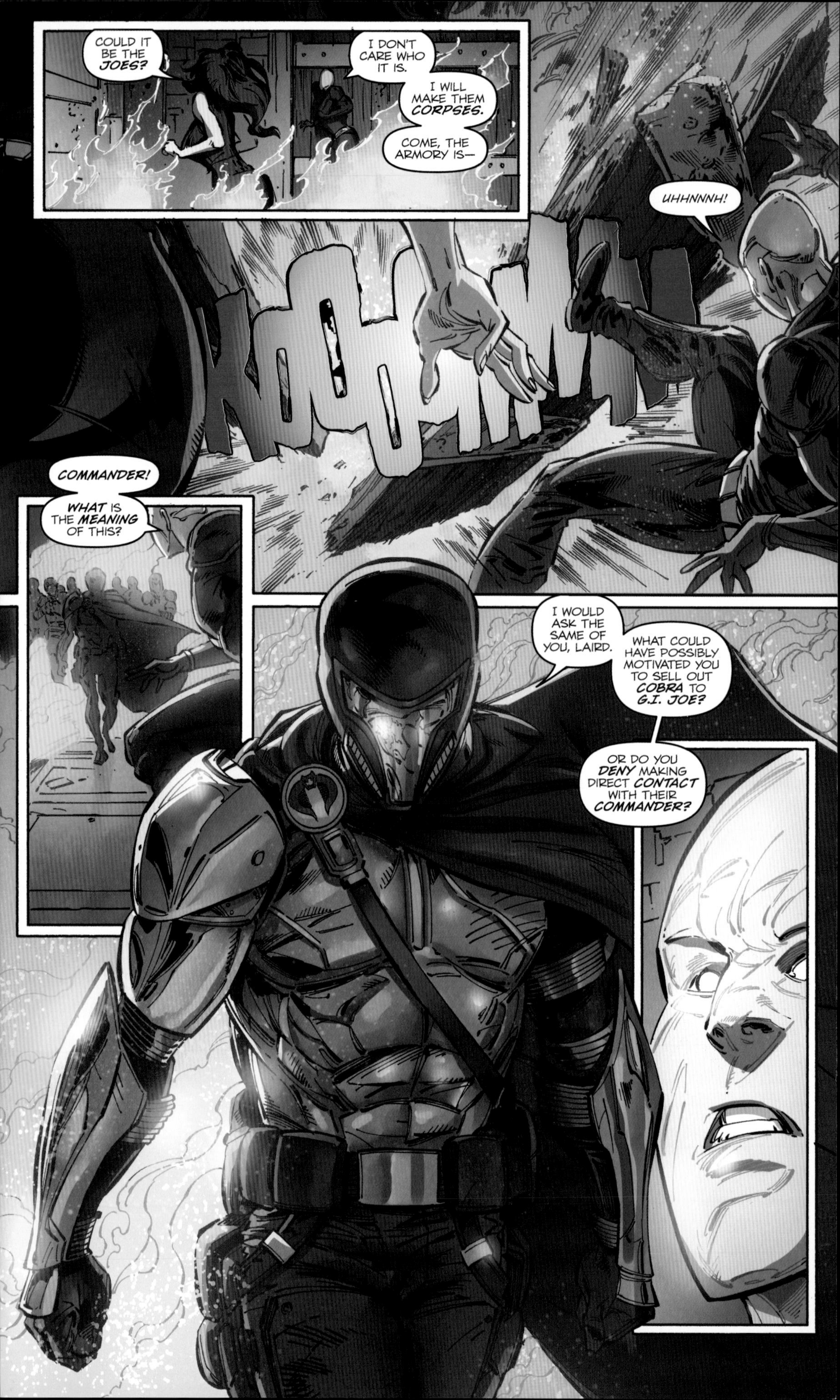
COULD IT BE THE JOES?
I DON'T CARE WHO IT IS.
I WILL MAKE THEM CORPSES.
COME, THE ARMORY IS—
UHHNNNH!
KOOOM
COMMANDER!
WHAT IS THE MEANING OF THIS?
I WOULD ASK THE SAME OF YOU, LAIRD.
WHAT COULD HAVE POSSIBLY MOTIVATED YOU TO SELL OUT COBRA TO G.I. JOE?
OR DO YOU DENY MAKING DIRECT CONTACT WITH THEIR COMMANDER?

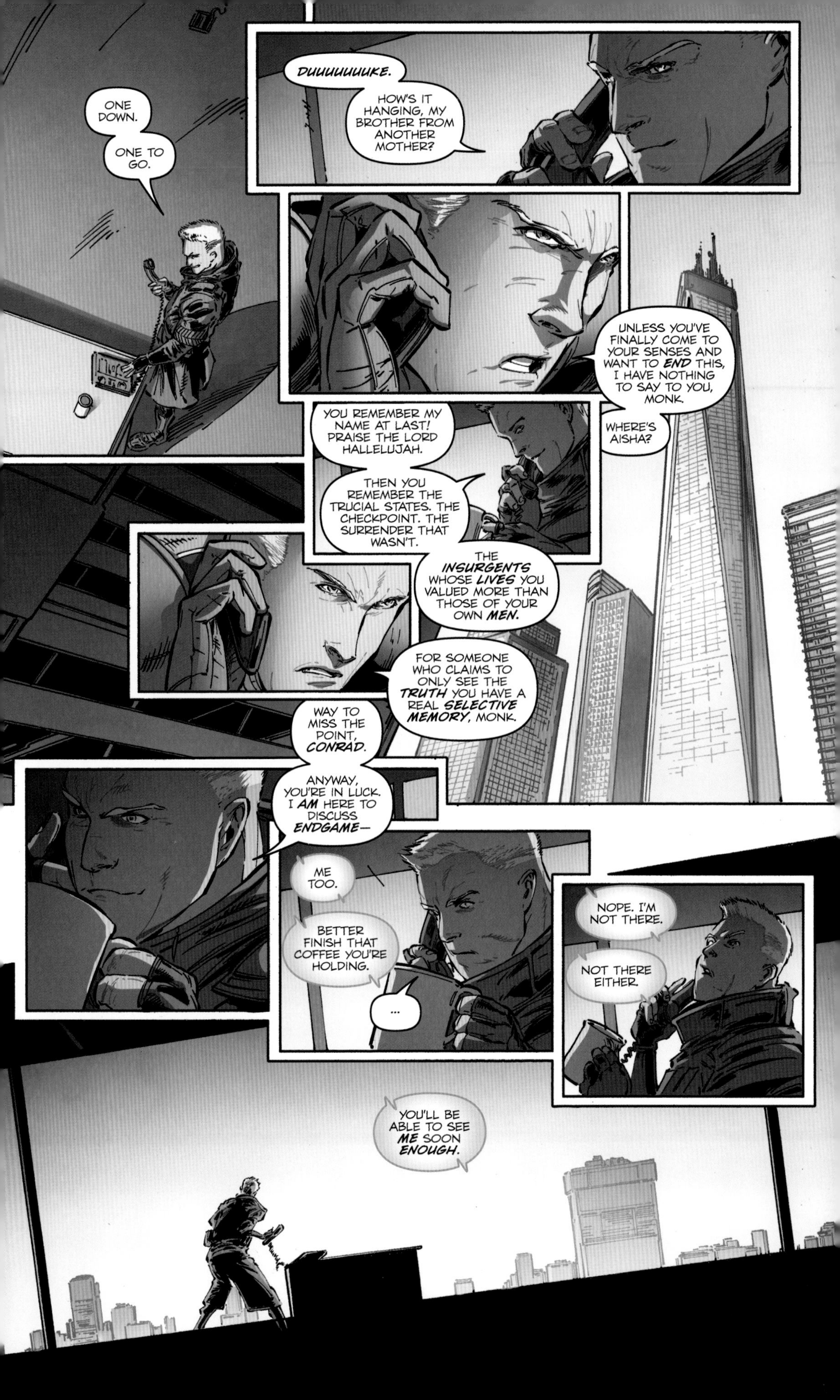
ONE DOWN.
ONE TO GO.
DUUUUUUUKE.
HOW'S IT HANGING, MY BROTHER FROM ANOTHER MOTHER?
UNLESS YOU'VE FINALLY COME TO YOUR SENSES AND WANT TO END THIS, I HAVE NOTHING TO SAY TO YOU, MONK.
WHERE'S AISHA?
YOU REMEMBER MY NAME AT LAST! PRAISE THE LORD HALLELUJAH.
THEN YOU REMEMBER THE TRUCIAL STATES. THE CHECKPOINT. THE SURRENDER THAT WASN'T.
THE INSURGENTS WHOSE LIVES YOU VALUED MORE THAN THOSE OF YOUR OWN MEN.
FOR SOMEONE WHO CLAIMS TO ONLY SEE THE TRUTH YOU HAVE A REAL SELECTIVE MEMORY, MONK.
WAY TO MISS THE POINT, CONRAD.
ANYWAY, YOU'RE IN LUCK. I AM HERE TO DISCUSS ENDGAME—
ME TOO.
BETTER FINISH THAT COFFEE YOU'RE HOLDING.
...
NOPE. I'M NOT THERE.
NOT THERE EITHER.
YOU'LL BE ABLE TO SEE ME SOON ENOUGH.

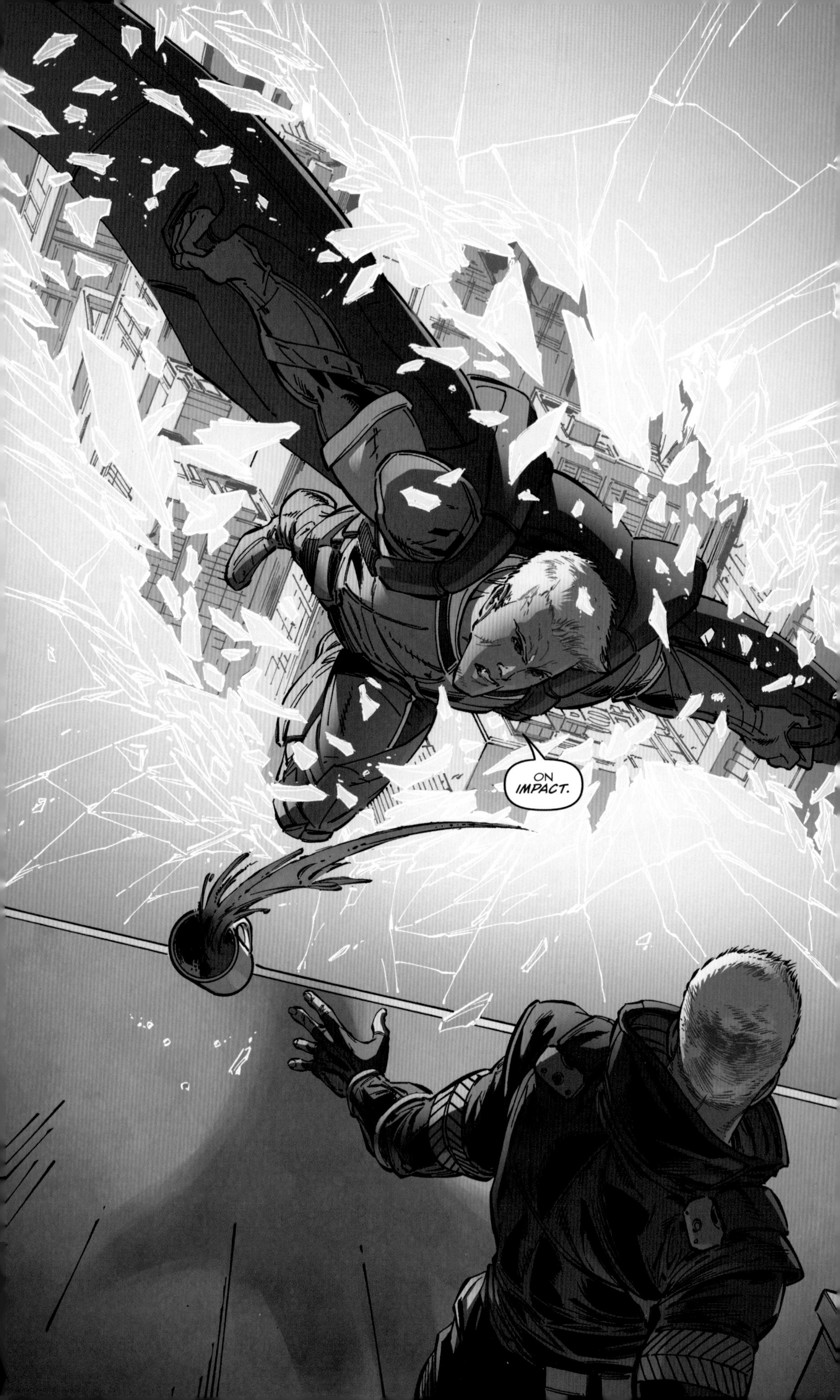
ON IMPACT.

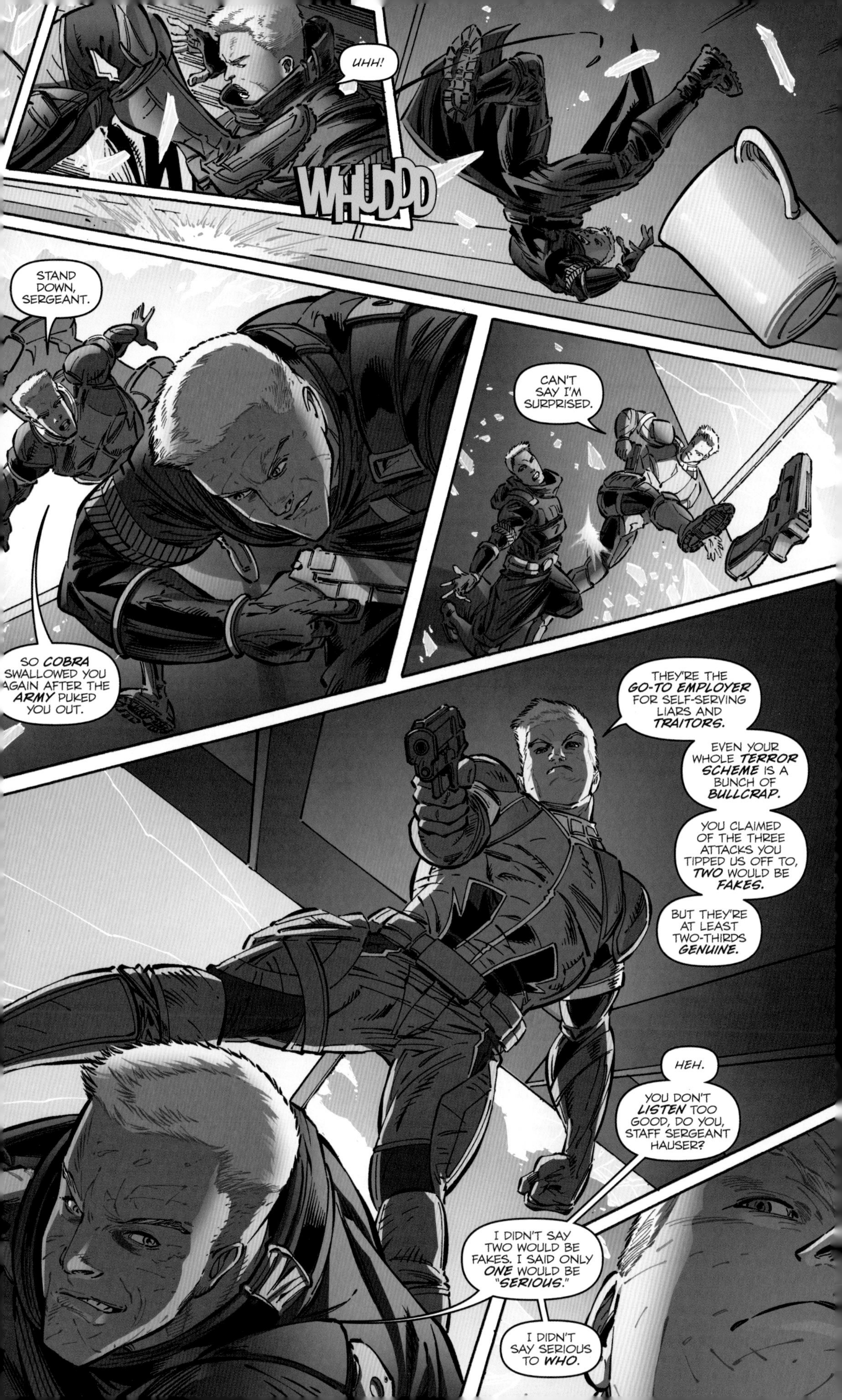

UHH!
WHUDDD
STAND DOWN, SERGEANT.
CAN'T SAY I'M SURPRISED.
SO COBRA SWALLOWED YOU AGAIN AFTER THE ARMY PUKED YOU OUT.
THEY'RE THE GO-TO EMPLOYER FOR SELF-SERVING LIARS AND TRAITORS.
EVEN YOUR WHOLE TERROR SCHEME IS A BUNCH OF BULLCRAP.
YOU CLAIMED OF THE THREE ATTACKS YOU TIPPED US OFF TO, TWO WOULD BE FAKES.
BUT THEY'RE AT LEAST TWO-THIRDS GENUINE.
HEH.
YOU DON'T LISTEN TOO GOOD, DO YOU, STAFF SERGEANT HAUSER?
I DIDN'T SAY TWO WOULD BE FAKES. I SAID ONLY ONE WOULD BE "SERIOUS."
I DIDN'T SAY SERIOUS TO WHO.

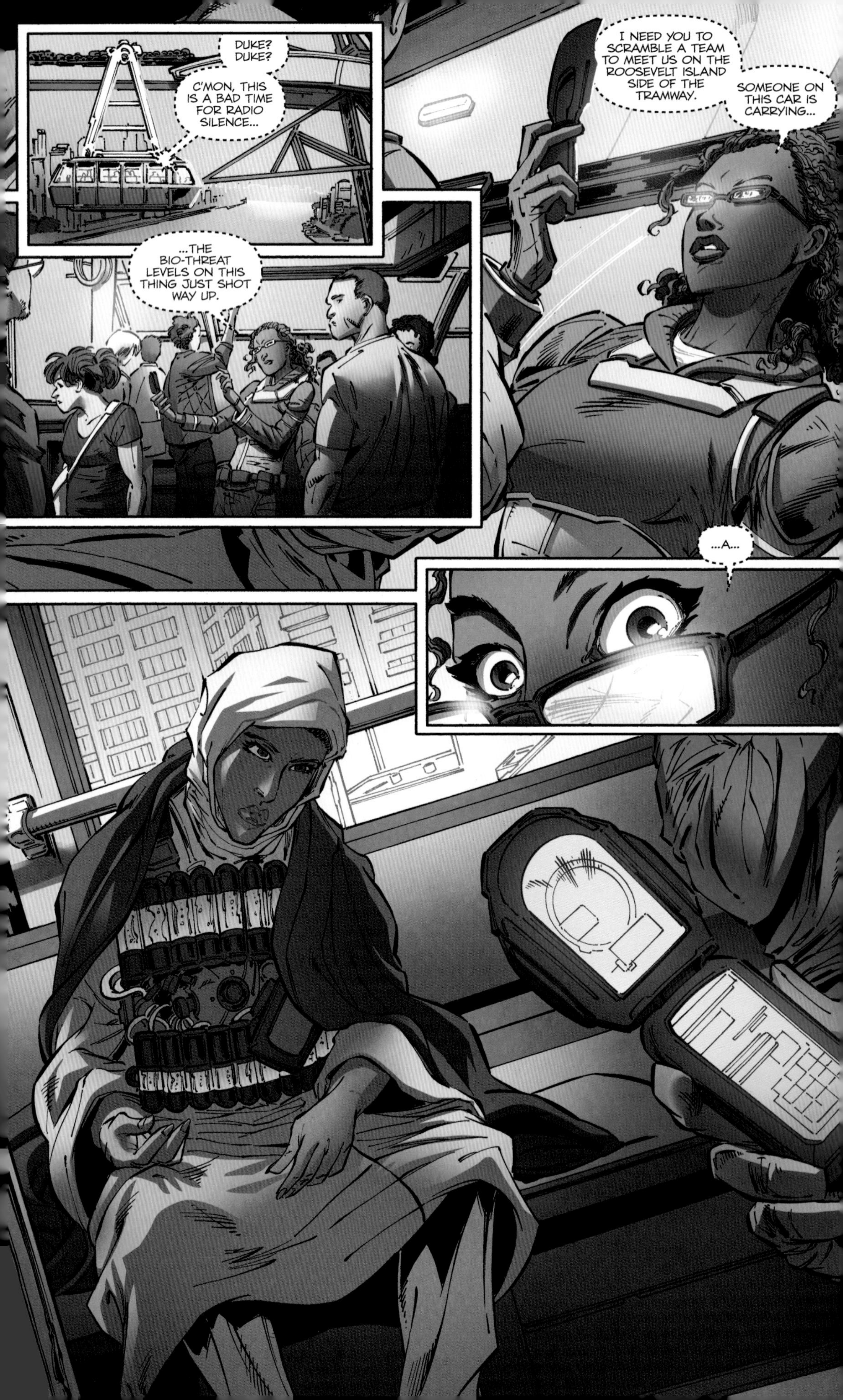

DUKE? DUKE?
C'MON, THIS IS A BAD TIME FOR RADIO SILENCE...
...THE BIO-THREAT LEVELS ON THIS THING JUST SHOT WAY UP.
I NEED YOU TO SCRAMBLE A TEAM TO MEET US ON THE ROOSEVELT ISLAND SIDE OF THE TRAMWAY.
SOMEONE ON THIS CAR IS CARRYING...
...A...

CHAPTER FIVE

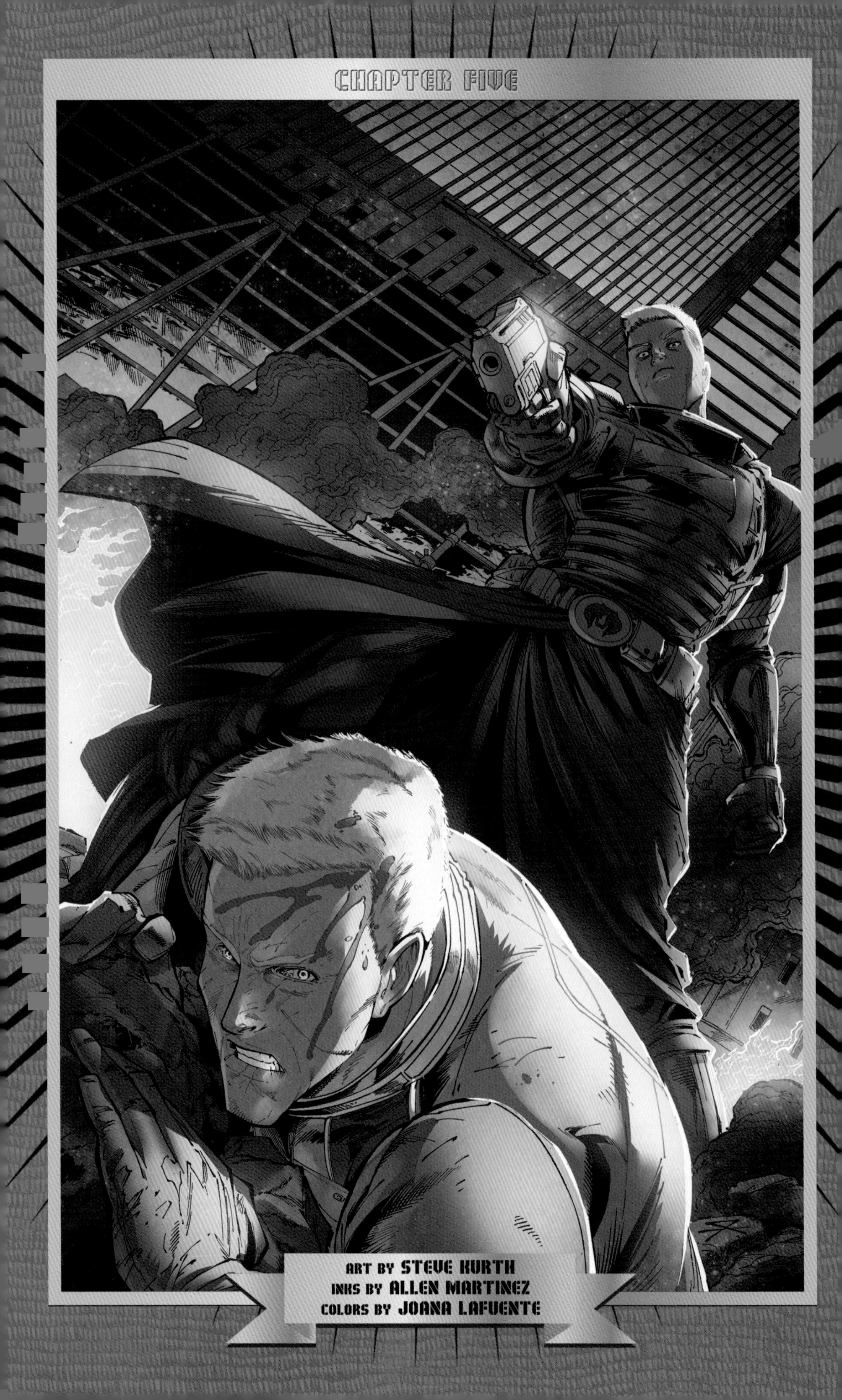

ART BY STEVE KURTH
INKS BY ALLEN MARTINEZ
COLORS BY JOANA LAFUENTE

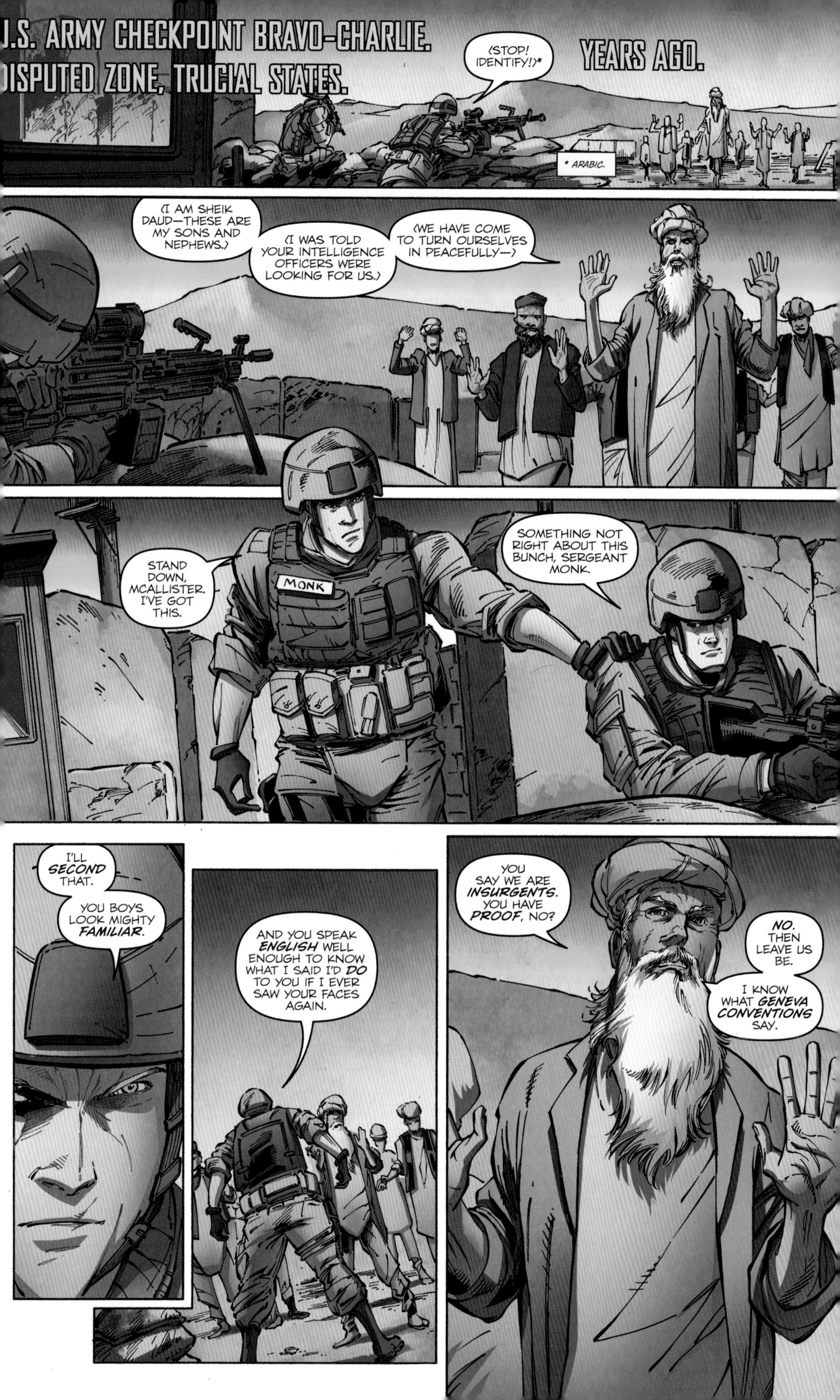
U.S. ARMY CHECKPOINT BRAVO-CHARLIE.
DISPUTED ZONE, TRUCIAL STATES.
(STOP! IDENTIFY!)*
YEARS AGO.
* ARABIC.
(I AM SHEIK DAUD—THESE ARE MY SONS AND NEPHEWS.)
(I WAS TOLD YOUR INTELLIGENCE OFFICERS WERE LOOKING FOR US.)
(WE HAVE COME TO TURN OURSELVES IN PEACEFULLY—)
SOMETHING NOT RIGHT ABOUT THIS BUNCH, SERGEANT MONK.
STAND DOWN, MCALLISTER. I'VE GOT THIS.
MONK
I'LL SECOND THAT.
YOU BOYS LOOK MIGHTY FAMILIAR.
AND YOU SPEAK ENGLISH WELL ENOUGH TO KNOW WHAT I SAID I'D DO TO YOU IF I EVER SAW YOUR FACES AGAIN.
YOU SAY WE ARE INSURGENTS. YOU HAVE PROOF, NO?
NO. THEN LEAVE US BE.
I KNOW WHAT GENEVA CONVENTIONS SAY.

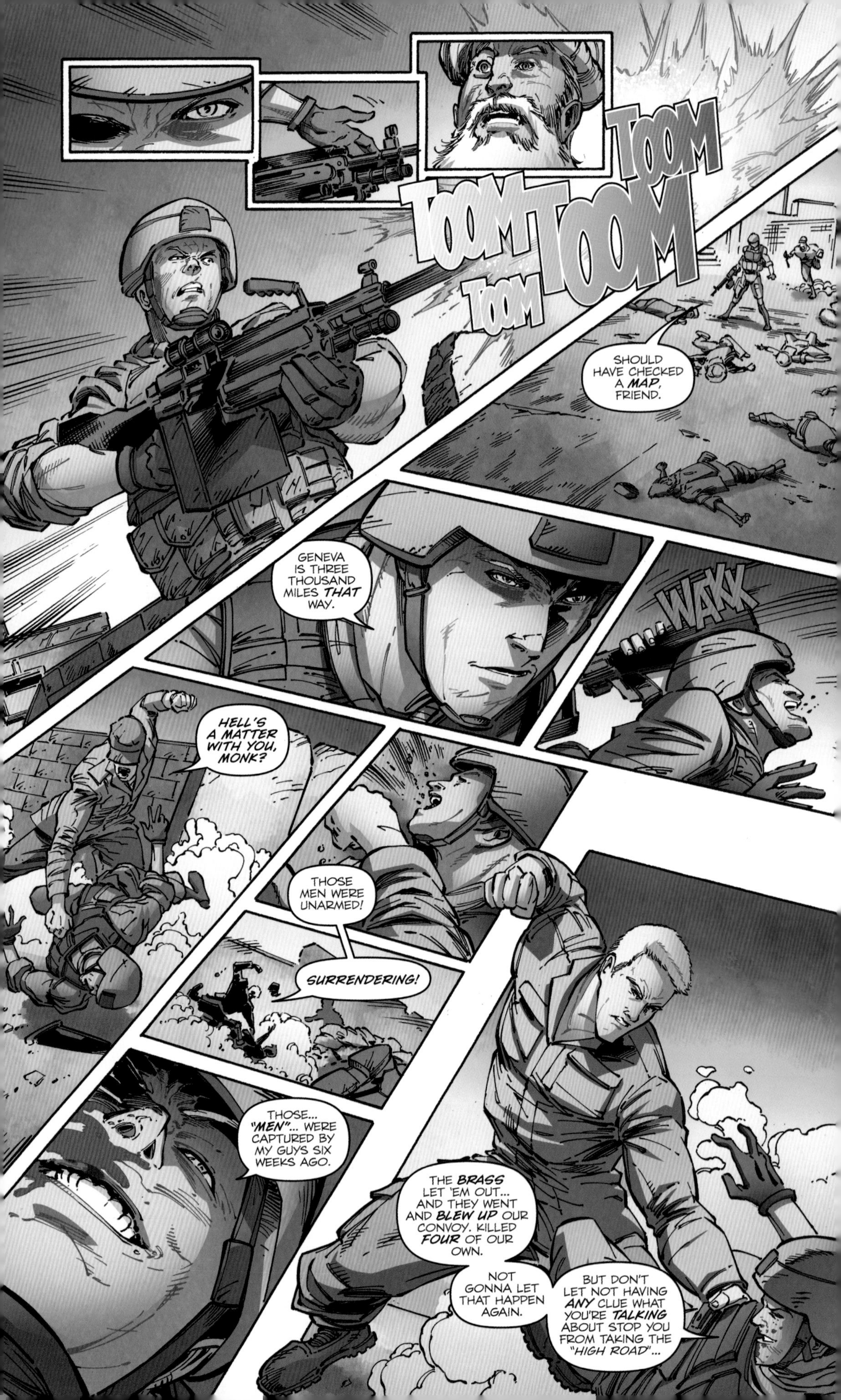
TOOM
TOOM
TOOM
TOOM
SHOULD HAVE CHECKED A MAP, FRIEND.
GENEVA IS THREE THOUSAND MILES THAT WAY.
WAKK
HELL'S A MATTER WITH YOU, MONK?
THOSE MEN WERE UNARMED!
SURRENDERING!
THOSE... "MEN"... WERE CAPTURED BY MY GUYS SIX WEEKS AGO.
THE BRASS LET 'EM OUT... AND THEY WENT AND BLEW UP OUR CONVOY. KILLED FOUR OF OUR OWN.
NOT GONNA LET THAT HAPPEN AGAIN.
BUT DON'T LET NOT HAVING ANY CLUE WHAT YOU'RE TALKING ABOUT STOP YOU FROM TAKING THE "HIGH ROAD"...

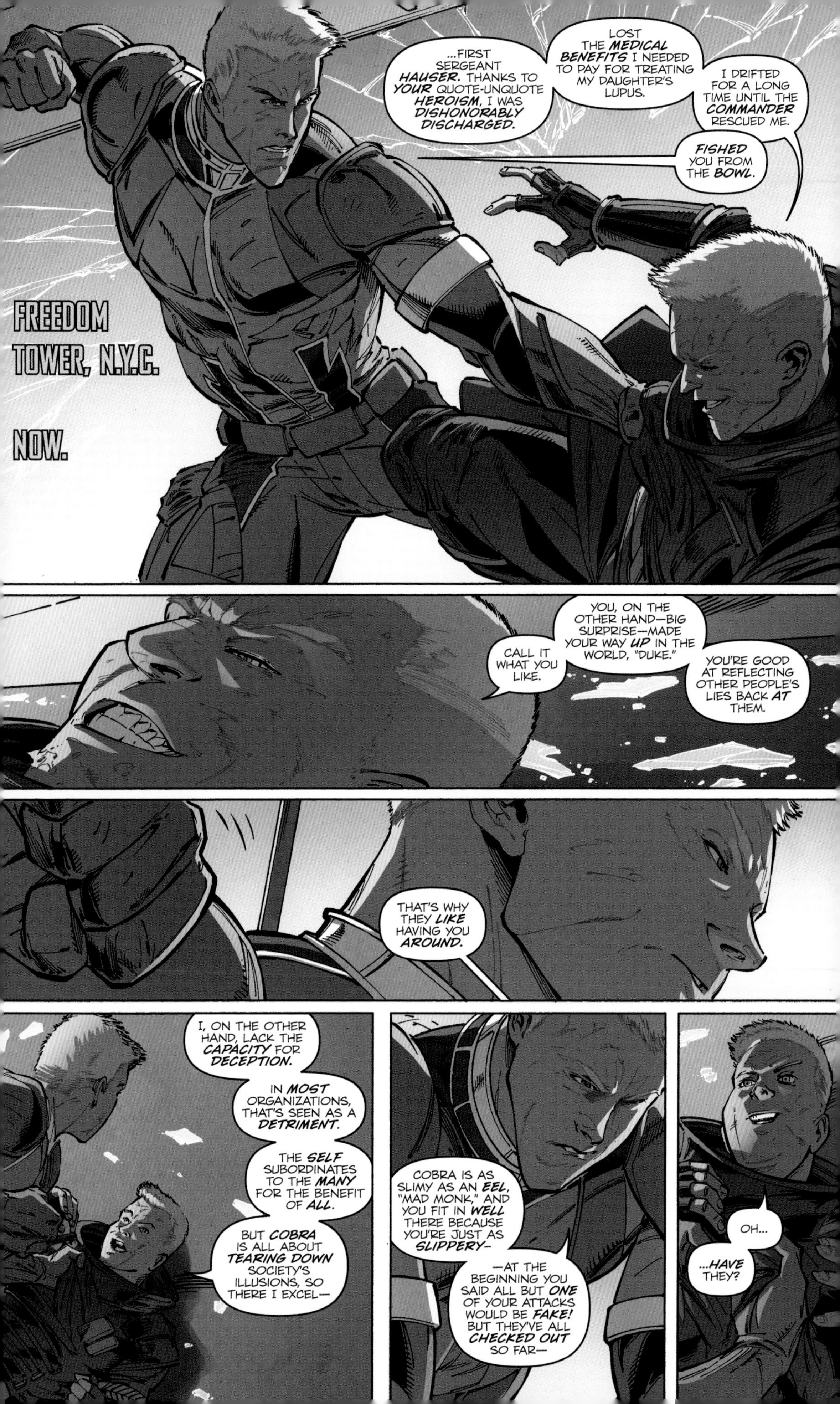
...FIRST SERGEANT HAUSER. THANKS TO YOUR QUOTE-UNQUOTE HEROISM, I WAS DISHONORABLY DISCHARGED.
LOST THE MEDICAL BENEFITS I NEEDED TO PAY FOR TREATING MY DAUGHTER'S LUPUS.
I DRIFTED FOR A LONG TIME UNTIL THE COMMANDER RESCUED ME.
FISHED YOU FROM THE BOWL.
FREEDOM TOWER, N.Y.C.
NOW.
CALL IT WHAT YOU LIKE.
YOU, ON THE OTHER HAND—BIG SURPRISE—MADE YOUR WAY UP IN THE WORLD, "DUKE."
YOU'RE GOOD AT REFLECTING OTHER PEOPLE'S LIES BACK AT THEM.
THAT'S WHY THEY LIKE HAVING YOU AROUND.
I, ON THE OTHER HAND, LACK THE CAPACITY FOR DECEPTION.
IN MOST ORGANIZATIONS, THAT'S SEEN AS A DETRIMENT.
THE SELF SUBORDINATES TO THE MANY FOR THE BENEFIT OF ALL.
BUT COBRA IS ALL ABOUT TEARING DOWN SOCIETY'S ILLUSIONS, SO THERE I EXCEL—
COBRA IS AS SLIMY AS AN EEL, "MAD MONK," AND YOU FIT IN WELL THERE BECAUSE YOU'RE JUST AS SLIPPERY—
—AT THE BEGINNING YOU SAID ALL BUT ONE OF YOUR ATTACKS WOULD BE FAKE! BUT THEY'VE ALL CHECKED OUT SO FAR—
OH...
...HAVE THEY?

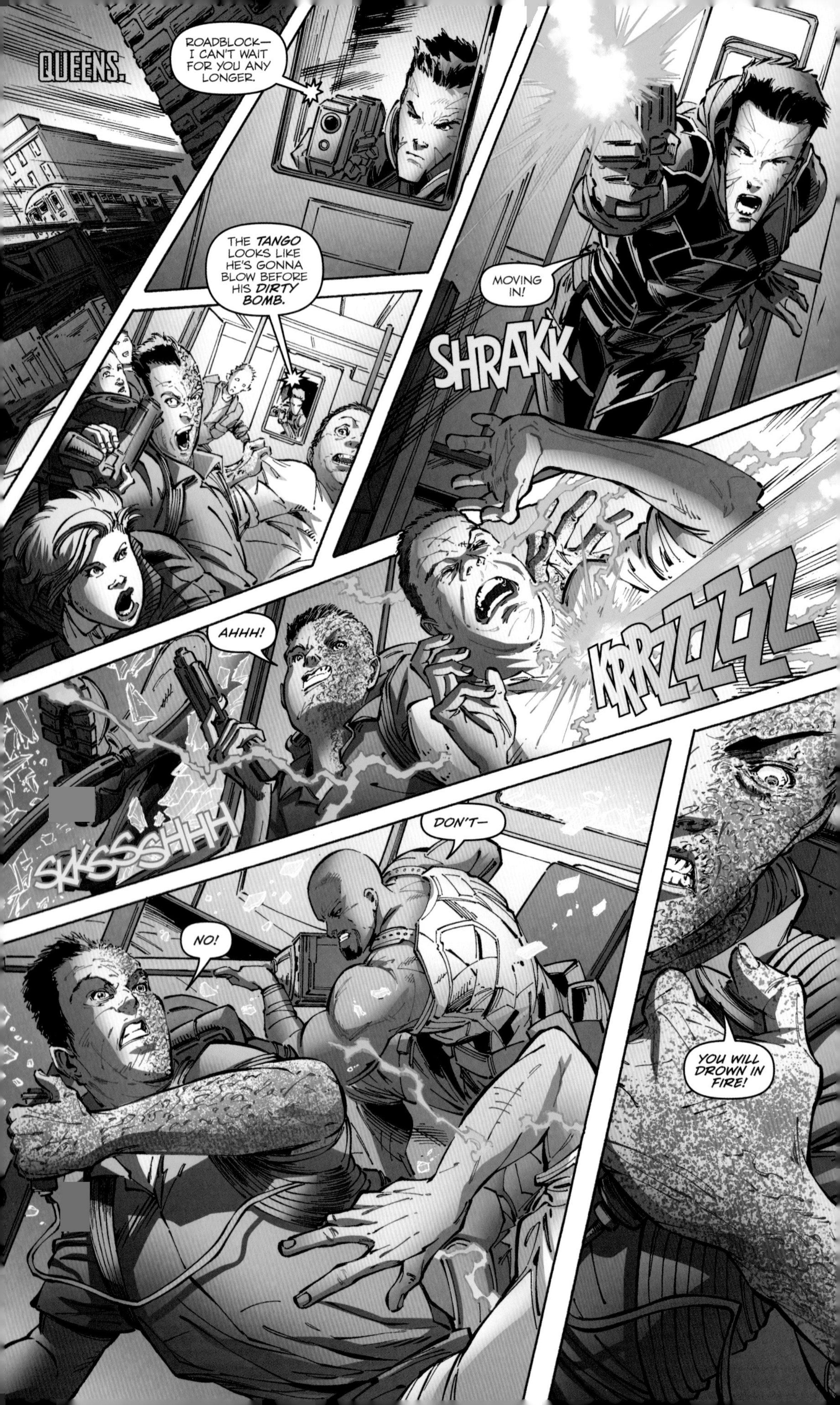
QUEENS.
ROADBLOCK— I CAN'T WAIT FOR YOU ANY LONGER.
THE TANGO LOOKS LIKE HE'S GONNA BLOW BEFORE HIS DIRTY BOMB.
MOVING IN!
SHRAKK
AHHH!
KRRZZZZZ
SKKSSSHHH
DON'T—
NO!
YOU WILL DROWN IN FIRE!

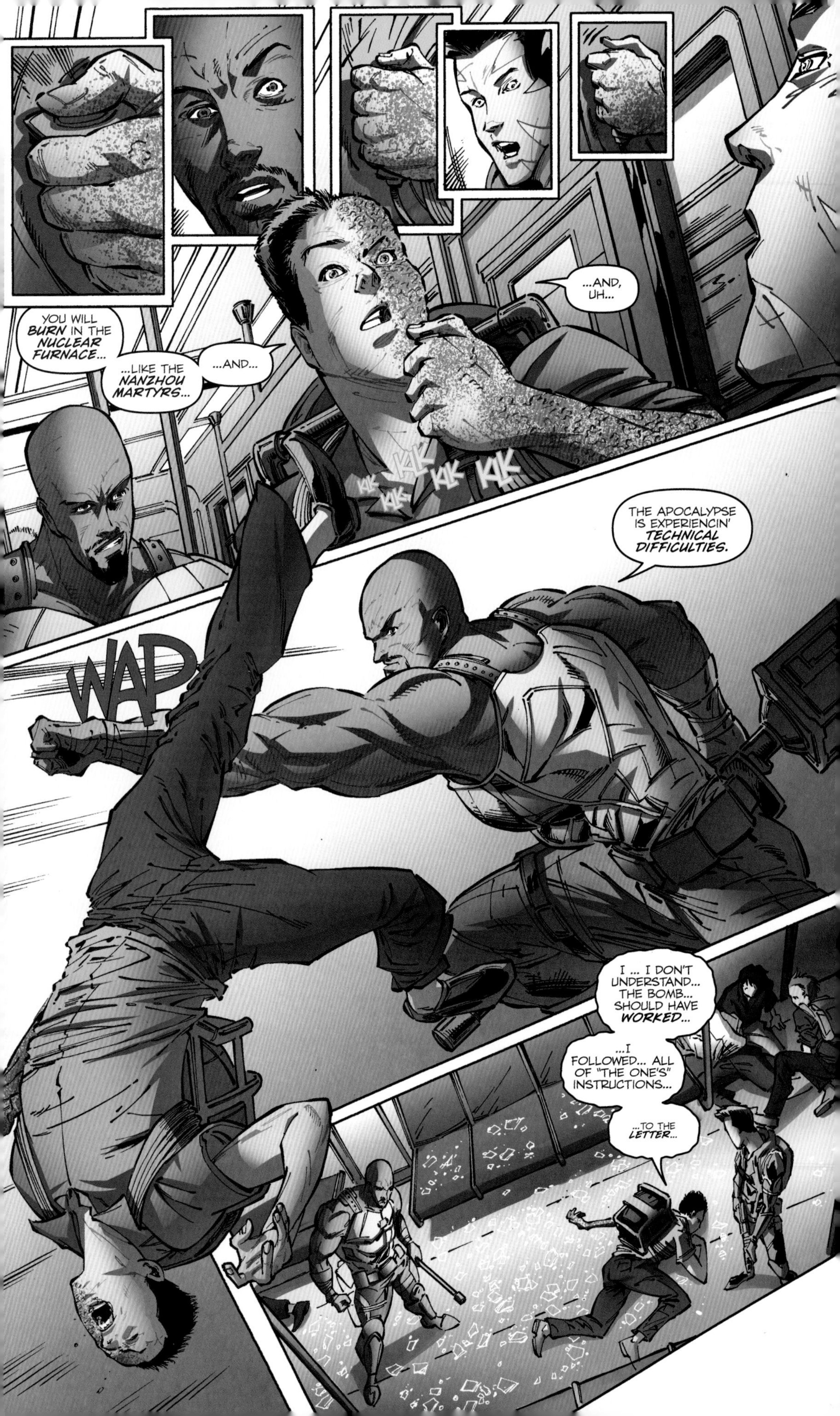
...AND, UH...
YOU WILL BURN IN THE NUCLEAR FURNACE...
...LIKE THE NANZHOU MARTYRS...
...AND...
KLK KLK KLK KLK KLK
THE APOCALYPSE IS EXPERIENCIN' TECHNICAL DIFFICULTIES.
WAP
I ... I DON'T UNDERSTAND... THE BOMB... SHOULD HAVE WORKED...
...I FOLLOWED... ALL OF "THE ONE'S" INSTRUCTIONS...
...TO THE LETTER...

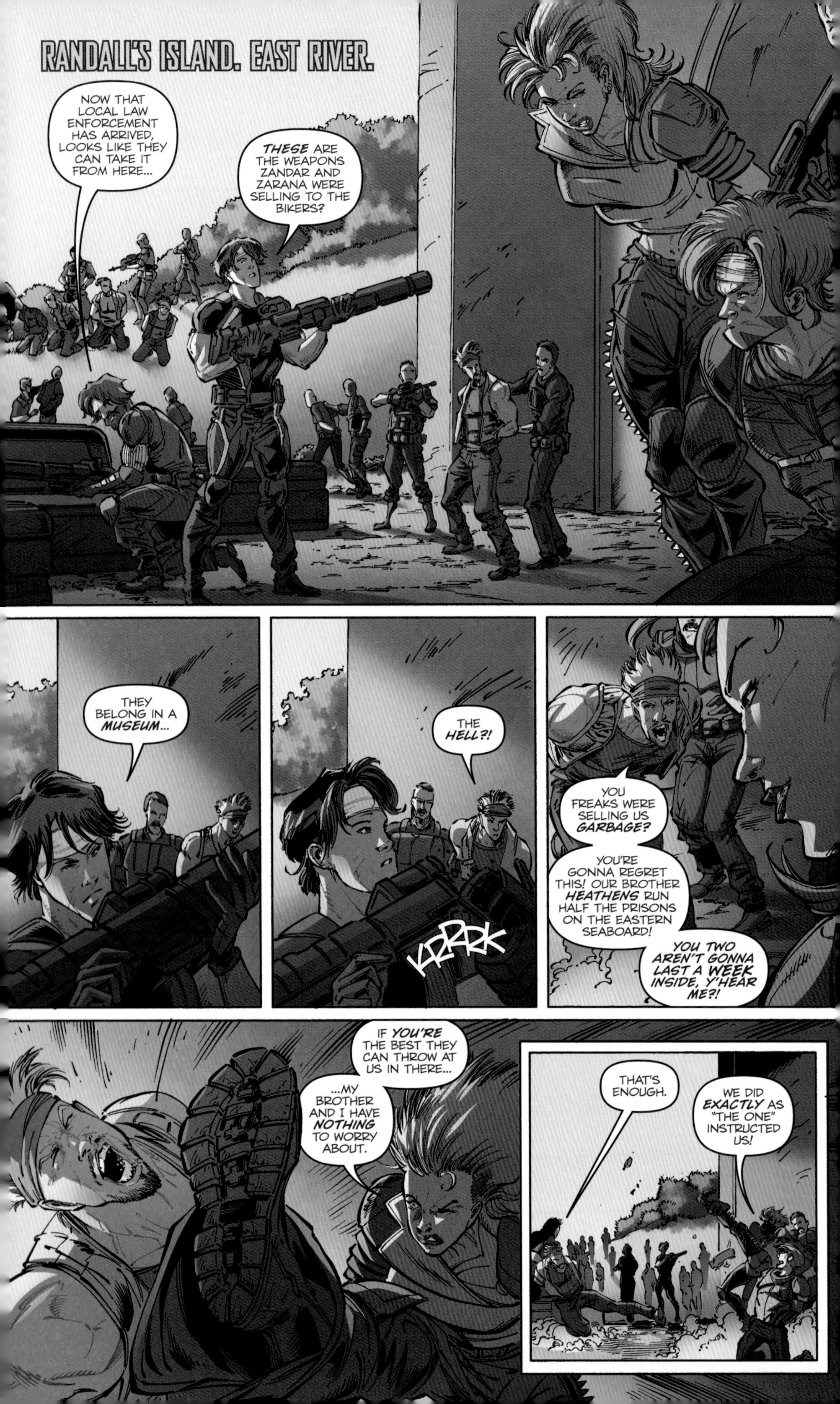
RANDALL'S ISLAND. EAST RIVER.
NOW THAT LOCAL LAW ENFORCEMENT HAS ARRIVED, LOOKS LIKE THEY CAN TAKE IT FROM HERE...
THESE ARE THE WEAPONS ZANDAR AND ZARANA WERE SELLING TO THE BIKERS?
THEY BELONG IN A MUSEUM...
THE HELL?!
KRRRK
YOU FREAKS WERE SELLING US GARBAGE?
YOU'RE GONNA REGRET THIS! OUR BROTHER HEATHENS RUN HALF THE PRISONS ON THE EASTERN SEABOARD!
YOU TWO AREN'T GONNA LAST A WEEK INSIDE, Y'HEAR ME?!
IF YOU'RE THE BEST THEY CAN THROW AT US IN THERE...
...MY BROTHER AND I HAVE NOTHING TO WORRY ABOUT.
THAT'S ENOUGH.
WE DID EXACTLY AS "THE ONE" INSTRUCTED US!

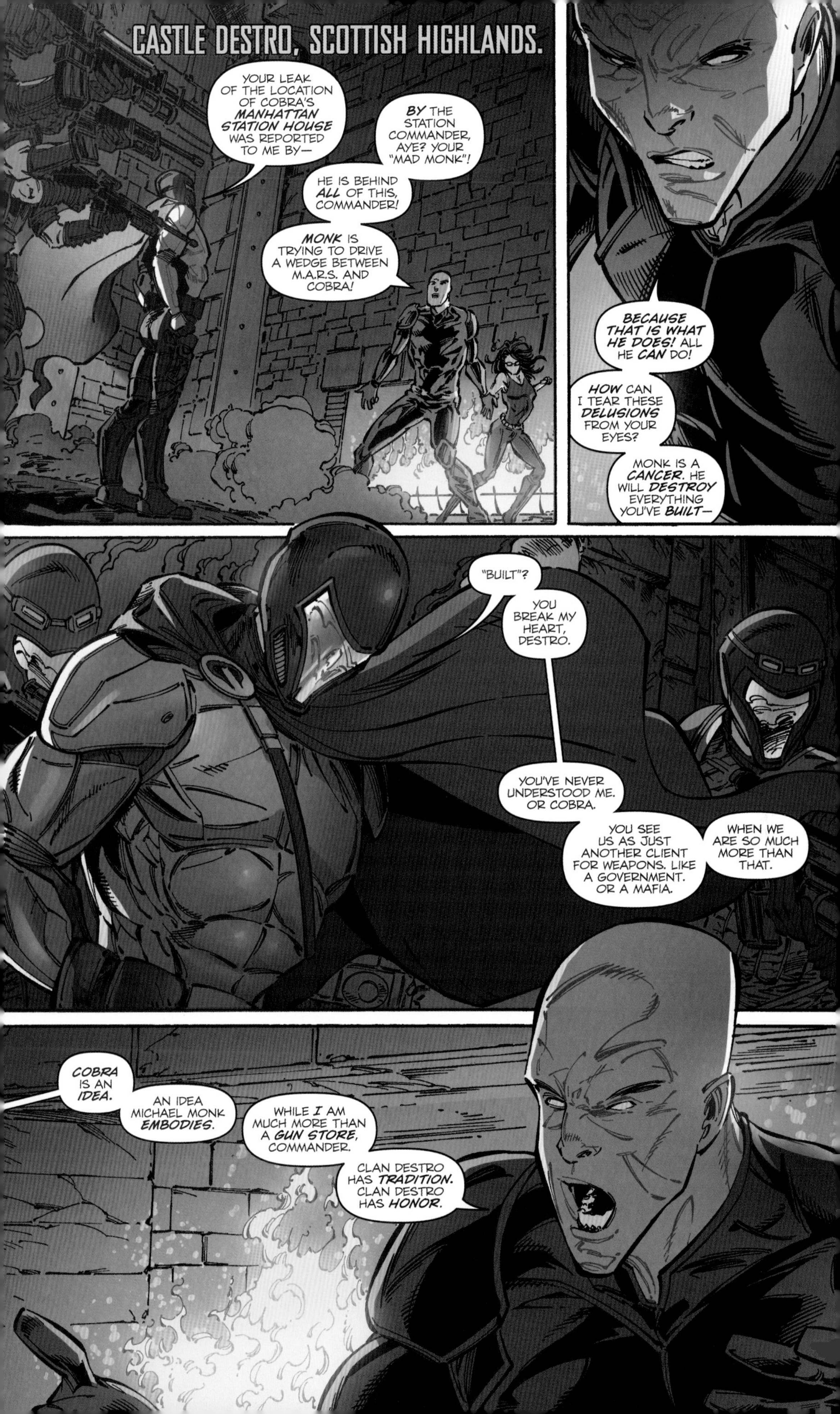

CASTLE DESTRO, SCOTTISH HIGHLANDS.
YOUR LEAK OF THE LOCATION OF COBRA'S MANHATTAN STATION HOUSE WAS REPORTED TO ME BY—
BY THE STATION COMMANDER, AYE? YOUR "MAD MONK"!
HE IS BEHIND ALL OF THIS, COMMANDER!
MONK IS TRYING TO DRIVE A WEDGE BETWEEN M.A.R.S. AND COBRA!
BECAUSE THAT IS WHAT HE DOES! ALL HE CAN DO!
HOW CAN I TEAR THESE DELUSIONS FROM YOUR EYES?
MONK IS A CANCER. HE WILL DESTROY EVERYTHING YOU'VE BUILT—
"BUILT"?
YOU BREAK MY HEART, DESTRO.
YOU'VE NEVER UNDERSTOOD ME. OR COBRA.
YOU SEE US AS JUST ANOTHER CLIENT FOR WEAPONS. LIKE A GOVERNMENT. OR A MAFIA.
WHEN WE ARE SO MUCH MORE THAN THAT.
COBRA IS AN IDEA.
AN IDEA MICHAEL MONK EMBODIES.
WHILE I AM MUCH MORE THAN A GUN STORE, COMMANDER.
CLAN DESTRO HAS TRADITION. CLAN DESTRO HAS HONOR.

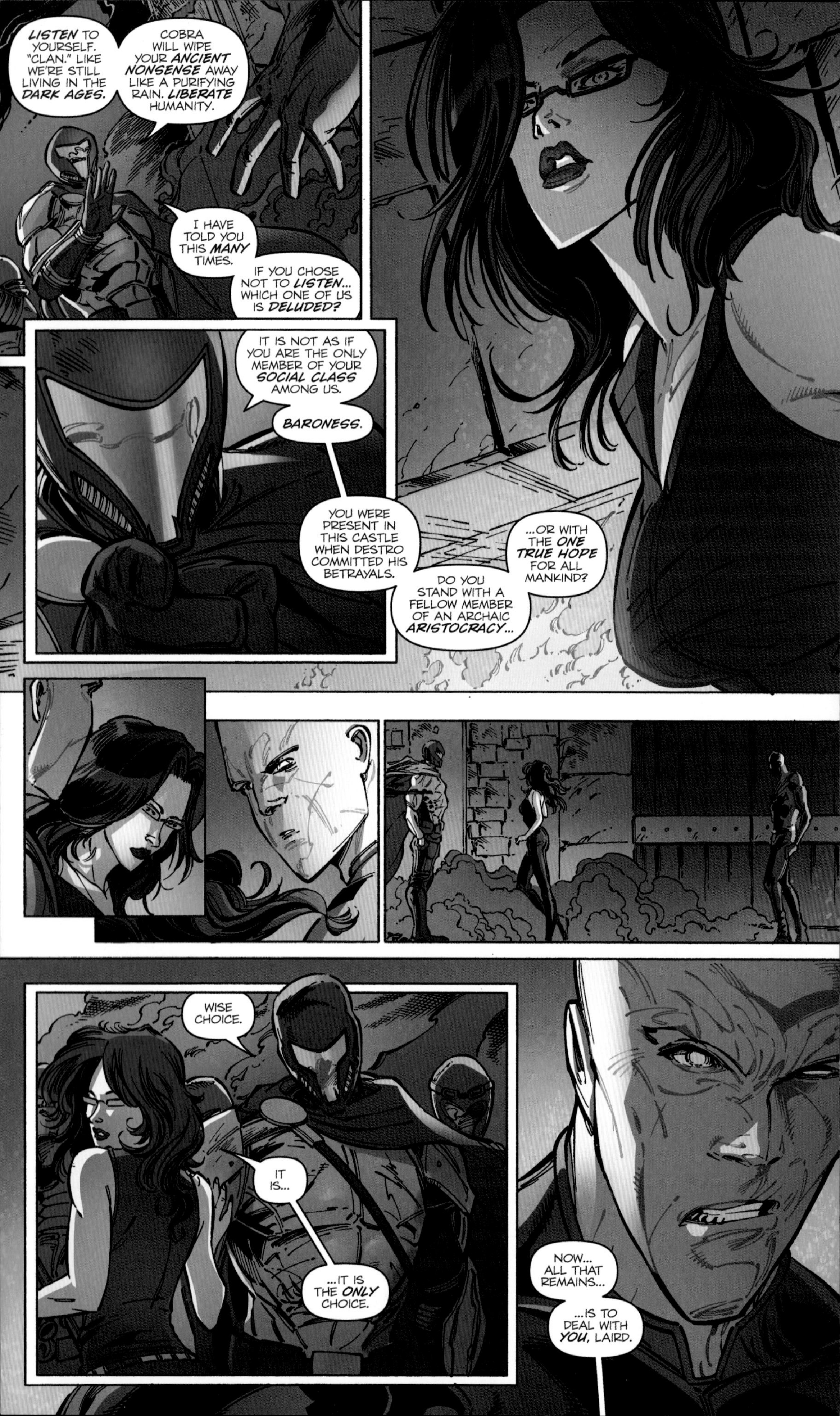
LISTEN TO YOURSELF. "CLAN." LIKE WE'RE STILL LIVING IN THE DARK AGES.
COBRA WILL WIPE YOUR ANCIENT NONSENSE AWAY LIKE A PURIFYING RAIN. LIBERATE HUMANITY.
I HAVE TOLD YOU THIS MANY TIMES.
IF YOU CHOSE NOT TO LISTEN... WHICH ONE OF US IS DELUDED?
IT IS NOT AS IF YOU ARE THE ONLY MEMBER OF YOUR SOCIAL CLASS AMONG US.
BARONESS.
YOU WERE PRESENT IN THIS CASTLE WHEN DESTRO COMMITTED HIS BETRAYALS.
DO YOU STAND WITH A FELLOW MEMBER OF AN ARCHAIC ARISTOCRACY...
...OR WITH THE ONE TRUE HOPE FOR ALL MANKIND?
WISE CHOICE.
IT IS...
...IT IS THE ONLY CHOICE.
NOW... ALL THAT REMAINS...
...IS TO DEAL WITH YOU, LAIRD.

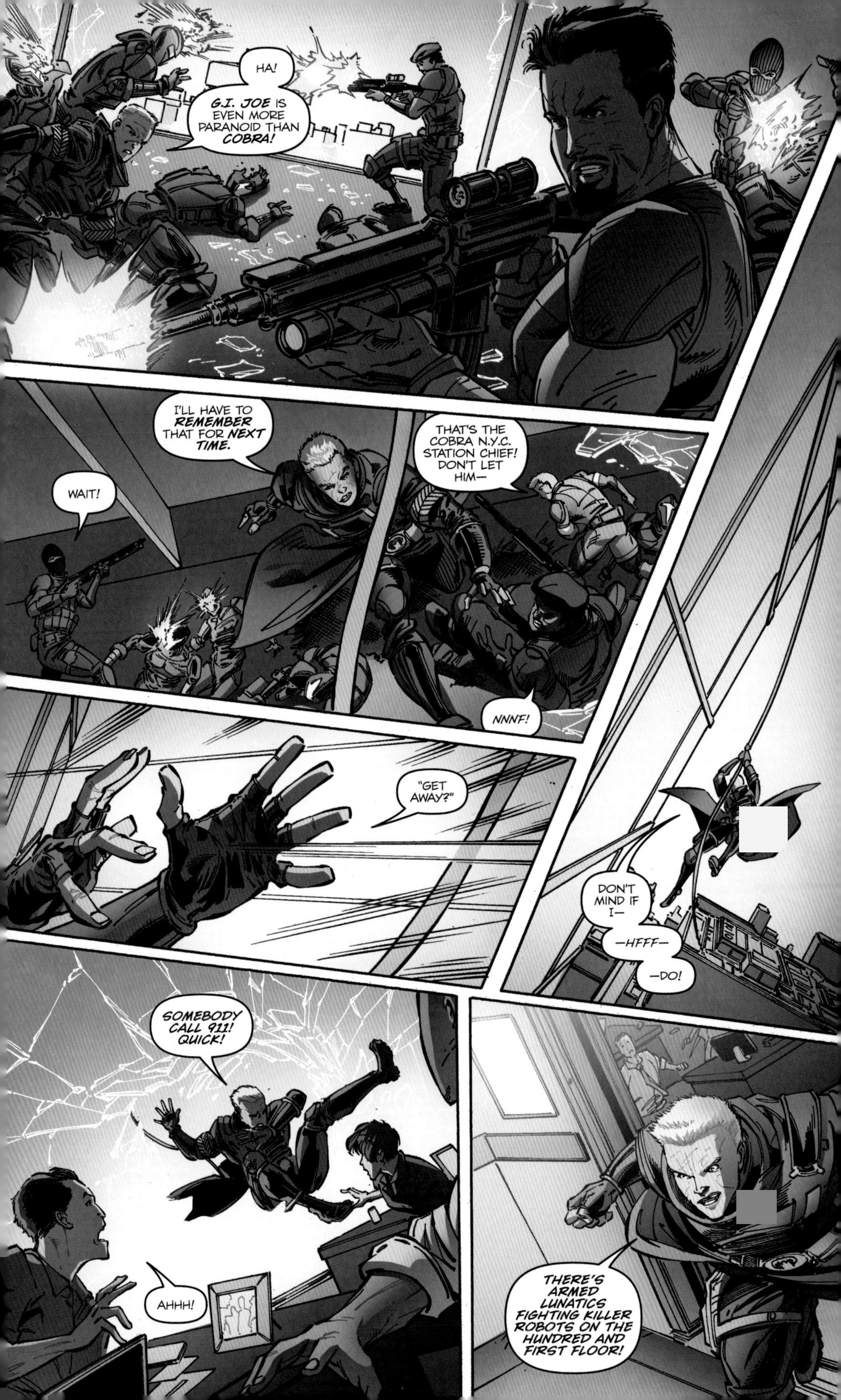
HA!
G.I. JOE IS EVEN MORE PARANOID THAN COBRA!
I'LL HAVE TO REMEMBER THAT FOR NEXT TIME.
WAIT!
THAT'S THE COBRA N.Y.C. STATION CHIEF! DON'T LET HIM—
NNNF!
"GET AWAY?"
DON'T MIND IF I—
—HFFF—
—DO!
SOMEBODY CALL 911! QUICK!
AHHH!
THERE'S ARMED LUNATICS FIGHTING KILLER ROBOTS ON THE HUNDRED AND FIRST FLOOR!

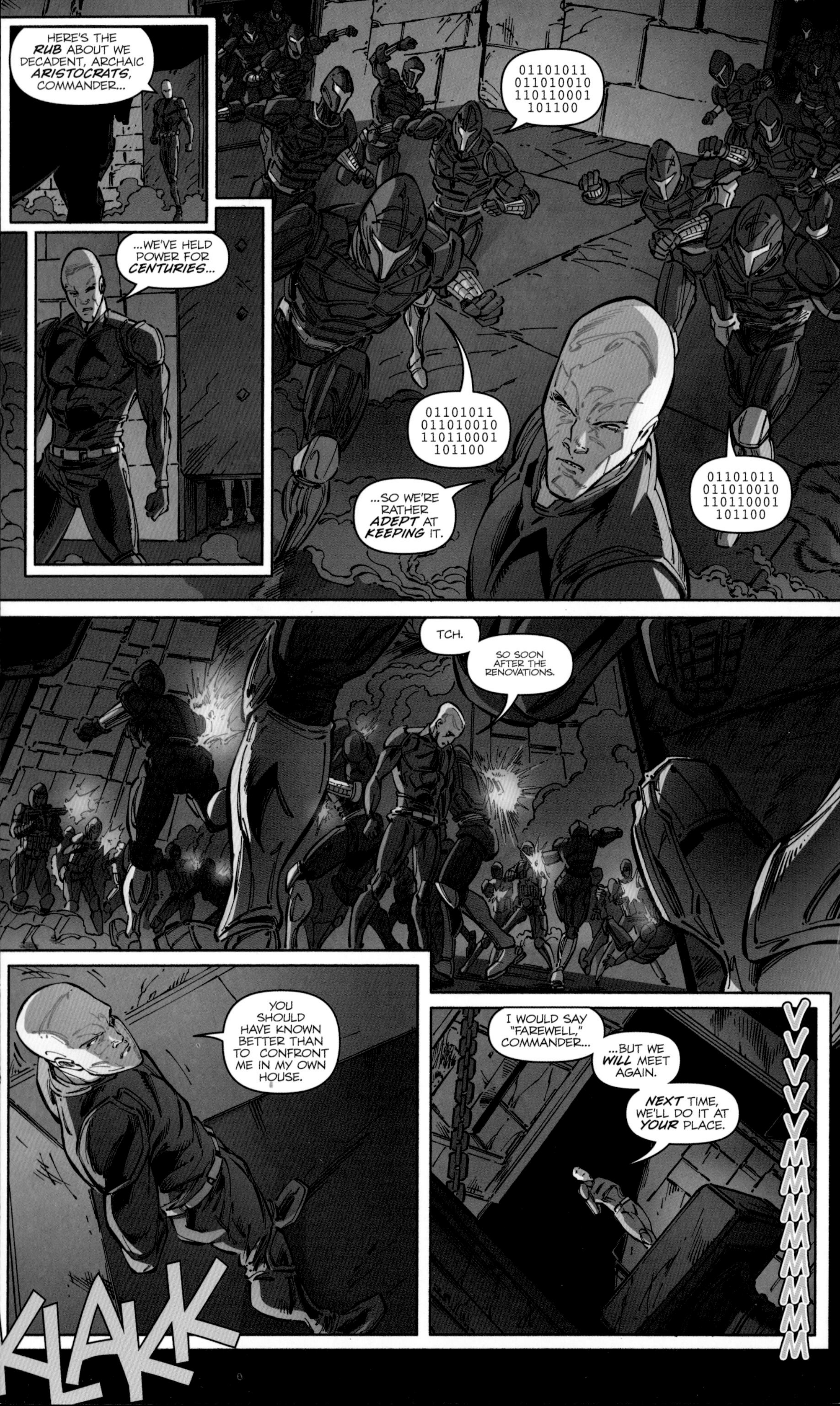
HERE'S THE RUB ABOUT WE DECADENT, ARCHAIC ARISTOCRATS, COMMANDER...
01101011 011010010 110110001 101100
...WE'VE HELD POWER FOR CENTURIES...
01101011 011010010 110110001 101100
...SO WE'RE RATHER ADEPT AT KEEPING IT.
01101011 011010010 110110001 101100
TCH.
SO SOON AFTER THE RENOVATIONS.
YOU SHOULD HAVE KNOWN BETTER THAN TO CONFRONT ME IN MY OWN HOUSE.
KLAK
I WOULD SAY "FAREWELL," COMMANDER...
...BUT WE WILL MEET AGAIN.
NEXT TIME, WE'LL DO IT AT YOUR PLACE.
VVVVVMMMMMMMMMMM

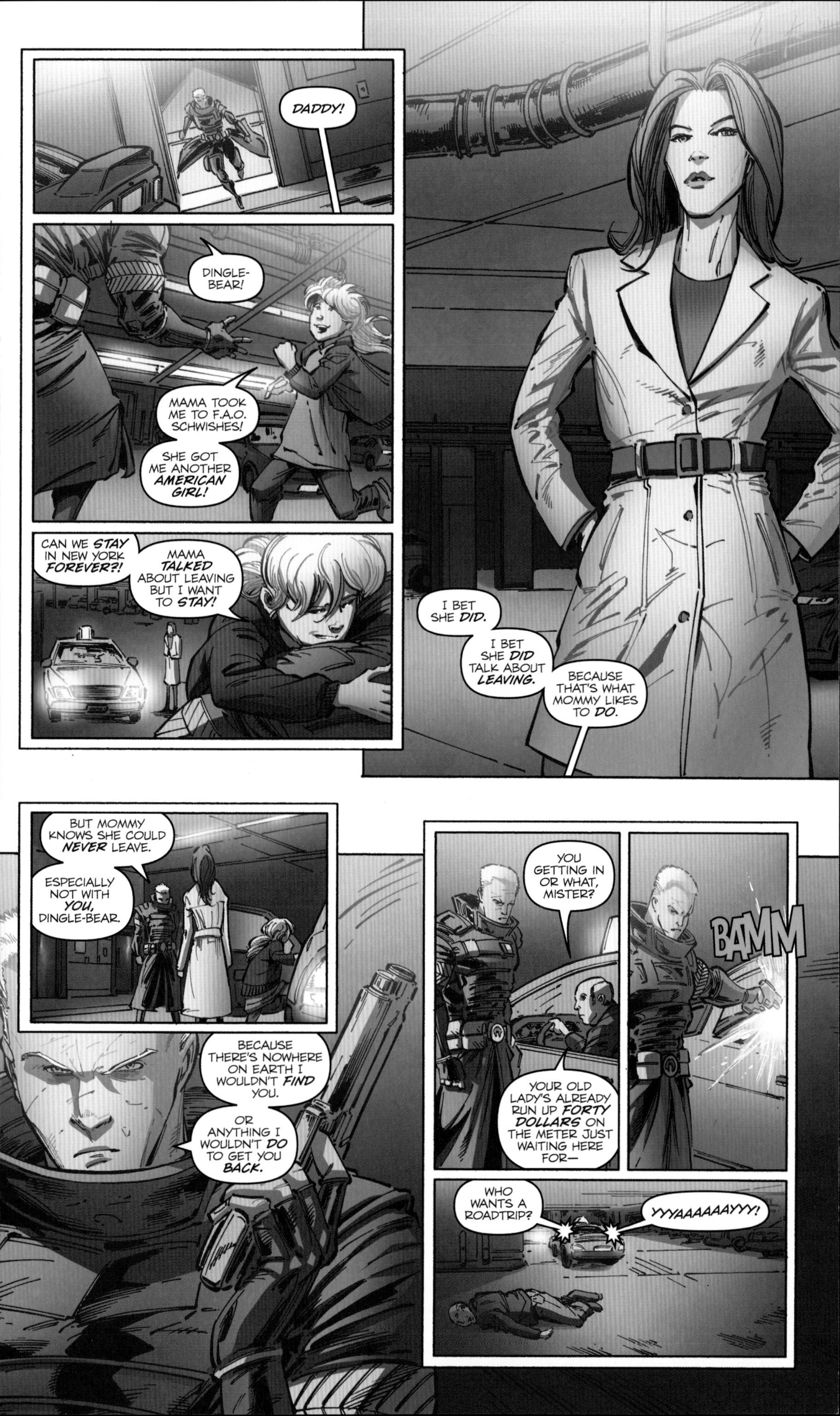
DADDY!
DINGLE-BEAR!
MAMA TOOK ME TO F.A.O. SCHWISHES!
SHE GOT ME ANOTHER AMERICAN GIRL!
CAN WE STAY IN NEW YORK FOREVER?!
MAMA TALKED ABOUT LEAVING BUT I WANT TO STAY!
I BET SHE DID.
I BET SHE DID TALK ABOUT LEAVING.
BECAUSE THAT'S WHAT MOMMY LIKES TO DO.
BUT MOMMY KNOWS SHE COULD NEVER LEAVE.
ESPECIALLY NOT WITH YOU, DINGLE-BEAR.
BECAUSE THERE'S NOWHERE ON EARTH I WOULDN'T FIND YOU.
OR ANYTHING I WOULDN'T DO TO GET YOU BACK.
YOU GETTING IN OR WHAT, MISTER?
YOUR OLD LADY'S ALREADY RUN UP FORTY DOLLARS ON THE METER JUST WAITING HERE FOR—
BAMM
WHO WANTS A ROADTRIP?
YYYAAAAAAYYY!

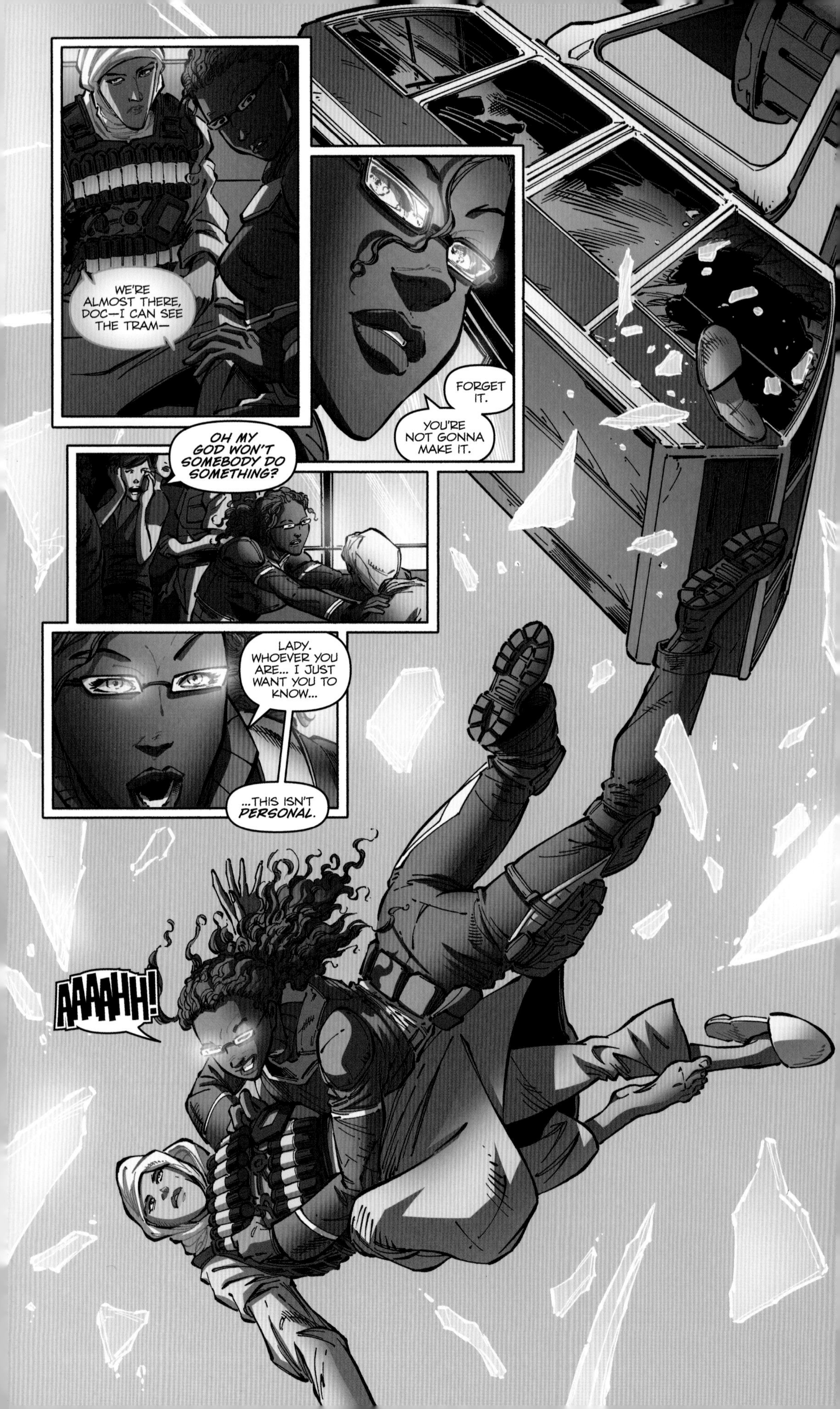
WE'RE ALMOST THERE, DOC--I CAN SEE THE TRAM--
FORGET IT.
YOU'RE NOT GONNA MAKE IT.
OH MY GOD WON'T SOMEBODY DO SOMETHING?
LADY. WHOEVER YOU ARE... I JUST WANT YOU TO KNOW...
...THIS ISN'T PERSONAL.
AAAAHH!

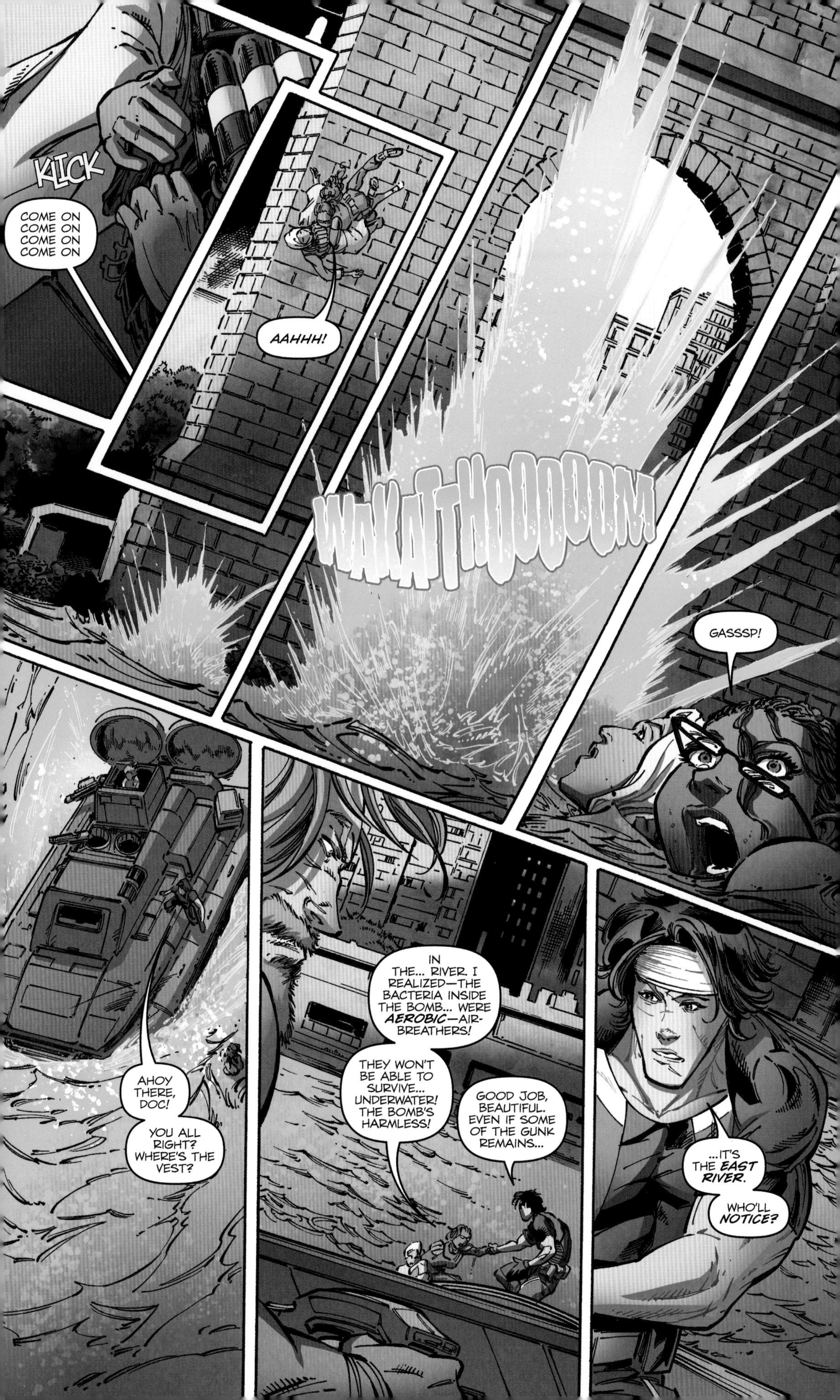
KLICK
COME ON COME ON COME ON COME ON
AAHHH!
WAKATTHOOOOOOM!
GASSSP!
AHOY THERE, DOC!
YOU ALL RIGHT? WHERE'S THE VEST?
IN THE... RIVER. I REALIZED—THE BACTERIA INSIDE THE BOMB... WERE AEROBIC—AIR-BREATHERS!
THEY WON'T BE ABLE TO SURVIVE... UNDERWATER! THE BOMB'S HARMLESS!
GOOD JOB, BEAUTIFUL. EVEN IF SOME OF THE GUNK REMAINS...
...IT'S THE EAST RIVER.
WHO'LL NOTICE?

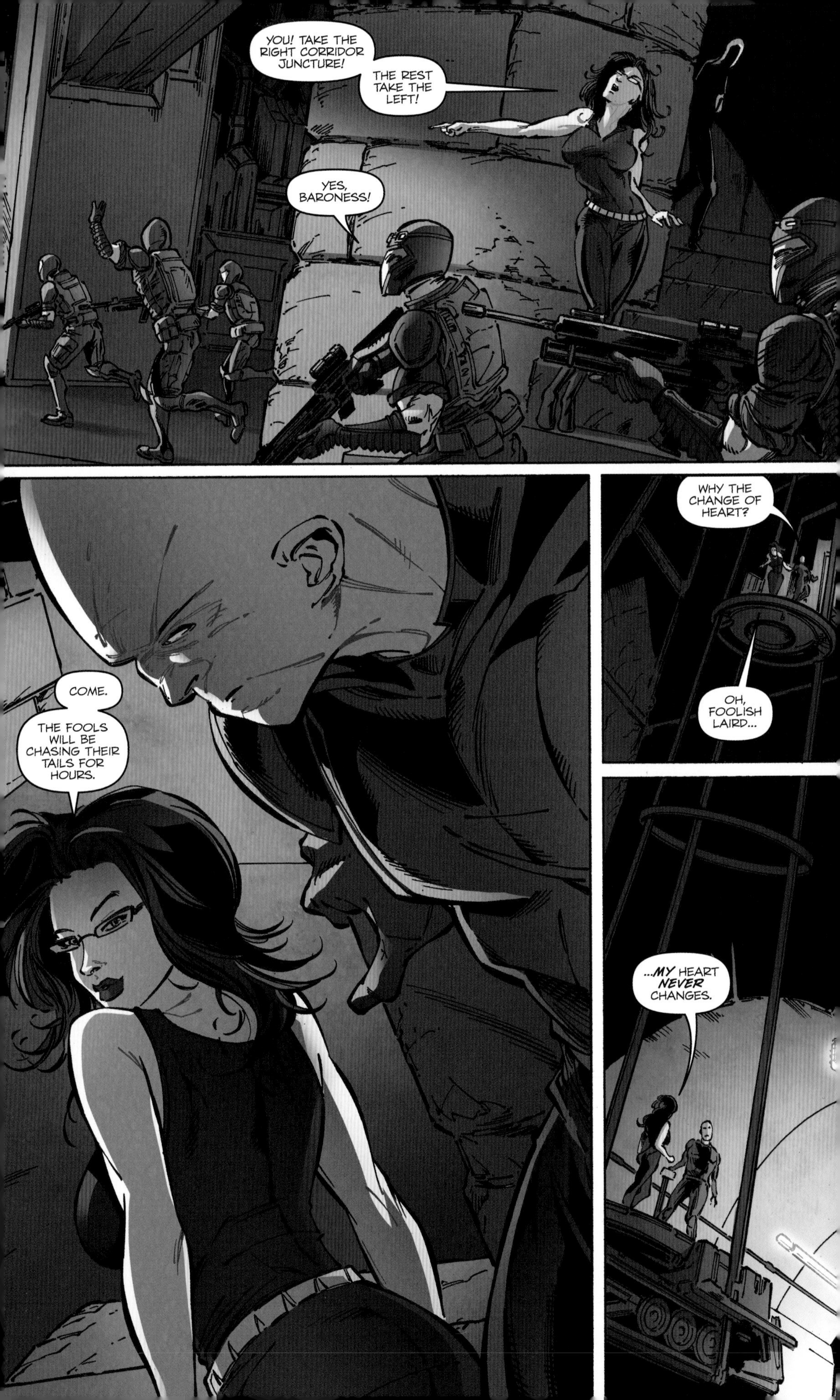

YOU! TAKE THE RIGHT CORRIDOR JUNCTURE!
THE REST TAKE THE LEFT!
YES, BARONESS!
COME.
THE FOOLS WILL BE CHASING THEIR TAILS FOR HOURS.
WHY THE CHANGE OF HEART?
OH, FOOLISH LAIRD...
...*MY* HEART *NEVER* CHANGES.

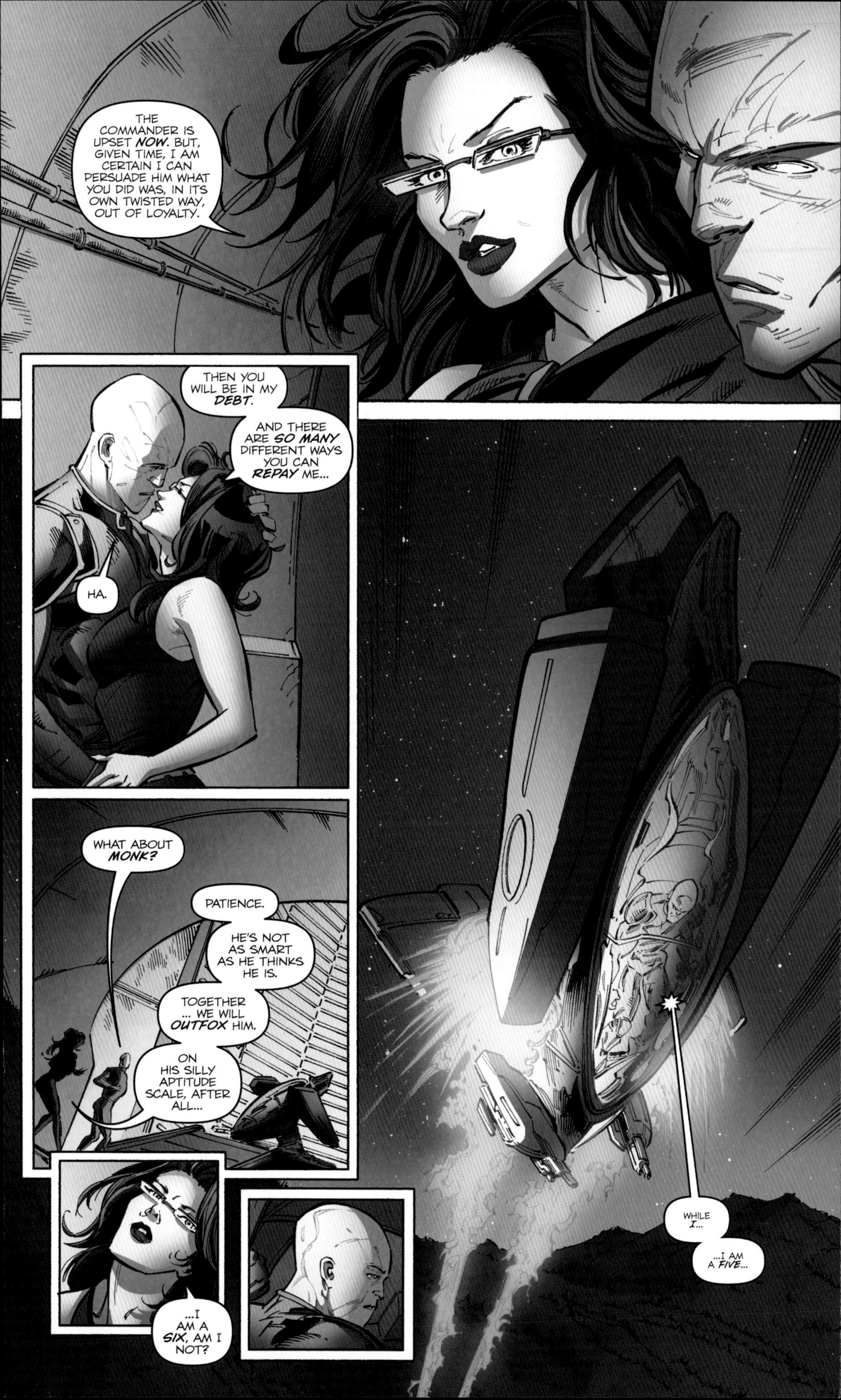
THE COMMANDER IS UPSET NOW. BUT, GIVEN TIME, I AM CERTAIN I CAN PERSUADE HIM WHAT YOU DID WAS, IN ITS OWN TWISTED WAY, OUT OF LOYALTY.
THEN YOU WILL BE IN MY DEBT.
AND THERE ARE SO MANY DIFFERENT WAYS YOU CAN REPAY ME...
HA.
WHAT ABOUT MONK?
PATIENCE.
HE'S NOT AS SMART AS HE THINKS HE IS.
TOGETHER ... WE WILL OUTFOX HIM.
ON HIS SILLY APTITUDE SCALE, AFTER ALL...
...I AM A SIX, AM I NOT?
WHILE I...
...I AM A FIVE...

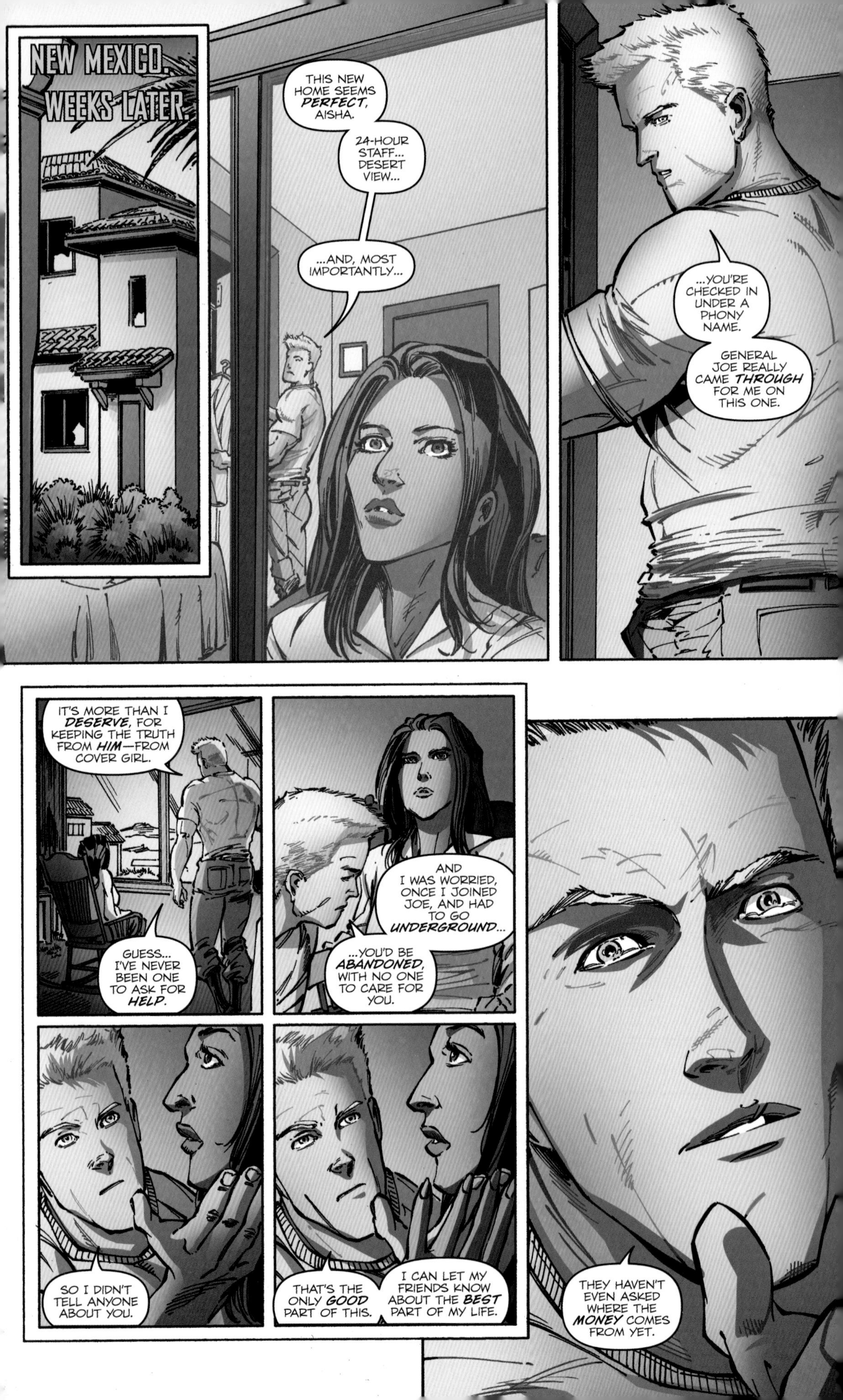
NEW MEXICO. WEEKS LATER.
THIS NEW HOME SEEMS PERFECT, AISHA.
24-HOUR STAFF... DESERT VIEW...
...AND, MOST IMPORTANTLY...
...YOU'RE CHECKED IN UNDER A PHONY NAME.
GENERAL JOE REALLY CAME THROUGH FOR ME ON THIS ONE.
IT'S MORE THAN I DESERVE, FOR KEEPING THE TRUTH FROM HIM—FROM COVER GIRL.
GUESS... I'VE NEVER BEEN ONE TO ASK FOR HELP.
AND I WAS WORRIED, ONCE I JOINED JOE, AND HAD TO GO UNDERGROUND...
...YOU'D BE ABANDONED, WITH NO ONE TO CARE FOR YOU.
SO I DIDN'T TELL ANYONE ABOUT YOU.
THAT'S THE ONLY GOOD PART OF THIS.
I CAN LET MY FRIENDS KNOW ABOUT THE BEST PART OF MY LIFE.
THEY HAVEN'T EVEN ASKED WHERE THE MONEY COMES FROM YET.

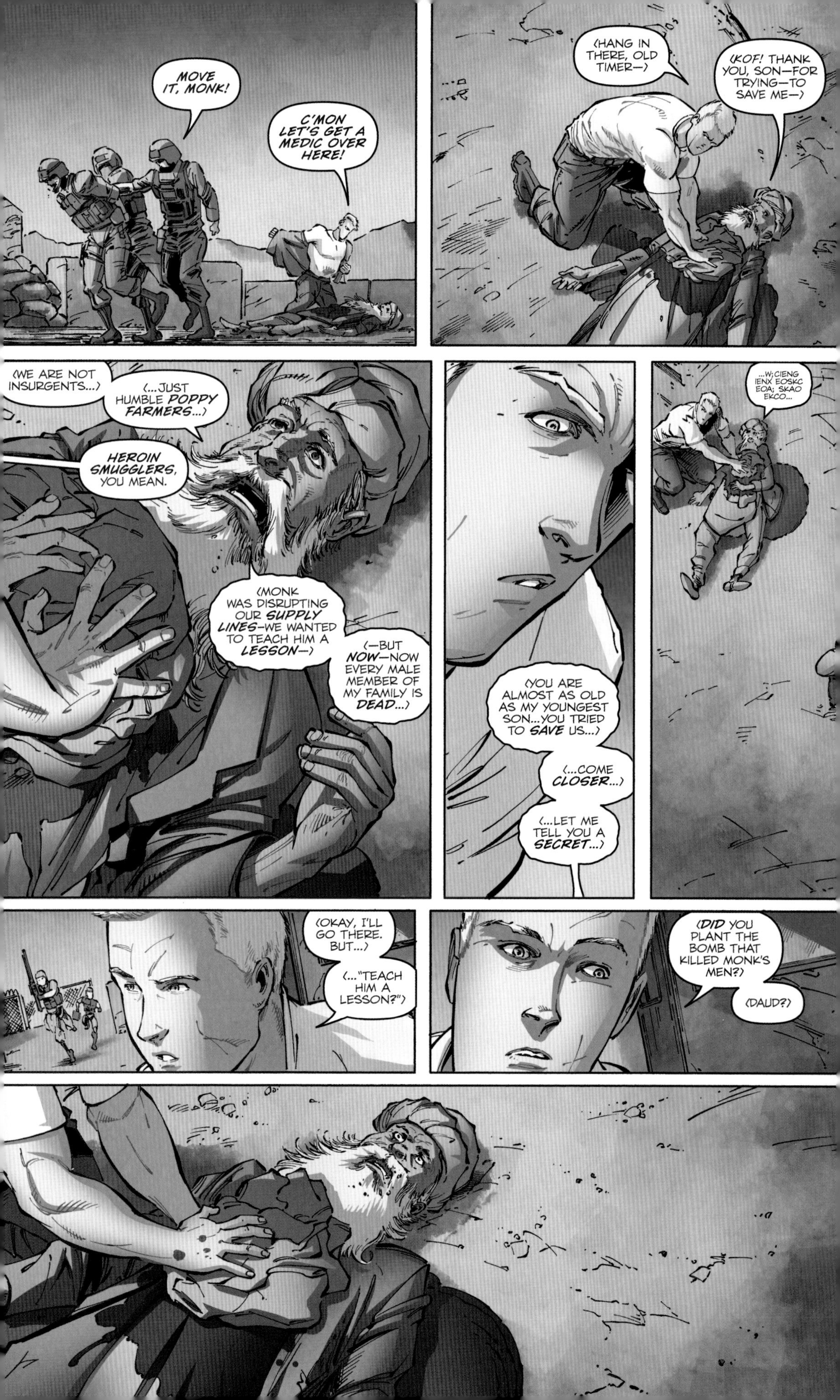

MOVE IT, MONK!
C'MON LET'S GET A MEDIC OVER HERE!
‹HANG IN THERE, OLD TIMER—›
‹KOF! THANK YOU, SON—FOR TRYING—TO SAVE ME—›
‹WE ARE NOT INSURGENTS...›
‹...JUST HUMBLE POPPY FARMERS...›
HEROIN SMUGGLERS, YOU MEAN.
‹MONK WAS DISRUPTING OUR SUPPLY LINES—WE WANTED TO TEACH HIM A LESSON—›
‹—BUT NOW—NOW EVERY MALE MEMBER OF MY FAMILY IS DEAD...›
‹YOU ARE ALMOST AS OLD AS MY YOUNGEST SON...YOU TRIED TO SAVE US...›
‹...COME CLOSER...›
‹...LET ME TELL YOU A SECRET...›
...W; CIENG IENX EOSKC EOA; SKAO EKCO...
‹OKAY, I'LL GO THERE. BUT...›
‹..."TEACH HIM A LESSON?"›
‹DID YOU PLANT THE BOMB THAT KILLED MONK'S MEN?›
‹DAUD?›

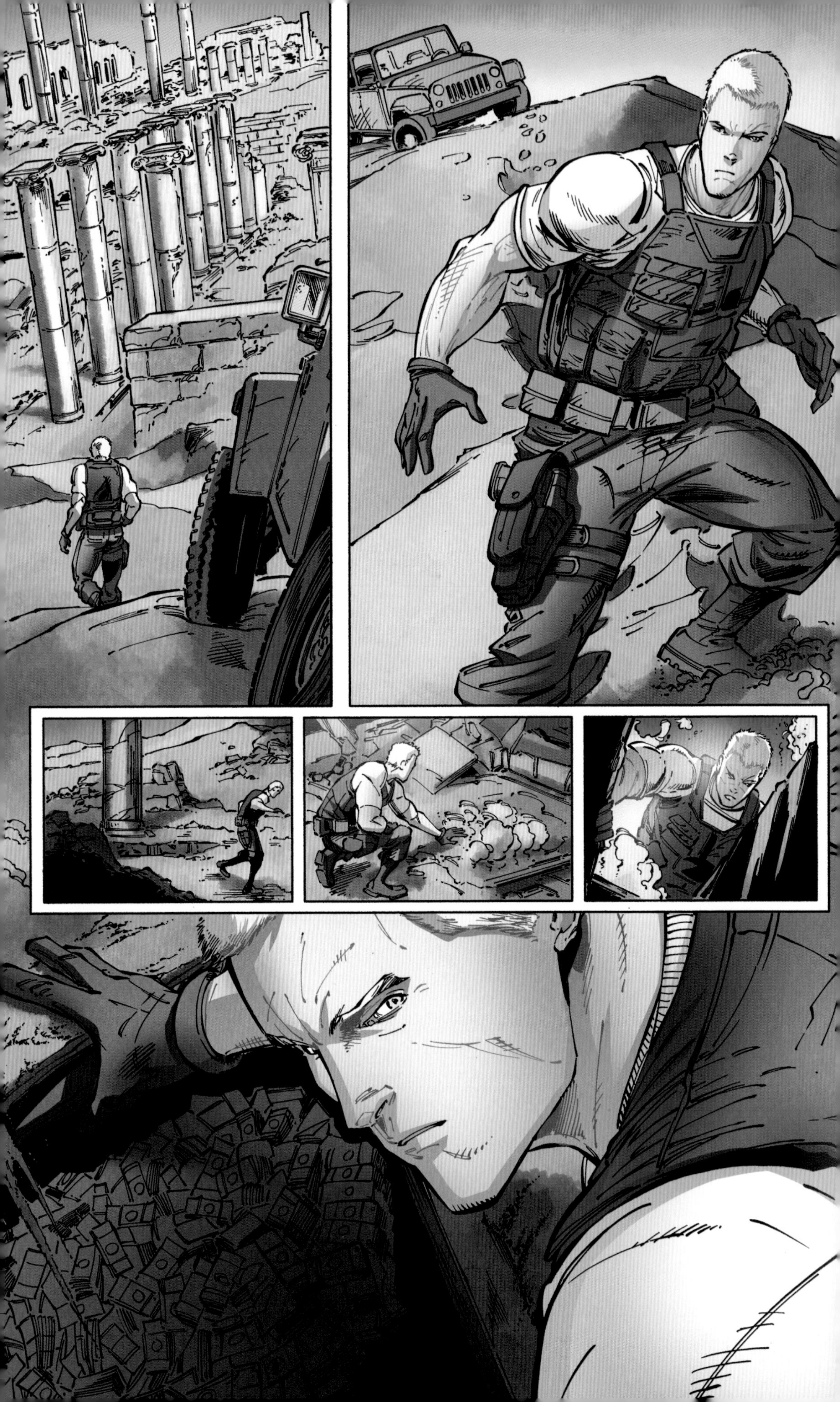

CHAPTER SIX

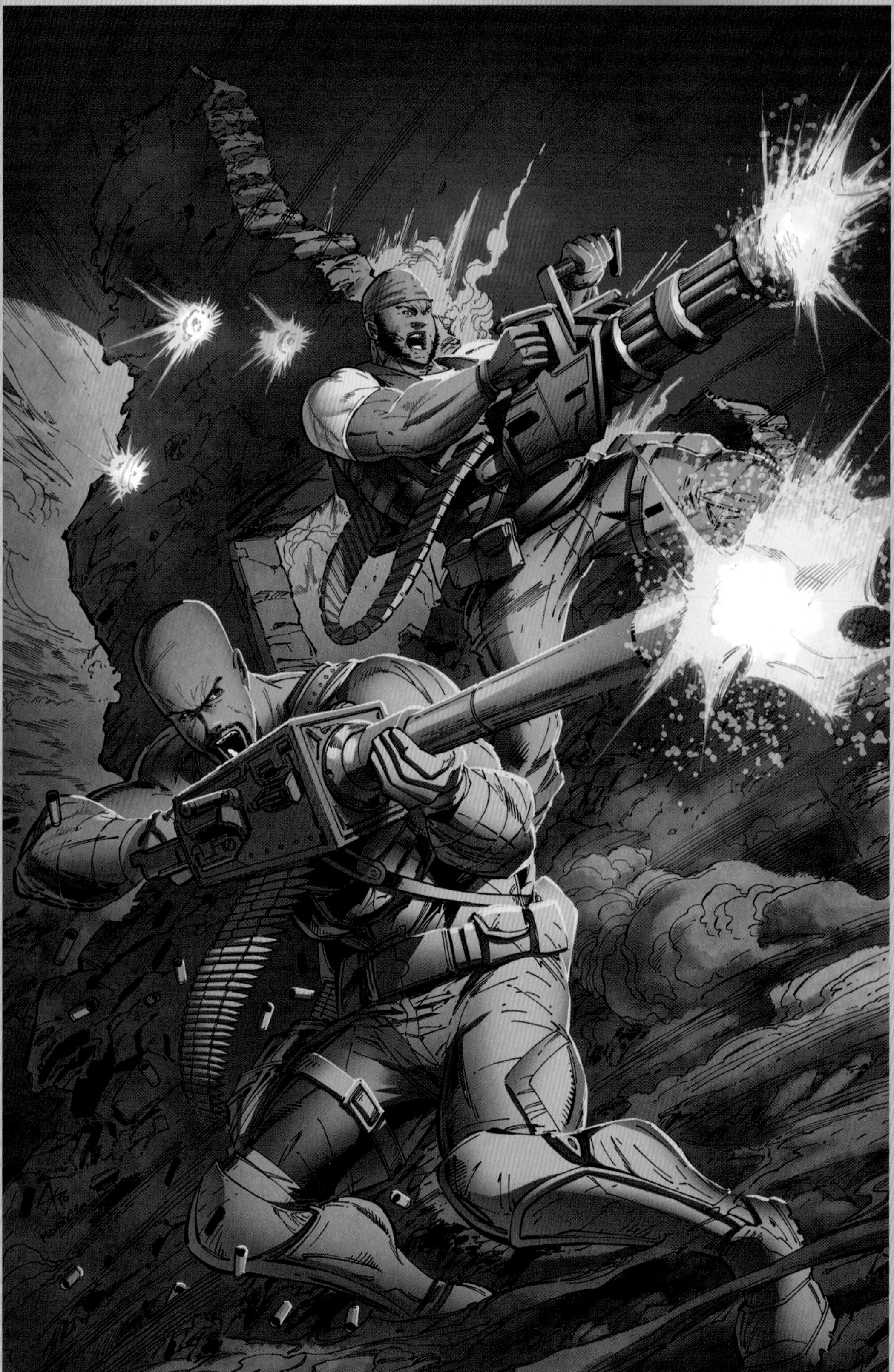

ART BY STEVE KURTH
INKS BY ALLEN MARTINEZ
COLORS BY JOANA LAFUENTE

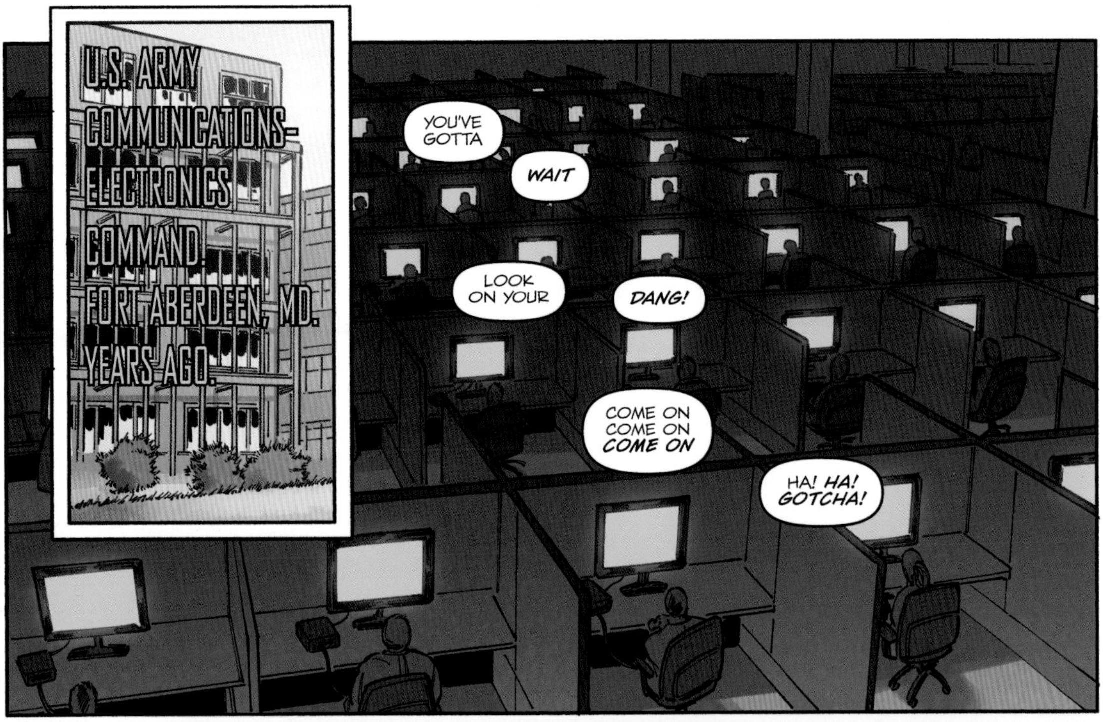
U.S. ARMY COMMUNICATIONS-ELECTRONICS COMMAND. FORT ABERDEEN, MD. YEARS AGO.
YOU'VE GOTTA
WAIT
LOOK ON YOUR
DANG!
COME ON COME ON COME ON
HA! HA! GOTCHA!

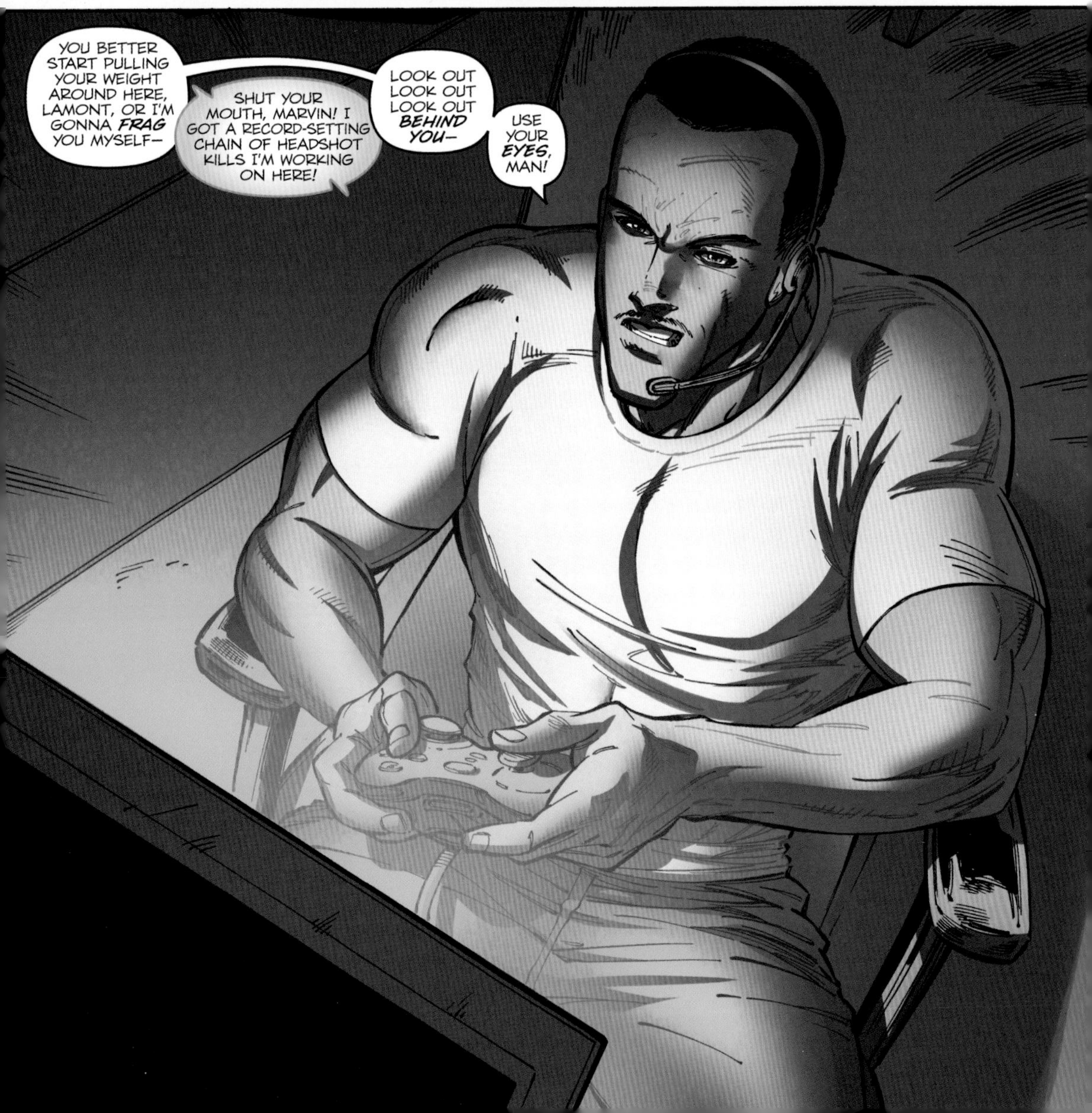
YOU BETTER START PULLING YOUR WEIGHT AROUND HERE, LAMONT, OR I'M GONNA FRAG YOU MYSELF—
SHUT YOUR MOUTH, MARVIN! I GOT A RECORD-SETTING CHAIN OF HEADSHOT KILLS I'M WORKING ON HERE!
LOOK OUT LOOK OUT LOOK OUT BEHIND YOU—
USE YOUR EYES, MAN!

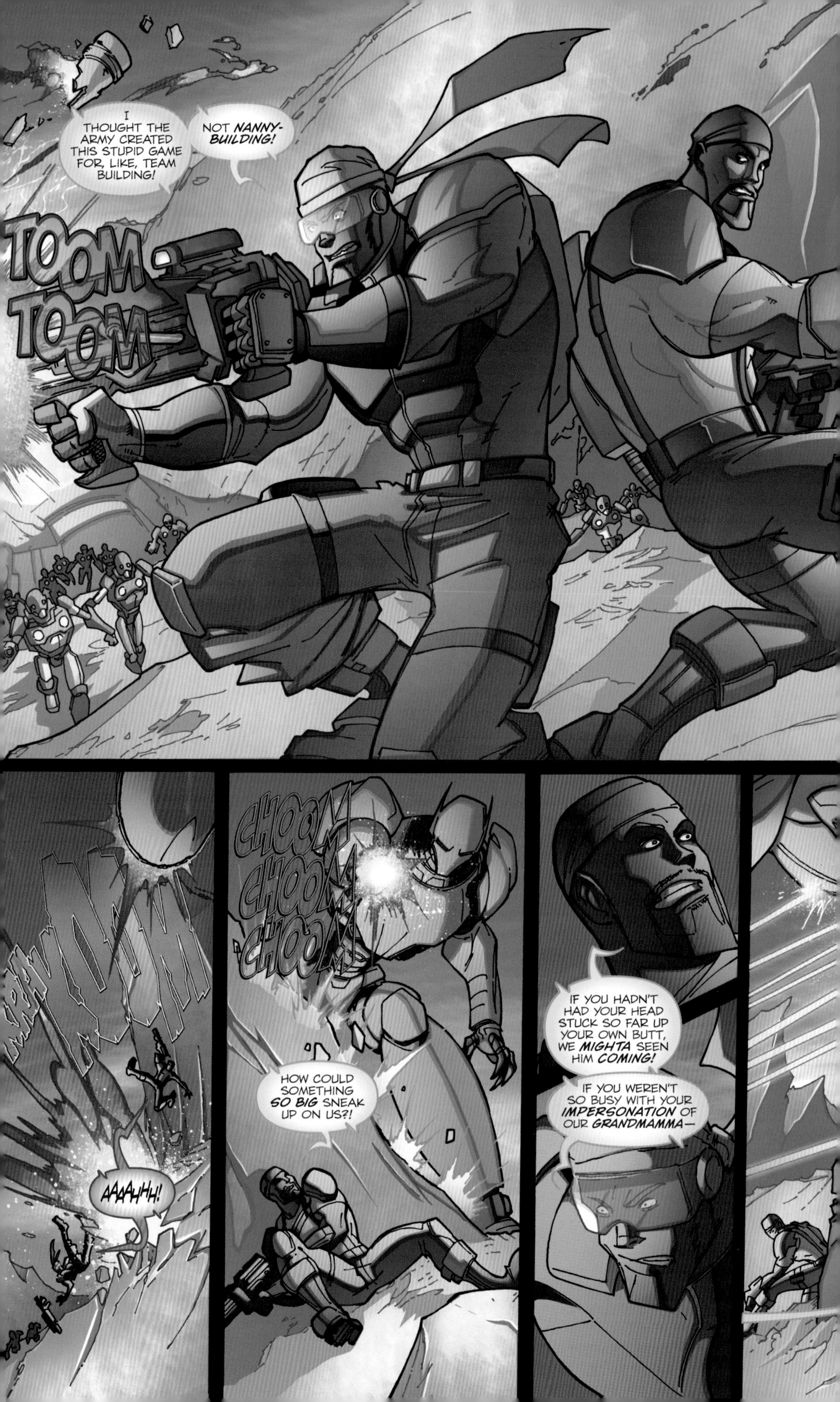

I THOUGHT THE ARMY CREATED THIS STUPID GAME FOR, LIKE, TEAM BUILDING!
NOT NANNY-BUILDING!
TOOM TOOM TOOM
AAAAHHH!
CHOOM CHOOM CHOOM
HOW COULD SOMETHING SO BIG SNEAK UP ON US?!
IF YOU HADN'T HAD YOUR HEAD STUCK SO FAR UP YOUR OWN BUTT, WE MIGHTA SEEN HIM COMING!
IF YOU WEREN'T SO BUSY WITH YOUR IMPERSONATION OF OUR GRANDMAMMA—

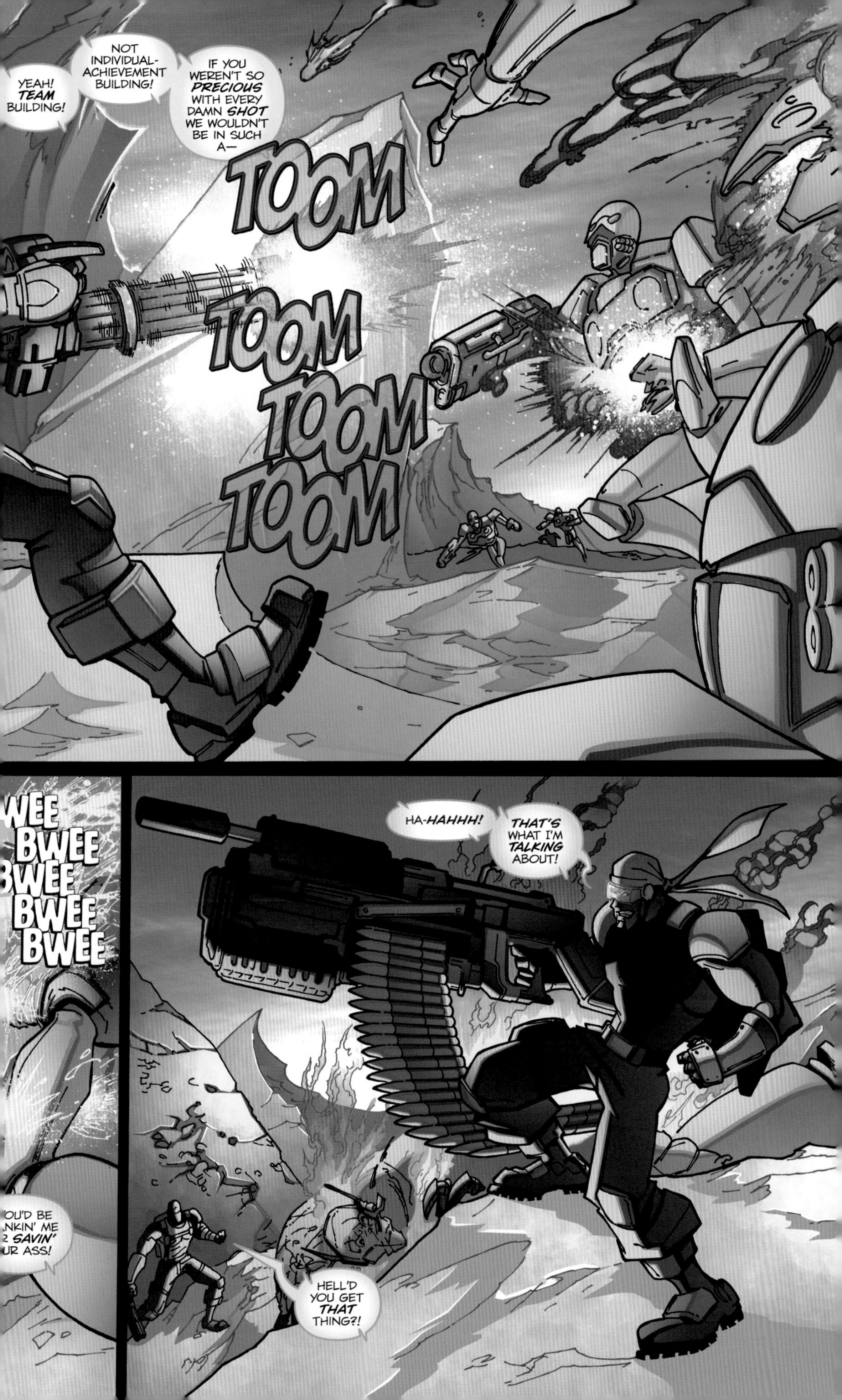

YEAH! TEAM BUILDING!
NOT INDIVIDUAL-ACHIEVEMENT BUILDING!
IF YOU WEREN'T SO PRECIOUS WITH EVERY DAMN SHOT WE WOULDN'T BE IN SUCH A—
TOOM
TOOM
TOOM
TOOM
WEE
BWEE
BWEE
BWEE
BWEE
HA-HAHHH!
THAT'S WHAT I'M TALKING ABOUT!
OU'D BE
NKIN' ME
SAVIN'
UR ASS!
HELL'D YOU GET THAT THING?!

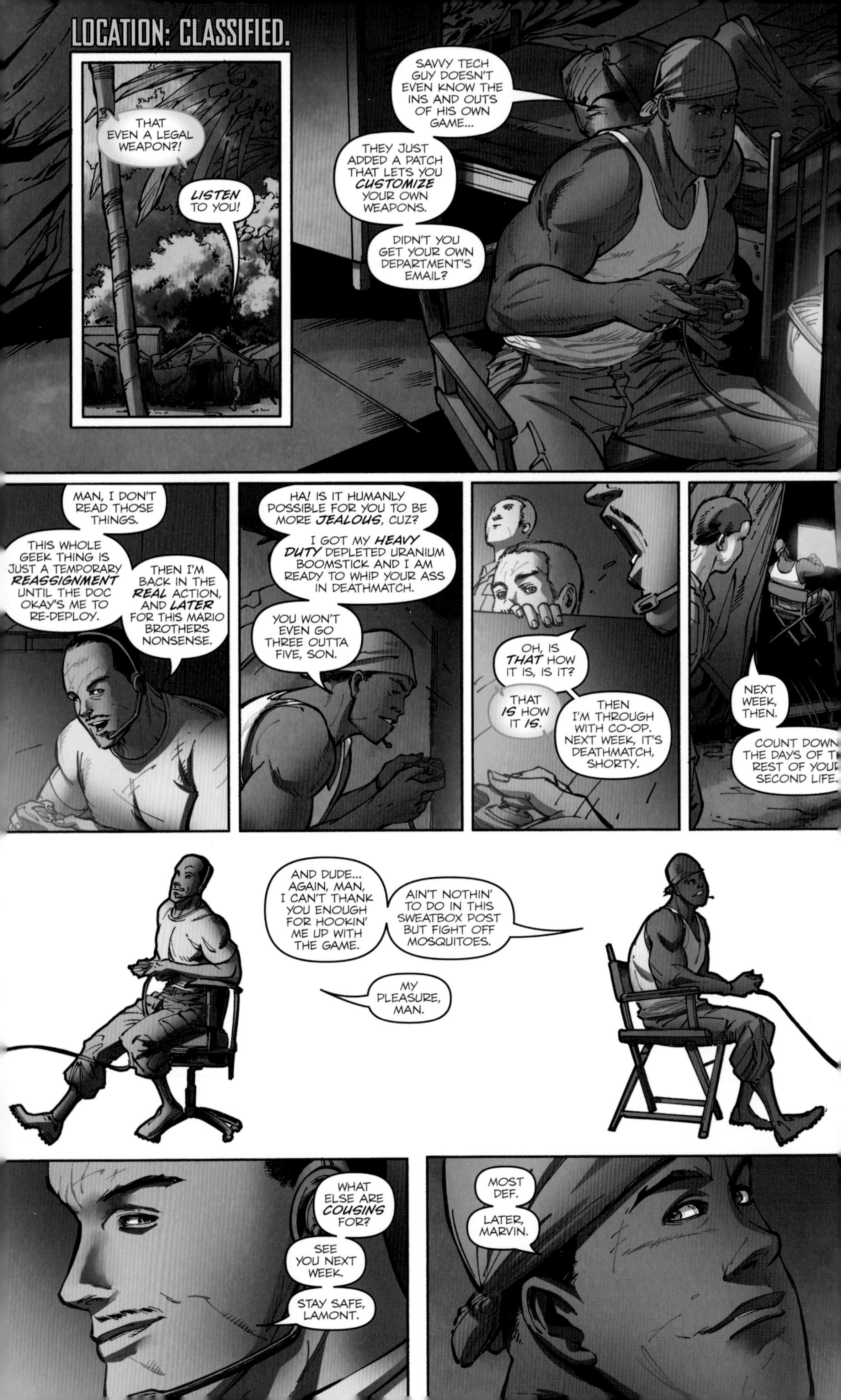
LOCATION: CLASSIFIED.
THAT EVEN A LEGAL WEAPON?!
LISTEN TO YOU!
SAVVY TECH GUY DOESN'T EVEN KNOW THE INS AND OUTS OF HIS OWN GAME...
THEY JUST ADDED A PATCH THAT LETS YOU CUSTOMIZE YOUR OWN WEAPONS.
DIDN'T YOU GET YOUR OWN DEPARTMENT'S EMAIL?
MAN, I DON'T READ THOSE THINGS.
THIS WHOLE GEEK THING IS JUST A TEMPORARY REASSIGNMENT UNTIL THE DOC OKAY'S ME TO RE-DEPLOY.
THEN I'M BACK IN THE REAL ACTION, AND LATER FOR THIS MARIO BROTHERS NONSENSE.
HA! IS IT HUMANLY POSSIBLE FOR YOU TO BE MORE JEALOUS, CUZ?
I GOT MY HEAVY DUTY DEPLETED URANIUM BOOMSTICK AND I AM READY TO WHIP YOUR ASS IN DEATHMATCH.
YOU WON'T EVEN GO THREE OUTTA FIVE, SON.
OH, IS THAT HOW IT IS, IS IT?
THAT IS HOW IT IS.
THEN I'M THROUGH WITH CO-OP. NEXT WEEK, IT'S DEATHMATCH, SHORTY.
NEXT WEEK, THEN.
COUNT DOWN THE DAYS OF TH REST OF YOUR SECOND LIFE.
AND DUDE... AGAIN, MAN, I CAN'T THANK YOU ENOUGH FOR HOOKIN' ME UP WITH THE GAME.
AIN'T NOTHIN' TO DO IN THIS SWEATBOX POST BUT FIGHT OFF MOSQUITOES.
MY PLEASURE, MAN.
WHAT ELSE ARE COUSINS FOR?
SEE YOU NEXT WEEK.
STAY SAFE, LAMONT.
MOST DEF.
LATER, MARVIN.

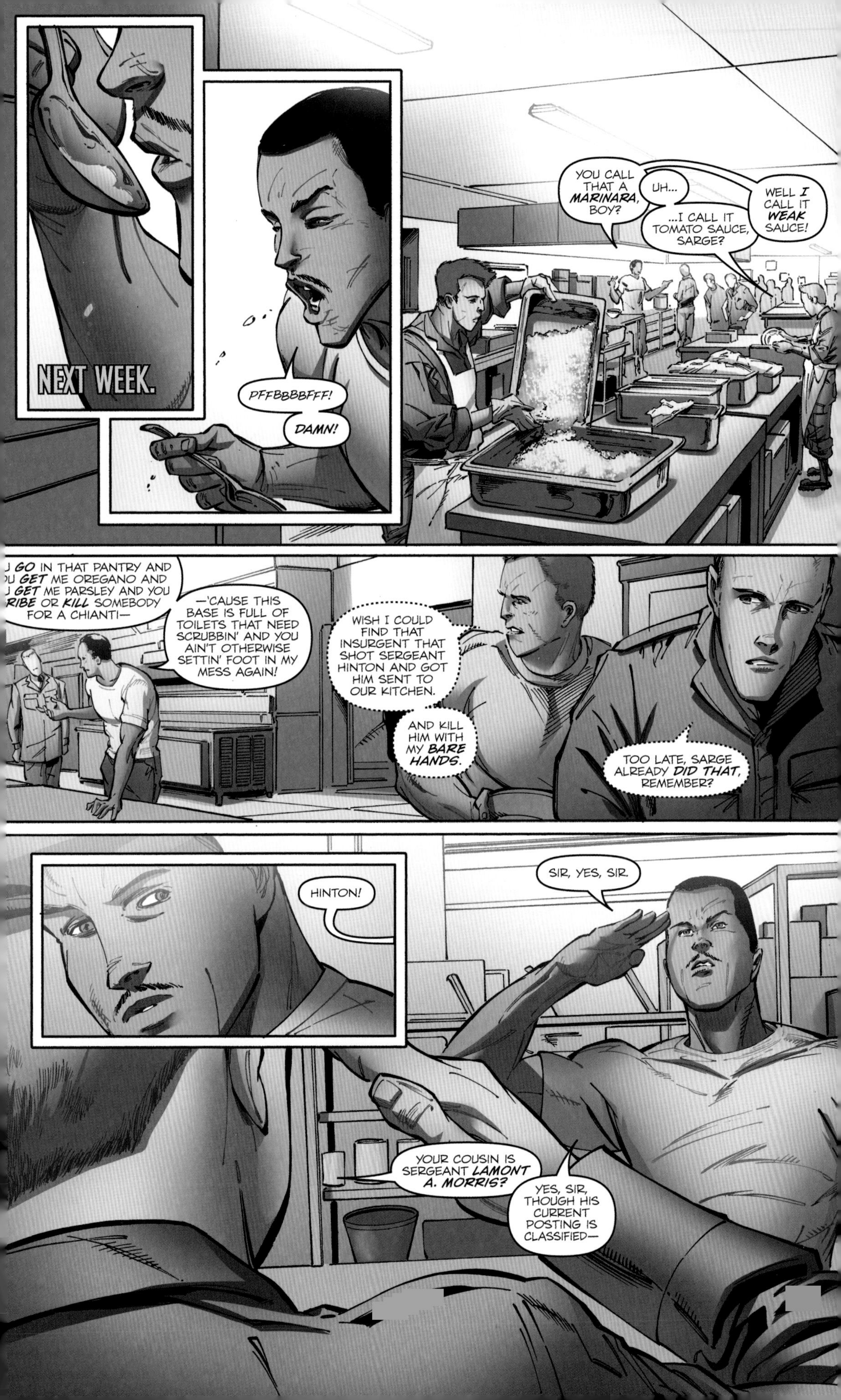
NEXT WEEK.
PFFBBBBFFF!
DAMN!
YOU CALL THAT A MARINARA, BOY?
UH...
...I CALL IT TOMATO SAUCE, SARGE?
WELL I CALL IT WEAK SAUCE!
U GO IN THAT PANTRY AND OU GET ME OREGANO AND U GET ME PARSLEY AND YOU RIBE OR KILL SOMEBODY FOR A CHIANTI—
—'CAUSE THIS BASE IS FULL OF TOILETS THAT NEED SCRUBBIN' AND YOU AIN'T OTHERWISE SETTIN' FOOT IN MY MESS AGAIN!
WISH I COULD FIND THAT INSURGENT THAT SHOT SERGEANT HINTON AND GOT HIM SENT TO OUR KITCHEN.
AND KILL HIM WITH MY BARE HANDS.
TOO LATE, SARGE ALREADY DID THAT, REMEMBER?
HINTON!
SIR, YES, SIR.
YOUR COUSIN IS SERGEANT LAMONT A. MORRIS?
YES, SIR, THOUGH HIS CURRENT POSTING IS CLASSIFIED—

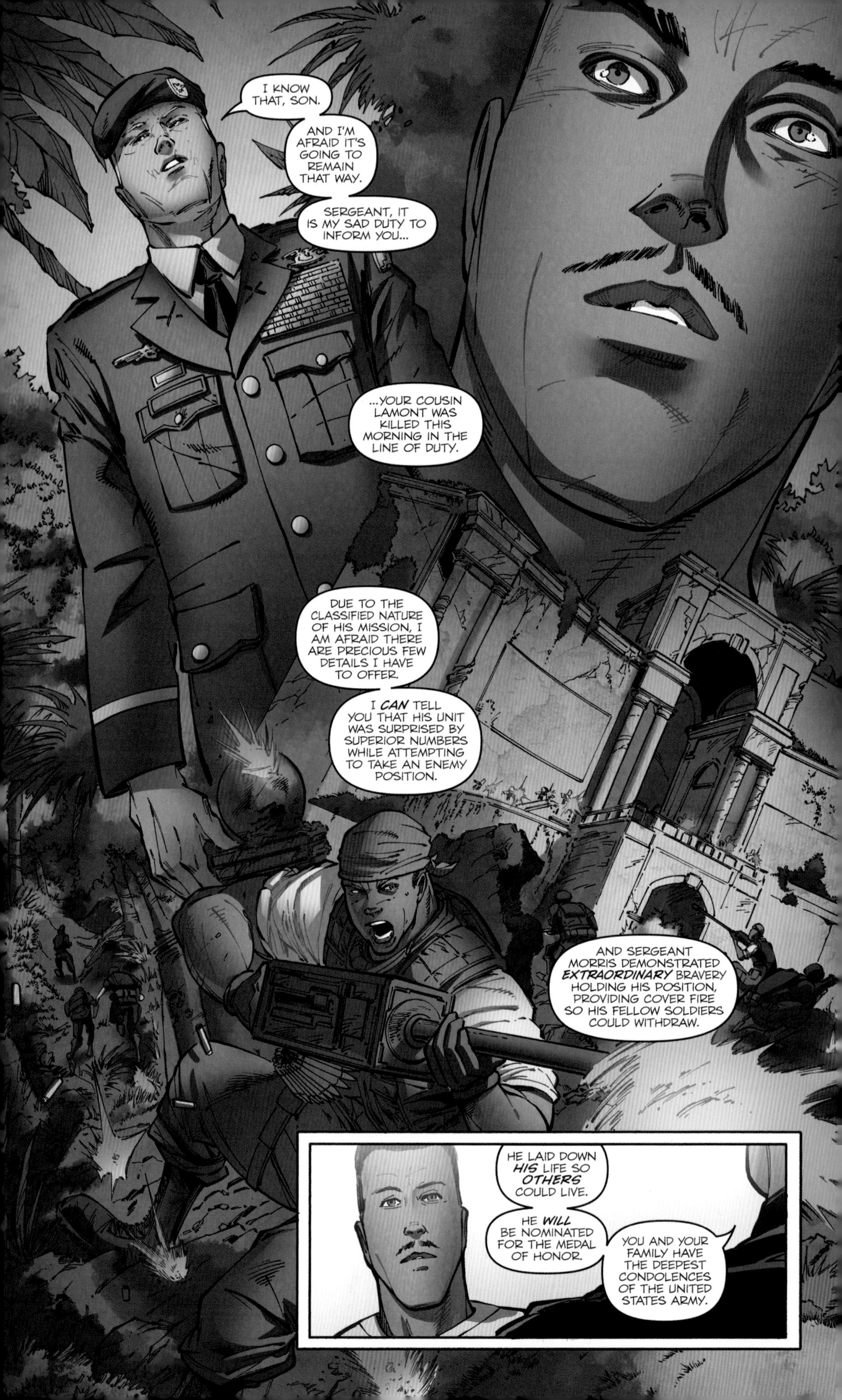
I KNOW THAT, SON.
AND I'M AFRAID IT'S GOING TO REMAIN THAT WAY.
SERGEANT, IT IS MY SAD DUTY TO INFORM YOU...
...YOUR COUSIN LAMONT WAS KILLED THIS MORNING IN THE LINE OF DUTY.
DUE TO THE CLASSIFIED NATURE OF HIS MISSION, I AM AFRAID THERE ARE PRECIOUS FEW DETAILS I HAVE TO OFFER.
I **CAN** TELL YOU THAT HIS UNIT WAS SURPRISED BY SUPERIOR NUMBERS WHILE ATTEMPTING TO TAKE AN ENEMY POSITION.
AND SERGEANT MORRIS DEMONSTRATED **EXTRAORDINARY** BRAVERY HOLDING HIS POSITION, PROVIDING COVER FIRE SO HIS FELLOW SOLDIERS COULD WITHDRAW.
HE LAID DOWN **HIS** LIFE SO **OTHERS** COULD LIVE.
HE **WILL** BE NOMINATED FOR THE MEDAL OF HONOR.
YOU AND YOUR FAMILY HAVE THE DEEPEST CONDOLENCES OF THE UNITED STATES ARMY.

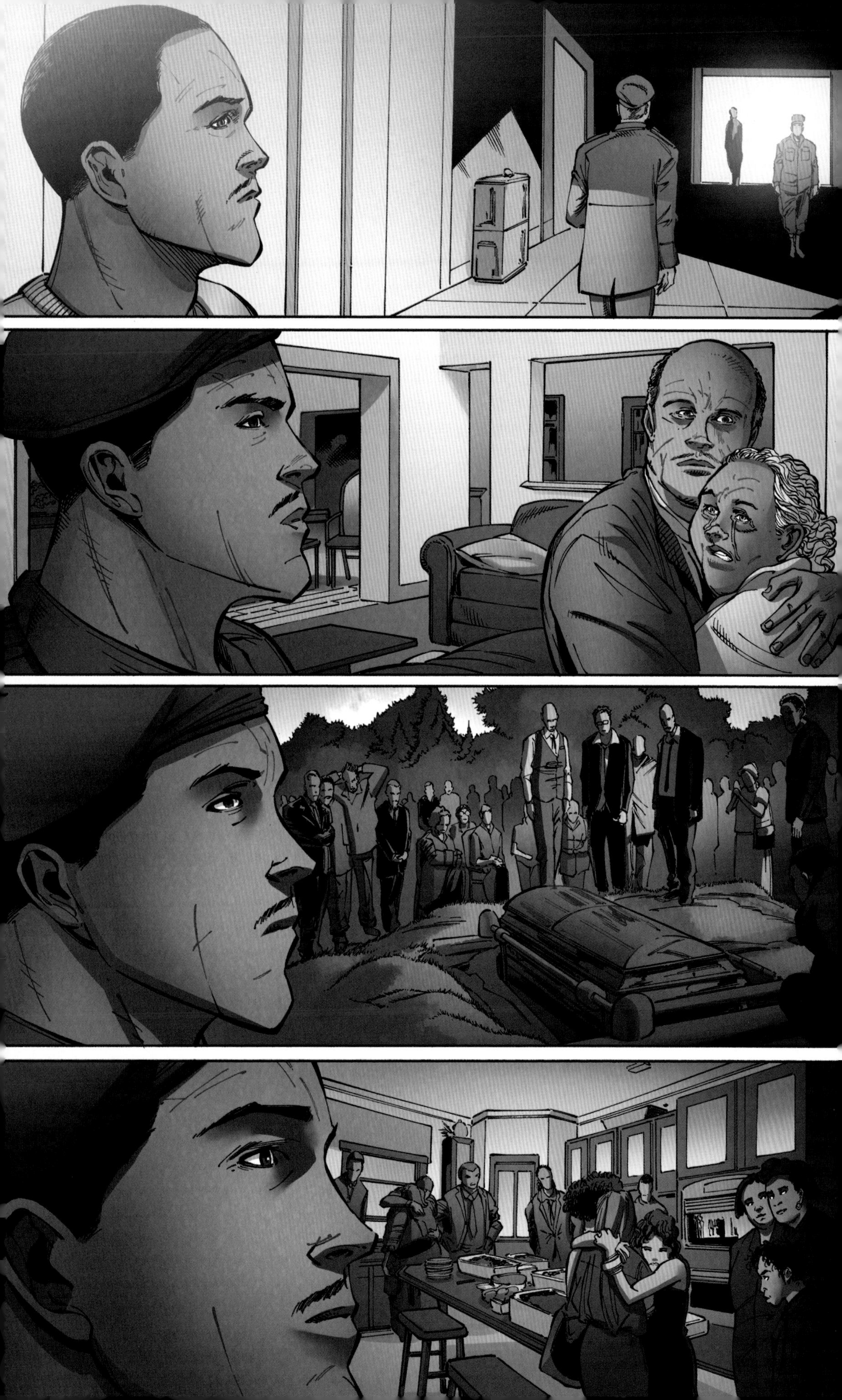

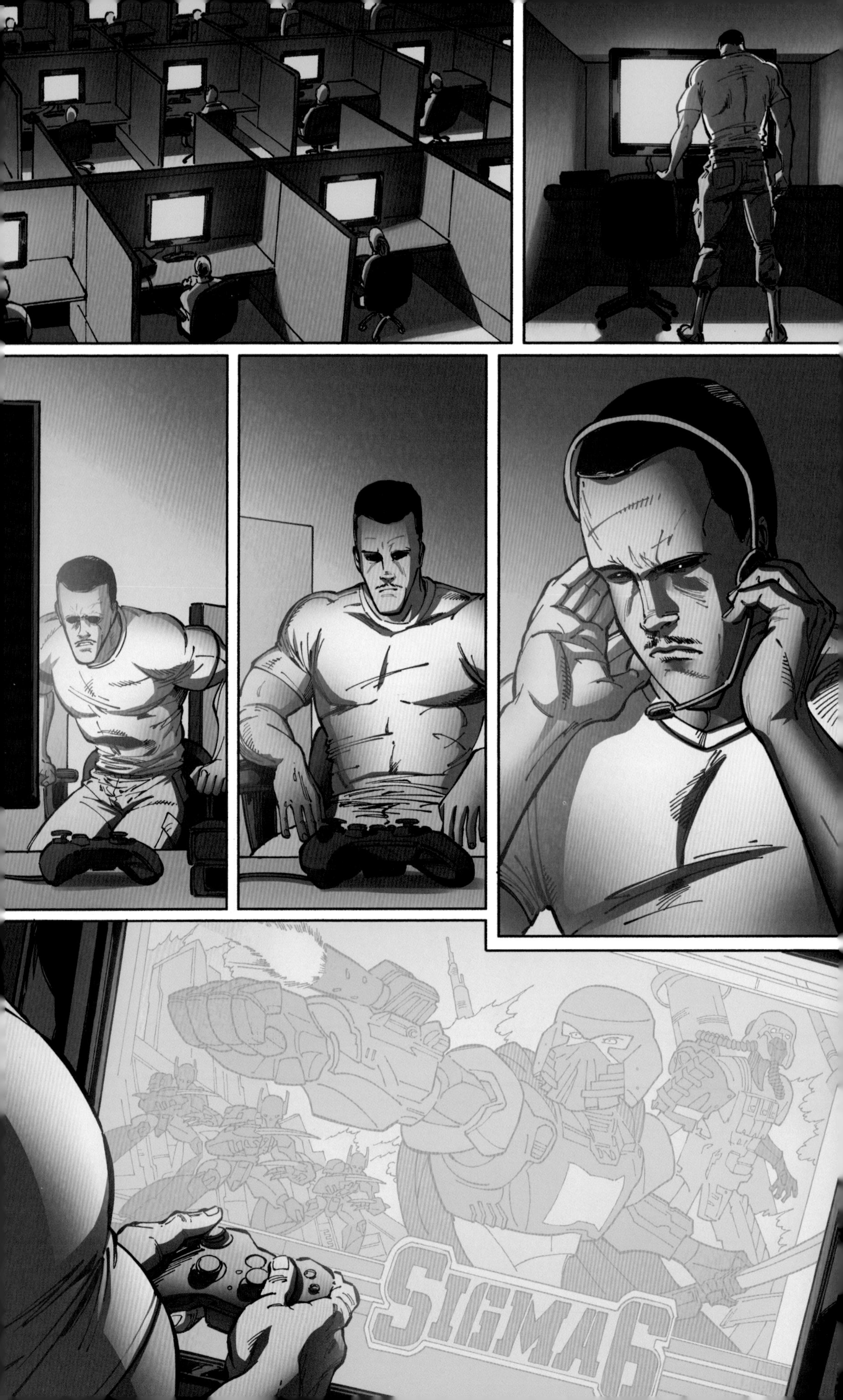
SIGMA 6

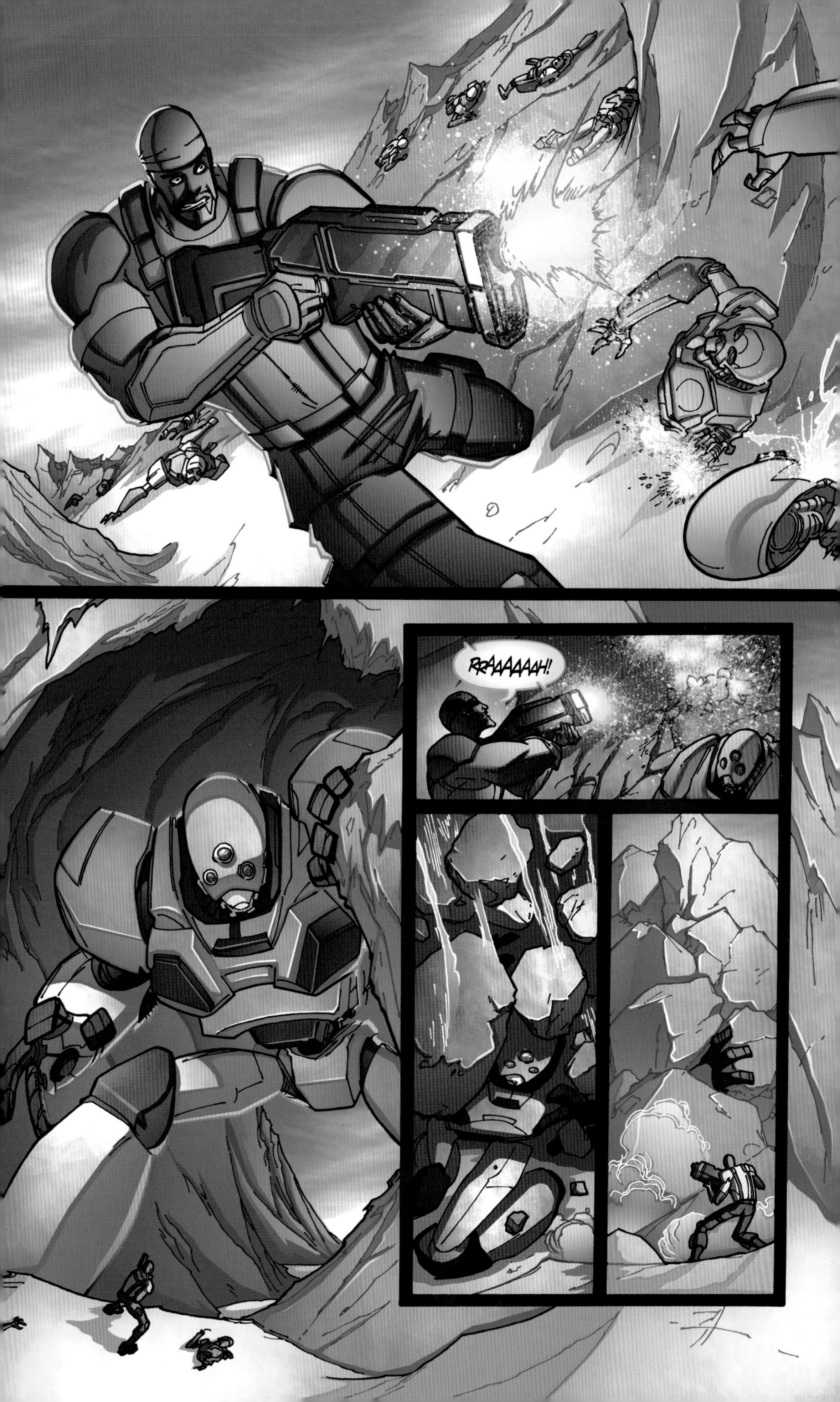
RRAAAAAAH!

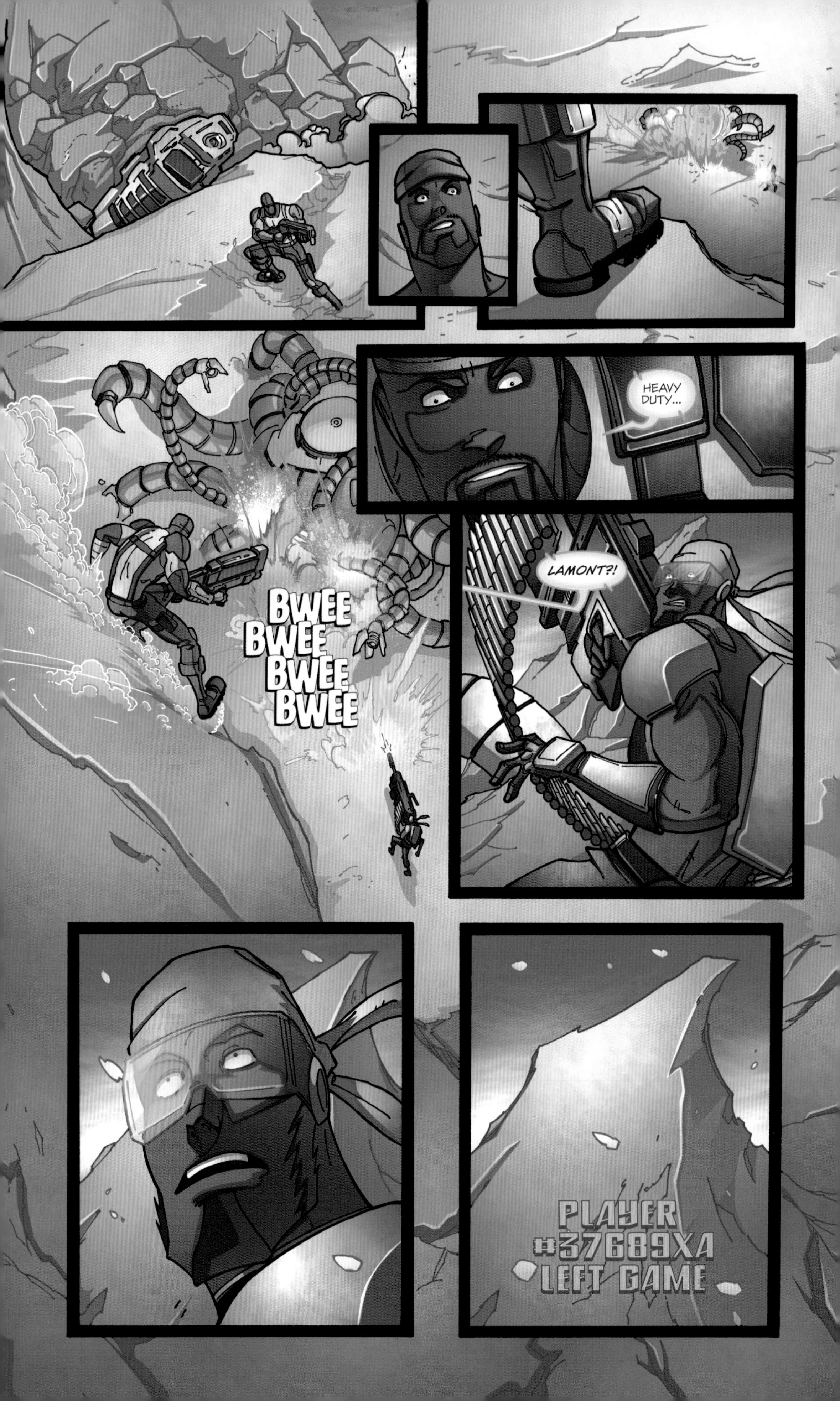

HEAVY DUTY...
LAMONT?!
BWEE BWEE BWEE BWEE
PLAYER #37689XA LEFT GAME

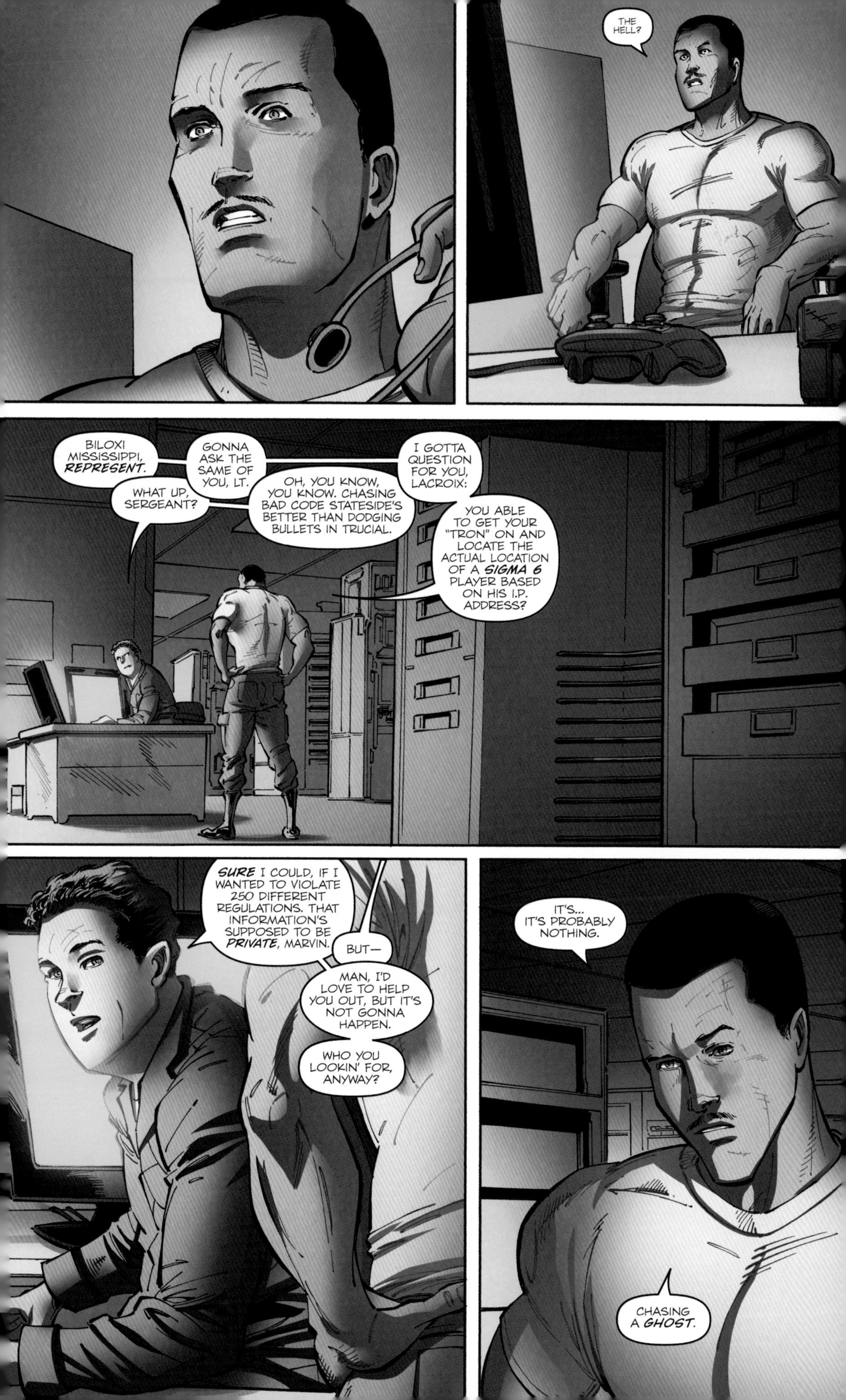

THE HELL?
BILOXI MISSISSIPPI, *REPRESENT*.
WHAT UP, SERGEANT?
GONNA ASK THE SAME OF YOU, LT.
OH, YOU KNOW, YOU KNOW. CHASING BAD CODE STATESIDE'S BETTER THAN DODGING BULLETS IN TRUCIAL.
I GOTTA QUESTION FOR YOU, LACROIX:
YOU ABLE TO GET YOUR "TRON" ON AND LOCATE THE ACTUAL LOCATION OF A *SIGMA 6* PLAYER BASED ON HIS I.P. ADDRESS?
SURE I COULD, IF I WANTED TO VIOLATE 250 DIFFERENT REGULATIONS. THAT INFORMATION'S SUPPOSED TO BE *PRIVATE*, MARVIN.
BUT—
MAN, I'D LOVE TO HELP YOU OUT, BUT IT'S NOT GONNA HAPPEN.
WHO YOU LOOKIN' FOR, ANYWAY?
IT'S... IT'S PROBABLY NOTHING.
CHASING A *GHOST*.

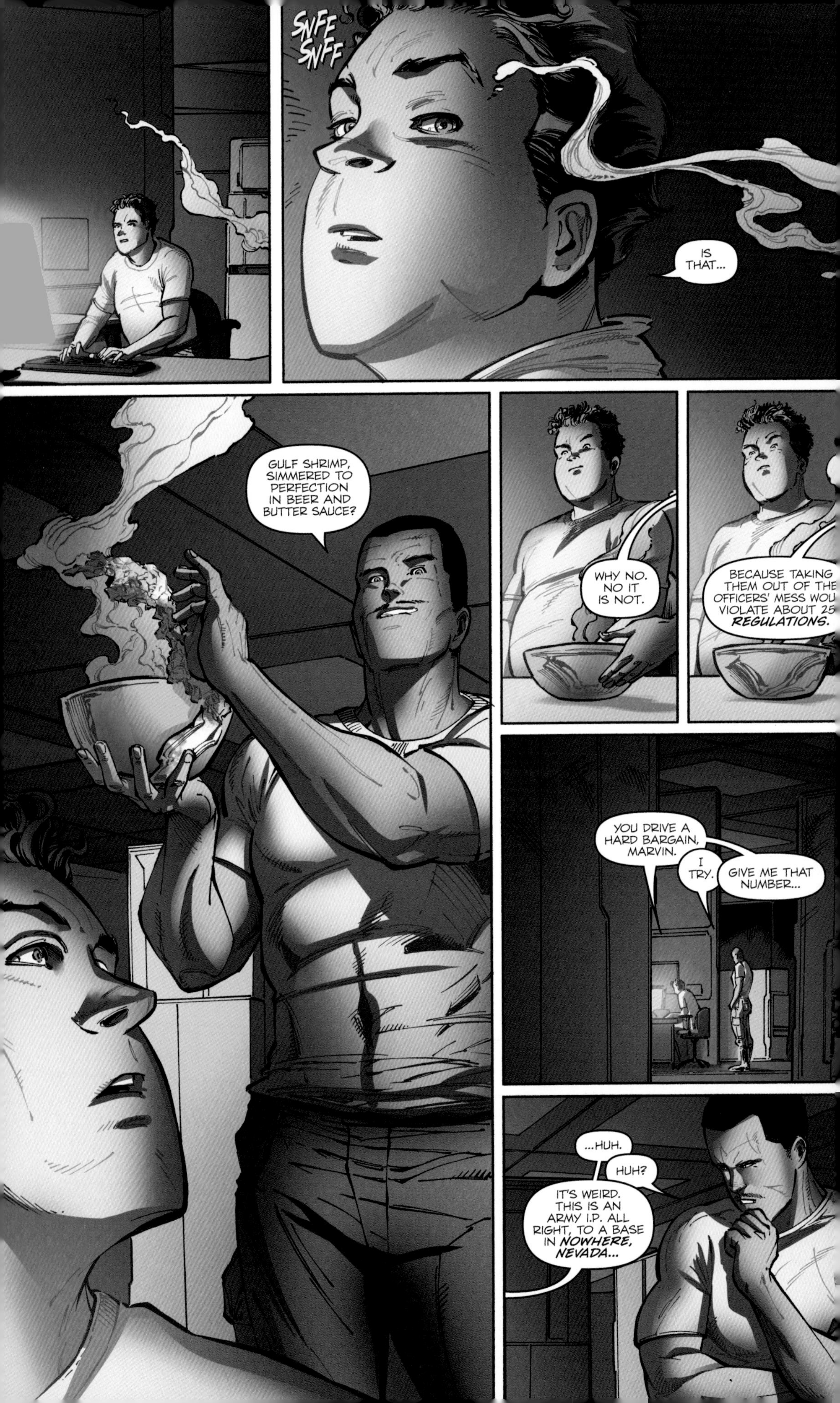
SNFF SNFF
IS THAT...
GULF SHRIMP, SIMMERED TO PERFECTION IN BEER AND BUTTER SAUCE?
WHY NO. NO IT IS NOT.
BECAUSE TAKING THEM OUT OF THE OFFICERS' MESS WOU VIOLATE ABOUT 25 REGULATIONS.
YOU DRIVE A HARD BARGAIN, MARVIN.
I TRY.
GIVE ME THAT NUMBER...
...HUH.
HUH?
IT'S WEIRD. THIS IS AN ARMY I.P. ALL RIGHT, TO A BASE IN NOWHERE, NEVADA...

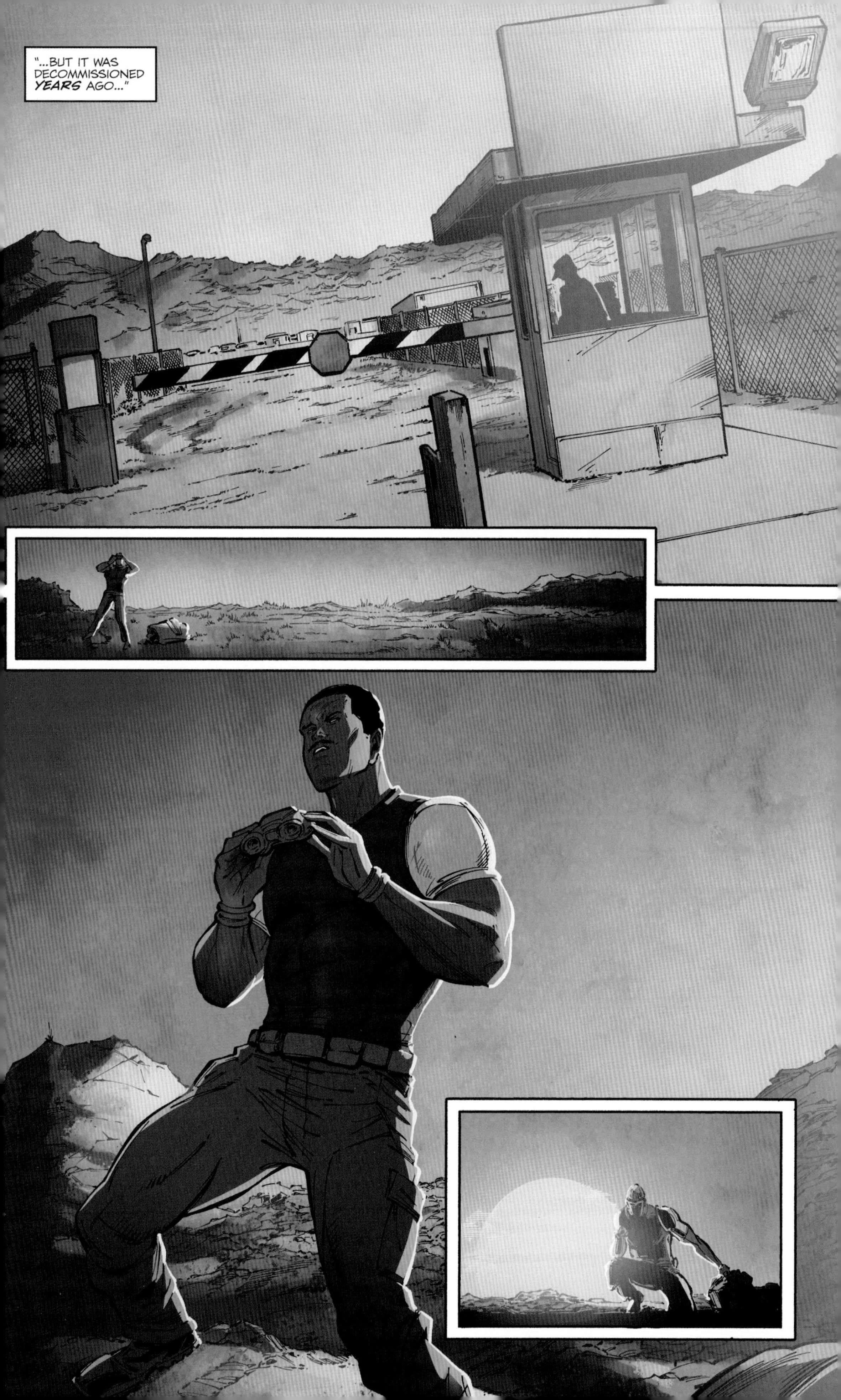
"...BUT IT WAS DECOMMISSIONED *YEARS* AGO..."

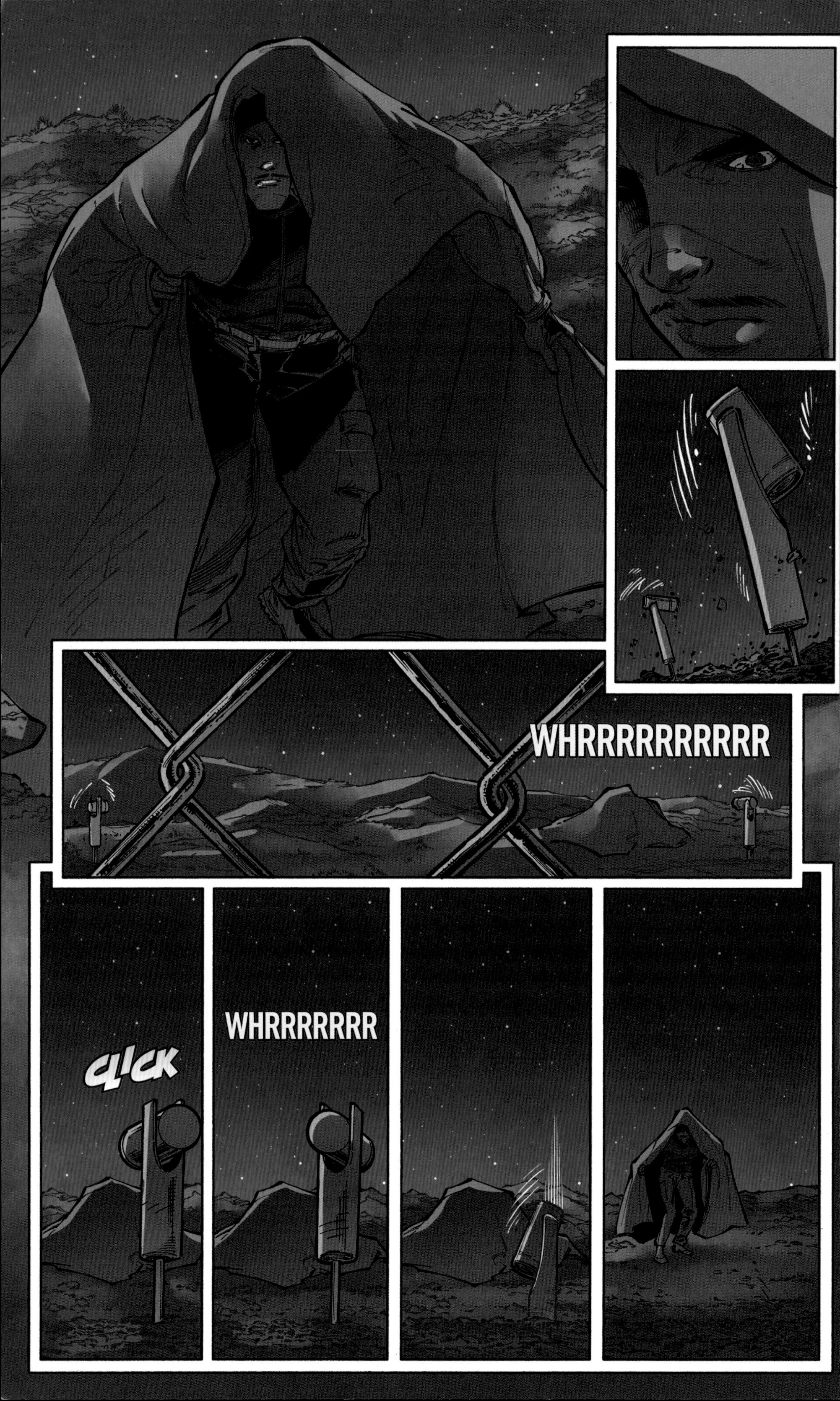
WHRRRRRRRRRR
CLICK
WHRRRRRRR

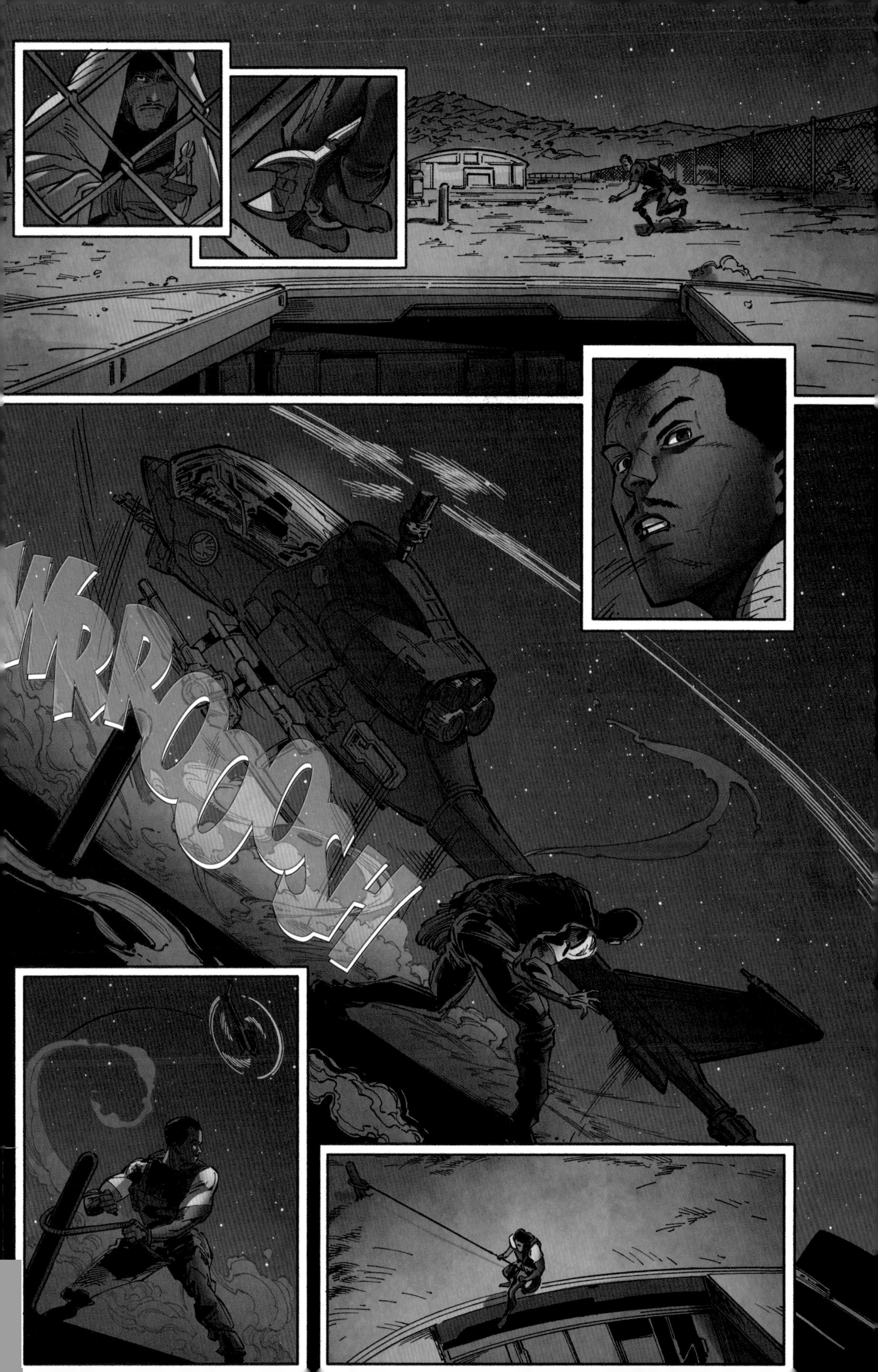
WRROOOOSH!

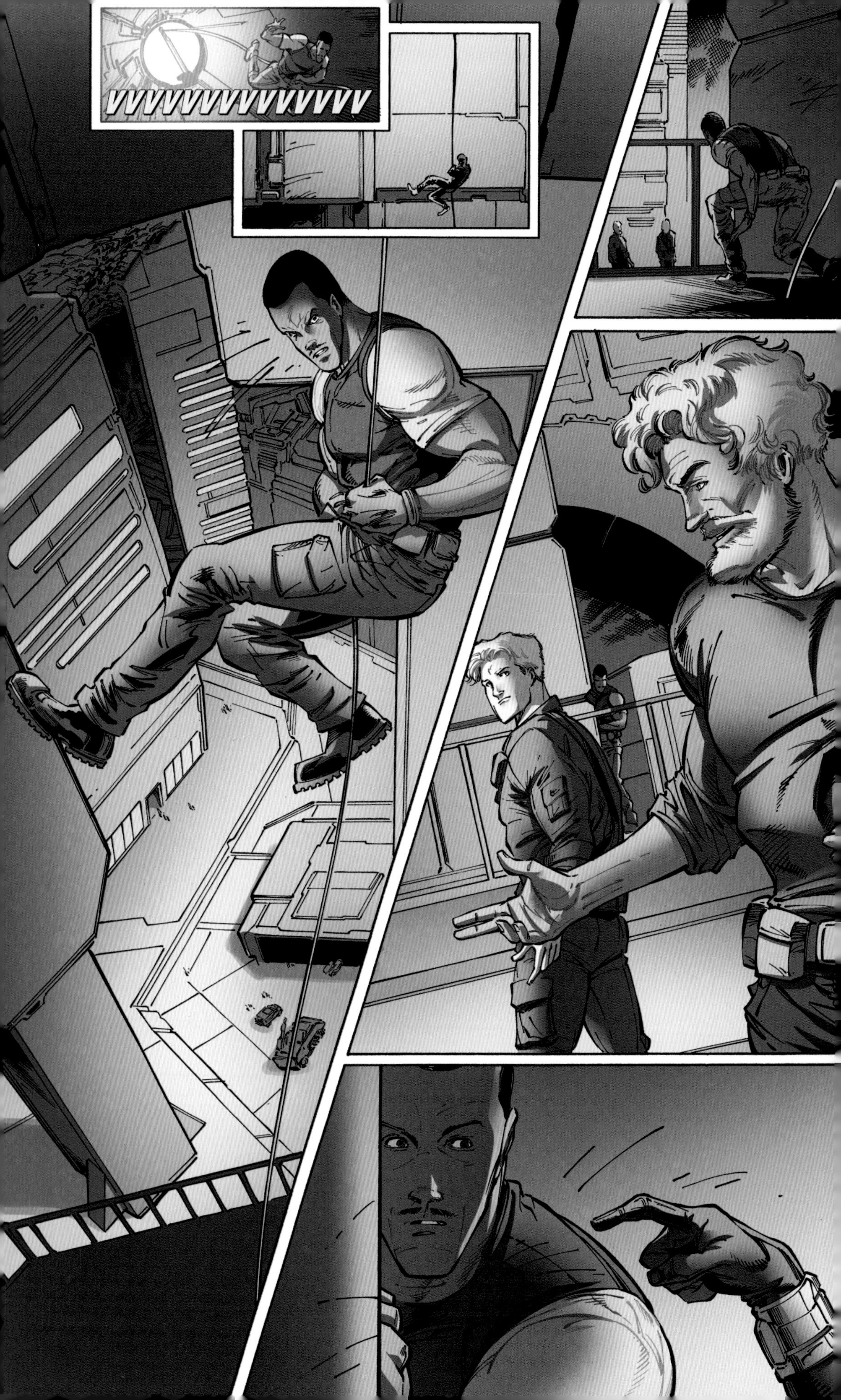
VVVVVVVVVVVVVV

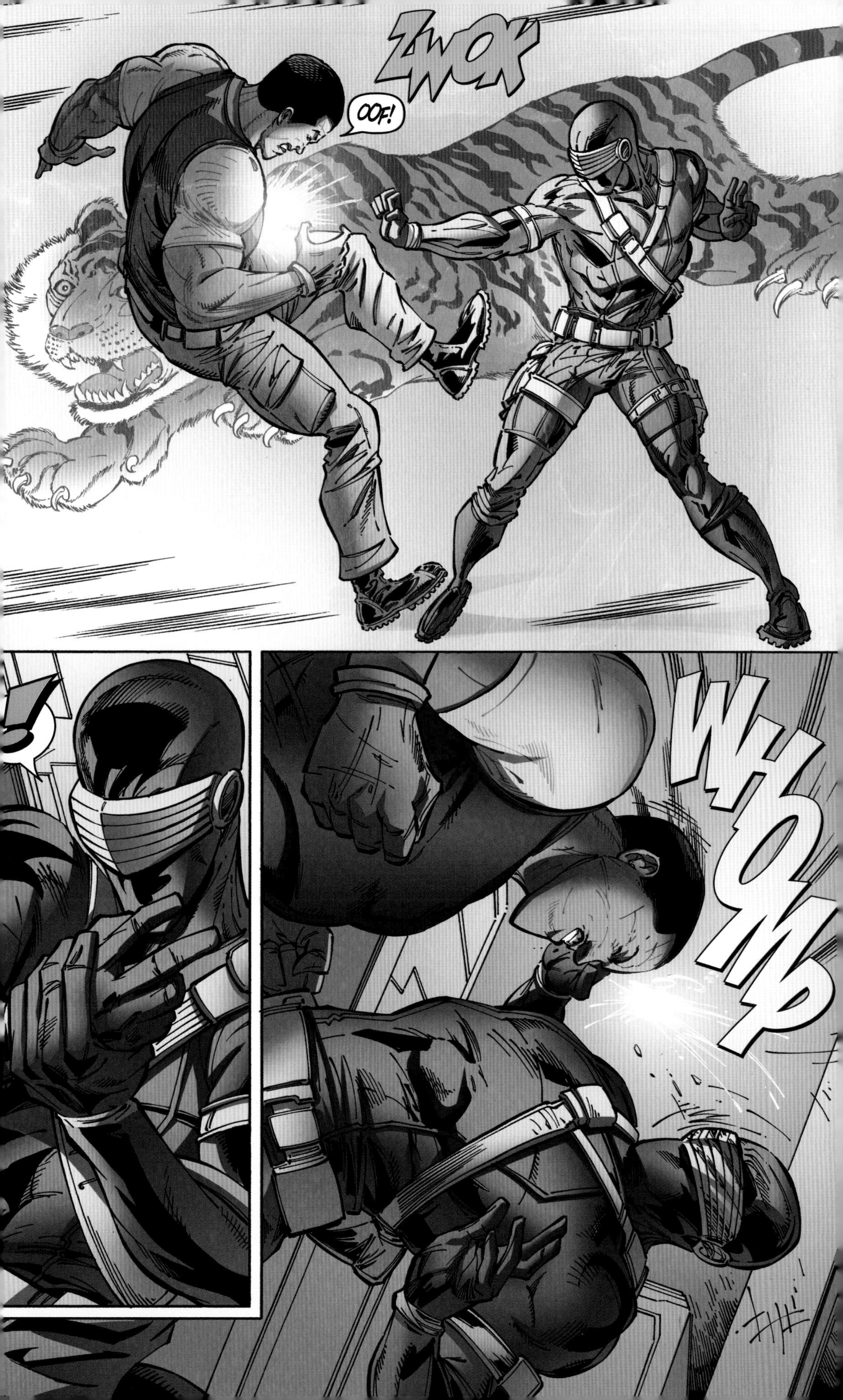
ZWOK
OOF!
WHOMP

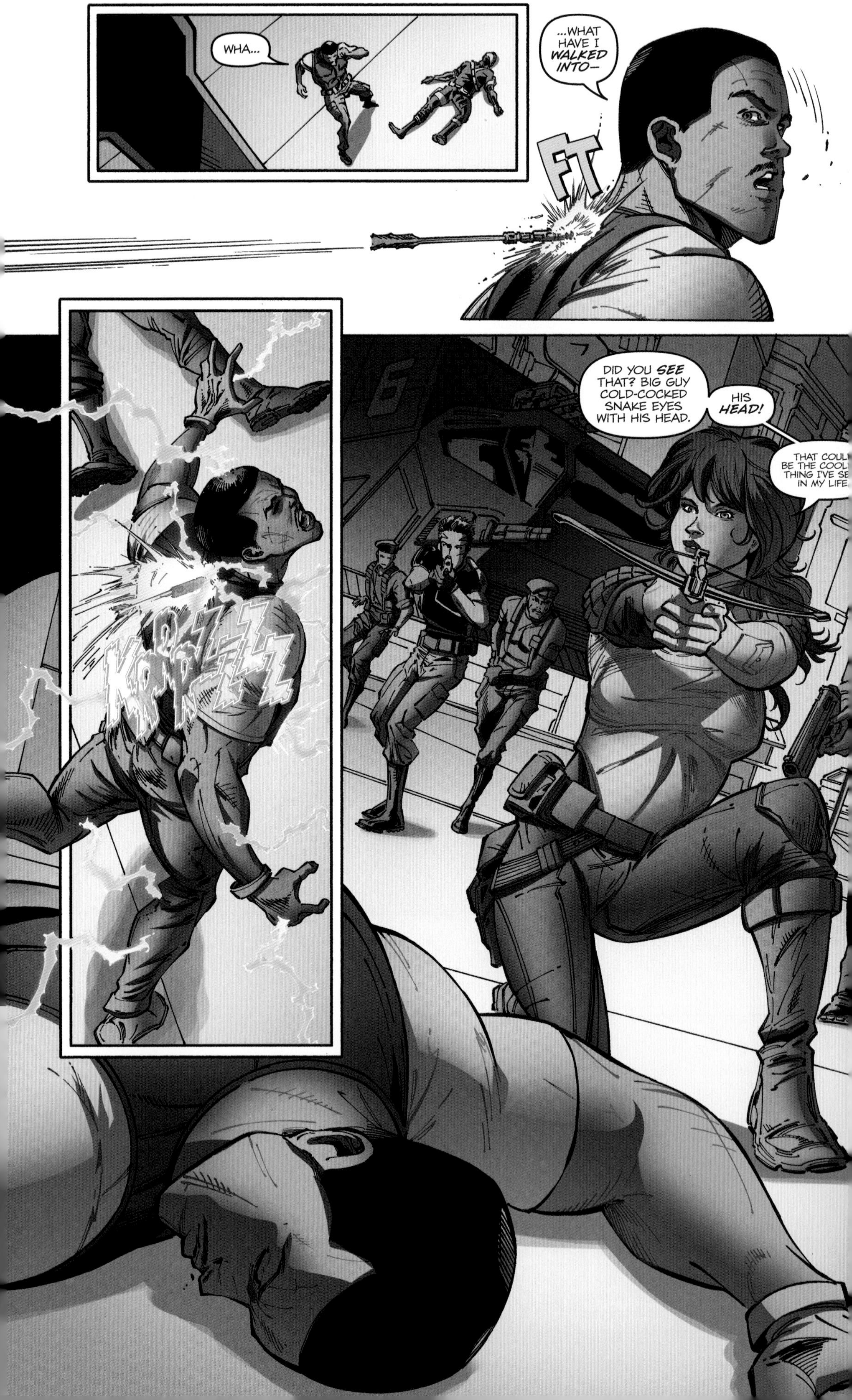
WHA...
...WHAT HAVE I WALKED INTO—
FT
DID YOU SEE THAT? BIG GUY COLD-COCKED SNAKE EYES WITH HIS HEAD.
HIS HEAD!
THAT COUL
BE THE COOL
THING I'VE SE
IN MY LIFE.

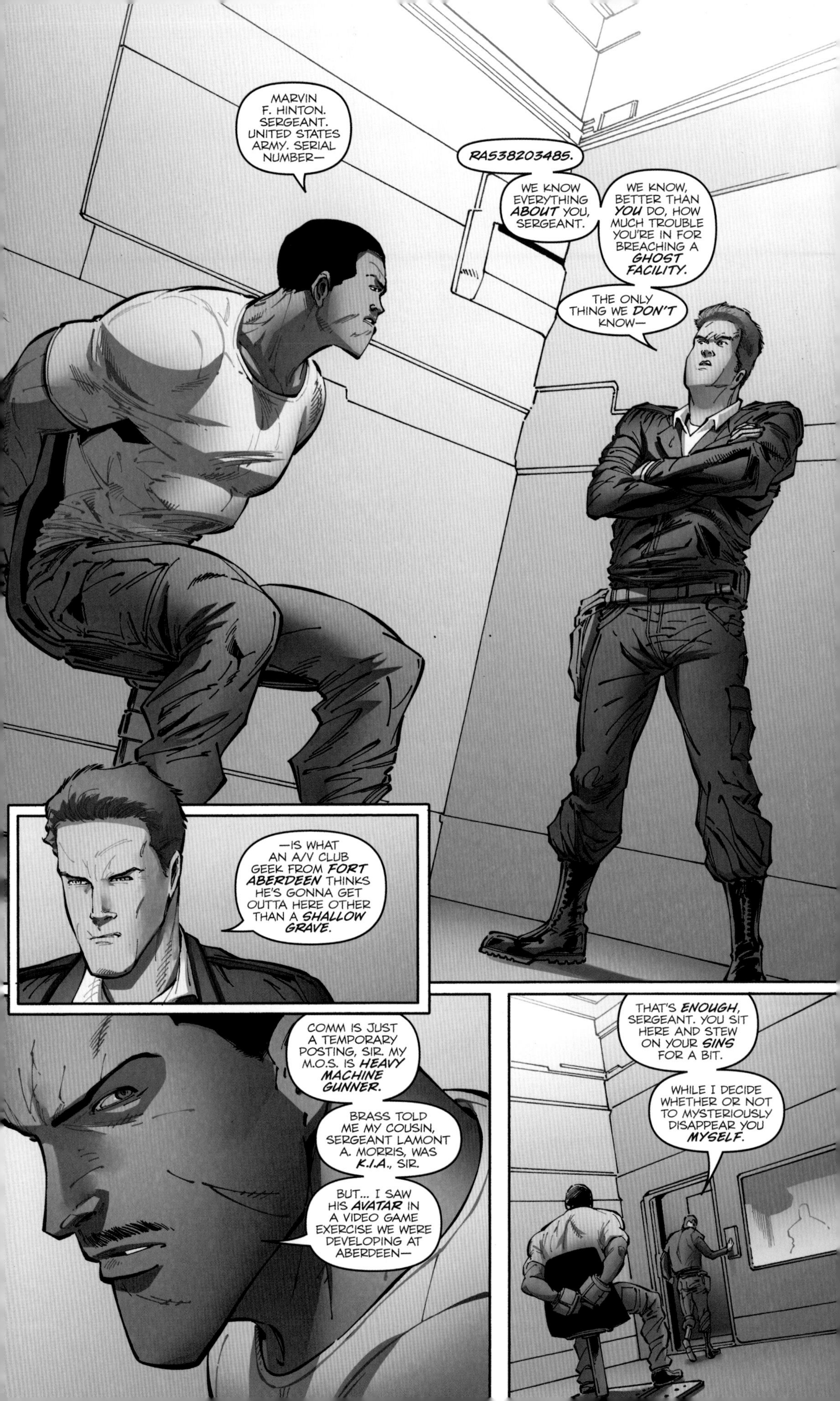
MARVIN F. HINTON. SERGEANT. UNITED STATES ARMY. SERIAL NUMBER—
RA538203485.
WE KNOW EVERYTHING ABOUT YOU, SERGEANT.
WE KNOW, BETTER THAN YOU DO, HOW MUCH TROUBLE YOU'RE IN FOR BREACHING A GHOST FACILITY.
THE ONLY THING WE DON'T KNOW—
—IS WHAT AN A/V CLUB GEEK FROM FORT ABERDEEN THINKS HE'S GONNA GET OUTTA HERE OTHER THAN A SHALLOW GRAVE.
COMM IS JUST A TEMPORARY POSTING, SIR. MY M.O.S. IS HEAVY MACHINE GUNNER.
BRASS TOLD ME MY COUSIN, SERGEANT LAMONT A. MORRIS, WAS K.I.A., SIR.
BUT... I SAW HIS AVATAR IN A VIDEO GAME EXERCISE WE WERE DEVELOPING AT ABERDEEN—
THAT'S ENOUGH, SERGEANT. YOU SIT HERE AND STEW ON YOUR SINS FOR A BIT.
WHILE I DECIDE WHETHER OR NOT TO MYSTERIOUSLY DISAPPEAR YOU MYSELF.

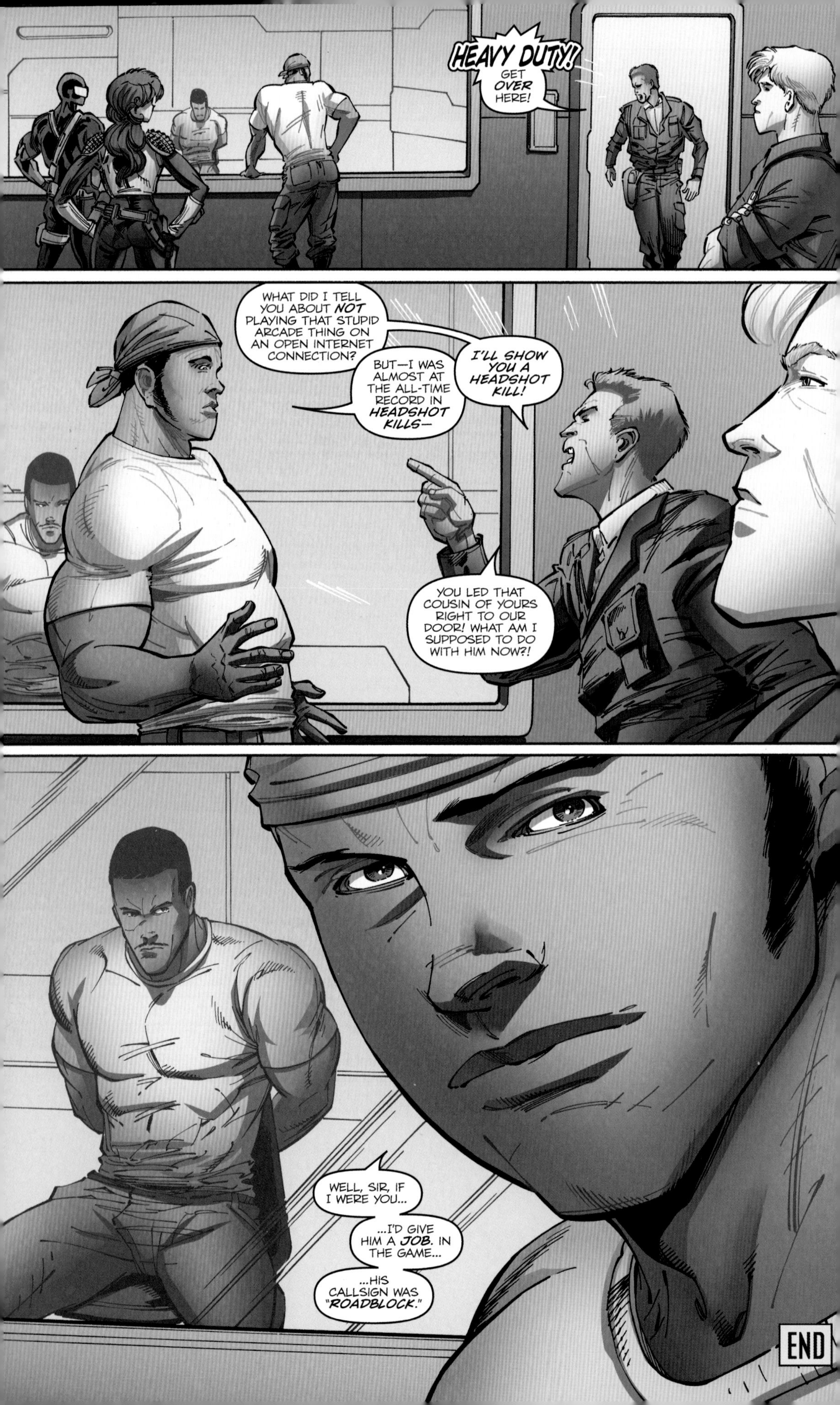
HEAVY DUTY!
GET OVER HERE!
WHAT DID I TELL YOU ABOUT NOT PLAYING THAT STUPID ARCADE THING ON AN OPEN INTERNET CONNECTION?
BUT—I WAS ALMOST AT THE ALL-TIME RECORD IN HEADSHOT KILLS—
I'LL SHOW YOU A HEADSHOT KILL!
YOU LED THAT COUSIN OF YOURS RIGHT TO OUR DOOR! WHAT AM I SUPPOSED TO DO WITH HIM NOW?!
WELL, SIR, IF I WERE YOU...
...I'D GIVE HIM A JOB. IN THE GAME...
...HIS CALLSIGN WAS "ROADBLOCK."
END

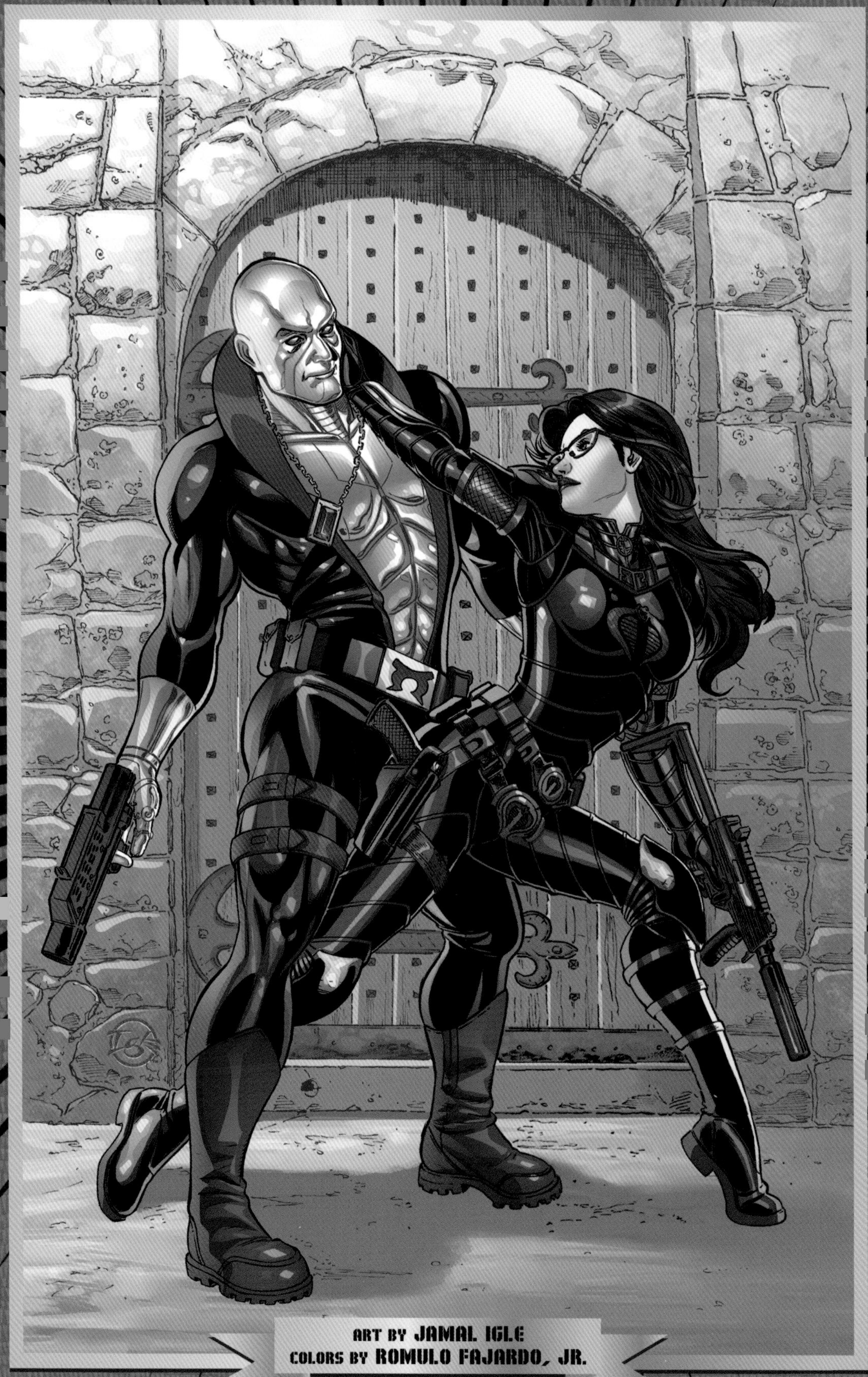

ART BY JAMAL IGLE
COLORS BY ROMULO FAJARDO, JR.

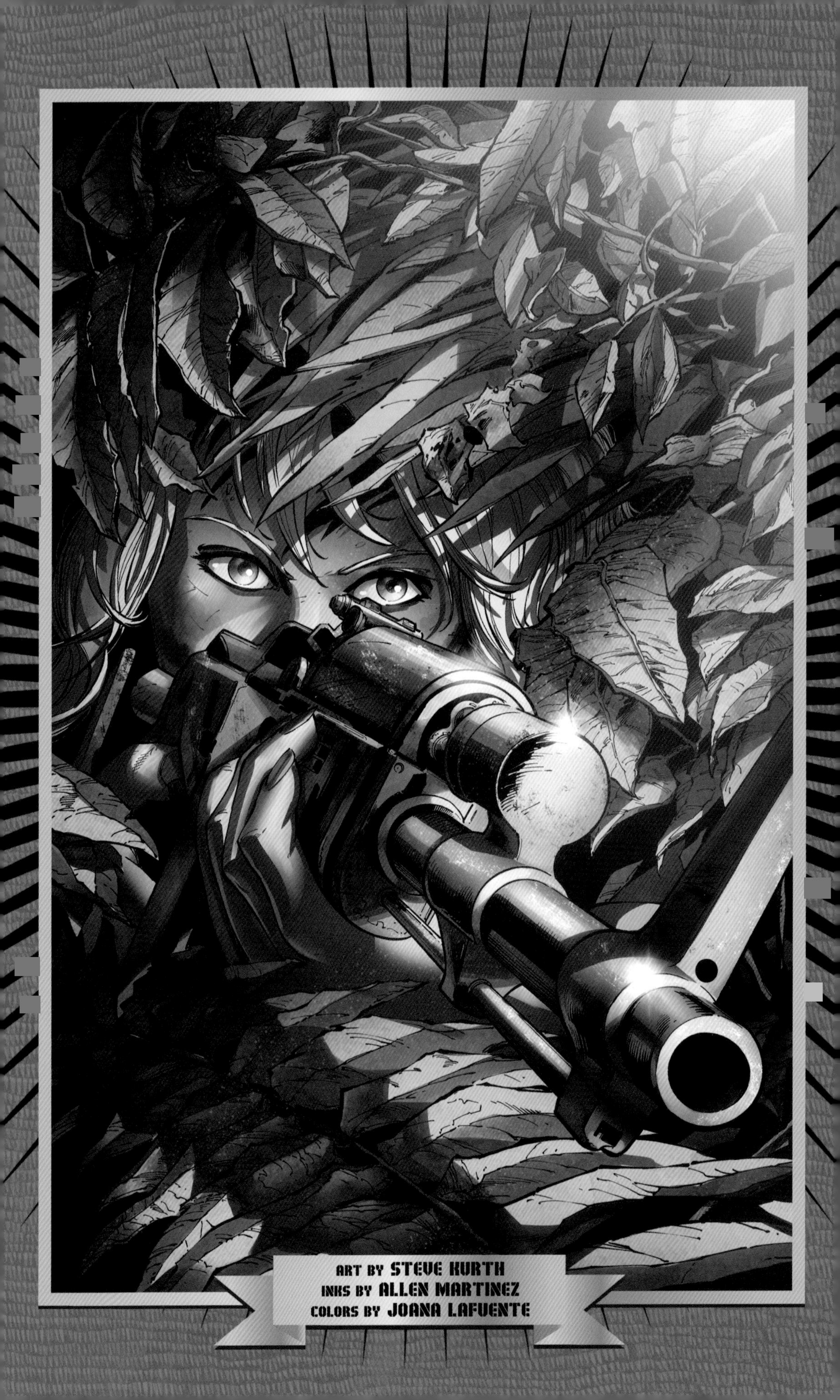
ART BY STEVE KURTH
INKS BY ALLEN MARTINEZ
COLORS BY JOANA LAFUENTE

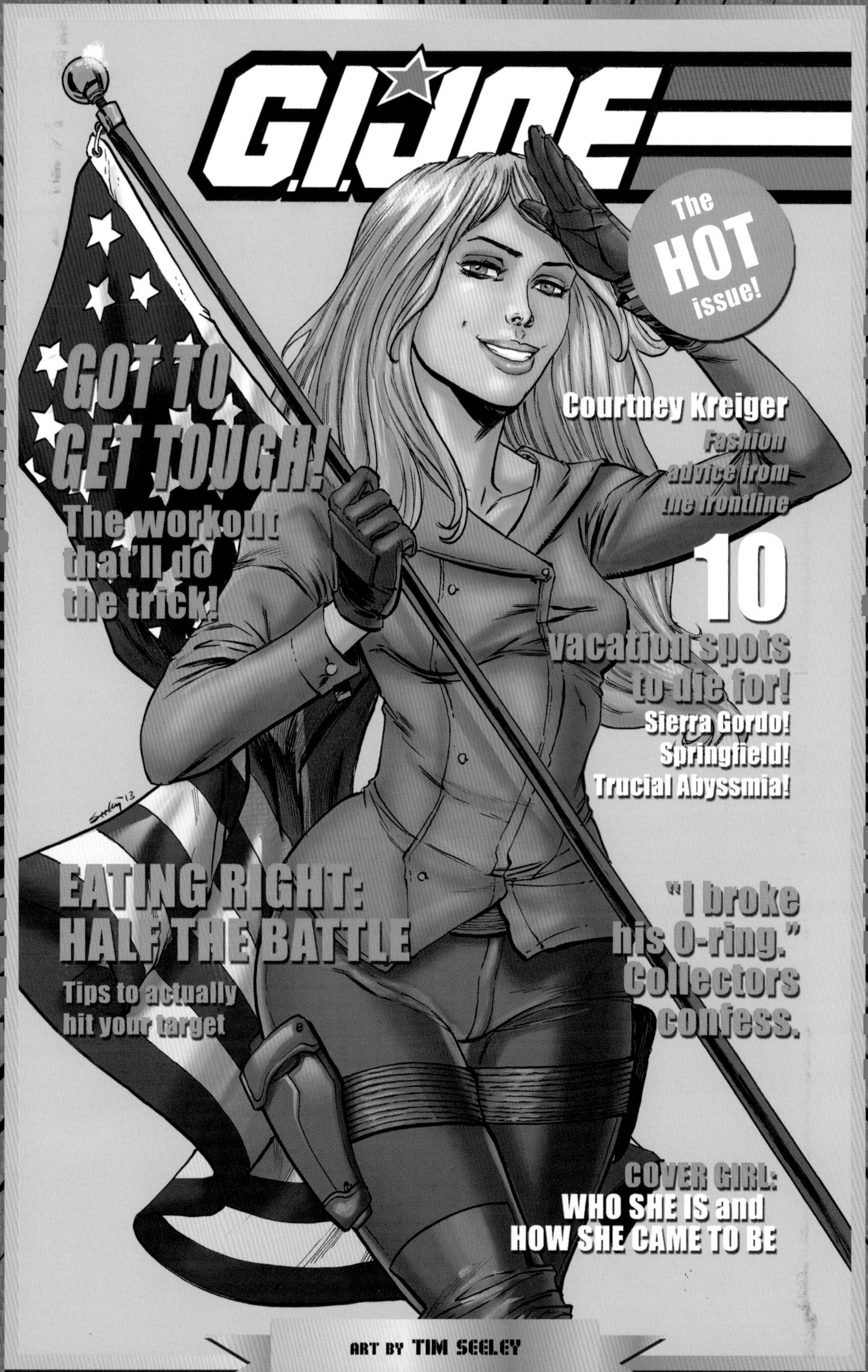
G.I. JOE
The HOT issue!
GOT TO GET TOUGH!
The workout that'll do the trick!
Courtney Kreiger
Fashion advice from the frontline
10 vacation spots to die for!
Sierra Gordo!
Springfield!
Trucial Abyssmia!
EATING RIGHT: HALF THE BATTLE
Tips to actually hit your target
"I broke his O-ring." Collectors confess.
COVER GIRL: WHO SHE IS and HOW SHE CAME TO BE

ART BY TIM SEELEY

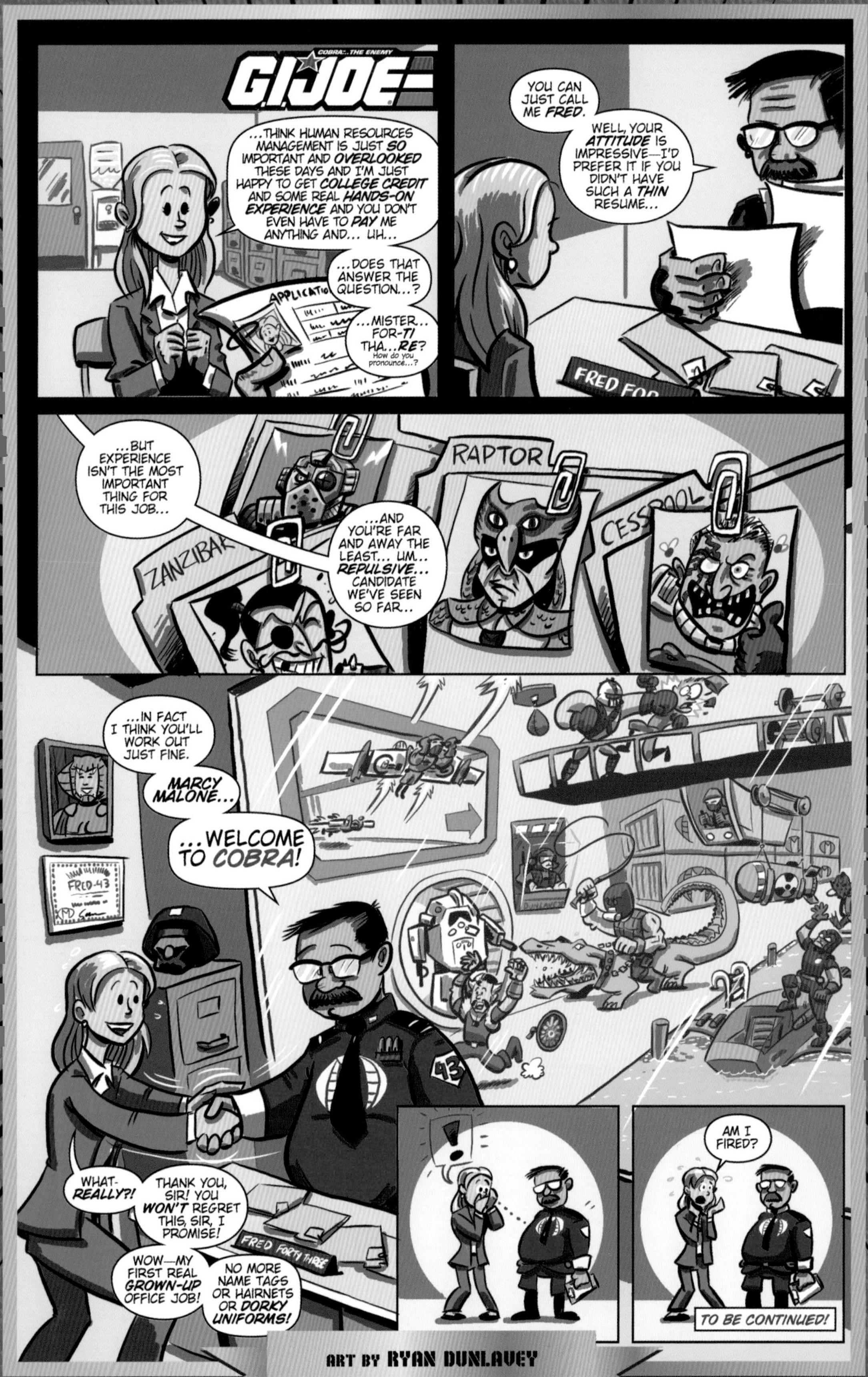
COBRA: THE ENEMY
G.I. JOE
...THINK HUMAN RESOURCES MANAGEMENT IS JUST SO IMPORTANT AND OVERLOOKED THESE DAYS AND I'M JUST HAPPY TO GET COLLEGE CREDIT AND SOME REAL HANDS-ON EXPERIENCE AND YOU DON'T EVEN HAVE TO PAY ME ANYTHING AND... UH...
...DOES THAT ANSWER THE QUESTION...?
...MISTER... FOR-TI THA...RE? How do you pronounce...?
APPLICATIO
YOU CAN JUST CALL ME FRED.
WELL, YOUR ATTITUDE IS IMPRESSIVE—I'D PREFER IT IF YOU DIDN'T HAVE SUCH A THIN RESUME...
FRED FOR
...BUT EXPERIENCE ISN'T THE MOST IMPORTANT THING FOR THIS JOB...
...AND YOU'RE FAR AND AWAY THE LEAST... UM... REPULSIVE... CANDIDATE WE'VE SEEN SO FAR..
RAPTOR
ZANZIBAR
CESSPOOL
...IN FACT I THINK YOU'LL WORK OUT JUST FINE.
MARCY MALONE...
...WELCOME TO COBRA!
FRED-43
WHAT-REALLY?!
THANK YOU, SIR! YOU WON'T REGRET THIS, SIR, I PROMISE!
WOW—MY FIRST REAL GROWN-UP OFFICE JOB!
NO MORE NAME TAGS OR HAIRNETS OR DORKY UNIFORMS!
FRED FORTY THREE
!
AM I FIRED?
TO BE CONTINUED!
ART BY RYAN DUNLAVEY

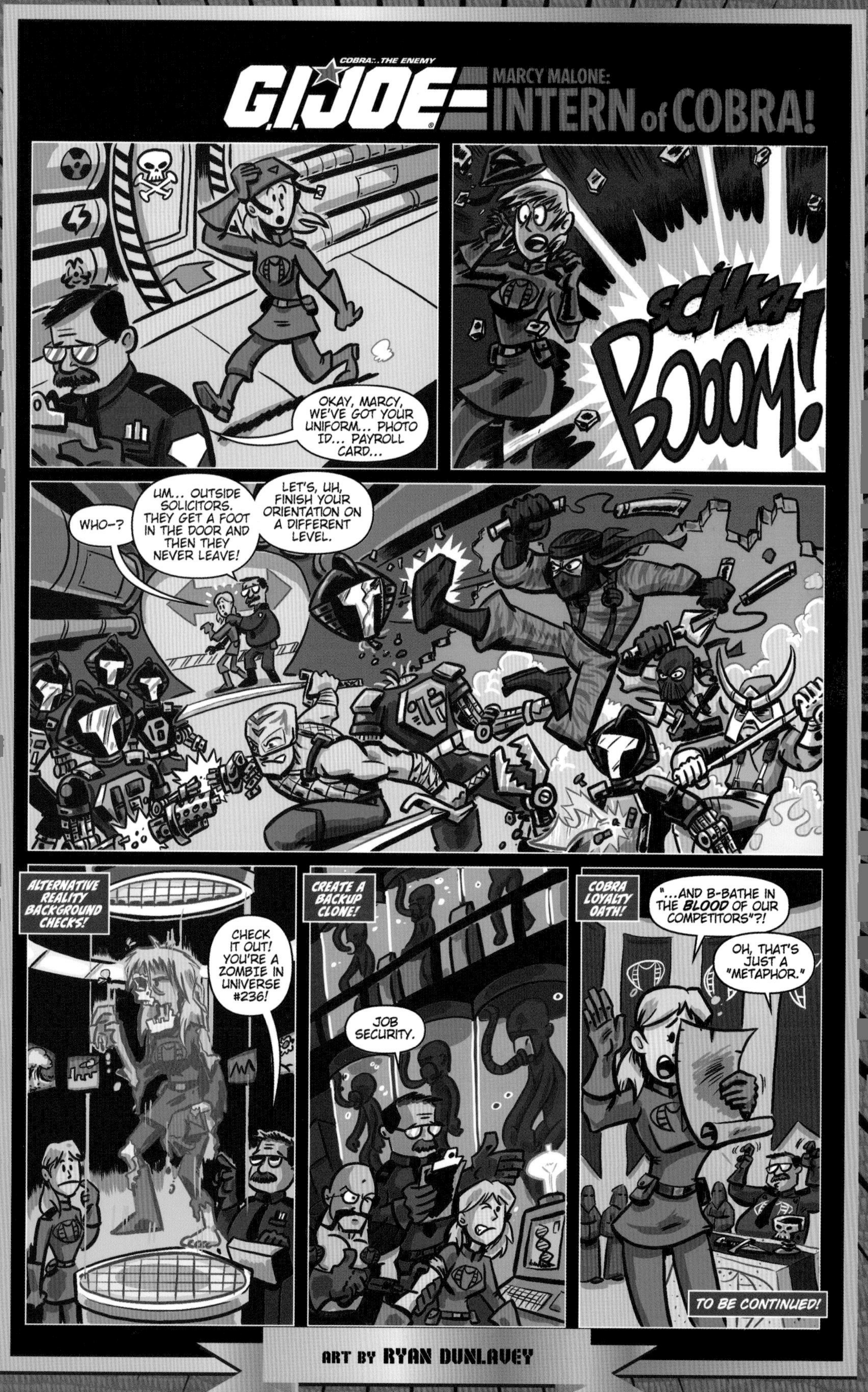

COBRA: THE ENEMY
G.I. JOE
MARCY MALONE: INTERN of COBRA!
OKAY, MARCY, WE'VE GOT YOUR UNIFORM... PHOTO ID... PAYROLL CARD...
SCHKA-BOOOM!
WHO-?
UM... OUTSIDE SOLICITORS. THEY GET A FOOT IN THE DOOR AND THEN THEY NEVER LEAVE!
LET'S, UH, FINISH YOUR ORIENTATION ON A DIFFERENT LEVEL.
ALTERNATIVE REALITY BACKGROUND CHECKS!
CHECK IT OUT! YOU'RE A ZOMBIE IN UNIVERSE #236!
CREATE A BACKUP CLONE!
JOB SECURITY.
COBRA LOYALTY OATH!
"...AND B-BATHE IN THE BLOOD OF OUR COMPETITORS"?!
OH, THAT'S JUST A "METAPHOR."
TO BE CONTINUED!
ART BY RYAN DUNLAVEY

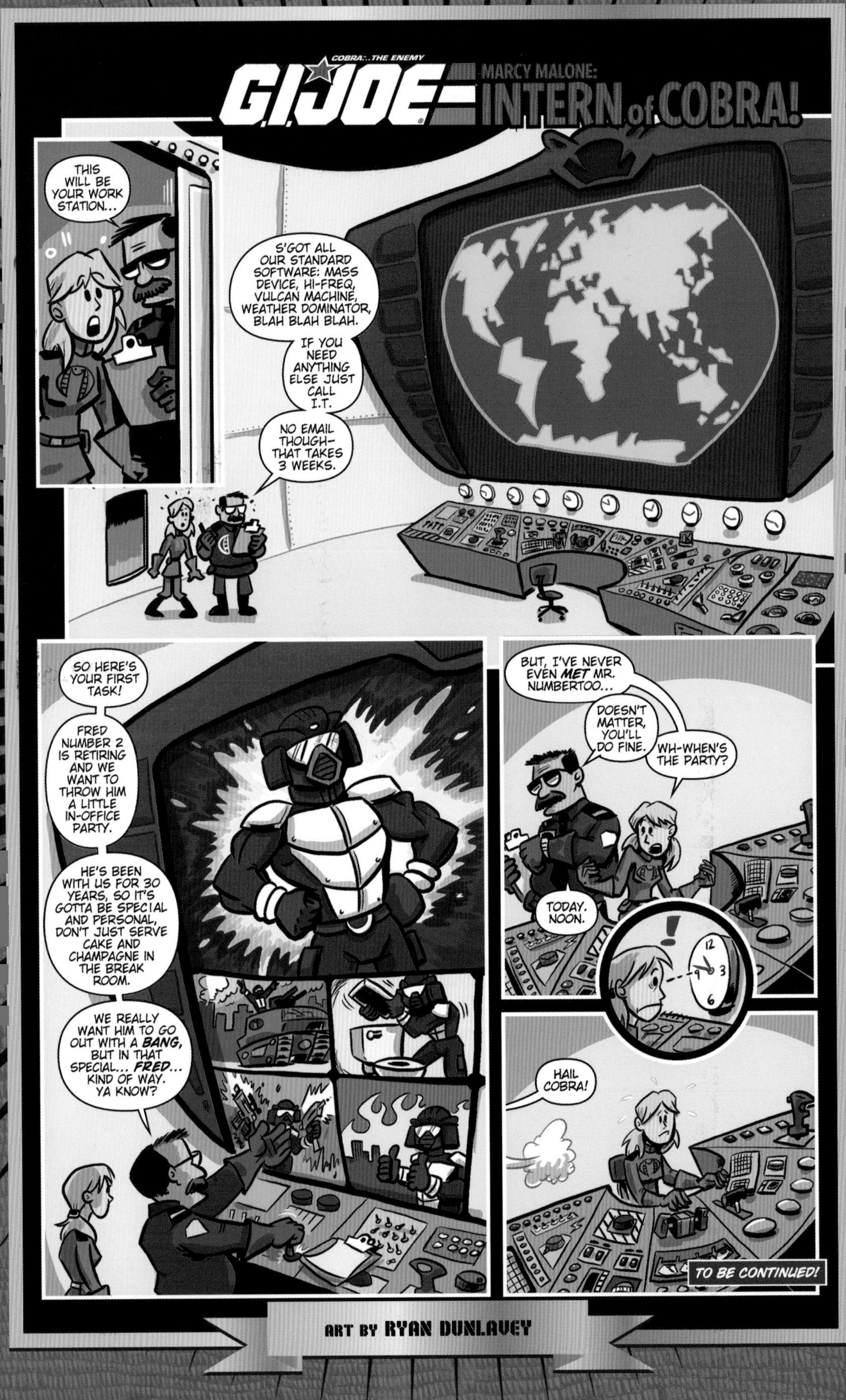
COBRA: THE ENEMY
G.I. JOE
MARCY MALONE: INTERN of COBRA!
THIS WILL BE YOUR WORK STATION...
S'GOT ALL OUR STANDARD SOFTWARE: MASS DEVICE, HI-FREQ, VULCAN MACHINE, WEATHER DOMINATOR, BLAH BLAH BLAH.
IF YOU NEED ANYTHING ELSE JUST CALL I.T.
NO EMAIL THOUGH-THAT TAKES 3 WEEKS.
SO HERE'S YOUR FIRST TASK!
FRED NUMBER 2 IS RETIRING AND WE WANT TO THROW HIM A LITTLE IN-OFFICE PARTY.
HE'S BEEN WITH US FOR 30 YEARS, SO IT'S GOTTA BE SPECIAL AND PERSONAL, DON'T JUST SERVE CAKE AND CHAMPAGNE IN THE BREAK ROOM.
WE REALLY WANT HIM TO GO OUT WITH A BANG, BUT IN THAT SPECIAL... FRED... KIND OF WAY. YA KNOW?
BUT, I'VE NEVER EVEN MET MR. NUMBERTOO...
DOESN'T MATTER, YOU'LL DO FINE.
WH-WHEN'S THE PARTY?
TODAY. NOON.
!
12
3
6
9
HAIL COBRA!
TO BE CONTINUED!
ART BY RYAN DUNLAVEY

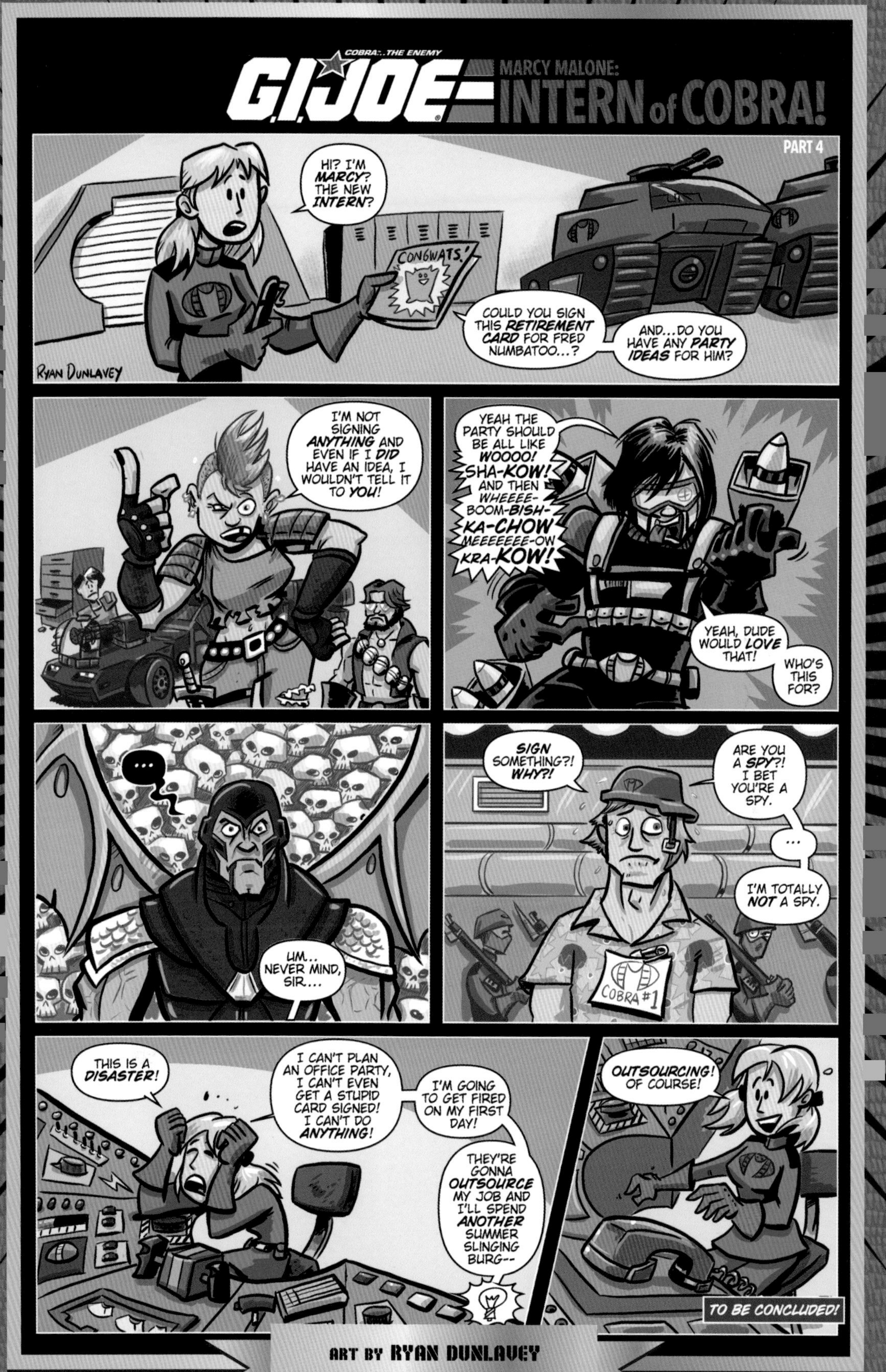
COBRA: THE ENEMY
G.I. JOE
MARCY MALONE: INTERN of COBRA!
PART 4
HI? I'M MARCY? THE NEW INTERN?
CONGWATS!
COULD YOU SIGN THIS RETIREMENT CARD FOR FRED NUMBATOO...?
AND...DO YOU HAVE ANY PARTY IDEAS FOR HIM?
RYAN DUNLAVEY
I'M NOT SIGNING ANYTHING AND EVEN IF I DID HAVE AN IDEA, I WOULDN'T TELL IT TO YOU!
YEAH THE PARTY SHOULD BE ALL LIKE WOOOO! SHA-KOW! AND THEN WHEEEE-BOOM-BISH-KA-CHOW MEEEEEEE-OW KRA-KOW!
YEAH, DUDE WOULD LOVE THAT!
WHO'S THIS FOR?
...
UM... NEVER MIND, SIR...
SIGN SOMETHING?! WHY?!
ARE YOU A SPY?! I BET YOU'RE A SPY.
...
I'M TOTALLY NOT A SPY.
COBRA #1
THIS IS A DISASTER!
I CAN'T PLAN AN OFFICE PARTY, I CAN'T EVEN GET A STUPID CARD SIGNED! I CAN'T DO ANYTHING!
I'M GOING TO GET FIRED ON MY FIRST DAY!
THEY'RE GONNA OUTSOURCE MY JOB AND I'LL SPEND ANOTHER SUMMER SLINGING BURG--
OUTSOURCING! OF COURSE!
TO BE CONCLUDED!
ART BY RYAN DUNLAVEY

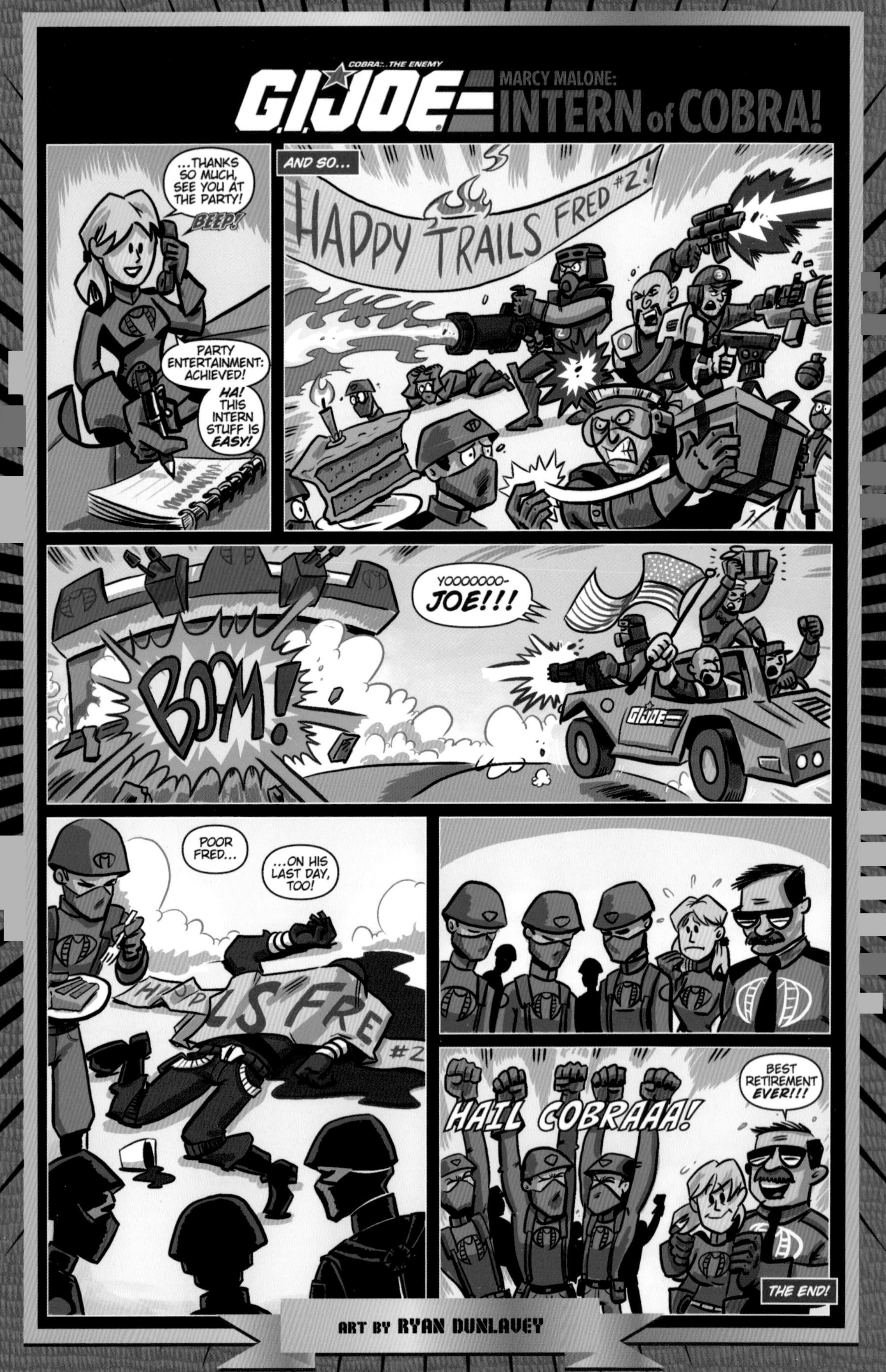
COBRA:..THE ENEMY
G.I. JOE
MARCY MALONE:
INTERN of COBRA!
...THANKS SO MUCH, SEE YOU AT THE PARTY!
BEEP!
PARTY ENTERTAINMENT: ACHIEVED!
HA! THIS INTERN STUFF IS EASY!
AND SO...
HAPPY TRAILS FRED #2!
YOOOOOOO-JOE!!!
BOOM!
G.I. JOE
POOR FRED...
...ON HIS LAST DAY, TOO!
LS FRE #2
HAIL COBRAAA!
BEST RETIREMENT EVER!!!
THE END!
ART BY RYAN DUNLAVEY